No Dominion

Louise Welsh

JOHN MURRAY

First published in Great Britain in 2017 by John Murray (Publishers)
An Hachette UK Company

First published in paperback in 2018

1

A CIP catalogue record for this title is available from the British Library

ISBN 978-1-84854-659-2
Ebook ISBN 978-1-84854-658-5

Typeset in Adobe Garamond by Hewer Text UK Ltd, Edinburgh
Printed and bound by Clays Ltd, St Ives plc

John Murray policy is to use papers that are natural, renewable
and recyclable products and made from wood grown in sustainable
forests. The logging and manufacturing processes are expected to
conform to the environmental regulations of the country of origin.

John Murray (Publishers)
Carmelite House
50 Victoria Embankment
London EC4Y 0DZ

www.johnmurray.co.uk

For David Miller

For that some should rule and others be ruled is a thing not only necessary, but expedient; from the hour of their birth, some are marked out for subjection, others for rule.

Politics, Aristotle

. . . the dead dieth no more; death hath no more dominion

Romans 6:9

Prologue

Seven of the children on the Orkney mainland were survivors of the Sweats. Each of them was billeted with a foster parent who was usually, though not always, the person who had found them. The children all claimed to remember the time before the Sweats. They boasted to each other of the cars their parents had driven, the countries they had travelled to; houses they once occupied, glittering with electricity. Their memories became more intricate as the years progressed. Each child could see their dead parents' faces; remember the scent of them. The children competed over details. They described the feel of their bedroom wallpaper, the view beyond the window, the colour of their grandparents' eyes, the taste of fast food and home cooking. Survivor children claimed to know the very atoms of the old world. But their memories only truly came alive when they were asleep, surfacing in dreams that woke their households and vanished upon waking.

The children were forbidden to enter abandoned buildings, but the grown-ups were often overwhelmed by the business of survival and left them to their own devices. Soon the small gang were daring each other into dead-eyed houses where they roamed through *Mary Celeste* rooms. Looting was a crime worthy of banishment, but the remnants of the old world were irresistible.

The adults had agreed that, although the children were not biologically theirs, the next generation must be a priority. There were no teachers, mathematicians, linguists, engineers, historians, writers or scientists left on the islands, but a small committee was established to set up a school and take turns at teaching the children what they could. It was a plan that floundered on the demands of the post-Sweats world. The education committee struggled to relearn forgotten lessons. They agreed that science and mechanics were essential to restore civilisation, but their knowledge of both was scant and the books in the islands' library difficult to understand.

The arts seemed an easier option, but the fledgling teachers failed there too. History stretched behind them, an infinite past. Literature was fathomless and music had the power to evoke emotions better left buried. It was hard to know where to start and so they let the landscape around them take charge. Classes consisted of hikes to brochs and standing stones. They inspected the Churchill Barriers and the Italian Chapel, roamed the cathedral and read the names inscribed on gravestones and books of remembrance. Once, the small class broke in to the war museum on Hoy. But the losses of the Second World War were puny compared with the devastation of the Sweats and, gradually, classes began to concentrate on the immediate past.

At first the children loved the frivolity of the pre-Sweats world. They drank in misremembered pop songs, half-recalled TV shows and confused accounts of video games. They beguiled their teachers with questions about the old days. Sometimes the adults would come to, wet-eyed, and realise that hours had passed while they had been lost in tales of life before the pandemic. As the children grew older classes began to resemble interrogations. Students tried to pinpoint details their instructors had forgotten, or never known.

Seven years after the outbreak of the Sweats the Orkney children all knew how to ride a horse, skin a rabbit, wring a chicken's neck, sail a boat and gut a fish. Even the younger ones could deliver a lamb and all were decent shots. They could each play the guitar well and build a shelter that would keep the rain out. The children could all read and count and most of the older ones could add, multiply and subtract. But there were gaps in their knowledge that in former times would have shocked a schools' inspector. Their understanding of the geography of the world beyond their islands was confused, their knowledge of chemistry, physics and astronomy rudimentary. The books they read were confined to chance and personal taste. They were prone to strange dreads and superstitions.

When the adults worried, as some of them occasionally did, that they had let the children down, they consoled themselves with the thought that you could not miss what you had never had. And there were still plenty of books in the library that would, in time, teach them what they wanted to know. The adults did not foresee that there would be a price to pay for keeping the children ignorant.

One

It was Easter Sunday and all but the lookouts were gathered in the upstairs lounge of the Stromness Hotel. Afternoon sunlight spilled through dust-glazed windows. Magnus McFall sat on the sill of the bay window with his back to the view of the harbour thrashing out one of the old songs. There were around forty-five people in the audience, most of them crowded around tables where tourists had once dined. The remainder stood on the edges of the room, leaning against its walls, as if readying themselves for a sudden getaway. Magnus looked to where Shug sat, balanced on a high stool by the bar, a bottle of Stella in his hand. Magnus would have preferred him not to drink, but the boy was now around fifteen years old and he had resolved not to fight battles he could not win.

> *Green grow the rashes, O;*
> *Green grow the rashes, O;*

The room joined in the chorus. Magnus risked a smile in Shug's direction. His son looked away and raised the bottle of beer to his lips. He was wearing a white denim jacket Magnus had not seen before. He wondered where the boy had found it. A faint blast of laughter gusted from the function room below where the smaller kids were watching *Young Frankenstein*. They had seen the film so many times they could join in with the dialogue, but the celluloid was fragile, the generator too precious to squander on fripperies and the screening remained a treat. A year ago Shuggie would have been with them, but here he was, lounging at the bar, torn-faced and half-drunk.

Magnus thought of the boy as his son, but as Shug had reminded him that morning, with enough force to make Magnus bunch his fists, they were not blood relations, just people the Sweats had thrown together. 'You need me more than I need you,' Shug had spat in his half-English, half-island accent. Magnus feared he was right.

What signifies the life o' man,
An' 'twere na for the lasses, O.

He followed Shug's gaze and saw Willow standing by the door. The girl had recently shorn her hair down to the bone. It was growing back in a dark fuzz that emphasised the curve of her skull. The loss of Willow's curls had seemed like an act of violence, but it had not made her less pretty. The girl's dark eyes met Shuggie's and then she slipped out into the corridor beyond. Shug caught Magnus watching him and scowled.

Her prentice han' she try'd on man,
An' then she made the lasses, O.

Magnus whipped the song to its final flourish. He acknowledged the applause, knocking back his beer to give himself an excuse to go to the bar. He was halfway across the lounge when Poor Alice caught his sleeve and asked, 'Did you write that tune, Magnus?'

The urge to pull away from the old woman's grasp was strong, but Magnus crouched beside her chair and admitted that Robert Burns had come up with the song.

'Well, he could not have sung it better than you.' Alice smiled her sweet vague smile and patted his hand.

'Thanks, Alice.' Magnus prised her fingers from the cuff of his shirt and kissed her cheek. Her rosewater scent gave him a shiver of déjà vu, but there were days when everything seemed like a memory and he did not try to pin it down. He stood up and looked towards the bar. Shug was gone. On the other side of the lounge Bjarne lumbered to his feet and began to push his way towards the door. Magnus saw the set of the big man's jaw and realised that he was not the only one who had been watching the boy. He caught up with him in the corridor. 'Bjarne . . .'

Before the Sweats, Willow's foster father had been an area manager for Ford motors, now he was one of the few islanders who traded beyond the Orkneys. The out-of-date Stella Artois they were drinking was courtesy of one of his deals. Bjarne had gifted a dozen crates of the stuff to the Easter celebrations as part of his election bid to become president of the Orkney Islands. He scowled at Magnus, his weathered face made even ruddier than usual by heat, drink and bad temper. They had talked about the children once before and Bjarne spoke as if they were midway through the same conversation.

'My lass, your boy, there's a difference.'

Magnus was tempted to reply that it was the differences between them that attracted the youngsters, but he knew what Bjarne meant. There was no doctor on the islands and the stakes were higher for women.

'I've spoken to him. He knows to treat girls with respect.'

The condoms Magnus had given Shug were well past their sell-by date. He worried the latex might have perished.

Bjarne's laugh was beery and sarcastic. 'My father spoke to me when I was his age.'

Magnus nodded. 'Mine too.'

'Did you listen?'

Magnus's father's contribution to his sex education had been succinct. *If you must tomcat around make sure it's not with an island girl and make sure you take precautions.*

'I was no saint, but I didn't get any lassies pregnant. If anyone got their heart broken it was me.' Magnus risked a hand on Bjarne's shoulder. The gesture felt odd. He took his hand away and let it hang awkwardly by his side. 'We need to trust our kids. If we don't we'll just push them closer together.'

He wanted to ask Bjarne what the Montague and Capulet shite was all about. Shuggie was a decent lad when he wasn't being a pain in the arse. Why was he so set against him?

The big man's feet were set wide apart, like a boxer making sure of his centre of gravity. 'I can read your mind, McFall. You think we should just let them get on with it.'

Magnus shrugged. 'They're teenagers. It's natural for them to want to spend time with the opposite sex.'

'My girl's only fifteen years old. She's too young to be thinking about any of that.'

There was no way of knowing precisely how old the children were. They had each been orphaned by the Sweats and their ages guessed at by the people who had found and adopted them.

Stevie Flint stepped from the lounge and gave them a questioning look. 'Everything okay?'

Bjarne ignored her. Magnus smiled. 'Aye, fine.'

Stevie's face was already burnished by exposure to the spring sunshine. She raised her eyebrows, but went back into the lounge where the trio of women who always sang 'Harper Valley PTA' were going into their party piece. Stevie stayed sober at island gatherings. The New Orcadian Council recognised the need for the occasional ceilidh, but getting drunk was a risky business and there was an unspoken agreement that a few clear heads were needed. There had been too many accidents, too many brains blown out under the influence, for alcohol to be taken lightly.

The women's voices reached into the lobby, stretched close to strangling point. The company in the lounge had started to clap in time, perhaps in the hope of hurrying the song along.

'Christ, please kill me now,' Magnus whispered.

'That can be arranged,' Bjarne said, his voice flat and free of threat. He turned and walked towards the stairs. The hotel corridor was dark after the sunlit lounge, but it was still possible to make out the stains on the carpet, the peeling wallpaper. They were living in the ruins of a civilisation they had no means of restoring.

Magnus swore softly under his breath and followed the big man. It was like running uphill. The Easter celebrations had endeavoured to cater to everyone and the day had been a long one. First there had been the church service in Kirkwall Cathedral. Then, in a spirit of cohesion, they had made their way in carts and on horseback through the blackened ruins of the island's burnt-out capital, back to Stromness, where they had embarked on a community lunch followed by a concert that was turning into a pub lock-in. Magnus had drank more than he was used to and his feet were not wholly his own.

'Even if you don't trust Shug, you should trust Willow.'

Bjarne did not bother to look back. 'I trust her, but she'd have no chance against that wee cunt.'

Magnus grabbed Bjarne by the arm. 'He's just a boy.'

Bjarne pulled away. He enunciated his words slowly, as if he was speaking to someone who had been hit on the head too many times.

'He's a randy little shit and I don't want him anywhere near my daughter.'

'Willow came looking for Shug. Maybe it's your daughter who's the randy one.'

Bjarne's breath touched Magnus's face, warm and beery. 'Watch your mouth, McFall, and tell that boy of yours to keep away from my Willow, if he wants to keep his bollocks. I've gelded enough calves to have developed a knack for it. A quick flick of the wrist with a sharp knife, that's all it takes.'

The blast of anger was sudden and hard to contain. 'Go anywhere near Shug and you'll wish I'd cut your balls off. I'll slit you port to stern.'

Bjarne's grin was satisfied, as if all he had really wanted was for Magnus to lose his temper. 'Thanks for the warning.'

They were standing at the top of the stairs, an intersection of light and dark. Sunshine flooded through the stairwell's high windows, outlining Bjarne's body in gold and casting Magnus in his shadow. It would be easy to shove the big man down the stairs, but Magnus had sworn that he was done with killing. He took a step backwards.

'I shouldn't have said that about Willow. She's a good kid. You don't need to worry about her.'

'I meant every word I said about Shuggie. He's a wee bastard. Keep him away from my girl.'

'She's not your girl, Bjarne, no more than Shug is my boy. They're both old enough to realise that now. We can look out for them, but we can't make them do what we want.'

'You'd better try, if you want him to stay in one piece.' Bjarne turned and jogged down the stairs.

Magnus reckoned he had held him there long enough for Shug and Willow to get to whatever hidey-hole they were bound for and did not bother to follow him. The big man was a problem that would keep till later. The hotel door slammed below. He wondered if he should have a word with Shuggie, but knew it would do no good. The boy, who had once depended on him for everything, now barely gave him the time of day.

'Fuck him,' Magnus muttered under his breath. 'Wee fucker.' He walked back to the lounge and another beyond-the-sell-by-date bottle of beer.

Two

Stevie Flint watched Magnus's progress towards the bar and wondered why they had never slept together. It was nothing to do with looks. The Orcadian had aged since his return to the islands, but his hair was thick and black, and he was still in decent shape. Stevie smiled and rubbed Pistol's ears. The dog set his head on her knee, smearing her trousers with saliva. Her mind always turned towards sex at island gatherings. She supposed that had been part of the purpose of get-togethers in the old days, to find mates.

Stevie scanned the room marvelling at how easily people had partnered up in the years their small community had grown. They were incomers like her, who had washed up on the islands alone, like driftwood after a storm. All of them had been bereaved. Some of the new couples were so devoted it was hard to believe their relationship had been forged from death. Other liaisons were more fluid, people slipping from one partner to the next. There were moralists on the island who looked down on women who had been with a lot of men. Stevie had not slept with anyone since the Sweats, but she had no problem with promiscuity. Seeking comfort in a warm bed was more natural than always being alone.

She watched Magnus put a bottle of beer to his mouth and saw the rise and fall of his Adam's apple as he glugged down its contents. His feet shifted as if he was trying to keep his balance and she realised that he was sliding from drunk towards fully tanked. He would be among the casualties sleeping it off between damp sheets in one of the Stromness Hotel's abandoned guest rooms that night. There was no shame in it. It was men like Bjarne that worried her.

Stevie had her own theory about why Willow had hacked her hair off and why her stepfather was so against young Shug. She ran a finger along Pistol's dark muzzle and wondered again if her suspicions were strong enough to act on. Bjarne's presidential ambitions meant her motives could easily be misconstrued.

'You could do worse.' Poor Alice nodded towards Magnus. Little Evie, the most recent post-Sweats child born on the island, was bouncing on the old lady's lap.

Stevie said, 'Have you been spying on me, Alice?'

'Spying on you, while you spy on him.'

Magnus had picked up his guitar. Stevie hoped he was not going to sing one of his own songs. As usual the islanders had turned to making things over the winter and there was a glut of poorly written plague memoirs, gloomy melodies and murky paintings.

Poor Alice bobbed Evie up and down, up and down. She grinned at Stevie over the toddler's head. 'Don't worry, your secret's safe.'

Evie's cheeks were bright red. She stretched, yearning towards her mother, Breda, wriggled free and slid gently to the ground.

Stevie gripped Pistol's collar. 'No secrets on an island, Alice. I like Magnus well enough, but I won't be tucking him into bed tonight.'

Poor Alice's smile revealed gummy gaps where her incisors should have been. 'He wouldn't be much use to you tonight right enough, but Magnus is a decent lad. He's done his best for young Shug and he's not one of those who are always drunk.'

Magnus was strumming out a tune, something soft and lively, that made Stevie think of sunlight shimmering through a waterfall. Most of the bar was chatting through the music but a few folk were swaying with the rhythm. Gentle songs were dangerous. They could evoke emotions best tamped down.

'I'm not looking for a man, Alice.'

The old woman shook her head. 'You'll dry up. Your skin will turn to leather and your twat will close tight as a clam . . .'

Stevie was about to tell Alice to mind her own business, but she saw young Connor barrelling into the room, only just avoiding a collision with the fully laden tray of drinks John Prentice was ferrying across the lounge. Stevie shook her head. 'Here comes a hurricane.'

The boy had recently gone through a growth spurt and was not yet used to the length of his limbs. Stevie had reckoned Connor ready for some responsibility. There had been recent talk of strange vessels sighted on the horizon. The number of lookouts had been increased and she had included Connor on the rota, setting him on watch in a hotel bedroom with a good view of the harbour.

'Whoa . . .' She caught hold of his arm, stopping him just short of their table. 'Where's the fire?'

The boy's face was red. Pistol gave his hand a friendly butt with his nose. Usually Connor would have rubbed the dog's ears, but he ignored him.

'There's a boat.'

'Where?' Stevie got to her feet and strode to the nearest window.

'I wasn't asleep.' Connor was on the edge of tears.

Stevie twitched back the curtains, careful to keep her body out of sight, and looked out. A handsome four-berth yacht was sitting just outside the harbour, its sails furled. A rowing boat was making its way steadily towards the quay. Stevie narrowed her eyes and was able to make out three people. Two of them were rowing and the vessel was making good progress.

'Jesus, Connor. A bit of warning would have been nice.'

The rowing boat docked and a man climbed from its stern, up the metal ladder onto the quay. Someone in the boat cast a rope towards him. He caught it and secured it around a bollard. The man was tall and rangy. As Stevie watched, the other passengers followed him onto solid ground: a blonde-haired woman, and another man, shorter than the first, but powerfully built. The distance between the boat and the barroom was too far for Stevie to be able to make out their features, but she knew everyone on the Orkneys and could already tell that the men and woman were strangers. The trio stood for a moment, in conversation. Stevie stayed by the window, caught between the need for action and an urge to observe them.

Connor whispered, 'I'm sorry.'

She tried to hide her irritation. 'You screwed up, now you have to help deal with it. Find Alan Bold and tell him he's wanted.'

The boy's face flushed a deeper shade of crimson. 'I think he's—'

'No doubt. Stop him mid-stroke if you have to.'

Connor nodded and scurried off, determined to redeem himself, his chin set against the embarrassment in store.

Stevie glanced out of the window again. The strangers were dressed in a combination of combat gear and outdoor wear that made them look like a cross between arctic explorers and Vikings. Their clothes had probably been top of the range when they had looted them, but now they were scuffed and dirty. They were armed, the obligatory rifles strapped to their backs. Stevie felt the same shrinking in her chest that she had sometimes experienced travelling on the London Underground when terror threat levels were high. Strangers were not unknown on the islands, but they usually arrived in the company of one of the lookouts and most were tired to the point of deference, not straight-spined and combat-ready.

The woman pointed at the hotel and the men turned their heads towards it. Stevie ducked behind the curtains, though there was little point in hiding. The sound of music and chatter must have drifted down to the harbour.

She pushed her way to the front of the room, touching Magnus's shoulder as she went, putting a finger to her lips. He gave her an irritated look, but strummed the tune to a clumsy conclusion. Stevie took the poker from its place beside the fire and banged it against the table in front of her, hard enough to crack the veneer. Pistol barked and the warm hubbub of laughter, chat and clinking glasses shivered into silence.

'We have some unexpected visitors.'

People seated by the windows looked down into the street. Stevie saw some of the islanders reach for their weapons and raised her free hand, telling them not to be hasty. 'Unexpected doesn't mean hostile. Remember, you were all unexpected visitors when you first arrived.'

Some of the islanders were getting to their feet. They said hurried goodbyes and hustled their small families out of the back door of the lounge. Stevie did not blame them. Adult survivors generally had some immunity to the Sweats, but children born since the pandemic were untested.

Stevie ignored the exodus. 'Please remember, we greet all visitors with courtesy.'

Brendan Banks stage-whispered, 'It's easier to be courteous once someone's been quarantined.' The Yorkshireman was sitting in the big bay window next to Magnus, a banjo resting on his lap.

Alan Bold stepped through the door, tucking his shirt into his jeans; his black hair and beard the usual wild tangle that had led the children to nickname him 'Scribble'. 'What's going on?'

'Three newcomers. I suggest we go down and greet them.' Stevie patted her thigh and Pistol trotted to her side.

Alan Bold's eyes were sleepy with drink and sex. His mouth had a bitter twist.

'Who fucked-up the lookout?'

Connor was standing, awkward and ashamed, on the edge of the conversation. Stevie gave the boy a smile and said, 'Me, I was in charge.'

'Yeah and I'm fucking Spartacus too.' Bold threw the boy a look.

Stevie said, 'Let's go down before it's too . . .'

It was already too late.

The sound in the room died and she looked up to see the strangers standing in the lounge doorway. The men were big enough to do some damage. Their beards were bushy and unkempt, their hair long and straggling. Stevie knew she should be cautious of them, but it was the woman who held her attention. She was dirty and travel-worn, her blonde hair kinked in matted waves across her shoulders. The woman's face was drawn and she would have been nothing much to look at, were it not for the scar that ran the length of the left side of her face, straight as a knife edge. The wound puckered her top lip and stopped short of her eye. The weapon that sliced her must have touched some ocular nerve, because her left pupil was dull and milky and no life-light gleamed inside. The scar emphasised the clean symmetry of her face and tipped her into beauty.

Pistol growled and Stevie caught hold of his collar, 'Shush.' She levelled her gaze at the trio. 'My name is Stevie Flint. I'm the elected president of the Orkney Islands. We operate a strict quarantine here. Please do not come any closer.'

Little Evie sensed the tension in the room and started to cry. Stevie kept her focus on the newcomers, careful not to catch any of the islanders' eyes. She felt the uncertainty of her position, the precariousness of her authority.

'None of us are sick.' The woman smiled and held up her hands, to show that she meant no harm. An eye was tattooed in the centre of each of her palms. They stared out at the company, unblinking. 'The boys and I are passing through. We heard your music and thought we should pay our respects. It looks like we chose a good day to arrive.'

Alan Bold said, 'This is an island. We're not on the way to anywhere. No one passes through.'

Stevie gave Pistol's collar a small tug, making the dog sit tall and straight. He was her gun. 'What's your business here?'

The woman said, 'This island is not on the way to anywhere and neither are we. It makes sense that our paths would intersect.'

Poor Alice said, 'Christ Almighty.' Her voice was heavy with sarcasm and somebody gave a boozy laugh.

Stevie glared at the old woman, silencing her. She tried to keep her irritation out of her voice. 'Peaceful visitors are welcome, as long as they make no trouble and contribute something to the community, but our islands are free of disease. We want to keep it that way. All newcomers must undergo two weeks of isolation.'

There was a murmur of assent from the people at the bar, but the woman's attention was no longer on Stevie. She stepped beyond the shelter of her companions, beyond the invisible quarantine line, towards the bay window where Magnus still sat, his guitar resting on his lap. This time her smile was genuine. It lit up her face and Stevie realised she would have been pretty, even without the scar. The people at Magnus's table shrank into the lee of the bay window and Stevie raised her voice, 'Stay where you are.' Pistol growled. She tugged his collar again, and the dog rose up on his back legs, barking.

'For fuck's sake.' Brendan Banks shifted back in his seat, holding his banjo in front of him as if it were a talisman against infection. He clamped his free hand over his mouth and nose. Beside him, Jenny Seybold raised her cardigan to her face, her eyes wide behind the makeshift mask.

Only Magnus seemed unafraid. He looked up, his expression cloudy, as if he recognised but could not place the woman. He shook his head. 'I don't . . .' Magnus set his guitar down and rose rustily to his feet. 'Belle?' His voice was tinged with shyness. 'What happened . . .?' He ran a finger down his face, mimicking the route of her scar, and took a step towards the woman. Brendan caught the hem of his jacket in an attempt to hold him back, but he tugged free of the Yorkshireman and held out his hands to the woman. Belle took them in hers, as if they were about to dance a reel, and Magnus pulled her into an awkward hug.

Stevie felt suddenly embarrassed. She glanced around the bar and saw that the islanders were staring at the couple. Even Brendan and Jenny, too close to the stranger for comfort, were caught in the drama. She said, 'You know each other?'

'Aye,' Magnus disengaged himself. 'This is Belle. I met her soon after I left London.' He nodded to his audience. 'She's okay.'

Stevie said, 'You vouch for her?'

'I vouch for her.' Magnus's voice was thick with drink, his smile as beery as a barroom darts champion's. He glanced at the two men, still standing broad-shouldered and silent on the edge of the room, their eyes wary and edged with deep creases that suggested long days of walking into the sun. Magnus gave an expansive grin. 'And I vouch for these lads too. If they're with

Belle, they're all right.' He put his arm around Belle's waist, pulling her close.

Poor Alice had edged her way to the front of the room, unable to resist being part of the action. She nudged Stevie. 'Looks like you missed your chance.'

Stevie whispered, 'Life is full of second chances, Alice. Otherwise you and I wouldn't be here to miss them.' She looked at Magnus. 'You can't vouch for people you don't know, and you can't guarantee they aren't carrying the Sweats. If they intend to stay, they must go through quarantine. I suggest you keep your distance if you don't want to join them.'

Magnus gave Belle a last squeeze and disengaged himself. 'She told you, they're clean.'

'For Christ's sake man, how many times did you hear that right before someone started coughing?' Brendan's usually mild voice was sharp. 'How many people do you know who looked in the pink, right up until the moment they dropped dead?'

One of the men said, 'We'll go into quarantine.'

Stevie had expected the demand to send the trio on their way. Their sudden acquiescence unsettled her. Pistol gave another low growl and she caught hold of his muzzle, silencing him.

'Leave the hotel. Keep a good distance from anyone you see. We'll make arrangements on the street . . .' They turned to leave, but Stevie called them back. 'Before you go . . .' she asked the question she asked all new arrivals, '. . . are any of you doctors?'

'I was an art history student and part-time coffee barista. Ed worked in a mobile phone shop.' Belle nodded towards the tall man. 'Rob's the only one who had a half-useful job.'

Ed glanced at his feet.

'I was a car mechanic,' Rob said. 'I worked for Kwik Fit.'

The mention of the cut-price tyre fitter with its jaunty advertising jingle made the lounge bar laugh.

Brendan said, 'I think you ripped me off for a set of new treads back in 2006.'

Rob gave a small smile. 'Could be.'

Someone shouted across the lounge, 'Have you any news from outside?'

The tall man levelled his tired gaze at the company. 'The news is, you're right to stay on an island and you're right to quarantine us, even though we're well. The cities are still burning. People are still dying.'

The islanders began to shout out names of towns and cities where they had once lived, asking for news of them. Stevie said, 'They need to go.' She nodded towards the door. The trio strolled from the room, taking their time.

The good feeling that had risen with the laughter of a moment ago was fractured. The younger children and families were gone, leaving hardened drinkers to the rest of the long night. The committee had rationed out bottles of branded beer the day before, but there was enough home brew on the islands to intoxicate a school of whales. Stevie knew that soon Mason jars and screw-topped bottles would appear on the tables, filled with liquid that spanned a spectrum of browns and yellows, making the lounge look like a busy day in an urologist's lab. She released her hold on Pistol's collar and went over to where Magnus was sitting.

'The only reason I'm not putting you in quarantine with them is because I know things are difficult between you and Shuggie at the moment. Don't make me regret it.'

Magnus stared her out. 'You want me to promise not to come down with the Sweats?'

His belligerence was out of character.

Stevie's hand tingled. 'I want you to stop being a wanker.'

She would have said more, but Alan Bold was heading out of the lounge, following the newcomers into the gloaming. Stevie caught a glimpse of her deputy's ruddy face, his cunt-struck eyes, and hoped he was not going to be trouble.

Three

Alan Bold's bravado seemed to have deflated in the dimness of the hotel lobby. He stood loitering in the entrance hall, amongst photographs of Victorian hunters armoured in tweed, posing with shut-faced gillies in front of their kills. One of Bjarne's election posters was pasted to the wall.

BJARNE for PRESIDENT!

VOTE BJARNE for ELECTRICITY
VOTE BJARNE for FUEL
VOTE BJARNE for PROGRESS
VOTE BJARNE for NORMALITY

For fuel in your tank & electricity in your home

VOTE BJARNE! BJARNE! BJARNE! BJARNE!

Stevie resisted the urge to rip the big man's empty boasts from the wall. She peered through the etched glass of the hotel's front door onto the quayside. The sun had started to sink towards the sea, so red it seemed the water might hiss with its descent. Pistol thumped his tail on the lobby floor and scratched at the door, keen to go out into the night.

Bold said, 'Where will you put them?' This was how it was with the deputy. He played the big man, but found it hard to make decisions.

'The usual place, it's well enough stocked, isn't it?'

Bold shrugged. 'As far as I know.'

Stevie nodded towards the strangers. 'What do you think it is with them?'

Bold put a hand on her shoulder. 'They're looking for somewhere to settle. We should hope they pick here.'

The deputy was right. The innovations of the last century had been lost and strong bodies were essential to the community's survival, but Stevie felt apprehensive. She pushed his hand away. 'There's something about them . . .' She let the sentence tail away. 'They look hunted.'

'We're all haunted.'

Stevie did not bother to correct Bold. She called Pistol to heel, pushed open the hotel door and stepped outside, hoping that whatever was hunting, or haunting the newcomers, would not follow them to Orkney.

The trio heard the door open and turned towards the sound. Stevie stopped six yards from them, resisting the reflex to hold out a hand in greeting. Pistol stood still by her right side, Alan Bold on her left, an irritating step beyond her eye-line. Stevie said, 'I'm sorry we couldn't give you a warmer welcome.'

Rob, the tall man, had olive skin and eyes almost as dark as his hair. The complexion of his companion, Ed, was pale with the faint blush that would have been described as English Rose, had he been a girl. Rob said, 'These are difficult times. You're right to be cautious.'

The door behind her opened, Stevie heard ragged footsteps on the cobbles and turned to see Magnus coming out of the hotel. Pistol got to his feet, wagging his tail.

'Don't worry,' Magnus said. He had sobered a little, but his walk still had a stagger to it. 'I'll keep my distance.'

Belle gave him a tired smile. Her good eye was cornflower blue, the damaged one a blue shade of white. She looked at Stevie, 'Do I address you as Madam President?'

'If you like, but most people call me Stevie. How long do you plan on staying?'

'We don't plan things.' Ed's voice was soft, with a faint burr which made Stevie think of warmer coastlines. 'We see where the wind blows us.'

She said, 'And it blew you here?'

'Not quite.' Belle gave a ghost of a smile. 'The last time I saw Mags he was headed this way.' She looked at Magnus. 'Did your family . . .?'

Magnus glanced away. 'They were gone before I arrived.'

That was how they spoke of people the Sweats had taken, as if they had set off on a long voyage.

Stevie said, 'We're sending you to Wyre for two weeks. There's a farmhouse about a mile from where you'll dock. It should be stocked with enough preserved food to keep you going for a few days and the foraging isn't bad at this time of year. I'm guessing you already have fishing rods and we'll drop fresh provisions on shore for you as and when we can. It's a short sail from here. Are you up to it?'

'We're up to it.' Rob wet a finger and held it in the air. 'But I'm not sure the wind is. We made the last stretch of the journey on the tide. The best we can do right now is row back to the boat and wait until it lifts.'

Stevie looked out to where their yacht sat; calm against the glassy sea. The vessel's mastheads rose like bare bones into the sky. She wanted the strangers gone.

Magnus said, 'The wind will lift soon enough.'

It was true. The wind swept across the islands, so fierce that few trees survived. Stevie loved the long vistas of uninterrupted green, the way the sky and the sea were hinged to the land.

She nodded. 'Do you need any supplies to take on board? Fresh water?'

Ed said, 'We filled our containers earlier.'

'Good.' Alan Bold was all business now. Stevie stood by while he instructed the trio on the coordinates of Wyre, directions to the farmhouse and the arrangements of how to get in touch should they need help. Magnus made an attempt to join in, but his contributions were drink-fuddled and after a while he raised a hand in farewell and lurched back towards the warmth of the hotel.

Stevie wondered where the newcomers had refilled their water containers and how long they had been on the islands. The coastline was full of sheltered bays where vessels could quietly dock. There were rarely glimpsed hermits on some of the islands, but it bothered her to think that there might be strangers hiding out, unknown to the community.

Alan had finished his spiel and was looking at her expectantly. 'Anything you want to add?'

'Just a question you've already been asked.' Stevie forced a smile. 'Do you have news from outside?'

Rob looked like he was about to say something, but it was Belle who spoke.

'We tried to skirt the bigger towns and cities, but once or twice we ventured in, to track down things we needed. It was like stepping into hell. Out here you can see what's coming towards you, in amongst the buildings you never know when someone is going to take a potshot. I was lucky to meet these guys. Without them . . .' She shrugged.

Stevie remembered her own flight from London in the stolen Jaguar, the stranger she had run over, the men she had shot.

Ed put a hand on Belle's arm. 'We're knackered. It's time to go.'

Belle let herself be led and the three of them made their way along the quayside to where they had moored the rowing boat. Alan Bold and Stevie stood outside the hotel, watching them go.

The deputy said, 'They would be an asset.'

Belle and her companions took it in turns to descend the rungs of the ladder strapped to the quayside. They stepped into the boat easily, each of them adjusting their weight to the lurch of the sea with the sureness of old salts. Stevie watched as Ed dipped the oars into the water and sent the vessel gliding slowly towards the becalmed yacht. 'I'm still not sure I trust them.'

'Magnus vouched for her.'

Stevie shrugged. 'He hasn't seen her since the first outbreak of the Sweats. A lot can happen in seven years. None of us are the same people we were.'

'No,' Bold said and stuffed his hands into his pockets. 'Some of us went from zero to hero.'

Stevie knew he meant her, but she did not bother to contradict him. He was right. The plague had been the making of her.

Four

Magnus's head was ringed by a band of pain, his throat dry. He heard movement in the kitchen and thought about shouting for Shug to bring him a glass of water, but he did not want the boy to see him in this state, not when he had Bjarne's warning to pass on.

Fuck.

Fuck.

Fuck.

Magnus rolled onto his front and pulled the pillow over his head, hoping to relieve the pressure on his skull. He could not remember how he had travelled the six miles from Stromness. His body ached, but it felt free of the bruises that usually followed a drunken cycle-ride home. Someone must have slung him into the back of their cart and dropped him off. The thought made him groan.

His memories of the evening were foggy, but he recalled Belle's arrival clearly enough to know that she had grown up. The girl he had first met at Tanqueray House, the ill-starred community he had briefly been a part of after he had fled London in the first wave of the Sweats, had been young and scared. She had come from privilege and seemed ill-suited to the privations of the post-plague world. This new version of Belle had the soldierly assurance of someone who had done a deal with death. The welt on her face lent her a battle-scarred look, but it was more than that. She had the air of a woman who would do whatever she needed to survive.

Magnus had closed the door on most of his memories of the period that had followed his flight from the city. Now he forced himself to remember the way Belle had taken his hand outside Tanqueray House while a mob closed in on him, baying for his blood. He owed her for that, even if he could not be certain that the new Belle would do the same.

Magnus dragged himself from bed, pulled on his crumpled jeans and padded barefoot into the lobby. The polished floorboards were cool against his soles. It was meant to be spring, but the day was dull and rain spattered the windows. The wind would be strong enough to send the becalmed boat to Wyre. A clatter of crockery came from the kitchen. The door was open a sliver. Magnus peered through the gap, but all he could see was a slice of flagged floor, a corner of a work unit.

'Morning.' His voice sounded cracked and old. The only response was the sound of dishes rattling into the sink. Magnus tried again. 'Hello?'

He half-expected to hear Belle's voice, but it was Shug who answered. 'Aye.' The word was all irritation and vowels.

Magnus stuck his head into the room. The kitchen was in its usual state of not quite chaos. A pile of his father's farm journals sat on the table, where he had left them a couple of nights ago, when he had been trying to work out some kind of sowing strategy. He had washed their work clothes earlier in the week and their overalls drooped from the pulley like hanged men. Shug was at the sink, cleaning the oatmeal pan.

'You have a good night?'

Shug dipped the pan into a bucket of rinse water on the draining board.

'Not as good as you from the sounds of it.' His jeans were fresh, his hair damp and slicked back, but Shug's eyes were dark from lack of sleep. Magnus wondered if he too was suffering from a hangover, or if something other than drinking had kept the boy up late. He was about to ask if he had mucked out the chickens and fed the pig, but it was the kind of question that led to an argument and his head was too sore for raised voices. He let the door swing to. Shug had been diligent at his tasks until a couple of months ago when he had become surly and prone to absences. It was part of growing up Magnus supposed, a means of disengaging from the mothership, except Shug had no mother.

Magnus took his waterproof from the peg in the hallway and slung it on, wincing at the feel of the cold, plasticky fabric against his naked torso. Then he shoved his bare feet into a pair of wellies standing by the door. He tried to conjure his own mother's voice in his head, but her presence was fainter than it had been. It was his father's voice that occurred to him more often these days, Big Magnus, the disciplinarian who had died in a combine accident caused by a moment's lapse of attention. Magnus shuddered. It hurt him to think of the blades slicing into his father's flesh, the instant of panic he must have felt as he pulled free the last of the blockage that had jammed the machine and realised, as it roared back into life, that he had not turned off the ignition.

He pulled open the heavy back door and went out into the yard. The rain had stopped, but the atmosphere was damp, the sky heavy, another shower building. A scatter of hens bustled towards him and he saw that they had not been locked up the night before. 'Aye, aye,' he said, in the soft voice he reserved for animals and seduction. 'You'll get fed soon enough.' Magnus lifted the cover from the water butt by the door, washed his face and scooped a palm-full into his mouth. The water tasted clean and ice-cold. He drank again and then walked to the vegetable plot and peed into the rhubarb.

'That's disgusting.'

Magnus turned and saw Shug watching him. He tucked himself away. 'It's the best way to fertilise rhubarb.'

'I hope Rab the pig enjoys it, because I'm not eating it.'

'You never complained before.'

The boy turned away. 'You fucking disgust me.'

His own father would have belted the boy, but Magnus looked down at his naked chest, goose-pimpled from the cold, his jeans stiff with stale beer and worse and thought that Shug had a point.

'I give the stems a thorough wash before I cook them.' He followed the boy across the yard, both of them ignoring the chickens fussing around their feet. Shug's spine was straight with indignation, his new white denim-jacket spotless. Magnus said, 'And cooking destroys any toxins.'

'Tell that to the pig, he'll be the one eating it.'

'Ach, you love my rhubarb pies, it's the urine that gives them that extra piquancy.'

Even a month ago Shug might have laughed, but now he ignored Magnus and took his bicycle from its place by the back door.

'Bjarne is after you,' Magnus said, as the boy he thought of as his son flung himself onto the saddle. 'He's got some bee in his bonnet about you and Willow.'

Shug was pedalling towards the gate, working hard against the gradient of the yard. He looked back over his shoulder and shouted, 'He can fuck off too.' Then he was through the open gate and down the road, a splash of white against the green fields beyond.

Magnus shouted, 'You didn't put the hens in last night.' His words were lost in the rising wind. He muttered, 'We're lucky a dog didn't massacre them,' and watched Shug disappear in the direction of Willow's house. He thought about Bjarne's bunched fists and wondered if he should risk humiliating the boy by following him. A hen tap-tap-tapped at the toe of his wellie with its beak and Magnus looked down at it. 'Hungry enough for rubber are you?' Rain was spattering the yard. He zipped up his jacket and pulled the hood over his head. 'Let's leave silly buggers to themselves while I fix you some gourmet mash.'

The sky was darkening, the rain building to more than a shower. Shug's fancy jacket would be no match for a storm. Magnus hoped the boy would shelter somewhere until it passed, but he knew that wild weather and hard fists were no match for young love.

Rab the pig bellowed in his pen.

Magnus muttered, 'Aye, aye, you'll get yours too.'

The thought of hard fists made him think of Bjarne again. Shug was at an age for beatings. He felt an urge to go after the boy. The pig shrieked. Magnus cursed and went to prepare its slops. He would see to the livestock first. Then he would ride over to Bjarne's and make sure that Shug was okay.

Five

Stevie put her feet on the desk and leaned back in her chair, trying to suppress a yawn. The night had been a long one. She had slept badly and had spent most of the morning with the clean-up group, putting the hotel to rights. 'I've got a bad feeling about them.'

'I don't see why you're getting your panties in a twist. They're young and able-bodied. They could be an asset.' Alan Bold's lips were red behind his beard. He had tried to kiss Stevie once. She had pushed him away and he had called her a frigid bitch. Now he rubbed his face as if he was trying to erase his hangover. 'Magnus vouched for them.'

'Magnus was seven sheets to the wind.'

Bold took a long drink of water and then raised the glass in the air, as if toasting something worth celebrating. 'In vino veritas.'

The New Orcadian Council had rejected the existing civic buildings as being too big, too haunted by the past. Instead they had made their headquarters in Stromness, in what had been a gift shop and cafe. Stevie liked the shop's large display windows which allowed anyone passing by to see inside. She suspected that Alan Bold was less keen on them. She glanced across the desk at her deputy and caught him scanning her legs, assessing them beneath her jeans.

'You can only be veritas regarding things you know something about.' She touched Bold's water glass with the toe of her boot, threatening to tip it over.

He shifted his eyes from her thighs and moved his glass beyond her reach. 'You want me to put a watch on them?'

'We're not the fucking Stasi.' Stevie had found herself fantasising about sailing to Wyre and observing the newcomers from some hidden vantage. She slid her feet from the desk and walked to the window. 'You can't start spying on people,' she said, half to herself.

When it became clear that their community had grown large enough to require some form of governance the freshly elected New Orcadian Council had toyed with the idea of perambulating across Orkney, holding meetings on each of the populated islands in turn, but the plan had proved impractical. It was not the weather that had stopped them. It was often wild in the dark months, but they could have planned their trips around the long bright summer nights that stretched into morning. It was the attitude of the outlying islanders that had hampered the council's urge to bring them into the democratic fold. Some islands were home to only one or two people, others to mysterious communities who preferred to be left to their own devices. In the end it had been decided that they would hold their small parliaments in the densest area of population, the town that had once been the second largest on the island, Stromness.

Stevie looked out at the cobbled street. The shop window was grimy and she could make out the faint outline of a long-gone window decal announcing *TEA & COFFEE, FRESH SCONES, SOUVENIRS*. The day was overcast, the street pitched in shadows that gave an impression of premature twilight. The wind was up, Belle's yacht on its way to quarantine. Stevie sensed the ghost of despair, the enemy of survival, hovering on the edge of her consciousness.

She had first come to the islands on a boat, with other survivors. They had been trying to outrun death and although they had known there was no way to put an ocean between them and the Sweats, the sea, grey and choppy, had seemed to offer possibilities. She had stood on the deck, beyond sight of land, and felt the salt spray sting her face, but the moment of cleansing she had craved had not happened. Instead, she had realised that the consequences of the pandemic would be waiting, wherever she landed. The only way to survive was to face them.

There had been no sign of any survivors on the islands until they had found Willow, bloody and malnourished, beneath her parents' bed. Stevie preferred to imagine that Orcadian survivors had fled, moved by the same urge that had brought her to their islands. It hurt too much to think that the entire population had either died of the Sweats, or taken the other way out: a gun to the head; looted packets of pills; a last look at the coastline from some high cliff; sailing rudderless into the storm.

Disposing of the bodies of people left behind had taken months. They had started by burying them in deep trenches, dug with the aid of a mechanical digger. Some people had joined in prayers and hymns over the mass graves in an attempt to give the occasion some dignity. Others had ignored all but the burials they had drawn in the lottery. They did their duty and then walked away, leaving the digger operator to cover the pit. Stevie was not religious, but she had volunteered for more burials than she was required to and had lingered on until the end of each one, mumbling her way through 'Abide with Me'. If it was an attempt to placate the dead, she had failed. They came to her most nights in dreams.

Eventually they had realised that, although the islands were small, it would take years to fumigate them. The longer they left the dead, rotting in their houses, the greater the danger from disease. In the end they had agreed to burn down the capital of the island, Kirkwall. They had given themselves two weeks to strip the place of useful goods. Stevie had assigned herself to a team clearing the library. They had loaded the books willy-nilly onto vans, not bothering to distinguish by title. Who could say what would prove useful? A detective novel might spark a thought process that inspired the invention of a new form of fuel; a cookery book might spawn a cure for bronchitis.

A fortnight had not been long enough. They had allowed another week's grace to ransack the place. Then one of their party had caught what might have been typhoid and died. The rest of the survivors had dosed themselves with antibiotics, built a firewall around the cathedral and set the capital ablaze. It had burned for days. Plumes of smoke had reached as far as Stromness and ash had drifted across the island, causing the survivors to fear they might be spreading the diseases they had hoped to avoid. But the worst thing had been the smell, a sickly mix of roasting flesh and melting plastic that had sent them temporarily fleeing mainland Orkney for its outlying islands.

Stevie watched as young Connor ran across the road towards the Pier Arts Centre. The rest of the school class followed close behind. A moment later Lorna Mills, who taught history and religion, came into view. Stevie counted five children and wondered vaguely who was missing.

Alan Bold said, 'Everyone spies on each other. That's how islands are. How often do you think you're on your own, then catch sight of the sun hitting off some nosy parker's binoculars?'

'Often, but that's different.' There was a hill with a good view of the farmhouse on Wyre, where she could lie in the long grass undetected. From up there the newcomers would look like ants. 'I'm not quite ready to turn into Poor Alice, poking my nose into everyone's business.'

Stevie turned her back on the window and the view of the children running along the street. 'Let's sort out the rotas. Then I can go home and sleep.'

They had finished allocating the communal tasks and Stevie had nudged Pistol from his slumber beneath her desk when the door opened. They had kept the jaunty shop bell and it jangled with the violence of a fire klaxon.

Candice was standing in the doorway. Her red hair had escaped its knot and her face was flushed and tearstained.

'What happened?' Stevie went to the woman and led her into the shop, closing the door behind them. Candice's horse stood obediently outside, its flank glossy with sweat. Candice and Bjarne's farmhouse was an hour's ride from the centre of Stromness, long enough for the woman to have calmed down, but she was still trembling.

Alan Bold started to get to his feet. 'This looks like a girl thing.'

Stevie threw her deputy a look that set him back in his chair.

Candice said, 'You need to get that little bitch out of my house.'

Stevie had no doubt who she meant, but she asked, 'What bitch?'

'That little whore Willow.'

Bold muttered, 'Christ Almighty.'

Stevie said, 'Alan, I think Candice could do with a cup of tea.'

Candice said, 'Fuck the tea,' but Alan Bold grumbled off to light the spirit stove and she allowed herself to be settled in the deputy's chair.

Candice and Bjarne were one of the couples on the islands who had gone through a formal marriage ceremony. Most people swore a set of promises at home in front of friends, but Candice had insisted on taking their vows in the cathedral. Stevie had thought it stupid swank, but later she wondered if the woman had wanted to draw on the building's gravitas in the hope of making their commitment stick.

She crouched opposite Candice and kept an arm around her, relieved to note that her face was un-bruised, her clothes un-torn. 'Do you want to tell me what happened?'

A long strand of curls had stuck to the tears on Candice's face. She peeled it free and took a deep breath. 'That little slut has put a spell on my husband.'

Stevie closed her eyes. She should have seen the crisis coming. 'You know I don't believe in things like spells.'

Candice ignored her. 'He follows her with his eyes. If she comes into a room he stares at her like a dog that's waiting to be fed. He doesn't stop staring until she leaves.'

'Poor kid.' The words were out before Stevie could stop them.

Candice shoved Stevie away. 'She's not a kid, not in the way you mean. None of them are.'

She looked towards the street and Stevie followed her gaze. The children had finished whatever had taken them to the arts centre and were retracing their route. Some of their earlier bounce had left them and even Connor was keeping pace with Lorna Mills. Stevie looked for Willow and realised that she and Shug were missing. 'They look like children to me.'

'They look like children, but they're not. There's nothing innocent about these kids. They're survivors.'

Alan Bold set two cups of steaming water packed with mint on the table. 'We're all survivors.'

The freckles on Candice's face were bold against her white skin. She looked like a woman who had once lived in the sun, but now hid from it in some unlit place. 'And we all did things we're ashamed of to survive.'

It was something they did not talk about on the islands; the things they had done to stay alive while everyone around them died.

Stevie said, 'She's lived with you a long time.'

'And now I want her gone.'

Stevie nodded. It would be a weight off her own mind to have the girl away from Bjarne and Candice's house.

'If you don't want Willow to live with you any more we'll find somewhere else for her. In the meantime, she can stay with me.'

Candice took a deep shuddering breath. Her words came out in a quick tumble of fear and relief. 'Bjarne mustn't know that I came to see you.'

Stevie felt suddenly sorry for the woman. She reached out and touched one of her hands.

'You don't have to be scared of Bjarne. If you want to leave him, we'll protect you.'

'Why would I leave Bjarne?' Candice slid her hand beyond Stevie's reach. Her stare was defiant, her eyes shiny with tears. 'We're married. All I need is that little whore to sling her hook and then everything will go back to normal.'

Stevie could barely recall Candice and Bjarne before they had fostered Willow. She wondered if the woman knew what she meant by normal.

'Where does Bjarne think you are just now?'

Candice blew her nose. Stevie's promise to take the girl had calmed her. 'I'll make something up. He hardly notices whether I'm there or not.'

Alan Bold said, 'If he fancies Willow, he'll notice when he's left alone with her.'

A single tear slid from Candice's left eye. She lifted her face to the ceiling to stop others following it.

Stevie said, 'Thanks, Alan, that's useful.'

The deputy shrugged. 'Willow's a pretty girl. She's getting to an age when men will look at her.'

Outside the wind was rising, clouds scudding across a darkening sky.

Stevie got to her feet. 'She's a child. That makes any grown-up who touches her a paedophile.'

Alan Bold's face flushed. 'I'm not saying it's okay, but you can't burn the eyes from men's heads.'

Candice had failed to stem the flow of tears. They ran a straight course down her face, like rain against a windowpane, but her voice was calm.

'I had children, two girls, Emma and Flora. They were children and they died. Willow isn't like them. She was old when we found her.'

Stevie said, 'She was no more than seven.'

Candice ignored her. 'Even when she was little, Willow knew things she shouldn't.'

Stevie put her face close to Candice's. She saw the brown flecks in the woman's green eyes, felt her breath warm against her own skin.

'She is a young girl in your care. I'll collect Willow this afternoon. In the meantime, if anything happens to that child, I'll blame you.'

Candice got to her feet. The tears were gone now, her expression resolute. 'It's your fault I took her in the first place.'

The accusation was a surprise. Stevie felt her own face flush.

'You begged to keep her. Don't you remember?'

For a moment it seemed that Candice might recall the way she had fastened her arms around the little girl with the long matted curls, the only island child they had found alive, and pleaded to become her mother. Then her expression shuttered. 'She was half-feral. Have you never asked how she managed to stay alive all by herself for so long?'

Stevie had a premonition of what Candice was going to say next and spoke quickly to stop her from saying it.

'Willow foraged as best she could. She was malnourished when we found her. She'd regressed to being a toddler. A few more days and she might have died.'

'Her mother and father were—'

Stevie interrupted, 'It was bad, but it was to be expected with so many dogs on the island.'

'She had blood on her face.'

'And scratches all over her body from foraging for blackberries. She's just a kid, Candice. If I hear that you've been spreading rumours about her, I'll have you and that child-molesting fuck you live with thrown off these islands.'

Alan Bold had been watching them, like an umpire at a tennis match. He leaned forward. 'Ladies . . .'

Stevie's voice was dangerously calm. 'Keep out of this, Alan.'

Candice got to her feet. She had been plump when she had arrived on Orkney, a sweet-faced cherub who had clung to Bjarne as if he was her only hope. Seven years had sucked the flesh and softness from her. Her cheekbones jutted from her face like stumps, her eyes gleamed deep in their sockets.

'You're a stuck-up bitch, Stevie Flint. You think you own this place, but it took a lot of deaths to make you important.'

It was the same thing that Alan Bold had said the night before. This time it forced the breath from Stevie's chest. Did the rest of the islanders believe that she had scaled the piles of corpses, stuck an island flag on them and made herself president?

Alan Bold showed no sign of recognising a kindred spirit. He grinned his fuck-and-be-damned grin and said, 'I hope we can still rely on your vote in the election?'

'You can stick your votes where they belong.' Candice tugged the stack of carefully charted communal rotas from the desk and threw them at Bold. The papers caught in the stale air of the old shop and fluttered to the floor, landing around her. She looked at Stevie. 'You think I'm jealous of Willow because she's young and beautiful with her whole life ahead of her and I'm an old woman at thirty-five.' She scuffed her work boots over the rotas, smearing the pages with the mud on the soles of her boots. Alan Bold groaned, but Candice ignored him. 'It's true. I am jealous of her. My children are dead, I've lost my looks and my husband wants to fuck our foster daughter, but that's not why I'm here.'

Stevie kept her voice low. 'So why are you here?'

Candice ran a hand through her hair. The copper that used to catch the sun, shining like fuse wire, had faded and there was grey amongst the strands, but a Pre-Raphaelite keen on witches might still have wanted to paint her. 'I'm here because if that little bitch stays another night under my roof, someone's going to die.' Candice lifted Alan Bold's glass of water from the desk, poured it over the rotas it had taken them hours to write and scuffed her boots through them again. 'I'm here to promise you that Bjarne and I will not end up like that little cannibal's real mother and father.'

Stevie said, 'It was the dogs . . .'

But Candice was at the door. She slammed it behind her, setting the bell ringing as loud as closing time in a sailors' pub.

Pistol had dozed through the row, but the bell woke him. He rose from his post beneath the desk and let out a bark.

Alan Bold scratched the dog's head, quieting him. 'That went well.'

Stevie could not bear to meet his eyes. She crouched down and started to peel the sodden pages from the floor. The ink had run, the words slid together; the carefully composed rotas ruined. She wanted to ask Alan if everyone thought she was glad the Sweats had killed the world. Did they really believe she was happier exiled on these treeless rocks surrounded by sea than she had been in London? Some nights she woke with the sound of high heels sharp against concrete still clattering in her head. Only in dreams could she recapture the heat of the city, the sweet sense of being alone in a crowd.

'Looks like you were right. I'm going to have to put off sleep for a while.'

The deputy knelt beside her and helped to gather the ruined pages.

'Night-time always comes around.' Bold knew better now than to touch her, but he gave her a smile. 'Even in a northern summer.'

Six

Magnus could not take much pleasure in his possessions. Even things that had belonged to his family, such as the croft and its contents, were prizes of the plague. They had come to him too soon and it felt wrong to take satisfaction in owning them. His Clydesdale horse Jock was an exception. It was impossible to look at the beast and not feel honoured to be the man who walked behind him, guiding the plough into a straight furrow. Jock was what Magnus's father used to call *show quality* but there were grey hairs amongst his chestnut coat; the horse was getting on. Magnus did not like to tire him, but when he went to saddle his usual ride Straven he saw that the horse was lame. That left him with the choice of Sid, the Shetland pony who not so long ago (it felt to him) had been Shug's pride and joy, the old Clydesdale or a bicycle. Sid the Shetland pony came up to Magnus's waist. He also had a Napoleon complex that made him inclined to biting and not averse to aiming a kick.

'You're worth ten of that wee bastard,' Magnus whispered to the Clydesdale. 'I'd take my bike, but by the time I got there, that cunt Bjarne might have gelded Shug, and we don't want that.'

He had given the horse some extra feed to apologise for the task ahead. The Clydesdale snorted and Magnus said, 'I know he could have had the bollocks off the boy by now, but Shug's canny enough to sidestep that big bear.' Jock's large head nodded, as if he understood. Magnus clapped his neck and clambered aboard, stretching his legs around the horse's barrel of a body. 'If I really thought there was going to be trouble I would have gone there straight away.'

Magnus had fed and mucked-out the pig and hens, his waterproof zipped tight, hood up against the building rain. He had hoped the weather would divert Shug from his course, but if the boy were any kind of boat he would be a tug, small and determined, able to withstand wild conditions and willing to tackle the largest battleships. Magnus had felt a rising sense of anxiety as he had gone about his tasks. Now he could feel panic building in his chest. He tugged the Clydesdale's reins, directing him to the left as they went through the gate and into the driving rain.

'Shug's too smart to walk into a beating.'

The horse kept his head high and plodded into the storm, his hooves clopping a familiar rhythm against the cracked tarmac. Sheep, lazing on the road, impervious to the weather, rose awkwardly onto spindly legs, and scurried out of the way, bleating lambs in tow.

Magnus resisted the urge to press Jock to go faster. There was no point in laming the horse for what was probably a wasted mission. Rain coursed down his face, it slipped through the scarf knotted around his neck and slid beneath his waterproof, onto his body. The urge to curse Shuggie was strong, but it was not the boy who was to blame, it was Bjarne. 'Bloody bear.' Magnus's knees pressed harder against Jock's sides and the horse obediently upped-pace. The movement had been involuntary, but Magnus did not bother to correct it. The bad feeling that had been building inside him had taken hold.

Before the Sweats, people had taken mobile phones for granted. When the satellites that powered them went down at the height of the pandemic, it had felt like a cruel joke. Magnus had been left with the suspicion that if he had texted less, or limited his calls to the purely necessary, he might have had one last conversation with his mother and his sister Rhona. It was a ridiculous notion, born out of survivor guilt, but he had heard other people talk about the way they used to *waste* and suspected they felt something similar.

He had grown used to a world where communications were limited, but now Magnus wished that he could simply take a phone from his pocket and call Shug to check that he was okay. He grimaced against the gale. Who was he kidding? The boy would have seen Magnus's name flashing on the incoming display and rejected the call.

Perhaps his anxiety was as misplaced as Bjarne's, a symptom of the knowledge that the boy was approaching adulthood and would leave him soon. For a fraction of a moment during the ceilidh, when Belle's face had come into focus, older and scarred in a way it had not been before, he had feared that she had come to claim the boy. But Shug was nothing to her, just a child they had rescued along the way. Magnus had often wondered what had happened to Belle. He was surprised to find that, now he was sober, he felt wary of her. 'She's not here for your boy,' he said out loud.

No, a small voice inside him answered, *but she's here for something*.

He was rounding a bend, a tight twist in the rise that was the highest point before they made the descent towards Bjarne and Candice's croft. Rain and mist obscured the view, but he could almost make out their house in the distance, a vague square of white against the greens and browns of the landscape below.

'Good boy.' He clapped Jock's neck. The old Clydesdale plodded on without acknowledging his touch. Magnus's face was numb with cold. He wiped it with his scarf but it was a useless gesture. The sky held infinite quantities of water and they were all descending on Orkney.

Some movement on the valley road below snagged his eye. Magnus drew Jock to a halt and leaned forward, sheltering his eyes. It was Shuggie. The boy had lost his dazzling white jacket, but he was unharmed and cycling for all he was worth.

'Stupid, wee bugger.' Affection coloured Magnus's voice. He knew he should turn Jock around and make for home before Shug discovered he had been about to interfere, but relief kept him there, watching the boy's progress.

Uncertainty touched him. Something was wrong. There was something about the way the boy was moving – a dissonance. Magnus had known Shuggie since he was a small child. He had washed, fed and clothed him, had comforted the boy from the nightmares that plagued him. Magnus had done his best to treat his childhood illnesses, including a bout of fever that had caused him to pray to God in a way he never had before. It was Magnus who had taught him how to sail a boat, skin a rabbit, and ride a horse. He was no longer privy to the boy's every thought and desire, but he knew how he moved, how he pedalled his bike. It was not Shug who was forcing his way up the hill, fighting against the gradient as if his life was at stake. Magnus dug his knees hard into Jock's side. He forgot that the horse was old and it was raining and hastened him into a trot.

Young Connor was red-faced and breathless, but he did not stop pedalling until Magnus and Jock were in front of him.

'Magnus, you've got to . . .' Connor's breath overtook him and he bent against his handlebars, gasping for air.

Magnus dismounted and clutched the boy by the shoulders.

'Is it Shug?'

Connor nodded.

'Where is he?'

'He's . . . he's . . .'

'Deep breaths.' Magnus resisted the urge to shake the boy. 'Point.'

Connor jabbed a finger, back in the direction he had come from.

'Shug's on the road . . . half a mile down . . . he's hurt . . . I think maybe he came off his bike.'

'You're a good lad, Connor.' Magnus was already clutching Jock's reins, pulling himself onto the horse's broad back. 'Catch your breath and then follow me down. I might need a hand.'

The road surface was fractured, the descent wet and winding. Magnus talked to Jock, urging him on, but the old Clydesdale was wise enough to know that he would lose his footing if he went too fast and he took the path at his own pace. The rain had faded to a drizzle, but man and horse were both wet to their bones.

Shug was lying at the side of the road, his white jacket sodden and dirty. Connor had put him in the recovery position. Magnus mentally blessed the lad and the first aid classes Stevie Flint had insisted on.

He slid from Jock's back and knelt beside the boy. 'Shug?' The rain had washed some of the blood from his face, but Magnus could see bruises blooming, dark and livid on his pale skin. One eye was closing and the bridge of his nose was swollen. 'Shuggie?'

Magnus took the sodden scarf from around his own neck and wiped the boy's face with it. He had experienced enough beatings to know the injuries were not the result of a bike accident. 'Can you hear me, son?' Shug's good eye fluttered. Magnus slipped a hand beneath the boy's head and raised him into a sitting position, unsure if he was doing the right thing. He ran his hands gingerly around the back of the boy's skull, relieved to find that the only wetness there came from rainwater.

'Dad?' Shug's voice was slurred.

'Aye, son, I'm here. Don't worry. I'll take you home.'

'Is Mirabelle with you?'

Mirabelle, a black collie only ever known as Mira, had died six months ago. She had developed a growth on her chest. Eventually, when the dog's suffering had grown too bad to bear, Magnus had taken her into the yard, given her a last hug and then shot her. There were plenty of puppies on the island, but Shug had refused to replace her and Magnus had not had the heart to force the issue.

He stroked the boy's forehead. 'She's waiting at the croft.'

Magnus heard the zip of Connor's tyres on the tarmac behind him and turned to look at the lad.

'Shuggie's had a nasty fall. I think he's concussed.' Magnus did not stop to question why he was pretending to go along with Connor's assumption that Shug's injuries were due to an accident. 'I need you to give me a hand to get him onto Jock's back and then make sure he doesn't fall off. Do you think you can do that?'

Connor looked doubtful, but he gave a brave nod.

The rain had died and the sun was coming out from behind the clouds; its warmth felt like an insult.

'Jock can't carry my weight as well as Shug's, but I reckon that together you're still light enough for him to manage.'

Connor said, 'Bjarne and Candice's place is closer than yours. I would have headed there, if I'd not heard Jock's hooves.'

Magnus gave what he hoped was an encouraging smile. 'He needs his own bed.'

Connor glanced at Shug. 'Are you sure? He looks . . .'

Magnus's voice became his father's, hard and certain. 'I know what I'm doing, Con.'

Connor nodded and went to help him.

Shug was heavy and slippery with rain and mud, but the old Clydesdale horse was patient and they managed to get him onto its back. Magnus gave Connor a leg up. He wrapped his arms around the injured boy and held on to the reins. Magnus walked beside the horse, ready to catch Shug if he began to slide off. It was a poor arrangement, but it would have to do.

Shug started to mutter something as they set off. Magnus looked at Connor. 'What's he saying?'

Connor leant forward, putting his ear close to Shug's lolling head. 'I can't make it out. Something about Willow.'

Magnus had not known of Willow's existence before the Sweats and had no idea of who her birth parents might have been, but he had always felt a sense of kinship with her. Willow's dark skin and black hair had declared her the child of incomers, but Magnus saw no contradiction in that. His own great-great-grandmother was reputed to have come from Newfoundland, spirited back to the islands by Magnus's great-great-grandfather after a whaling expedition. He had liked Willow and even imagined she might be the glue that kept Shug on the islands. Now he felt a hot stab of bitterness towards the girl. She was the reason Shug was in this state.

Magnus said, 'Willow would do well to keep away.'

'No, Dad . . .' Shug's voice was slurred but he was back in the land of the living. 'Willow needs to come and live with us. Promise you'll go and get her.'

Magnus would have promised to fly to the moon on Sid the Shetland pony, if he thought it would help the boy.

'Aye, son, I'll get her.'

'Promise?'

'I promise on my life.'

Shug put his face against Jock's neck and closed his eyes.

Seven

The rain was clearing as Stevie and Alan Bold left the old shop, dark clouds gusting away on the breeze, to reveal blue skies. Stevie stretched her arms out, enjoying the feel of the wind on her skin.

'Sailing weather.' Alan Bold's hangover seemed to have lifted with the storm. He set a straw hat at a jaunty angle on his tangled fuzz of hair, as if he were preparing to promenade along a pier in Brighton or Torquay. 'You should take a turn on the water. Get that woman out of your system.'

For a moment Stevie thought he was talking about Belle, then she realised he meant Candice.

'I promised to collect Willow. Who knows what state she's in? I need to get her settled at my place and start thinking about where she can live long term.'

Crows were strutting across a patch of grass outside the shop, looking for worms drawn to the surface by that morning's rain. Stevie hated the birds. They had pecked the eyes from corpses, grown fat on their flesh. She touched Pistol's head lightly, '*Go, boy.*' The dog tore across the road and onto the bit of green, scattering the carrion.

Alan Bold watched the dog's progress. 'If you go now Bjarne will guess Candice is behind it.'

The same thought had occurred to Stevie. It made her uneasy but she shrugged.

'That's Candice's problem.'

The deputy took a pair of Ray-Bans from his shirt pocket and put them on.

'Not if Bjarne beats Candice up, or worse. Then it becomes everyone's problem.'

Pistol trotted back to Stevie's side, wagging his tale sheepishly, as if embarrassed not to have caught any crows. She gave his head a reassuring pat. 'I'm not sure it's safe to leave Willow where she is.'

Alan Bold shrugged. 'If I go, Bjarne can't see it as some feminist conspiracy. I'll tell him Poor Alice has had a fall and needs someone in the house with her, in case she takes another tumble. I'll make it sound like a temporary thing. After a week or so it'll become a fait accompli.'

Stevie looked up at the sky. The sea would mirror that same sharp blue, frosted with foam. With the breeze behind her she could be on Wyre in less than an hour.

'I don't know . . .'

Alan Bold took his Ray-Bans off. 'Is it because of what I said?'

Stevie raised her eyebrows. There was salt in the air. Her boat was waiting in the harbour, its sails ready to be unfurled. 'Am I supposed to know what you mean? You say a lot.'

Alan Bold's voice was impatient. 'What I said about Willow coming to an age when men will find her attractive. I might have let my cock lead me into trouble a few times, but I'm not a paedo.'

'I know you're not. It's a good plan, it's just . . .' Stevie let the sentence tail away.

'Just what? You don't trust me?'

She turned to face the deputy. 'Why are you so keen?'

The sun was shining in Alan Bold's eyes, shrinking his pupils to pinholes, but he did not replace his sunglasses.

'It was me who found Willow, remember?'

Stevie remembered. It had been Alan who had coaxed the small girl from her hiding place beneath her parents' bed. Stevie would have closed the door to the room to stop Willow from escaping, shifted the bed and grabbed her, but Alan Bold had insisted it was important the child came to them, rather than be captured. He had lain on his stomach, his eyes level with Willow's, ignoring the stink of the rotting corpses on the mattress above, and had spoken softly to her until eventually she emerged, dirty and bloody into his arms.

'I may be a bit of a prick at times, but I do have some sense of responsibility.'

Stevie glanced at her watch. Some of the islanders had let time go, but she was scrupulous about winding her Timex each morning.

'Meet me back here with Willow at three. I want to know what's been going on in that house.'

Alan Bold said, 'You know what's been going on. Willow has the hots for Bjarne and it's threatening his marriage.'

Stevie shook her head. 'Every time I start to like you, you say something like that. I can guarantee you Willow does not have *the hots* for Bjarne and even if she did, she's a child in his care. That makes her out of bounds.'

The deputy looked at her over the top of his sunglasses. He was handsome in spite of his wild hair and unkempt beard. The kind of man some women thought they could tame.

'I don't need to be reminded she's out of bounds, but you're wrong about the other thing. Candice is right. Willow has set her cap at Bjarne.'

'Trust me, Alan, that girl is not in love with her foster father.'

'Who said anything about love?'

Alan Bold was no longer looking at her. Stevie followed his gaze and saw Lorna Mills. The teacher had finished her classes for the day and was walking home. She was wearing a cropped red jacket, tight blue skirt and high heels that had been on the cutting edge of fashion when the Sweats hit. Stevie wondered if Lorna had cherished the shoes all this time, or if they had belonged to a fashionable Orcadian. Most of what they wore had belonged to the dead, but it seemed wrong to look so good in their clothes.

Stevie said, 'Willow is not in love, or in lust with him.' But Alan Bold was already halfway up the street, hailing Lorna like a comic-book lothario. He drew level with the teacher and said something that made her laugh. 'Three o'clock,' Stevie called after him.

Alan Bold waved a hand in acknowledgement, but his attention was on Lorna and it looked as if he was shooing Stevie away.

Pistol ran the length of the boat's deck, sniffing the briny air, trying to keep pace with the waves. A seagull swooped towards the boat and the dog made a lunge for it, his jaws snapping. The bird wheeled beyond his reach, its cry tearing through the rush of salt and wind like manic laughter. In the old days people had believed gulls were the souls of dead sailors and it was true that there were more of them since the Sweats had killed the world.

Stevie pulled her cap low and brushed a stray hair from her eyes. She would dock at the ferry port, in easy view of anyone who cared to look. She was still not sure why she was heading to the island, but experience had taught her that sometimes it was good to follow your instincts. The strangers had been on the fringes of her mind since their unexpected arrival. Perhaps seeing them would put an end to the pulse of curiosity that was making it hard for her to concentrate.

Pistol was dancing on his hind legs, barking at the gulls. She called his name and he ran to her, mouth open in a doggy grin, tail wagging.

'Sit.'

He sank his haunches obediently, but the seagulls were too big a temptation to be easily relinquished and his backside hovered a fraction above the deck.

Stevie lowered her voice. 'Sit!'

This time the dog obeyed her.

Belle's yacht was moored by the ferry dock. The ferry itself was some way off, tipped at an angle; one half of its keel below the water, the other black and barnacled, exposed to the sky. Stevie slid her boat to the quayside and heard the rush of her vessel's wake boom inside the half-sunk ferry. She snared a mooring pin, drew her boat in, secured it and hopped onto the quay. Pistol followed her, so close his feet padded in the dark of her shadow.

Before the Sweats, Stevie's priorities had been sales commission, sex, nightclubs and clothes. Now she could appreciate a drift of light, a foam of waves, a sequence of starlings, flocking and fracturing and flocking again. Sometimes she wondered if she would always have become who she was: hard and lean, a practical woman. It was one of the cruelties of the pandemic. It made survivors doubt who they were.

Pistol was ahead of her, nosing in the grass beyond the quay. Stevie tucked her jeans into her socks and made a mental note to check the dog for ticks when they got home. She shouldered the small rucksack of supplies she had packed as an alibi and began to make her way towards Cubbie Roo's Castle. The grass was long and tufted with tussocks that added a spring to her progress, but which Stevie knew had the potential to unfoot her.

The island was two miles long. It felt like a raft of land set on the ocean, the sky and sea fused into one element. During the fires she had sometimes camped alone here, on the far side, facing away from the main island and its plumes of smoke. The sea and sky had been a comfort to her then, their soft blues and greys an antidote to the hard red of the flames.

The castle was on a high mound, a climb from the shore. Pistol knew the way and bounded ahead, marking interesting scents; occasionally doubling back to check that Stevie was still with him. It had been grazing land before the Sweats, fields hemmed by wire fences, designed to keep cattle contained. The cattle were gone, the fences slumped and rusting. Once, according to the information sign that still stood beside the remains of the castle, a square tower had dominated the hill, but over the centuries it had been attacked by the elements and dismantled by crofters, who had their own uses for the stones the ancients had gathered. Only fragments of King Cubbie Roo's fortifications were left, a windbreak rather than a shelter. Stevie liked it there. Raised up above the small strip of land, surrounded by sea and sky, she felt like she was at the centre of the world, king of the derelict castle. The farmhouse lay below her. Stevie had meant to spy on it, but instead she wrapped herself in the travel rug she had taken from the boat, lay on her back in the lee of the ruins and looked up at the sky.

Way above the atmosphere, in the space station orbiting the earth, a discreet drama must have played out. She wondered again if the astronauts had succumbed to the Sweats or if they had run out of supplies; cannibalising each other or starving. Were they aware of the devastation taking place on earth? Or had communication simply stopped? She imagined them shaking each other's hands and then going one by one into the airlock and flushing themselves into starry blackness. Surviving the first onslaught of the Sweats had been hard, but it had engaged all of her wits. Living beyond the catastrophe required a different kind of stamina. Perhaps that was why the newcomers had snared her attention. She was secretly longing for some danger to make life seem important again.

Pistol sensed that she would stop on the hilltop for a while and disappeared on an expedition of his own, hunting for voles and stoats; chasing gulls across the island. Stevie closed her eyes. She would lie there, soaking up the healing blue and green of Wyre and then leave, dumping the pack of supplies at the farm gate, without spying on the newcomers. There would be time later to learn more about Belle and her boys. One thing the post-Sweats world guaranteed was time.

Eight

Magnus told Connor to help himself to the rhubarb pie in the kitchen cupboard and settled Shug on his bed. He stripped his son and soaped his body with water warmed on the stove. The bruising was bad, but as far as he could tell there were no broken bones. It was the boy's head that worried him. Shuggie was half in the present, half in the past. His ramblings slipped between Willow and Mira the dog, both of them beloved, both in danger.

Magnus put a cold compress on Shug's head and took *The Home Doctor*, which had been like a bible to him when the boy was younger, down from its shelf. The book told him to give Shug some paracetamol and if symptoms persisted, to take him to hospital. Magnus bolstered the boy's body with pillows to stop him from rolling onto the floor and jogged downstairs to the kitchen where he kept a tin of medical supplies.

Connor was standing awkwardly in the hallway. The boy had pie crumbs on his jumper and a purple-red splash of rhubarb juice on his face.

'Is Shuggie going to be okay?'

Magnus went into the kitchen and took the medicine tin from its place on top of a cabinet, where he had elected to keep it, back when Shug was waist-high.

'I hope so.' He opened the tin, found the paracetamols and

pocketed them. 'You did well today, Connor. Shuggie and I both owe you. You make sure you collect.'

Connor had followed him into the kitchen. He nodded uncertainly.

Magnus dipped a jug into the water butt by the door and took a clean glass from the draining board. 'Anything you need, you come to me.'

'I don't need anything, Magnus.'

Magnus put his hand on the boy's shoulder. 'You don't have to collect straight away, but there'll be a time when you need help. When that time comes, you call on me, okay?'

Connor's eyes were wide. 'How do you know?'

'That's the way life goes, everyone needs help sometimes.' He squeezed the boy's shoulder. 'When your time comes around, come to me.'

'Okay.' The prospect seemed to alarm Connor. He took his windcheater from the back of a kitchen chair where he had hung it. 'You'll tell Shug I helped him?'

'I'll tell him.' Magnus scanned the kitchen for something he could give the boy. The half-eaten rhubarb pie was still sitting on the table. He wrapped it in a dishtowel and handed it to the boy. 'Do me a favour, Con.'

Connor stood by the door, one hand on the latch, the other holding the pie. 'What?'

'Don't say anything to anyone about Shug's accident.'

The boy gave a mute nod of his head and was gone.

Nine

It was Pistol who woke her, shoving his wet nose into her face while she slept. Stevie opened her eyes on his wide grin, his meaty breath. She made a noise of disgust and the dog's head darted forward, welcoming her back to the world with a lick that narrowly missed her mouth.

'Get off.' She pushed him away. The springy grass that carpeted Cubbie Roo's Castle had made a good mattress and she had slept more deeply than she had meant to. She looked at her watch. It was not yet two. She would easily make her meeting with Alan and Willow.

Pistol was not easily offended. He crouched down, a stray rock between his front paws, and barked for her to throw it.

'You're a pest, Pistol.' Stevie was still wrapped in the tartan blanket, like some highlander of old, swathed in plaid. She disentangled herself, sat up and lifted the rock above her head, ready to send it over the remnants of the tower. That was when she saw Belle, sitting on one of the ruined walls, watching her.

Belle's long hair hung loose, framing her face. It seemed blonder than it had before; the colour of corn-stubble left by the harvest. Their eyes met, their gazes held. Stevie froze, her throwing arm still aimed towards the woman. She saw Belle's damaged pupil move beneath the cloudiness, like an imp trapped inside a bottle. It focused on Stevie and she realised there was still some sight in it.

Pistol barked and the spell was broken. Stevie corrected her aim. She threw the stone in the opposite direction and the dog bounded after it.

'He's not much of a guard dog.' Stevie wondered how long Belle had been sitting there, watching her sleep.

Belle was wearing a pair of leather trousers and a black, slash-neck mohair sweater. She looked spare and strong, a rock-chick Valkyrie.

'He checked me out and decided I was okay.'

'I'm not sure that's his call.' Stevie got to her feet and brushed herself down. She had tucked the rucksack beneath her head, as a pillow. She lifted it and slung it in Belle's direction. 'I brought you a few supplies.'

'Thanks.' Belle's smile made the clumsy gesture seem ungracious. 'The boys will appreciate it.'

'You're all still healthy?'

Pistol bounded back and dropped the stone at Stevie's feet. It was a game he never tired of.

Belle grinned, 'Fit as your dog.'

Stevie lobbed the stone. 'But brighter, I hope.'

Belle shrugged. 'The three of us have done all right since we teamed up. Whether it's due to luck or intelligence . . . who knows? How about you? How did you end up here?'

It was the way people got to know each other, telling the story of their survival. Some told it lightly, compulsively. Others were more guarded, though whether their reluctance was due to trauma or shame was not always clear. Stevie knew it could be difficult to trust people who kept silent about their escape from the Sweats and the chaos that had followed, but she preferred to forget her last days in London. It was not just that the memories were painful. During her flight she had discovered a talent for violence that she would rather remain buried. She started to fold her blanket.

'Is there anything else you need?'

'We'll manage.' This time Pistol dropped the rock at Belle's feet. She threw it in an arc, out into the green scrubland, and turned her gaze back to Stevie. 'Are you in a hurry?'

Stevie felt an unexpected urge to tell Belle about Willow and Candice, the hatred the woman held for the child she had once begged to take care of. She set the folded blanket down on the grass, and sat on the square of tartan.

Stevie glanced at her watch again. 'Not really. I'd like to know how things are out there. The only news we get comes from the occasional newcomer, or people who venture out to trade. We've not heard much recently.'

Belle looked out to the sea beyond the islands. Stevie followed her gaze and saw white gulls floating on air pockets; an advance of white horses breaking against the shore.

Belle said, 'I can see why you stay here. It's beautiful.'

'It's not to everyone's taste.'

'I guess not, but an island is safer than the mainland. At least you have an idea of who's around.'

'We didn't see you coming.' Stevie wondered why everything she said to the woman sounded churlish.

'We sailed into your harbour in full view.'

It was true. The trio had made no effort to conceal themselves. Stevie wondered again why she mistrusted them. She said, 'What happened to your eye?'

Belle smiled, as if amused by the boldness of the question. 'Wrong place, wrong time.' For a moment it seemed that this was all she was going to say, but then she lifted her fingers to the scar on her face, as if touching it might help her tell its story. 'I joined a group of travellers called the Kinfolk.' She smiled. 'I guess it sounds less sinister than The Family. We were sick to death of death and so we tried to have a good time.' She shrugged. 'Or maybe we were just trying to drown our misery by making a racket – drink, drugs, sex, the usual stuff. Sometimes we came across other groups. Usually it was an excuse for a powwow and a piss-up. But then . . .' She faltered.

The sound of the gulls and the rhythm of the sea grew louder, carried on a gust of wind that bent the grass and raised goosebumps on the back of Stevie's neck. A horsefly landed on her wrist. She slapped it away and prompted, 'But then?'

'But then we met some people who weren't so friendly.'

Stevie had her own experiences of the post-Sweats world beyond the islands and so this time she did not ask what had happened. Instead she said, 'How bad was it?'

Belle looked towards the sea again. Pistol was chasing something across the fields, snapping at the breeze. 'Bad enough. They were organised.' She met Stevie's eyes. 'Has Magnus told you about the place where we met?'

Stevie shook her head. 'He's never talked to me about it.'

'Let's just say, it was fucked up. But one good thing it did was to put me on my guard. The Kinfolk suited me. I smoked ganja, snorted the odd line, drank whatever was going and joined in the dancing and the singsongs round the campfire, but I was always armed and always prepared.'

'Sounds dangerous.'

'It was reckless, but I reckoned the only way to stay alive was to be prepared to die. We weren't a bunch of peaceful hippies. We'd faced-off people we didn't like the look of before, but the group who joined us that night seemed okay. There were less than a dozen of them. Mainly guys, but there were a few women too.' Belle tore some long strands of grass from the hillock and started to weave them together. 'Looking back, that was what made it seem okay, there were women too. We partied around the campfire, drinking and swapping survival stories, like we usually did when there were newcomers. People drifted off to bed in the early hours. I'm not sure how long I slept, but I woke up to lights and shouting. I was in my boots and out of my campervan before I knew I was awake. It took me a moment to realise what was happening, then I saw that the group we had welcomed had been joined by other men, guys we would have pointed our guns at, if we'd seen them coming. They were rounding people up.'

A breeze caught Belle's hair, lifting pale strands of it into the air. The same breeze caressed Stevie's skin.

Belle said, 'I had my gun in my hand, but all my shooting prac-tice, all my boasts about fighting to the death, were useless. I stepped out of my van, some guy grabbed me from behind, snatched my gun and that was that.' Belle's fingers traced the white scar that puckered her lip and robbed her left eye of colour. 'I got this the first time I tried to escape.'

Stevie knew agonies lurked in the gaps in Belle's account, but some suffering was best left buried. She asked, 'How long did they hold you?'

'Too long.'

'I'm sorry.'

Belle shrugged. 'I used to spend hours talking about boys when I was a teenager, trying to decipher what a look meant, whether they liked me or not. But I never tried to make anyone like me as much as when we were captured. I wanted to belong to one man and one alone. I reckoned that way I had a chance of survival.' She levelled her gaze. 'I would do anything to survive.'

The statement sounded like a warning, but Stevie knew that whatever had happened to Belle could easily have been her own fate. 'You survived.'

'So far.' Belle nodded, her expression serious. 'So have you.'

Stevie got to her feet. 'It's an ongoing struggle.' She put her fingers in her mouth and sent a high whistle across the fields, signalling to Pistol that it was time to go. 'There's a crisis with one of the younger members of our community. I should already have left.'

If Belle resented being the only one to tell her history she did not show it. She got up from her rocky seat, still keeping her distance from Stevie, and brushed a strand of hair from her eyes.

'I was rude to you last night, when you asked for news of the outside world.'

Pistol came haring over the wall. He dashed to Stevie's side, tail flapping, delighted to be reunited. She clapped her thigh and he came to heel.

'Impatient, not rude. We've heard tales of tribes forming, territories being claimed. I'd hoped some kind of order was reasserting itself.'

Belle's expression was grave. 'There is some kind of order, but not the kind I'm guessing you were hoping for.'

Stevie glanced at her watch. It was quarter past two. She had promised Alan that she would collect Willow from him at three, but she had a sense that this was the revelation Belle's story had been building towards. 'Tell me.'

Belle leaned against the remnants of one of Cubbie Roo's walls. She looked past Stevie, southwards, where somewhere beyond the sea a new order was emerging.

'The raiding party that took us wasn't just in it for sex, or the thrill of the fight. The world is full of useful things that we might never be able to make again. The tribes are stripping and hoarding as many assets as they can. That's what the raid was for. They wanted to make slaves of us.' She met Stevie's gaze. 'You asked for news of how things are beyond your islands. They're hellish and pretty soon that hell will be coming your way.'

Ten

Magnus woke into a grey-gloaming. He was slumped in a blanket, in an armchair he had dragged from its usual spot on the landing to the side of Shug's bed. The chair was too big for the room and he was close enough to hear the boy's breathing. Shug was awake, his eyes shining in the dying light of the day.

Magnus reached out and touched the boy's forehead. It was cool with none of the clamminess that had worried him earlier. Shug flinched and Magnus took his hand away. He poured the boy a fresh glass of water and passed it to him.

'Thanks.' Shug raised his head from the pillows and drank.

It was the same room, the same bed that Magnus had slept in as a boy. The walls were still painted the same pale-blue his mother had chosen. Magnus had not wanted to change anything she had done. He took the glass from Shug and set it on the bedside table.

'How do you feel?'

'Crap.' An undercurrent of belligerence was back in the boy's voice.

'Do you remember what happened?'

Shug pulled himself up, leaning his back against the headboard. His pyjama top was half unbuttoned, a juvenile scrub of hair bloomed on his chest.

'I remember you helping me onto Jock. I thought Mira was there.'

Magnus was relieved that the dog had been returned to the land of the dead.

'And before that?'

Shug looked at the wall.

'I was worried about Willow. Candi and Bjarne are fighting all the time and Candi blames her. I thought maybe she could come and stay with us for a while.' He wiped a hand across his eyes.

Magnus reached for the handkerchief in his pocket and then stalled. Shug would not want him to acknowledge his tears.

'Did Bjarne do this to you?'

'We've got a signal. If he's home Willow half shuts her bedroom curtains. If he's away she leaves them open.'

'And the curtains were open?'

'She mustn't have had time to close them. I snuck in the back way, but Bjarne was waiting for me in the yard.'

'I'll kill him.' Magnus's words were low and resolute.

Shug's voice was cracked, as if it had not just been his head that Bjarne had damaged, but his whole vessel. 'Willow saved me.'

'She got you into this, son. If it wasn't for her, you wouldn't be lying here now.'

His rifle was in its cabinet by the door. Magnus would take it with him when he went to see Bjarne, but it would be the Glock that he would point at the bully who had beaten his son. The gun he had found after his flight from Tanqueray House.

Shug was insistent. 'If it wasn't for Willow, Bjarne would have killed me. He jumped on me before I knew he was there. I'm fast, you know that.'

The boy was wiry but he was not fully grown and although they were not blood kin, he had inherited Magnus's weakness as a fighter. He lacked what Big Magnus used to call 'killer instinct'.

Magnus reached out a hand and laid it softly on top of the covers.

'You dance like a butterfly, sting like a bee.'

Shug shook his head and frowned, as if the movement had pained him.

'I stung like a midge, less than a midge, they leave a mark. He was killing me, but then Willow came out of the farmhouse and pointed a shotgun at him. Bjarne had me on the ground by then. He was too busy with his boots to notice her at first. Willow fired into the air and he paid attention. I begged her to come with me, but she told me to go.'

Magnus was not ready to concede any credit to the girl.

'She should have stayed with you, made sure you were okay.'

'You didn't see Bjarne. If she'd moved that shotgun he would have been on me. I used my bike like a crutch. My head was swimming, but I just lent on the handlebars and put one foot in front of the other, like you used to tell me to when I was wee and didn't want to walk any further.' He looked up at Magnus, as if something had just occurred to him. 'Where did you find me?'

'Halfway up the rise. I'd come looking for you, but it was young Connor who found you first.' A feeling of foreboding had crept over Magnus as he listened to Shug's account. He asked, 'Did you hear another shot after you left the farmhouse?'

'I don't think so.' The significance of the question did not seem to strike the boy. 'Willow said she would hold him until I was clear.'

'What about Candice?'

'I don't know where she was. She hates Willow.' The hostility was gone from the boy's voice. His eyes met Magnus's. They were swimming with tears. 'Dad, we have to get her away from that place.'

The word 'Dad' tugged at Magnus's heart. He reached out and took the boy's hand in his.

'I'll go first thing in the morning.'

He would get there at first light, use the element of surprise to humiliate Bjarne the way he had humiliated his boy.

'Tomorrow's too late.' Shug pushed away the bedclothes and started to get out of bed. 'I need to make sure she's okay.'

Magnus grasped him gently by the shoulders. The boy tried to shove him away, but Magnus held him there, making the same soft, soothing noise he had used on poor Mira before he put her out of her misery.

'I'll go. On condition you stay in bed.'

'Promise?'

'I promise, but you have to promise too, that you'll stay where you are.'

'I promise.'

Shug lay back on his pillows closing his eyes. It was as if he were a child again; secure in the faith that nothing could defeat his father. Magnus kissed the boy's forehead and went downstairs to fetch his gun.

Eleven

The wind, which had rushed across the landscape like ghosts through a battlefield, died when Stevie was halfway to the main island, leaving her becalmed. Pistol ran a circuit of the boat, intrigued by their loss of progress. When he realised that they had not yet reached land he skittered his way down the steep steps to the cabin below, where he curled up on the bunk and went to sleep. Stevie knew she should take her cue from the dog and get some rest, but instead she took out her fishing rod, baited it and cast off into almost still waters. She sat watching the gently lapping waves, thinking about Willow and wondering if Belle's story, about prisoners forced into scavenging gangs, was true.

The light was draining from the sky as she sailed into Stromness harbour. Candles flickered in the windows of the hotel bar and the sound of Brendan Banks's banjo drifted across the quay. She felt premature nostalgia, an urge to hold on to that moment; the sinking sun, the music sparkling from golden windows. Stevie wondered if her time on the islands had been an interlude between episodes of violence. What was this urge to stay alive?

Pistol had been nosing round the quayside. Now he ran towards her and sniffed, with feigned disinterest at the fish in her bag.

'Get off.' She gave him a friendly shove. 'That's Willow's dinner, not yours.'

She shouldered the bag and walked away from the hotel.

Alan Bold's house was in darkness. Stevie rattled its letterbox and when there was no reply told Pistol to *stay*, opened the door and stepped into the gloom. Bold's house had a musty, bachelor smell; overflowing ashtrays, spilled whisky and unwashed laundry. Stevie wondered if the impression of being unable to fend for himself was another of Bold's seduction techniques. A grandfather clock stood at the end of the hall, ticking into the shadows. She disliked the shape of it, tall and vaguely human; its hundred-year-old heart still marking time. Stevie opened the door to the lounge. The oil lamps were unlit, the stove cold.

'Alan?'

Her voice sounded loud in the empty room. There was no one there but something, an invisible movement in the air, made her return to the hallway and call again.

'Alan?'

There was a bang from the ceiling above her head, a muffled voice, followed by the sound of heavy footsteps.

'Jesus Christ, Stevie, did you never learn how to knock?' Alan Bold was naked except for a pair of hastily pulled on jeans. He fastened his belt buckle as he loped down the stairs. 'Where were you?'

Unexpected warmth touched Stevie's cheeks.

'I went for a sail, like you suggested. The wind died on me. Did you get Willow?'

Bold stopped on the stairs. Stevie had always thought of her deputy as skinny, but his chest was broad, his biceps well defined. Three names were tattooed across his heart in cursive script, too small for Stevie to read. He ran a hand through his mop of black hair.

'I went to Bjarne and Candice's place, but there was no one there. I hung around for a while, but no one turned up, so I left.'

Stevie noticed a cropped red jacket hanging amongst the fleeces, waterproofs and jaunty hats on the coat stand by the door. A pair of once-fashionable lady's shoes was tucked neatly next to Bold's walking boots.

'And you had a certain schoolteacher to see.'

'That's none of your business.' Alan Bold's face creased into a grin that indicated she had riled him. 'I did what we agreed. It's not my fault it didn't work out. Willow has survived seven years in that house. One more night won't kill her.'

He turned his back on Stevie, ready to climb the stairs to his warm bed and Lorna Mills.

Stevie put a hand on the newel post of the staircase.

'Do you know that for certain? Did you search the place?'

Bold turned to face her again. Some of his assurance had left him and he was no longer grinning his angry grin.

'I put my head round the kitchen door and called hello. No one answered so I sat at the table, drank a glass of water and when no one came I went on my way.'

'You didn't check any of the rooms?'

'I respect people's privacy.' Alan looked uneasy. 'The girl didn't know we were coming. She's probably off somewhere with young Shug. Candice was no doubt hiding, so she wouldn't be there when we confronted Bjarne, and as for him – he could be anywhere.'

It was all true, but Stevie felt a premonition of fear.

'Do you have the motorbike keys?'

'They're in the ignition.' Alan Bold descended the final steps to the lobby. He grabbed a checked shirt that was hanging on the coat stand and put it on, fastening the buttons. 'This isn't an emergency. Candice only came to us this afternoon.'

'Her visit wasn't entirely a surprise. I've been worried about Willow.'

'I've been worried too.' Lorna Mills was at the top of the stairs, her skin almost as pale as the white, cotton sheet she had wrapped around her nakedness. She shone like a phantom against the dark. 'When she cut her hair . . .'

Stevie whispered, 'I wondered then too . . .'

Lorna said, 'I spoke to her . . . she insisted everything was okay . . .'

Alan Bold looked from one to the other. 'Girls cut their hair, so what?'

The women ignored him. Lorna said, 'I think you should go there. Maybe it's nothing but . . .'

Stevie nodded. She dropped her bag of fish in the hallway and went back out into the darkening night, shutting the door on the realisation dawning on her deputy's face.

They kept the motorbike fuelled and serviced in a shed behind Alan Bold's house. It was a community resource, only to be used in emergencies. Stevie ordered Pistol – 'Home, boy.' She pushed the bike from the shed, pulled on the helmet dangling from its handlebars and kicked the engine into life. The sound broke through the silence, loud and unfamiliar. A shape came out of the darkness towards her. Stevie gasped and then recognised her deputy's silhouette; his long legs, his cartoon hair.

'You should have told me.' Alan Bold handed her a stiff, leather jacket.

Stevie took the jacket from him and pulled it on. 'I wasn't sure.'

Bold was wearing motorbike leathers. He took another helmet from a shelf in the shed.

'It doesn't matter. If I'd had any inkling that there was a chance Bjarne was abusing Willow, I would have stuck around until I got her.'

'Even when you had a hot schoolteacher waiting for you?' The fear that she had put Willow in danger made Stevie angry.

'For Christ's sake.' Alan Bold's curse was muttered and impatient. 'You decided to become a nun, good for you. It doesn't mean the rest of us have to.' He put a hand on her shoulder. 'Shift up.'

'Piss off.'

Bold gave an exasperated laugh.

'This isn't an anti-feminist thing. I've been a biker since I was sixteen. We'll get there faster if you let me drive.'

Stevie shifted back on the saddle, leaving room for her deputy to sling his leg over the bike. Alan Bold put his helmet on, revved the engine and knocked the kickstand free. Stevie wrapped her arms around Bold's body and flattened her face against his back. A whiff of leather and petrol filled her nostrils, mixed with the peat smoke that scented the night. Then they were on their way, out of the yard and into the darkness, speeding along the road beneath the stars.

Twelve

Magnus liked nothing about his journey. He did not like leaving Shug alone with his injuries. Nor did he like his stolen mount. Rebel was a well-named chestnut, a prized possession of Magnus's nearest neighbour Les. He had tempted the horse from its field with a bag of pony nuts and slyly saddled and ridden it away without permission. Magnus did not like the darkening night, the scent of rain on the air, or the thought of the steep hill down to the valley where Candice and Bjarne's croft lay. Top of the list of things Magnus did not like about his mission was its destination. The Glock sat heavy in the pocket of his jacket but, now that he was on his way, he knew he did not want to kill Bjarne. Another death would sit too heavy on him. He simply wanted the violent bastard gone.

He met no one on the road. Rebel's hooves rang quick and skittish against the fractured tarmac. The moon was full-faced and low in the sky, shining silver on their progress. Magnus cursed it and held tight to the reins as they flew down the hill at a sickening canter. He glanced at the spot where he had found Shug and the memory strengthened his resolve. Bjarne was not the kind of man who responded to reason. Magnus would point the gun at the bastard's head and tell him that if he so much as glanced at Shug again, he would blow his brains from his skull. Then he would invite Willow to come and stay at their place.

It was a poor plan. Bjarne would simply bide his time, order the girl home and take some violent revenge. Magnus wondered what his father would have done. Despite his modest croft, Big Magnus had been a kingpin in the local farming hierarchy. His word carried the heft of a district and to oppose him was to oppose dozens of other men. Magnus had friends he could call on, but they were musicians like Brendan Banks. He imagined the stocky Yorkshireman fending off Bjarne with his banjo and groaned. There was nothing for it but to threaten to kill him and follow through when he did not comply.

He could see the vague outline of the croft further down the valley. The lower floor of the house was in darkness, but there was a faint light shining in one of the upper windows. They were home and not yet in bed. Killing the big man would mean the end of the life Magnus had tried to build. The New Orcadian Council would exile him from the islands.

Magnus pulled on Rebel's reins, drawing the horse to a sudden halt. He had been stupid. He had got used to thinking of the world as a lawless place where people were forced to make their own justice, but things were changing, order being reasserted. Bjarne had beaten Shug so badly that only Willow's intervention had saved him. Magnus would take his case to the council, harness the support of the community and have Bjarne thrown off the Orkneys.

Somewhere an owl screamed. Rebel whinnied and pawed the ground, eager to be on their way. Magnus shucked the reins and the horse resumed its progress. He would avoid violence, take his case to law and win retribution, but that did not mean he would break his promise to Shug. He had told the boy that he would collect the girl and he was not going to let him down.

The farmyard was almost in darkness by the time Magnus reached it. He had expected his arrival to be announced by the farm dogs and had unsheathed his gun, in case any of them attacked the horse, but the place was silent. He was surprised to see hens pecking in the yard. For all the man's faults, Magnus had always thought of Bjarne as a good crofter, but it seemed that here too chores occasionally went neglected, chickens left to the mercy of stoats and wild dogs. Rebel flattened his ears, as if the yard made him nervous. Magnus patted the horse's neck and dismounted.

'Shhh, they're just wee chicks, they won't do you any harm.'

He looped the horse's reins around the post Bjarne had made for that purpose and scanned the empty yard. Now that he had decided to go to law, Magnus was keen to avoid confrontation. He wondered belatedly if he should have snuck in the back way, sought out the girl's room and stolen her off.

Rebel whinnied and pawed the ground. 'Shhhh.' Magnus wished again that his own horse, steady Straven, had been fit to ride. He looked up at the lit window. The candlelight was pale and flickering. He edged round the side of the house, saw the shape of the peat stack and realised that there was no scent of smoke. Its absence and the missing dogs gave him a strange feeling. He wiped his palms against his jeans and crept on. Something lay slumped on the ground at the corner of the house.

'Christ.' The word was half-curse, half-prayer. Magnus edged forward. 'Willow?'

He drew closer and saw that the shape was too small to be the girl. Magnus touched it with his toe, recoiling at its softness. It was one of Bjarne's dogs, a sleek Dobermann, lying shot through the head. *Fuck*. Magnus reached out a hand and felt the dead beast's neck. The flesh beneath the black fur was cold and stiff. It had been dead for some time. *Shit*. Magnus sunk to his haunches beside the dog. His breath came in short, panicked stabs.

Fuck, fuck, fuck.

What was he doing here? Magnus got to his feet and turned the corner, keeping close to the wall. His body tensed, expecting to feel the impact of a bullet at any moment.

A second dog lay dead beside the back door, a large Alsatian. Magnus knew what had happened. Bjarne had gone mad. It had happened to men on the islands before. The traumas the Sweats had inflicted could lie dormant for years and then break out in violence and suicide. If Magnus had been a praying man, he would have prayed that Bjarne had not decided to take Candice and Willow with him.

The farmhouse door creaked as he opened it. Magnus slipped into the kitchen. It was darker inside than it had been in the yard and he stood still for a moment, letting his eyes adjust to the gloom. The room was neat. The counters clean, floor swept, chairs tucked beneath the table. It looked like no one had started to prepare dinner yet. Magnus crept into the hallway. Candice liked to paint and some of her canvases were hung on the wall. The pastel shades she favoured were not to Magnus's taste and he had not paid much attention to her pictures at the exhibitions of survivors' art the New Orcadian Council had organised. Now, in the shadows that drained the colour from the canvases, he realised they were strangely proportioned cityscapes. Buildings loomed over tiny people, rendered insignificant by towering skyscrapers.

Bjarne was in the sitting room, a broad shape slumped in an armchair by the window. Magnus pointed his gun at the big man, before he realised that Bjarne was no longer a threat. He lowered his weapon and stepped into the room, looking for the gun Bjarne had shot himself with. A book lay splayed on the ground by his feet, its pages spattered with gore. Magnus had never imagined the big man reading. He crouched over it and read the title, *Killing Your Rage: A Man's Guide to Anger Management*. The self-help book sent a shudder through him, as if the corpse had reached out and touched his hand.

Magnus scanned the floor. He was so sure that Bjarne had shot himself it took him a moment to realise that there was no gun. He looked again at the corpse; saw the way the blood and brains had splattered in front of the body, the forward slump of the man's ruined head. Bjarne had been shot from behind.

Shit.

Bjarne's hard fists and quick temper had gained him enemies across the Orkney Islands, but it was Willow who had aimed a shotgun at him that afternoon. Magnus took a white throw from the couch and draped it over the mess that had once been Bjarne's fierce brain. There were no forensics any more and he thought covering the corpse might save someone else from the horror, but it looked worse than before. The throw was not big enough to cover Bjarne's arms and legs. The fabric clung in folds around the corpse, dipping into the space where the man's skull should be, sucking up the blood-claret. Bjarne's hands poked out from beneath the drapes, giving the impression that he might snatch the cover away at any moment and show off the chaos beneath.

Magnus found it hard to take his eyes from the Halloween joke, but he closed the sitting-room door softly behind him. He felt the pull of the road beyond the farmhouse, strong as a lighthouse beam, but the girl might be hiding somewhere, scared or even wounded, and so he turned his back on escape and tiptoed upstairs. Willow's name was spelt out on the door to her room in little-girl glitter that belied her shaven head, her efficiency with a shotgun.

'Willow?' He whispered her name, his finger on the trigger of the Glock. 'It's Magnus, Shug sent me.'

There was no reply. He pushed the door open. The bedroom was a jumble of clothes, books and make-up. Magnus had not lived with a teenage girl since his sister Rhona left home and the bright colours, cut through the darkening shadows, making it hard to distinguish the contents of the room. The bed was small. It was pressed against the wall and sheltered by gauzy fabric, spangled with sequins. The covers were humped in a pile beneath the sparkly netting.

'Willow?' Magnus's voice was hushed. He took a deep breath, sank his hand through the net and tugged at the duvet. A threadbare teddy stared vacantly at him from the empty bed. 'Thank Christ.' He checked beneath the bed and took a quick look in the wardrobe, but the room was empty.

A faint glow of candlelight leaked from the half-open door at the end of the hallway. Magnus took a deep breath, slipped through the door and into the room. He smelt fresh blood a moment before he saw Candice's curls, a riot of red against the pillows.

'Candice?' He did not want to get any closer to the bed, but he forced himself to tiptoe closer. 'Candice?'

He knew before he touched her, but his hand reached out and tugged the bedclothes away. Candice had been in bed, curled on her right side, her back towards the door, when she was shot. The shot had hit her between the shoulder blades, making a bloody well in her back, severing her spine and stopping her heart.

The candle flickered on the windowsill, throwing his shadow, large and trembling, against the wall. Magnus struggled for breath. He was muttering something, a prayer of *fucks* and *nos*. He pulled the bedclothes over Candice's head, as if the murder was her shame, something to be hidden from the world.

'Willow?' Magnus's voice quivered. 'Don't be frightened. You're safe.' Every hair on his body was erect, every atom primed. He opened the doors of the fitted wardrobe, but there was no space for anyone to lurk amongst the jumble of clothes.

Remembering how Willow had first been discovered, lying beneath her dead parents' bed, he dropped to his knees and lifted the valence, but there was only dust.

The house was old and full of places to hide. Even if he searched them all, the farmyard was ringed by a complex of outhouses, milking parlours and stables. Beyond them lay fields and ditches. Willow had grown up on the farm. She would know where to seek cover. The thought made Magnus uneasy. He took the candle from the windowsill and slid from the room keeping close to the wall.

Downstairs a door opened.

Thirteen

Stevie and Alan Bold were picking up speed when they saw the woman in the middle of the road. The moon was full but she was dressed in black and Bold had to swerve to avoid her.

'Christ.' He took his helmet off. 'I almost fucking hit you.'

Breda's ex was nicknamed 'the sperm donor'. She had kicked him out as soon as she had discovered she was pregnant and was rarely seen without her daughter, eighteen-month-old Evie. But now she stood on the faded white lines that intersected the road, alone and tearstained, her hair a wild nest.

Alan Bold's fists were still clamped around the handlebars of the motorbike, as if the shock of the near-miss had fused them there.

'Why didn't you move when you heard the bike? You could have killed us.'

Stevie took her helmet off. 'Breda? Is there something wrong?'

'Evie's gone.' The woman's voice was close to a wail. 'I thought I heard something, so I went into the nursery to check on her. She wasn't there. Someone's stolen my baby.'

Stevie got off the bike, went to Breda and put her arms around her. The woman had rushed from her house without bothering to put on a coat and she was trembling with cold and shock. Stevie took off her leather jacket and draped it over her shoulders.

'She won't have gone far. Little Evie's an adventurous little girl. She must have woken up and gone exploring. We'll find her.'

Breda shook her head. 'Evie's too small to get out of her cot by herself. She wouldn't manage to open the front door, it's too heavy.'

'Children surprise you.' Alan Bold spoke as if he knew what he was talking about. 'They're growing and learning all the time. One day they can't reach something, the next they can. I'll get a search party together.'

Breda ignored him. 'The front door was open. Someone came in and took her.'

Survivors who had chosen to live in town tended to cluster together. Most of Stromness was unoccupied, but for a few streets where people lived side by side. Alan Bold was already banging on the door of the nearest house. A rusty halo surrounded the full moon. A bitter chill had crept over the island and it would be frosty tomorrow. Stevie took Breda by the shoulders.

'Go indoors and put on something warm. Alan's right, we'll find her, but we need as many people in the search party as possible. That includes you.'

Alan Bold was on the doorstep of the next house, talking to Breda's neighbour, Grant. Grant reached back into the hallway, grabbed a coat and scarf and stepped into the night. He squeezed Breda's shoulder as he passed. 'She won't have gone far.' He headed out to alert others. The search party would quickly grow.

Breda gulped back her sobs. 'What if Evie comes back and I'm not here?'

Stevie said, 'We'll ask Poor Alice to wait in your house.' A thought struck her. 'We should give your place a thorough search, in case she's hiding there.'

'I already looked.' Breda's voice was fractured by sobs.

Doors were opening, people emerging from their houses. Some brought oil lamps with them and their glow added a festive air at odds with the anxious voices straining against the chill night.

Alan Bold was uncharacteristically decisive, dividing people into groups and issuing instructions on where to search. He paused, on his way to organise another cluster of neighbours. 'Stevie's right. Kids hide in places that would never occur to us. You need to go through your house from top to bottom.'

Breda snapped, 'What would you know about it? You don't have any children,' but she hurried indoors.

Stevie followed her, leaving a wounded-looking Bold to organise the search. Willow would have to wait.

Fourteen

Connor was standing in Bjarne and Candice's kitchen, drinking a glass of water. 'Cool gun, Magnus. Can I have a look?'

'No.' Magnus tucked the Glock safe inside his jacket pocket. 'What are you doing here?'

'I help Bjarne with the milking. That's where I was going when I found Shug. He'll be finished by now, but my mum told me to come back and tell him why I didn't show up. He's promised her some beef to salt when he slaughters his next beast and she didn't want to get on his bad side.' If Connor thought there was something incongruous about Magnus walking through Bjarne and Candice's farmhouse with a candle in one hand and a gun in the other, he did not show it. 'How's Shuggie?'

'Recovering.'

'My mum's always saying that boys have thick heads.' Connor nodded towards the interior of the house. 'What kind of mood is the big man in?'

Magnus set the candle he had taken from the bedroom windowsill on the table. It gave a Christmas glow to the room. Candice had lit it before she died, her life snuffed out before the flame.

'Peaceful. I'd leave him alone for the moment.'

Connor's face creased in a frown. 'But my mum . . .'

'I told Bjarne how you helped Shuggie. He knows you had a good reason for not showing up.'

Connor grinned. 'I wasn't looking forward to telling him.'

'Now you don't have to.' Magnus tried to return Connor's smile. 'Did you see anyone else out there?'

'Only Rebel. Did Les lend him to you?'

'He owed me a favour.' Chances of returning the horse undetected were narrowing. Connor roamed the settlements of the main island, dispensing news and gossip with an absence of guile or judgement. Magnus said, 'It's dark outside. You'd best head home. I'll walk with you to the road.'

'I don't mind the dark.' Connor pulled out a chair and sat at the table, at ease in Candi and Bjarne's kitchen. 'My mum says there's nothing to fear, not like in the old days, before the Sweats killed all the bad folk.'

Connor's foster mother was one of the religious people who believed the Sweats had been sent by God.

'All the same, Candice and Bjarne are going to their bed and it's time for us to head to ours.'

Connor's chin set in a stubborn jut. 'Candi usually gives me a slice of cake for the road.'

Magnus glanced around the kitchen, but everything had been tidied away. There was no cake in sight and he did not have the stomach to search the rows of kitchen cabinets and explore Candice's neatly stacked provisions: the dried pulses and pickled veg, the jams and preserves, set against a future that would never come. He said, 'It's not so long since you had rhubarb pie.' It was surreal, bickering with an eleven-year-old boy about cake, while Candice's and Bjarne's corpses cooled in the rooms beyond. For a moment it seemed that Connor might argue his case, but he got to his feet.

'Magnus, remember you said I could ask you for anything and you'd give it to me?'

'Yes?' Magnus blew out the candle. He placed a hand on the boy's shoulder and steered him out of the kitchen, into the chilly darkness of the yard.

'Can I have your gun please?'

'No.'

The boy looked up at him. 'I knew you'd say that.'

'So why did you ask?'

Connor shrugged. 'No harm in asking. Magnus?' His voice rang through the dim, deserted yard.

'Keep your voice down, Connor. Candice and Bjarne are in bed.'

'Okay,' the boy whispered. 'I just wanted to ask, did you shoot Rocky and Satan because Bjarne beat Shuggie up?'

Rocky and Satan were Bjarne's dogs. Magnus glanced towards their bodies, dark shapes on the edge of the farmyard and wondered if the boy really believed he might have killed the creatures.

'I'd never punish an animal for something its owner had done.' Magnus put his hands on Connor's shoulders. He turned the boy to face him and crouched level with him. 'How did you know that Bjarne had beaten up Shuggie?'

'I know more than people give me credit for. I've got a good pair of eyes in my head. They see things.'

'What did you see tonight?'

'I saw you and your gun in Candi and Bjarne's kitchen.'

It had not occurred to Magnus that he might be blamed for the killings, but now he saw how it would look. He took the gun from his pocket and placed it in the boy's hand.

'Is the gun hot or cold?'

'Cold.'

'That's because it hasn't been fired in a long while. What does it smell of?'

Connor raised the Glock to his nose and gave a cautious sniff. 'Nothing – metal maybe, but metal doesn't really smell.'

'If I'd fired that gun you'd be able to tell. I brought it with me because I wanted to protect myself from Bjarne, but he and Candi were in bed so I went away without speaking to them.'

'You said you'd spoken to Bjarne and told him why I'd missed milking. You said he was peaceful.'

The boy was staring at the gun as if it was a holy relic. Magnus took it from him and returned it to his pocket.

'That was a wee white lie to get us out of there.'

'How do you know they're in bed?'

It was hard to tell in the gloom of the yard, but Magnus thought that Connor's expression had an unfamiliar, sly cast to it. He said, 'Where else would they be at this time of night?'

'I don't know.'

He shrugged free of Magnus and walked to his bicycle, propped against the same post that Rebel's reins were tied to. The horse snickered. The boy rubbed its nose, mounted his bike and started to freewheel towards the gate.

Magnus shouted after him, 'Have you seen Willow?'

Connor looked back over his shoulder. 'She's at your house.' His bicycle tyres crunched against the gravel and then were absorbed into the unquiet hush of the night.

Fifteen

It looked as if Breda had looted every toy on the Orkney Islands. Three large playpens stuffed with primary-coloured plastic dominated Evie's nursery. The floor was strewn with an untidy mess of dolls, cuddly creatures, cars and plastic animals. A four-storey dolls' house lurked Gothically in a corner, half obscured by a pedal car that had crashed into the building's facade, sending dolls and furniture flying. It was against the ethos of the islands. Manufactured goods, considered disposable before the Sweats, had become irreplaceable and were meant to be used with care. Stevie picked up a headless Barbie, stripped down to dolly nakedness. The doll's breasts were large and ridiculous, her hips non-existent. Stevie tossed it back onto the floor.

'Is there a particular toy that she's fond of? A teddy bear or something she doesn't like to be parted from?' A train set snaked around the room, its carriages derailed by a smiling, fluffy elephant. Stevie disliked the nursery's mismatch of scale and objects. It made her think of the Sweats, the implosion of order. 'If it's missing, we'll know there's a good chance she's wandered off.'

Evie's cot was standing in the middle of the nursery, amongst the debris of toys. Breda went to it, rifled the bedding and held up a disreputable-looking monkey. Stevie thought she could remember the child dragging the ugly creature around.

'Evie won't go anywhere without Charlie.' Breda was crying again.

'She might still be in the house somewhere.'

'I told you. She's too little to get out of her cot by herself. Look how high the sides are. She couldn't climb over them without hurting herself.'

Stevie tried to conjure an image of little Evie in her mind. The cot's sides were high, but Alan Bold was right, the girl was growing. As the youngest child on the islands, born on the wash of a wave of deaths, Evie was spoilt, and wilful. All the children were. They were the only hope for the future and the grown-ups had deified them.

Stevie said, 'No one would take her.' She resolved to write up a list of suspects. It was possible that some woman, desperate for a baby, might have stolen into the nursery and spirited her off. 'You start upstairs, I'll look down here.'

Breda turned away. Stevie heard her footsteps climbing the stairs and then her voice, calling for her child. Furniture shifted overhead. The shouts of the search party had been getting fainter, moving ever further from Breda's door, Evie's name travelling through the air on soft echoes. Now there was a rupture in the rhythm of the calls.

'Thank God.' Stevie went into the hallway, ready to step out and greet whoever had found the child. Breda had heard the shouts too. She stood on the landing, her expression fearful. Stevie met her eyes and smiled. 'I told you she couldn't have got far.'

She opened the front door. The night smelled of lamp oil and burning torches. Alan Bold was running up the street, his arms empty. He stopped when he saw her. Even in the dim light she could see that his eyes were wild. Stevie's hand went to her mouth. She closed the door behind her and stepped into the street, so Breda would not hear what Alan Bold was about to say. Her deputy was panting, trying to catch his breath. Stevie said, 'Is she . . .?'

He shook his head. 'Other kids are missing.'

Sixteen

Magnus knew the house was empty as soon as he walked through his back door. The air inside was cold and still as undrawn breaths. He lit a lantern and ran up the stairs to the boy's room. The door was open, the bedclothes mussed, the bed empty.

'Shug?' His shout was a puff of fog in the chilly room. 'Shuggie?' Magnus crossed the landing, his shadow large against the wall. He checked his own bedroom, the bathroom and then ran downstairs. The rarely used lounge was empty. So was the office where he kept his father's farm journals and the financial accounts from before. When accounts were things that could be marked in black or red, one side of the ledger or the other. 'Shug?'

The boy had vanished. Magnus's legs were trembling. He set the lantern on the kitchen table and sat down, trying to think. Bjarne had many enemies, but Magnus did not know anyone with a grudge big enough to want to murder him. He groaned and put his head in his hands, remembering that a few short hours ago he had taken the Glock from its hiding place and set out, ready to kill the big man.

Bjarne had lived his life in a way that invited violence, but Candice was different. She had been beautiful when she arrived on the islands. Life and her choice of man had snuffed the spark out of her. It was hard to imagine someone taking the time to kill her. Magnus closed his eyes, trying to see the murder scenes again; Candice curled on her side in the master bedroom, Bjarne sitting in his chair in the sitting room. If Bjarne had been killed first, the sound of the shot would surely have woken Candice. Magnus tried to remember if there had been any pills on the bedside table, sleeping tablets that might have pulled the woman so far under, she would not have woken. He had been in shock, but he was pretty sure he would have noticed them, had they been there.

It was impossible to imagine Bjarne remaining in his chair while a shot rang out in the room above. Had there been two killers, two gunshots, timed closely enough to deny the couple any warning?

Magnus knuckled his skull, trying to think. Shug had been safe at home in bed when the killings had happened, Willow at the farm. The girl had been in trouble with her foster parents. He pictured her in the yard, pointing the gun at Bjarne while Shuggie staggered to safety. It was easily imagined, but killing Candice as she slept? Standing behind Bjarne's chair and blowing the top of his head off as he sat reading a book on how to manage his anger? Those images were harder to conjure.

Magnus got to his feet. If Connor had not discovered him in Bjarne and Candice's kitchen with a gun in his hand, he might have been tempted to keep the news of the killings to himself. He could have taken to his bed, pulled the covers over his head and let the bodies be discovered by someone with no motive for murder. As things were, he had to report them.

Magnus took a dry scarf from the back of the door and swapped it for the damp one around his neck. Stevie Flint had a way of picking on a detail and worrying at it until whatever problem she was working on unravelled. Magnus was too tired to be a match for her. He would cycle over to Alan Bold's house. The deputy was more likely to take his statement at face value and perhaps Magnus would meet Shug on the way.

He had been trying not to think too much about his son, but a wave of anxiety washed over him. The blows to the boy's head had been savage, the beating Bjarne had given him harsh. Shug was in no state to go adventuring with Willow tonight.

Magnus took a bottle of whisky from the kitchen cupboard and poured himself a dram to help keep the night air out. He knocked it back and then poured himself a second, drinking it like the medicine it was.

He muttered, 'Candice didn't deserve to die, but I'm glad someone killed you, you violent cunt.'

It was bad luck to speak ill of the dead. Footsteps crunched on the gravel outside the kitchen window. Magnus took the lantern and went quickly to the door.

'Shug?' It was dark outside, the moon behind some cloud. 'Shuggie, is that you?'

His whisky breath clouded the air. He raised the lantern and saw a figure on a horse.

'It's me.' Brendan Banks did not have his customary banjo slung over his back. 'Little Evie's missing. There's a search party.'

'Since when?'

'Since her mother went into her room and found her gone.'

There was no reason to assume the events of the night were connected, but Magnus had a bad feeling in his belly. He grabbed his cap from the hook by the front door and shoved it on his head. Rebel was still standing where he had left him. The horse pawed the earth, impatient to be fed. Magnus clapped the beast's neck. 'Sorry, boy, there's more work for you tonight.'

Brendan said, 'Did Les say you could borrow his pride and joy?'

'There wasn't time to ask.'

'You must have been in a hell of a hurry then. I wouldn't like to be in your boots.'

Magnus pulled himself onto the horse. 'You've no idea how true that is, Brendan.' He gripped Rebel's flanks with his heels and shucked the reins, setting them on their way. 'No idea.'

Seventeen

The search was too ramshackle to be comprehensive. The island was too big and too dark, the search party too small. Stevie wrote a list of every household with children and began dispatching riders to check that they were okay. There were less than a dozen families, but the radius where they had settled was wide. It would be a while before she knew whether the children were safe at home, sleeping in their beds.

So far, in addition to Evie, three were confirmed missing. The other children were two girls and a boy, all in their early teens. They were survivors of the Sweats, fostered by adults who had kept travelling north, until somehow they had landed on the Orkneys.

Stevie had watched the foster parents closely as they related the details of their evening, up until they found their children gone. They had each looked worried, but they were not distressed in the way that Breda was. Perhaps it was simply that their children were older and more able to look after themselves or maybe they feared something else. It was a strange coincidence, a missing toddler and three absent teenagers. It made her uneasy.

Stevie wondered if the younger child's disappearance could be an ill-thought-out prank. The islands' teenagers had an odd, collective sense of humour that excluded the adults. She glanced at the list she had made of homes with children. She had spread a map of Orkney Mainland across Breda's kitchen table, but knew the island too well to have to refer to it.

Joe Archibald walked into the kitchen. He was a tall, good-humoured man; gentle, but capable of holding fast in a crisis. He took his hat off, like men must have done in the old days, when hat-wearing was the norm and women to be treated with formal respect.

'Someone said you were looking for me.'

Stevie was relieved to see him.

'Can you go to Candice and Bjarne's place and check on Willow, please? There's been a bit of tension there, so watch how you go.'

'Bjarne been playing up?'

'Possibly.'

Joe nodded as if he had heard all he needed to know. He shoved his hat back on and made for the door.

'Joe.' Stevie called him back. It seemed like an age since she and Alan Bold had been careering through the dark to fetch Willow. 'Step into Magnus McFall's place on the way and make sure Shuggie is with him. You might want to take Magnus with you, for backup.'

Joe smiled. 'Magnus McFall is the last person I'd take to Bjarne's farm. There's been bad blood there ever since Mags's lad took a fancy to Bjarne's lass. Anyway, Brendan went to fetch him a while ago, when the search started. They'll no doubt be here soon.'

It was as if his words conjured the men's presence. The kitchen door opened. Alan Bold stepped into the room followed by Magnus and Brendan. The night air followed them in, a fresh chill tinged with peat.

'Speak of the Devil and smell smoke.' Joe gave Magnus a friendly clap on the shoulder. 'I'm away to see your nemesis.' He tipped his hat onto his head and stepped back into the darkness.

'Where's he off to?' Alan Bold's hair was a tangled forest, his face ruddy with cold.

Stevie said, 'He's going to get Willow.'

Alan looked at Magnus. 'Tell her what you just told me.' He hurried after Joe, slamming the door behind him.

Magnus McFall smelt of whisky. He pulled out one of the kitchen chairs and sank wearily into it. They sat in silence and then Magnus asked, 'Have you seen Shug or Willow?'

Stevie looked at him. 'No. Are you worried about them?'

Magnus wiped a hand across his mouth. Stevie saw the misery on his face and wanted to tell him to keep whatever his bad news was to himself. She said nothing and after a while Magnus began to speak.

Eighteen

Connor sat on a chair in his mother's kitchen, tears and snot running down his face. A lantern glimmered on the table beside the boy, illuminating his pale skin, his half-formed features. There was a splash of purple on his cardigan that looked like blood, but which Magnus knew was rhubarb juice.

'Connor, no one's accusing you of anything.' He had not told the boy of Candice and Bjarne's deaths yet. Magnus reached into his pocket for a hanky to give the boy, but he had lost it somewhere along the way. He considered passing Connor his scarf, to wipe his face with, but the wind was rising, the weather growing wild, and who knew how far he would have to travel that night. 'There's been some odd goings on. Little Evie is missing. So are some of your pals. We need to know where they are, so we can make sure they're okay.'

Magnus had expected Stevie to go with Alan Bold to view the bodies, but the deputy had taken Brendan and Joe, and promised to report back. Stevie had stuck with Magnus. She was standing just out of his sightline, leaning against the kitchen units, watching him question the boy. Magnus tried again.

'Connor, have you any idea where Shuggie and Willow might have gone? Did they take little Evie away as a joke? You won't get into trouble if you tell us. I promise.'

Magnus had described the murder scene to Stevie and the others. He had told them about the dead farm dogs, the way the contents of Bjarne's skull had been splattered in front of his body, mentioned the self-help book on the floor. Describing Candice's body had been harder. His voice had faltered but he had forced himself on, seeing her red curls made lustrous again by blood. 'I don't think they suffered,' he had said. 'It looked too quick for them to have realised what was happening.' But how could he know?

Magnus took his scarf off and passed it to the boy. 'Wipe your face and take a deep breath.' He had not told Stevie or the others why he had gone to Bjarne's place. He had left the Glock out of his account too. It was stupid. The boy was bound to refer to the gun. Magnus would be left looking shifty; worse than shifty, guilty. It was his own fault.

Connor lifted Magnus's scarf to his nose. He blew into it vigorously and then held it out to Magnus. 'Thanks, Mags.'

'That's all right, son. You keep it.'

'Really?' The boy gave a ghost of a smile.

'It's yours now.' Magnus leaned forward, aware of Stevie Flint's eyes on him. 'I've got some sad news, Connor.' The boy held Magnus's gaze. His eyes had grown larger, his mouth smaller. He must have been around four years old when the Sweats had taken his birth family. He knew the pitilessness of circumstance and feared it. 'Do you remember when we met in Bjarne's place?'

'Yes.' The boy nodded. 'You were—'

'I was there.' Magnus cut him off before he could mention the gun. 'I probably looked a wee bit strange.'

'You did, you—'

'I'd had a big shock. I wanted to get you out of there, before you had one too.'

'Rocky and Satan were dead. I thought you—'

'I know you did, son. But I didn't touch Bjarne's dogs. Somebody did though. The same person that killed them shot . . .'

The boy clamped his hands over his ears. 'I don't want to hear any more.' The tears were coursing down his face again.

Magnus took the boy's hands in his and held them. 'Candi and Bjarne are dead. Someone shot them.'

He let Connor's hands go and sat quietly while the boy sobbed into them. The kitchen was cold. A soft glow leaked in from the adjoining room where Connor's mother sat, reading her Bible by the light of a candle. Magnus wondered why she had not stayed with them. He would not have stopped her. He cast a look towards Stevie, her face half hidden in the shadows. She held his gaze until he looked away. The sound of the boy's weeping filled the room. Magnus battened down an urge to get to his feet and walk from the kitchen. 'Connor, son.' He rubbed the boy's arm.

Connor looked at him. 'Did you shoot them, Magnus?'

'No, son. Shooting people isn't my style. I was angry with Bjarne, but I had no problem with Candi. I went there to make sure there would be no more fighting between Bjarne and Shug.'

Stevie shifted behind him. Magnus had not told her about Shug's beating or his argument with Bjarne.

'You're sure they're dead?'

'I'm afraid so.'

The boy nodded. He had seen enough deaths to know that sometimes there was no doubt. He took a deep shuddering breath. His mouth pursed, as if he was locking his lips.

The wind gusted outside and the flame in the oil lamp flickered. Magnus wondered where Shug was and hoped he was sheltering somewhere. He did not like to think of him outside in the rising storm so soon after his beating. He could not imagine the boy stealing away the toddler. They would find her safe somewhere.

'You get around, Connor, you see things.' Magnus tried to smile. 'Has anyone mentioned taking little Evie away from her mum?'

The boy shook his head.

'Do you have any idea who might have wanted to kill Bjarne and Candice?'

'Apart from you?' The boy's question was guileless.

'Apart from me.'

'The new folk?'

He was like a poor arithmetic student, guessing at answers, but Magnus said, 'What new folk?'

'That blonde woman and her men.'

Stevie Flint spoke for the first time. 'They're under quarantine on Wyre.'

Connor looked away. 'She said it was boring.'

Stevie stepped out of the shadows. 'Who said it was boring?'

'The blonde woman – Belle. Willow said she isn't very bonny, but she is. She only has one eye, but that doesn't stop her being pretty.'

Connor had been in the Stromness Hotel when the trio had arrived, but there was immediacy to the statement that made Magnus ask, 'When did you last see her?'

Connor's mouth pursed again. 'I promised not to tell.'

Stevie said, 'It isn't always bad to break a promise. Whoever killed Bjarne and Candi is still out there and little Evie is missing.'

The boy flinched. 'Will it be like the bad days before the Sweats saved the righteous?'

Magnus cast Stevie a look. He gave the boy's arm a reassuring squeeze. 'Not if we find whoever did this. Tell us about Belle and her men.'

Connor's shoulders slumped. 'Willow and Shug went to visit them. It was Willow's idea, but Shug does anything she says.'

It was true. Magnus had found his son's devotion to the girl irritating and amusing in equal measure. He had thought he would grow out of it. Now he wished he had given Shug a talking to. He had never raised his hand to the boy, never thought he had the right to hit him. He asked, 'Did you go with them?'

Connor's eyes were lowered. 'Willow wouldn't let me.'

Magnus gave the boy's shoulder a sympathetic squeeze.

'Boys and girls pair off when they become teenagers. They want to be alone together. It'll happen to you sooner or later.'

'No it won't.' Connor's voice was fierce with remembered hurt. 'Anyway, they didn't want to be on their own. They wanted to visit the strangers and they didn't want me to go with them.'

Stevie drew out a chair and sat opposite Connor. 'Why did Willow want to visit the strangers?'

Connor shrugged. 'She wanted to know what it's like.'

'What what's like?'

Connor's voice was patient. 'What the world is like. She wanted to know what it's like in other places.'

Stevie asked, 'And what did Belle say?'

Connor's eyes teared. 'They wouldn't tell me, but then they came over.'

'You saw Belle and her friends on the main island?'

'They had a beach barbecue. Moon and Sky were there too. So was Adil.'

All three children were missing.

'A barbecue?' Stevie sounded bemused. 'When?'

Connor shrugged.

'A couple of days ago. They built a fire and roasted some fish. I hid on top of the dunes but Willow saw me and shouted at me to get lost. I thought Shug would tell her to let me join in, but he pretended not to see me. Willow threw a stone and the others laughed.' There was a loose thread on the cuff of Connor's jumper. He plucked at it, his eyes downcast. 'I didn't go away. I had as much right to be on the beach as anyone. I sat on the dunes, where they couldn't see me, and watched.' Connor raised his eyes and looked at Magnus. 'Willow says I spy, but I don't. I just want Shug and me to be pals, like we were before.'

Magnus gave the boy's shoulder another squeeze but it was Stevie who spoke, taking on the bad cop role, as if they were on a TV show, from back when crime could be considered entertainment.

'If you were up on the dunes, how do you know Willow asked Belle what things are like beyond the islands?'

Connor looked at his cuff again, the unravelling thread. The boy was a poor liar. Keeping quiet was his only defence against self-incrimination.

Magnus said, 'You're not in trouble, Con. You're a good help. We need to find Shug and the others, especially little Evie.'

'I want you to find Shug and Evie, but I don't care about Willow.' Jealousy tightened Connor's features. Magnus caught a glimpse of how the boy might look when he was older: prominent chin and cheekbones framing deep-set eyes.

A breath of cold air gusted beneath the kitchen door and through the window's untrue frames, sending the light within the lantern dancing and shadows jagging across the walls. A child of Evie's age could easily die from exposure on a night like this.

Magnus put some steel into his voice. 'Answer Stevie's question. How do you know what Willow asked Belle?'

'She was always going on about it.'

A picture of Jesus with his burning heart in his hand hung above the unlit stove. Connor glanced at it and Magnus knew that there was more. He prompted the boy. 'And?'

'And I was hungry. I knew they wouldn't give me anything to eat. But I thought maybe if I got closer, I could grab something and run away. I hid in the seagrass and crept down, like a commando.' He looked from Magnus to Stevie, staring them both in the eye. 'It's not true what Willow says. I'm not a spy. I was hungry.'

Stevie said, 'What were they talking about?'

'They were drinking and smoking. One of Belle's men put his arm around Willow. Shug's face went red, the way it does when he's about to fight someone, but Willow didn't seem to mind. Belle told the man not to act stupid and he let Willow go.'

Shuggie was a brooder, prone to long silences and introspections. Magnus knew he would not easily shrug off the insult or Willow's betrayal.

He said, 'What did Belle say about the cities?'

Connor's stare was defiant. 'They need young people.'

Stevie took a sharp intake of breath; the quick sound of someone being stabbed in the guts. 'Are you sure that's what she said?'

The boy's chin jutted out. His voice grew belligerent. Soon he would be a teenager.

'Everyone here, all the grown-ups, are always going on about how dangerous everywhere is once you get off the islands. All you talk about is gangs and looting and guns and fighting. It's all lies. Belle told us the cities are back. They have electricity. People are driving cars again and at night they play music. Proper music, not the rubbish Magnus and Brendan Banks play on their stupid guitars and banjos. People dance. They're warm and they always have enough to eat.'

Stevie said, 'We have enough to eat here.'

'Maybe *you* do, but me and mum don't always.' Connor glanced at the adjoining room where his mother sat and lowered his voice. 'There's only the two of us. Maybe everyone thinks we don't need much. But we need more than we have.'

Magnus felt ashamed. Connor had often eaten at the croft and he usually sent him home with something for his mother, but since Shug had taken up with Willow it had happened less often. He felt a blast of annoyance at his son.

'I'm sorry, Con. We'll make sure you're both better cared for. I promise.'

'Don't worry about me. I'm going to the city too.'

'You're staying here.' Connor's mother stood in the doorway of the kitchen, her Bible hanging loose in her hand, like a weapon. She was a small, thin woman with grey hair, cropped short like a man's. She looked at Magnus and Stevie. 'Have you finished?' Her voice was dry as cigarette papers. She looked at Connor. 'I never thought you would bring trouble to my door.'

Stevie got to her feet. 'He's not in trouble, Mrs Taylor.' Connor's mum was always Mrs. 'We thought he might be able to help us find out where his friends have gone.'

The woman looked through her. Her voice was imperious, edged with a hint of whisky-slur. 'Connor has a long day tomorrow. It's time for him to go to bed.'

Magnus stood up, but he kept his eyes on Connor's. 'What city are they headed for?'

The boy's voice was small. He hung his head, all defiance gone. 'Glasgow.'

'Did Belle mention little Evie?'

'No.'

'Or anything about taking a child, a baby?'

The boy shook his head.

His mother said, 'He's told you all he knows. He needs to go to bed now, if he's to be any use tomorrow.'

Magnus's eyes met Stevie's. The kitchen was cold and neither of them had taken their coats off. He took his cap from the table and pulled it low, over his ears.

'I'm sorry we disturbed your evening, Mrs Taylor.' He shook Connor's hand and pulled him into a hug. 'You do as your mother says. Whatever Belle might have told you, the cities are not good places. There's no electricity, cars, lights or dancing.' The words conjured pictures in Magnus's mind. He felt how the children might be mesmerised by them. He squeezed Connor's shoulder, trying to ground them both in the reality of survival: hard work and long, cold winters. 'You're better off here.'

Connor pulled away. His eyes met Magnus's.

'Why wouldn't they take me with them?'

Nineteen

The islanders met in the chill nicotine dawn, in the offices of the New Orcadian Council. The old gift shop was too small to accommodate them all comfortably and they were forced to huddle together, most of them standing, all of them haggard from cold and lack of sleep. They had scoured the mainland through the night, the search party growing as those in outlying districts were woken and drawn into the quest. Five of the school-age children on the island, including Shug and Willow, were missing. Those who remained, with the exception of Connor, were younger kids, who would burden a group wanting to travel fast.

'Not as big a burden as Evie, she's only eighteen months old. She won't be able to walk far,' Alan Bold had said as their small contingent of searchers made their way home to Stromness in the back of a cart, the rain running through their clothes and onto their skin. The sleepless night had turned his complexion waxy yellow. 'She has special value to whoever took her.'

Alan Bold, Magnus and Stevie had travelled in the middle cart of a convoy of three. Stevie had stolen a glance at Magnus. His head was bowed, eyes closed, but the steady jut of his neck told her that he was not asleep. She said, 'Belle didn't strike me as the maternal type. If she's got little Evie, my guess is she's taken her to sell, or exchange for something she needs more.'

Magnus had looked up, eyes red-rimmed. 'I vouched for Belle. It's up to me to fix things.'

The wind dropped and for a moment they could hear the sound of the rain beating against the tarpaulin covering the bodies of Candice and Bjarne, lying together in the cart up ahead. Stevie wished she had been more patient with Candice. The woman had irritated her and she had sided with Willow without bothering to examine the evidence. The results of jumping to conclusions were cold and bloody. She said, 'If I'd paid more attention to Candice things might have gone differently.'

She remembered waking to find Belle watching her from Cubbie Roo's Castle walls, the wind lifting her fine, corn-spun hair into the air. The woman had recounted her survival story; the raid that had resulted in the loss of her eye, the loss of her freedom. From now on, Stevie resolved, her decisions would be based on hard facts, rather than gut feeling and prejudice. She said, 'We shouldn't leap to false conclusions. Belle and her men might still be on Wyre. The children could be with them, or hiding somewhere else. Teenagers have a silly sense of humour. It could be a joke that's got out of hand.'

Alan Bold's face was the colour of cold porridge. 'We'll know soon.'

They had sent a boat to Wyre. It had been beaten back by the waves on its first attempt, but was on its way now.

Magnus's eyes were on the wagon ahead, the muffled shape of the bodies beneath the tarpaulin. The small convoy shared a delayed rhythm, the rear carts mimicking the lurch and pitch of the leader as they went over the same ruts and potholes in turn. He said, 'We should have remembered there's a world beyond here, full of people ready to kill for what we have.'

Stevie wiped the rain from her eyes. It was a futile gesture. The deluge was unrelenting. Belle had told her she would do anything to survive, but she had also said the world beyond their islands was hellish, *pretty soon that hell will be coming your way*. Stevie had thought it a friendly warning, but perhaps it was a disguised threat, a secret promise. She wiped her face with the edge of her sleeve. The wind was biting, her lips dry and chapped despite the rain.

'We don't know what's happened yet,' she said.

Magnus turned to look at her. 'We know what happened. They took our children.'

The New Orcadian Council office's spirit stove could not provide warm drinks for more than a few people at a time and hip flasks and bottles were circulating. Stevie followed their progress, saw the islanders tip and swallow. Most drank more than one long, throat-burning draught, but the alcohol had little visible effect. Someone passed her a bottle and she raised it to her lips. The liquid scoured her mouth, but she swallowed it down without coughing, eager for some warmth in her belly. She shoved the rotas that she and Alan Bold had carefully rewritten to one side and clambered onto her desk. Everything she had worked for was coming undone. She looked into the gathering of islanders, felt their misery and knew the sting of misplaced pride.

Breda was sobbing softly beside the makeshift stage. Parents with small children held them close. Those with missing teenagers looked side-whacked, but their eyes were dry. They reminded Stevie of horses turning their flanks to the wind; stoical against the storm.

'Candice and Bjarne are dead.' Stevie's voice sounded thin and cracked. She delivered the news without emotion, a human telecaster. 'They were shot in cold blood in their own home.'

Word of the murders had already circulated. There were no exclamations of horror, no gasps of surprise.

Brendan Banks said, 'Bjarne was an angry man. Are you sure he didn't do the deed himself?'

'Positive.' Stevie tried to make eye contact with as many people in the room as possible. Their closed expressions made it hard for her to read their mood. 'I can go into details of why we're so certain later, but for now let's just say that we're sure.' Candice had come to her for help and she had sent her away. Stevie's eyes teared but she pressed on. 'Five teenagers are missing. So is Breda's eighteen-month-old daughter, little Evie.' Lorna Mills had an arm around Breda. The woman buried her face in the teacher's embrace. 'We have no evidence that these disappearances are related, but it's too big a coincidence to dismiss. We suspect the children have gone to the mainland with a view to making their way to Glasgow.' Connor was standing beside his mother at the back of the shop. Stevie had promised the boy she would keep his testimony to herself. She made sure not to catch his eye. 'We also suspect the newcomers we quarantined on Wyre have something to do with their going.'

'Suspect or know?' a voice shouted from the crowd.

'Strongly suspect.' Stevie had not forgotten her resolution to follow facts. 'A boat has gone to Wyre to check if they're still there. If they've gone, we'll conclude they're at the heart of this.'

'The newcomers didn't make them go.' Poor Alice had looked after the younger children while their mothers joined the search party. She looked tired and brittle, as if she had spent a night in the hills. 'I'm not saying Belle and her boys don't have a motive for playing Pied Piper, but the youngsters were bound to leave eventually. That's what young people do. They go in search of adventure. You can't hold on to them, no matter how much you want to.'

A mutter of protest slid through the meeting; surf on a wave.

Lorna Mills slipped her arm from around Breda's shoulder and turned to face the islanders.

'Poor Alice is only half right. These islands were never going to be big enough for personalities like Willow. But they weren't ready to leave yet. They're young for their years, easily influenced. I don't know who killed Bjarne and Candice, but I did suspect that something unhealthy was going on in that house. I know some of you did too.' She glanced at Stevie. 'Now I wish I'd followed my intuition instead of waiting until I was certain. Belle may have lured them away, for whatever purpose, but I spend my working days with these kids. I know them. They wouldn't up and leave for no reason. Stevie was right when she said the murders of Candice and Bjarne could have something to do with their disappearance.'

'My boy had nothing to do with any murders.' A woman in the centre of the room pulled back the hood of her parka, baring her face. She was dark-eyed and olive-skinned, her hair pinned up in a windswept bun. 'Adil was always asking me what things were like before the Sweats.' She stretched her lips into the semblance of a smile. 'I knew he'd leave the islands one day, but we had years yet. He's still a boy.'

The door to the council offices opened and the bell swung into its customary clanging. Joe Archibald stepped into the old shop, his face red and wind-burnt from the crossing to Wyre. His mate Raja was with him. Both men had hats pulled low over their faces. Joe shook his head and Raja said, 'The farmhouse on Wyre is empty. It looks like they set off suddenly. They left a meal half-eaten on the kitchen table, but they took all their gear with them.'

Magnus McFall pushed his way through the crowd towards the exit. Stevie called after him, 'Magnus, you're part of this.' But the crofter lifted a bottle to his lips and stepped into the street, setting the shop bell ringing again. The door slammed behind him. Stevie closed her eyes in despair.

When she opened them the olive-skinned woman had lifted a young child from the floor and was bundling it against the cold. 'Adil won't last two minutes in a city. Every second we waste talking, our kids are getting further away.'

Stevie remembered the woman's name now. Francesca was one of the few islanders with more than one child. She and her three boys lived on the edge of Stromness in a large, messy house surrounded by a well-tended vegetable garden.

'You say your son won't last two minutes in the city, how long do you think you'd last, Francesca?'

The woman's face flushed. 'I was in London when the Sweats hit. I know what to expect.'

'In that case you'll know that you're risking your life and the lives of your other kids if you chase after Adil with them in tow.' Stevie let her gaze scan the room, taking them all in. 'We thought we were safe on the Orkneys. We were wrong. Belle warned me that the hell of the cities was headed this way. She might have already known that she was going to make off with our teenagers, the cream of our crop, but what if she meant more than that? What if Belle and her boys were just an advance party? Maybe we're going to have to fight for the privilege of living in peace.'

The room erupted into a confusion of voices. Stevie held up her hand, but it was Alan Bold who strode across the room and swung the door backwards and forwards, making the shop bell clang, until the islanders gave in to silence.

Stevie threw him a grateful look. 'I'm not saying we abandon our runaways to their fate, but we have to accept that we're not in a position to send half the island chasing after them.'

Alan Bold reached up and stilled the bell with his hand. 'Who's to say that isn't part of their plan? Get the most able-bodied men off the island and then strike.'

Lorna Mills took her arm from around Breda's shoulder. The prospect of a potential attack had given nervous energy to the deadened atmosphere, but the teacher's voice was composed. 'Where do the murders fit into this?'

'I don't have all the answers.' Stevie held Lorna's gaze. 'But I do know we're in danger of making ourselves vulnerable.'

Francesca's face was red. The child in her arms started to cry. 'So we abandon our children to the cities and hope for the best?'

Breda shouted, 'Evie's a baby. She won't know where her mummy has gone. She'll think I abandoned her.'

Stevie held up a hand. 'I told you, I'm not suggesting we forget about the children. But it's essential we make sure we don't lose what we've built here.'

The parents whose children were missing were gathered together at the front of the small crowd. Sonny Renton stepped closer to the desk and looked up at Stevie.

'None of this means anything without the kids.' Renton was a small man in his mid-fifties, the foster father of Sky. He had damaged his leg badly in a scything accident during the island's first harvest and walked with a limp. He turned to face the gathering.

'Each of us lost everything in the Sweats. Everything we worked for, everyone we loved. We call ourselves survivors, but most of us are only just holding on by our fingertips. Our kids keep us going, even though most of them aren't ours by birth. These islands are nothing to me, if I lose my daughter.'

There were a few muttered assents, but most of the islanders kept their silence. Some looked at their boots.

Renton raised his voice. 'Who'll come with me and help bring our kids back?'

Francesca put her hand up. So did Breda and the other parents whose children were missing, but the majority of the islanders kept their hands by their sides.

Renton said, 'You bunch of bastards. How would you feel if it was your child?'

'It's not that we don't care.' Brendan Banks took his cap from his head and wrung it between his hands. 'We don't know what to do for the best. What if Stevie's right? We've made a life here. We can't give it up without a fight.'

Someone else said, 'It's almost harvest time. If that fails, we all fail.'

Stevie got down from the desk. 'You elected me president of the council because you trust me. I've done my best to live up to your trust by working hard, being straight with you and not making promises that I can't keep.' There were a few murmurs of assent from the crowd, but not as many as she needed. She said, 'Have I ever lied to you?'

This time the response was louder, 'No.'

Stevie focused on the parents of the missing children and asked the question again, her voice low, as if the conversation was solely between them.

'Have I ever lied to you?'

Their response was mumbled and reluctant, but it was the answer she wanted – *No*.

Stevie nodded. 'I'm going to make a promise to you. I intend to keep it, or die trying. I promise to track the children down and bring as many of them back as will come with me.' Some of the parents started to speak, but Stevie talked over them. 'Francesca's right. The longer we delay, the further your sons and daughters get from us. Any chance we have of bringing them home relies on speed. That's not going to happen if we take the time to assemble a big team. They already have a day's travel on us.' She looked at the parents of the missing teenagers. 'Sonny, I know you want to be the one who brings your girl home, but your leg slows you down. Francesca, you have two other boys who need you here.

Breda, this is a task for someone who can kill.' She scanned the crowd. The islanders' faces were turned towards her. Their expressions were grave, but they were survivors and had learned to grasp at slim spars of hope. 'I'll take one person with me.'

Alan Bold took his hat from his pocket and put it on his head, ready to set out.

Stevie caught his eye and looked away, focusing on the faces of the islanders lifted towards her. 'You elected Alan Bold as my deputy. While I'm gone he will continue with the day-to-day running of the council and lead preparations for our defence in case of an attack.' She looked to where Joe Archibald stood, broad-shouldered and earnest at the back of the room. 'Joe, you're a good sailor and a decent marksman. Will you consider coming with me?'

Joe Archibald gave her his steady smile. He shook his head.

'I'm sorry, Stevie. I promised myself when I landed here that this is where I'll die. If there's going to be a battle for Orkney, I'd rather stay and be a part of it.' He adjusted his cap, embarrassed at turning her down in front of so many witnesses. 'I'm not the one you should be inviting. Magnus McFall is a better sailor and as good a shot as me. His boy is one of the missing kids. He'll stop at nothing to bring him home.'

Stevie had anticipated the suggestion. Magnus was popular, but he was too emotional – too inclined to drink and take chances – to be a good choice. There was another reason she wanted to avoid his company too. One she could not share with the rest of the islanders.

She said, 'Magnus walked out on our meeting half an hour ago with a bottle in his hand. He'll be well on his way to drowning his sorrows by now. I need someone I can rely on.'

Poor Alice shook her head. 'Magnus likes a drink, but there are plenty of people in this room who would beat him to the title of island drunk. My bet is, while you've been up there jawing, Magnus has been down at the quayside getting his boat ready. You'd better shift yourself, if you want to catch him.'

Stevie looked at Brendan Banks.

The banjo player nodded. 'He thought he'd have more chance on his own.'

'And you didn't think it worth mentioning?'

Brendan shrugged. 'It's his boy, his decision.'

'No, Brendan . . .' Stevie unlocked her desk drawer, took out the gun and boxes of ammo she kept there and shoved them in her rucksack. Pistol had been asleep beneath the desk. He got up and nudged her legs, eager to be outdoors. She ignored the dog. 'It's not Magnus's boy, Magnus's decision. These children don't belong to anyone. Not to us, not to the islands. They're their own people. It might be that they don't want to come back, in which case I'll have to respect their choice.' The dog nudged her again and she shoved it away. 'Alice is right. We can't hold the children here for ever, but they're young and inexperienced. They've been duped into thinking the world is safer than it is. We have to take some responsibility for that. The Sweats gave us no second chances, but if I catch up with the kids quickly enough, I may be able to offer them one.'

Alan Bold had taken a rifle from a locked cupboard. He shouldered it, ready to walk with her down to the quayside. Stevie thought he looked relieved not to be going with her.

Francesca said, 'Don't listen to Adil if he tells you he wants to stay. He thinks he's grown-up, but he's still a child.'

The parents clustered round Stevie, reminding her of their children's names, giving her messages for them, telling her of childhood ailments. She touched each of them in a swift embrace and headed to the door, Pistol at her heels, Alan Bold at her side. The meeting followed them into the street. The crowd was quiet.

There were none of the smiles or catcalls she imagined had accompanied soldiers heading to war.

Stevie knew she had not been entirely straight with the islanders. She had let them think the children's welfare the sole purpose of her search, but she had a second motive. The murders had been forgotten in the confusion of child runaways and threatened invasion. Bjarne had been unpopular, Candice a pale ghost of the woman she had once been. They had no friends or family to vouch for them.

Whatever the age of Candice and Bjarne's murderers, whoever's son or daughter they were, Stevie was determined to bring them home to face justice. It was the reason she had not wanted to team up with Magnus McFall. Magnus would fight to the death for his son, even if Shug turned out to be a killer.

Twenty

Magnus was loading final provisions into his dinghy. Tiredness made him clumsy, but he could not afford to take a break. The tide would turn soon and he needed its help if he was to reach open waters before the end of the day.

A dog barked. Magnus looked up and saw Pistol lolloping along the pier. Stevie would not be far behind.

'Shit.'

He had hoped to be on his way before anyone realised he was gone. Magnus ran his eyes over the gear still waiting on the quayside, calculating what was essential.

'Wait up, McFall.' Stevie's voice carried over the lap of the harbour waves and the cries of the seagulls. The weather had cleared a little and her parka was unzipped. She held a rifle in her left hand, muzzle pointing towards the ground. A rucksack was strapped to her back. The population of the island followed in her wake.

Magnus remembered a TV advert for bread, or had it been a bank? A whole village inspired to run through the streets for love of some product. The villagers in the advert had been dizzy with joy. His fellow islanders looked like a Highland funeral. Magnus wondered if he would ever rid himself of trivial flashbacks.

Pistol ran back to greet Stevie, tail wagging. Magnus had resolved to save the potcheen for emergencies, but he opened the bottle, lifted it to his lips and took a quick swig.

Stevie crouched on the edge of the pier, looking down at him.

'Confident you and your white lightning can find the kids and bring them back?'

Magnus tipped the bottle again, though he knew it made him look foolish.

'We'll give it a good shot.'

Stevie draped an arm around Pistol's neck. 'My dog's got more sense than you.'

'Then I must be bloody thick. Your dog's the stupidest mutt on Orkney.'

Magnus was not sure why he was being rude to her, except that it made him feel better. He was tired and hungry and his boy was missing.

'Not just thick, arrogant.' Stevie looked like she wanted to smack him with her rifle. A quick jab in the solar plexus would send him into the water. Magnus braced himself, but Stevie held the gun firm, its stock resting against the ground, business end pointing towards the sky. 'You really think you could bring them back without any help?'

She was right. It was reckless to tackle the sea crossing solo. Stupid to think he could find Shug and his friends on his own, but Magnus did not want anyone with him. Even before the Sweats he had preferred to travel alone. Had never minded late-night drives along the familiar motorways that linked the comedy circuit, that night's gig still playing in his head.

He looked at the crowd gathered on the pier. Some of the islanders had lifted the last bags of provisions, ready to help him pack them on the boat. Magnus forced a smile.

'I can't fit you all on board.'

Stevie said, 'You don't have to. I'm the only one coming with you.'

The news surprised him. He had expected a squad of boats to head for the mainland.

'How come?'

'I'll explain once we're underway.' Stevie grabbed Pistol by the collar and said to Alan Bold, 'Look after him for me. He'll be a pest on the boat and cities were never good places for dogs.'

The deputy gripped the collar. They had talked quietly of how long the search should go on for. What to do if she did not come back. Bold said, 'He'll miss you.'

The dog looked from one to the other and whined. Stevie scratched his head. She had raised him from a pup. They had never been parted before.

'I hope he doesn't interfere with your love life.'

Bold glanced to where Lorna Mills was standing. 'My wandering days are drawing to a close.'

Stevie gave him a quick hug and whispered, 'Which is not quite the same as saying they're over.'

The deputy held her tighter than she expected. Stevie hoped that he had not taken her words as an invitation. She pulled away and climbed into the dinghy.

Pistol broke free just as the rowing boat pushed off from the quayside. Alan Bold made a move to catch him, but the dog was swift. Magnus dipped the oars again, sending the boat on its way before he realised that the dog had escaped. Pistol did not hesitate. He leapt, hurtling over the water.

There was a moment when the dog seemed to hang in the air, an ungainly mess of legs, tongue, ears and tail, and then he landed, splay-pawed and awkward amongst the supplies. The boat rocked like a leaf in a river at full swell. They looked certain to overturn, but the little craft righted itself.

'Shit.' Stevie pushed Pistol to the floor. She pressed her hand on the top of his head – '*Bad boy*' – keeping him still, letting the dog know who was in charge. She could do nothing about his tail which thump, thump, thumped against the rowing boat's hull.

'Let him stay.' Magnus had regained his rhythm. He dipped the oars and they pulled further away from the pier, closer to his sailing boat. 'He's a good omen.'

Pistol grinned, but he was a dog. He lived in the moment and knew nothing of the task ahead.

Twenty-One

Magnus and Stevie took turns napping in the yacht's single bunk during the crossing. The sky shifted through a palate of greys and blues but the wind stayed with them, gusting the sails full-bellied, away from the Orkneys. They were careful beneath their recklessness, as behoved true survivors; wearing their lifejackets above and below deck; clipping themselves to the vessel for fear of being tipped overboard. Magnus was the better sailor. Even stumbling with tiredness he could still anticipate the pitch and roll of the deck. Before the Sweats, Stevie had never captained anything larger than a pedalo. She had learned quickly, but possessed none of Magnus's natural instinct for the craft or the water. Every act she made on board was conscious; each correction of the sail or shift of the boom a calculation.

Pistol grew miserable from lack of exercise. His tail lost its usual buoyancy and he prowled from deck to cabin to deck, head hanging like a guilty thing. Magnus saw the dog slink beneath the sails and thought that it could be his own miserable soul roaming the boat.

Stevie's footsteps sounded on the cabin stairs. She had found a yellow cagoule and was wearing it on top of her lifejacket. She pulled its hood over her head as she came up on deck.

'You're some banana.'

Magnus had greeted her with the same joke ever since she had taken to wearing the yellow waterproof. Stevie did not think it funny. Neither did he.

Stevie unpeeled the lid from a tin of baked beans. She ate half of the can and handed it to Magnus, the spoon still resting inside. Their journey had been full of such unacknowledged intimacies. They had taken a turn at sleeping between the same sheets, but had barely talked during the crossing, shifting politely around each other.

Magnus tried to savour the beans. Processed food was a rare luxury, saved for journeys like these. The sauce tasted sweeter and saltier than he remembered. He wondered if they had gone bad, but he was hungry. He finished them and set the empty tin by the wheel, ready to stow beneath the deck. Aluminium was a luxury too.

He took the wheel, kept his eyes on the horizon and waited for Stevie to say something. The air was more alive at sea than on land. Even at the top of a mountain, peaked high above everything else, the wind did not rush with the same vitality, touching every exposed part of skin, grabbing at hair, reaching up sleeves, down backs and necks. Magnus tightened his scarf. There were more gulls in the sky. He nodded towards them.

'We'll reach land soon.' They had not discussed what they would do when they got there.

Stevie kept her silence. Magnus said, 'We're assuming Connor told us the truth and the kids are headed to Glasgow. But they could have steered him wrong to throw us off the scent. They might be halfway to Norway by now.'

Belle's blonde hair and pale skin made her look like a Viking warrior. It was not hard to imagine her there.

'I know.' Stevie's features were hidden in the shadows of her hood. 'If we could have spared the people I would have sent a boat in that direction too, but it's too risky. They're lucky we're coming after them at all.'

Magnus heard the resentment in her voice. He said, 'I'm surprised you left, if you think our hold on Orkney is in danger. You'd make a better general than Alan Bold, or is this part of your election campaign?'

Stevie ignored the jibe.

'I don't know if I made the right decision.'

She pulled her hood back, showing him her face. It was a conscious gesture of openness. Magnus was not sure that he trusted it.

Stevie said, 'It's not certain the islands will come under attack, but we know the children are gone. I think there's a chance I can find them.'

'And if the islands fall?'

'I'll have made the wrong choice.' Pistol rested his head against Stevie's leg. She ran a hand along his muzzle. 'Poor dog, not long now.' She glanced up at Magnus. 'I don't mean I could save the islands. But if something were to happen there, I'd want to be a part of it, for good or for bad. You feel the same way.'

Magnus nodded. 'But here we are, sailing in the wrong direction.'

The dog left Stevie's side and loped to starboard, sniffing at the air. Magnus wondered if it could scent land. He said, 'It was necessary for me to come. Shuggie's my responsibility. I'm not sure what compelled you.'

Stevie shrugged. 'I promised their parents.'

Magnus checked the compass in the centre of the wheel, making sure they were still on course, and then trained his eyes on the horizon.

'You did, but I'm guessing you didn't do it just to be kind.'

The wind was high, spray dashing over the deck. Stevie pulled her hood up, protecting her face from icy stabs of water, hiding her expression.

'So why do you think I'm here?'

Magnus's eyes met hers. 'Either you're electioneering or you want to find out who killed Bjarne and Candice.'

Stevie looked away. 'You found their bodies. Don't you want to know who did that to them?'

'I want to find Shug more.' He waited for her to say that perhaps they were searching for one and the same, but Stevie was silent and he added, 'What makes you so certain it wasn't me?'

'You didn't kill them.'

'How can you be sure?'

'Bjarne's brains were splattered across the living room. Whoever shot him would have been covered in blood and grey matter. When Connor found you in the house you were wearing the same clothes you'd had on earlier that day. The only marks on them were mud.'

Magnus thought of Shug's white jacket. It had been streaked with mud and blood.

He said, 'I could have stripped off, murdered them in the scud and put my old clothes back on.'

'You could have. But I'm guessing that would have set Bjarne on his guard. Whoever killed him had the advantage of surprise.'

A thin strip of darkness was sandwiched between the sea and sky. Magnus pointed towards it.

'Land ahoy.'

Stevie took a set of binoculars from the pocket of her cagoule and trained them on the horizon. The dog was running up and down the deck, snapping at the seagulls reeling around the boat, his tail waving, as if to tell the birds that it was all in fun. Magnus watched the horizon take shape and wondered what waited there. He might have been an astronaut about to step onto an uncharted planet. Stevie passed him the binoculars. 'Look.'

Magnus focused the lenses. He had thought the terminal, where ferries loaded with cars, lorries and containers had once begun their journeys to the islands and beyond, might have decayed and slid into the sea. But it looked in decent shape. He squinted and saw a thin pall of smoke curling from the chimney of one of the flat-roofed buildings. Belle's boat was moored in the harbour.

'Someone's there.'

'Good.' Stevie retrieved her rifle from the cabin and loaded it. 'Maybe whoever it is saw our kids.'

Magnus nodded at the rifle. 'Go easy with that thing.' But he took his pistol from the inside pocket of his jacket, where he had stowed it safe against the salt spray, and checked the ammunition clip. He raised the binoculars to his eyes again. A figure stood on the quayside, watching their boat approach. It was too far for him to make out any details, but Magnus thought it was a man. He felt a shiver of apprehension. It was as if he was seeing himself, waiting by the shore.

Twenty-Two

The man was called Rees. He was bald beneath his knitted cap, a surly Cornishman with no resemblance to Magnus except for the gun on his hip and a tendency to favour his own company. His pair of ridgebacks hurtled towards Pistol; a rush of sharp teeth and slavering jowls. He called them and they loped to his side, hackles erect. Stevie held Pistol by the collar, outgunned.

'Leaving your boat there?' Rees sheltered a roll-up from the wind in the curl of his hand.

'Any objections?' They were barely one up from the dogs, Magnus reflected, a step away from a snarl.

'None.' Rees ruffled the head of one of the ridgebacks. The beast panted, its tongue lolling. 'I'll keep an eye on it for you.'

Stevie cast a look around the empty ferry terminal, at the expanse of cracked tarmacadam and squat ferry offices that quickly gave way to hills. The three of them were exposed; visible from sea, high land and the shelter of the buildings. She said, 'How many people are settled here?'

'Just me.' Rees cast a glance in the direction of the hills. 'I live here alone.'

'Must get lonely.'

'I've got the dogs.' He flicked the ash from his cigarette onto the ground. 'And people come and go.'

'People returning to the cities?'

He shrugged. 'I don't ask where they're going, or where they've come from for that matter. I'm a trader; goods and services.'

'What did they trade?' Stevie nodded to where Belle's boat bobbed in the water.

Rees shrugged. 'The usual, tobacco, drink, weapons. I don't remember.'

Stevie said, 'We're looking for the crew of that boat.'

Rees dropped his roll-up and ground it into the tarmac with the heel of his work boot. 'Sometimes I trade information, at a cost.'

Then he turned his back on them and led the way to a row of shipping containers set along the quayside. Magnus tensed as the Cornishman unfastened the padlocks that secured the door of the first container. Locks and confined spaces set him on edge.

Stevie caught Magnus's faint intake of breath and gave him a searching look. He shook his head to show it was nothing.

Rees pulled the final chain from the hasp. 'You'd best leave your dog outside.' Stevie hesitated and he said, 'Don't worry. There's nothing to harm him here. Wolves don't venture close during the day.'

'Wolves?'

Rees grinned. 'Wolves are the least of it. When the Sweats took hold some idiots had the great idea of opening up the zoos. There are lions and all sorts out there. Mostly they keep to themselves, but it's best to have your wits about you after dark.'

Stevie fondled Pistol's ears and then sent him out towards the cracked tarmacadam lot, still marked with lanes, where cars had once formed orderly lines as they waited to board the ferry. 'Lions couldn't survive in Scotland, it's too cold.'

'We're not the only ones who are adaptable.' Rees pushed open the door to the container and they followed him inside.

Narrow window slits let in arrow points of light. Rees lit a couple of oil lamps, and the interior glowed into focus. The sides of the container had been faced with hardwood, the floor coated with deck paint. A counter along one wall acted as a kitchen, a small platform in the corner as a bed. A table and chair set by the far wall hinted at a spartan life. He shut his own dogs in the adjoining container. The briefly opened connecting door offered a quick glimpse of shelves stacked with boxes.

Rees set a tin kettle of water on a lit stove. 'They sailed in, same as you did. Three girls and two boys with a blonde woman and two men. She had something wrong with one of her eyes.'

Magnus said, 'How did the kids look?'

The kettle screeched; a barn owl on the kill. Rees took it from the hob, poured boiling water into three mugs and added something black and dried from a canister on the countertop.

'Nettles and mint.' He stirred the mugs and passed them each one. 'Tastes like piss, but you get used to it.'

Magnus took a sip. The liquid was thin and grass-tainted.

'One of the boys is my son. His name's Shuggie.'

'They looked okay.' Rees did not ask which of the boys Shug was. 'Tired, but you'd expect that.'

Magnus knew it would make him look weak but he said, 'He was in a fight not long before he left.'

'That was him, was it?' Rees looked amused. 'His face was a few pretty shades – a nuclear sunset – but no lasting damage I'd say.'

'Good.' Magnus resented the trader's smile, his own gratitude at news of Shug.

In the room beyond the ridgebacks were whining. Exiled in the car park, Pistol picked up the noise of the other dogs and barked. He butted the container door, eager to be inside.

Stevie said, 'Did they have a toddler with them?'

'Why do you ask?'

She had meant to say that Evie belonged to her, but paused a beat too long.

'She's the daughter of a friend.'

Pistol barked again.

Stevie went to the door and opened it. 'Go.' She pointed towards the parking lot and the dog trotted off, head hanging. A splash of yellow by one of the low buildings snagged Stevie's eye, a small shape moving against the concrete. She narrowed her eyes and saw that it was a child. As she watched a figure appeared, snatched up the child and hurried indoors. Stevie thought the person looked in her direction, but the distance was too far for her to make out their features. She could not be sure that they had seen her.

She shut the door and turned back into the container's dim, metallic gloom. 'Evie's eighteen months old. They kidnapped her.' The word sounded strange in her mouth. 'She'll be missing her mother.'

'She looked happy enough when I saw her.'

Rees's beard was grey and neatly trimmed. Stevie wondered who he groomed himself for.

'Her mother's distraught.'

'So why isn't she looking for her?'

'She thought we would do a better job.' Stevie had slung her rifle across her back. She fingered the clasp on the strap crossing her chest. 'She's right.'

Rees looked her up and down; the quick, reflexive flit from breast to crotch to breast that Stevie had grown used to.

'That remains to be seen.' He took a sip of his drink and leaned against the counter, regarding her. 'Like I said, the kid seemed happy enough. They all did.'

Magnus took a sip of his brew. It tasted no better than before, but he swallowed it.

'Did they mention where they were going?'

Rees shrugged. 'Where does anybody go? You were young once, you know the script – bright lights, big city.'

'Is that what they told you?'

'They didn't need to.'

Rees pulled out the only chair and offered it to Stevie.

She rejected it with a brief shake of the head. 'Didn't you think it odd, a gang of teenagers with three adults and a toddler?'

He settled himself on the chair. 'I don't know where you've just come from, but round here nothing's *odd*.' He emphasised the word, making it sound absurd. 'People come, people go. Sometimes they need something. Sometimes they've got something I need. We trade and they go on their way.'

Magnus said, 'Did you ever do business with a man called Bjarne? A big guy, a Yorkshireman settled on the Orkneys?'

'Ammunition and guns trade well.' Rees hid his expression behind his mug. 'Maybe I'd remember him, if I had a brace of rifles and half-a-dozen boxes of bullets in my hands.'

Magnus snorted. 'I'd want to know what you were going to tell us was worth it, before I handed over a bloody arsenal.'

'I think you'll find it a good deal.' Rees took a small tin box out of his pocket. He extracted a small bag of tobacco and some rolling papers. 'But that's the trouble with trading information. You never know if it's worth the price until you've paid it.'

Stevie's fingers returned to the clasp on the strap that held her rifle in place. 'You're a brave man. There are two of us, one of you.'

'Maybe I lied about being on my own.' Rees sprinkled a thin line of tobacco onto one of the papers. He looked up from his task and grinned. 'There could be an army hiding in these buildings yonder. Anyway, if you shoot me, you'll never find out what I know.'

'Depends on where I shoot you.'

The trader's grin widened, but Stevie thought she sensed unease beneath the stretched lips, the exposed teeth. He rolled the loaded paper and ran his tongue along it, sealing the cigarette. 'You don't strike me as the type.'

Stevie smiled her best salesgirl smile, the one that had once stoked her salary with commission.

'Inflicting pain makes me feel bad, but I can do it.'

A small flake of tobacco stuck to Rees's lip. The trader caught it on his tongue and spat it free. He set his cigarette on the table and placed his hands on his thighs, in easy reach of the rifle stationed by his side. Pistol whined at the door and the dogs in the adjacent container barked, as if they could sense the tension rising.

'We don't need any trouble.' Magnus resisted the urge to reach inside his jacket for his gun. 'We're just anxious about our kids.'

'Your kid.' Rees's eyes were on Stevie. 'I'm guessing she doesn't have any.'

Stevie detected a hint of superiority in his voice that made her think her suspicion about the toddler she had caught a glimpse of was right. She said, 'None of the children are mine, but I care about them. Guns and ammo are a small price to pay.' She looked at Magnus. 'Stay with him. I'll fetch the rifles from the boat.'

'Stevie . . .' Magnus took a step towards her.

She held up her hands; too low for surrender, but wide enough for apology.

'We need some form of transport and we need to know anything that might help us track down the kids. You can shoot him in the leg, torture it out of him, or we can trade.' She looked at Rees. 'We hid the guns inside the boat. It'll take me a while to get them.'

Magnus said, 'Need a hand?'

She nodded towards the Cornishman.

'I'd rather you kept an eye on him.'

They both knew there were no rifles in the boat and that whatever ammunition they had was precious. Magnus gave an even nod, his expression neutral. 'Be careful.'

Stevie treated him to a smile. 'Don't worry. It's like the man said, the wolves only come out after dark.'

Pistol gave her a rapturous greeting. Stevie had never quite cured him of jumping up and had to push him away. '*Down!*' The remains of a rabbit lay bloody on the ground by the shipping container. The dog had ripped the meat and innards from the carcass and discarded the bones and pelt. The rabbit's head lolled in her direction, large eyes dull and unsurprised. Once it would have made Stevie retch; now she was merely glad to know that the dog had eaten.

She looked towards the terminal building where she had seen the child. Its windows were boarded up, but she suspected there were gaps in the makeshift shutters, where someone could keep lookout. She checked her watch and jogged away from the buildings, down towards the quayside and onto the boat. Pistol followed her, tail wagging. She ordered the dog into the cabin and shut the door on him, hoping his recent meal would send him to sleep.

The next part was more difficult. Stevie slipped off the boat and ran in a wide arc around the quayside, skirting the shipping containers. She was dressed in black and kept her body low, hoping the greys of tarmac, concrete and sky would camouflage her, but there was little cover and she was dangerously exposed to view. She had slid a knife into her left boot and could feel it, loose in its sheath, rubbing against her ankle, a counterpoint to the weight of the gun in her jacket pocket. She glanced at her watch. Three minutes since she had left Magnus and Rees.

There was an edge of scrubland beyond the tarmac. Stevie used it as her guideline and changed direction, making for the building near where the toddler was hidden. The child looked the same shape and size as Evie, but only a mother could tell one child from another at that distance. Stevie was nearing the building now. She could hear the wind shaking the trees that had colonised the hills beyond the ferry terminal. As she drew closer she heard another sound below the hiss of the breeze and trembling leaves – a song sung in a wavering falsetto.

> *Cry baby Bunting,*
> *Daddy's gone a-hunting*
> *Gone to get a rabbit skin,*
> *to wrap the baby Bunting in . . .*

And beneath the wavering voice, she heard the sound of a child sobbing.

> *Cry baby Bunting,*
> *Daddy's gone a-hunting . . .*

Baby Bunting kept on crying. Stevie drew level with the building, edging close to the windows. Chipboard had been nailed across them. The compressed wood had proved unequal to the northern climate. The boards had swollen and warped; their edges pushed free of the window frames. Stevie crawled along the side of the building and put her eye to one of the gaps. She glimpsed a slice of kitchen – maroon linoleum, a white enamelled cooker, an edge of grey, stainless-steel sink. It was a cold space, the kind that defied cleaning. As far as she could tell it was empty. Stevie felt a surge of sympathy for whoever lived here, caught in squalor on the edge of nothing, but she kept her gun in her hand and crept forward. Time was ticking on. It was six minutes since she had promised Rees the guns and ammo. Instinct told her the trader did not believe the Sweats were a sign that the world needed to slow down. He would be getting impatient.

The terminal building's pebbledash was sharp against Stevie's cheekbone. She moved quietly and peered through the next gap in the boarding and into the eyes of a small child.

> Cry baby Bunting,
> Daddy's gone a-hunting . . .

The toddler was being rocked to and fro, its head resting on the shoulder of the singer, who had her back to the window. It stopped in mid-cry and stared at Stevie, large eyes brimming with tears.

'Shhhh . . . Shhhhh . . .' The woman jiggled the child. It raised a hand, waved a teething ring towards Stevie and cawed an unintelligible greeting.

The woman turned and Stevie ducked out of sight. The child had lifted its head as it called to her and she had seen its face. It was younger than Evie, its head bald except for a downy covering of baby hair.

'Is someone there?' The woman's voice was high and determined. 'I've got a gun.'

Stevie crouched beneath the window. She had hoped the child was Evie, but now suspected it might belong to Rees. There was a weight in her chest; shame at what she was about to do; fear that it might kill her. She took a deep breath and slid the blade of her knife into the breach in the chipboard. The damp wood gave way easily. Stevie levered the knife's handle and the board let out a hollow crack as it split. The woman shouted, 'Rees?'

Stevie sprinted to the front door and crouched by the step, her rifle pointing upwards. She held her breath and waited. Time passed. The wind shook the trees. A tuft of grass beside the step bent with the breeze. Stevie's joints began to stiffen. She risked a quick glance at her watch. Nine minutes since she had left Rees and Magnus. She wanted to look towards the sea and the shipping container where the two men waited, but stared instead at the door handle, willing it to turn. The space between her shoulder blades prickled and she imagined Rees making his way across the flat expanse of tarmac towards her, raising his gun as she came into range.

The child had not let out a sound since it greeted her. Stevie wondered how the woman had silenced it. A feeling of dread crept over her. Who knew how much the woman had suffered? Fear could trigger desperate acts. One of the first new mothers on Orkney had drowned her baby before cutting her own wrists. They had been discovered in the bath, their bodies cradled together in the pink water.

Stevie was half out of her crouch when the door handle slowly began to turn. She braced herself and watched as the door opened a crack. It was all she needed. She rammed the muzzle of her rifle into the gap and sprang to her feet. The gun rose with her. The woman screamed. Stevie said, 'Stay where you are.'

The woman's eyes were wide in the darkness of the hallway. Stevie's rifle rested horribly against the crown of the child's head.

'Don't hurt her.' The woman's voice was hoarse.

It was an effort to keep the gun where it was, pressed against the child's soft skull. The baby gave her a glassy look. Stevie said, 'Open the door and throw your gun outside, beyond the step.'

The woman pulled the door wider. She had dark hair and the raw complexion of someone used to working outside in all weathers. She said, 'I took the safety catch off. I need both hands to fix it.'

Stevie stroked the child's cheek with the barrel of her gun. 'I won't ask twice.'

The woman's eyes were wild with fear, the set of her jaw determined. She was short and wiry, dressed in a grey T-shirt and running bottoms.

'It's liable to blow all our heads off when it hits the ground.'

To let the woman put both hands on the gun was to invite her own death. Stevie said, 'That'll put an end to all our worries.'

The mother's glance flitted across the hills and down to the bay. She must have seen no chance of help because she did as she was told and tossed the gun beyond reach. Stevie tensed as the weapon hit the tarmac but the woman did not blink. Stevie saw that she had been lying and knew that, given a chance, the mother would kill her. She nodded towards the child. 'What's her name?'

'Mercy. I named her for the times.'

'Why isn't she crying?'

'I gave her something to keep her quiet.' The woman put her hand on the baby's skull, her fingers dangerously close to the barrel of Stevie's gun. 'How did you know I'd open the door?'

'I didn't. But it's the only point with a clear view of your man's storerooms. You'd already risked stepping outside since our boat docked. I thought that if I got you rattled, you might risk it again.'

She could have added that most survivors ran towards trouble. If they had to die they preferred to be on their feet.

The woman stared Stevie in the eye. 'Rees is a crack shot. He'll have the legs from you before you even know he's there.' Her voice broke. 'I know children fetch good prices, but they're high maintenance. Put your rifle down and I'll make sure he gives you goods to trade.' Her fingers stroked the child's thistledown hair.

'Take your hand away from the gun.' The target between Stevie's shoulder blades burned, but she dared not turn to see if Rees was behind her.

The woman slid her hand free of her daughter's head, all the while keeping her eyes locked on Stevie's.

'Mercy's getting over a bad cold. She might not survive a long journey. Let us both go and my husband will give you guns.' She tried to smile. 'High value, no hassle.'

It was a good slogan, the kind any salesperson would be proud of. Stevie said, 'What's your name?'

'Lucy.' The woman kissed the top of her child's head, her lips almost brushing the barrel of the gun. 'I can see you're a good person. You wouldn't shoot a child.'

'Are you willing to take the chance?'

Lucy held Mercy close and cast her eyes downwards, as if it hurt her to look at Stevie.

'Whatever you want, you can get it without threatening a baby.' She stepped from the house. The strain was beginning to tell. The hands that held the child were trembling. 'If you have to aim a gun at someone aim it at me.'

Stevie's biceps ached with the effort of keeping her rifle steady; there was a knot in her right shoulder where she would feel the recoil if the gun fired.

'We're going to your husband's man-cave. Stay in front of me and keep a steady pace. I don't want to hurt either of you, but if you trip or make a break for it, I will shoot you both.' Stevie heard the conviction in her own voice and felt afraid.

There was no longer any need to seek cover. They walked across the tarmac, Lucy leading the way with Mercy in her arms. Stevie followed a breath behind, her rifle still aimed at the child's head. A thin spatter of rain drove in from the sea, hitting them in their faces. The baby whimpered, but whatever Lucy had given her had taken hold and she did not cry.

Stevie saw Rees and Magnus step from the shipping container and was glad the Cornishman had time to take in the scene: his wife and child, her rifle. Rees reached for his pistol. Magnus said something to him and he dropped it. The Cornishman raised his hands in the air to show that he was unarmed and then slowly lowered them.

Magnus picked up the abandoned gun from the ground. Stevie expected him to point it at Rees, but he held it by his side. She felt a blast of impatience. The scent of moral superiority was typical of the Orcadian.

She waited until they were close and said, 'Ready to trade?'

The Cornishman ignored her and looked at Lucy. 'Are you all right?'

Lucy nodded. 'Give her what she wants.'

Rees lifted a hand, as if he was about to touch his wife and daughter. It hung in the air, an incomplete gesture. He let it fall to his side and looked at Stevie. 'Name your terms.'

The wind blew Stevie's hair across her face, but she dared not move a hand to brush it away.

'We want to know everything you can tell us about where our kids are headed and anything you know about Bjarne, the trader from Orkney.' She kept her eyes trained on Lucy. The woman's hips were taught, her spine straight; back muscles defined beneath her thin cotton top. Stevie realised Lucy was tensed for flight and whispered in her ear. 'It'll be over soon. Keep your cool and I promise everyone will walk away in one piece.'

She thought about telling Magnus to make himself useful and point his gun at the woman, but was afraid he might refuse and that the slender power balance would be broken.

Rees said, 'Why don't you give my wife and daughter a break? I've already promised to tell you what I can.'

Stevie kept her gun steady. 'The sooner you tell us, sooner they'll go free.'

Mercy whimpered and Lucy made a soft shushing noise.

Rees said, 'Your kids are headed south. They think they're going to civilisation, but the people they're with will sell them to the highest bidder. If they're lucky they'll go straight to one of the big scavenging gangs. If they're unlucky there may be a few detours along the way.'

Magnus moved to Stevie's side. He pointed the gun he had lifted from the ground at the trader. 'What kind of detours?'

Rees looked him in the eye. 'Use your imagination.'

Magnus said, 'Is this guesswork or do you know for sure?'

'No one announced it, but I could tell that was the plan. The kids were high on adventure and the adults were keeping them that way – spinning them a line, full of promises about how things would be when they reached Glasgow – electricity, cinemas, Internet, hot- and cold-running water.'

Stevie said, 'Belle was held captive by a gang trading in women. She wouldn't get involved with people trafficking.'

'What planet have you been living on?' Lucy's back was still to Stevie, pinned in place by the threat of the rifle. 'Ex-slaves make the best traffickers. People are commodities. That's why I hide Mercy every time a boat docks. Babies are scarce.'

Magnus said, 'Little Evie's eighteen months old. My son's only fifteen. He's a tall lad, but he's just a boy.'

Lucy looked at her husband. 'You said they were all old enough to know what they were doing. You never told me there was a baby.'

Rees gave a weary shrug. 'There was no point in upsetting you. Whatever price they'd put on her would be beyond our means. I wanted them gone before they started poking about and discovered Mercy.' He looked at Magnus. 'You'd think the Sweats left plenty to go round, but you'd be wrong. It left a lot of technology no one knows how to use. That makes manpower valuable. The kids you're looking for are young and fresh. They're in for a hard time.'

'Is that what this is about?' Lucy's voice was dangerously low; thunder before a lightning storm. 'They asked you for help finding stolen kids and you pushed them for a deal?'

Mercy wriggled in her mother's arms and started to cry. Lucy shushed her again, but the child refused to be silenced.

'The teenagers are old enough to take their chances, the baby is gone.' Rees looked from Stevie to Magnus, his expression a contradiction of shame and defiance. 'This life makes monsters of everyone.' He nodded towards Stevie's rifle. 'I bet you never thought you'd hold a gun to a child's head. Well I never thought I'd use some kids' disappearance as a chance to scam ammo, but if we want to keep warm and fed this winter we need merchandise to trade.' Rees shook his head. 'I used to work for the HMRC. I thought it was stressful.' He dragged a hand across his face. 'There's no point in a Mexican fucking stand-off. Let's go inside the cabin. Keep your guns on us if you want, but Mercy's heavier than she looks. Lucy won't be able to hold her for much longer. I'll tell you what I can.'

Lucy risked a glance over her shoulder at Stevie. Her face had lost some of its hardness.

'I would have made him help earlier, if I'd known.' She turned slowly until she was facing the gun barrel and held her child out to Stevie. It had stopped crying and gave a drowsy smile. 'Put down your gun. Hold Mercy instead.'

Stevie lowered her rifle.

'Hold her,' Lucy persisted.

Magnus stepped forward. 'I'll take her if you like.' He slid his gun into his jacket pocket and reached for the child.

It happened quickly. Rees grabbed a pistol from the back of his belt and pointed it at Stevie. He risked a quick glance at his wife. 'Get that mad bitch's gun.'

The harshness in her father's voice set Mercy crying again. Lucy jiggled her on her hip as she took the rifle from Stevie.

Rees gave Magnus a shove. 'Let's leave the girls to talk make-up and babies, while we get the guns from your boat.'

Stevie was about to say that she had invented the cache of weapons, but Lucy shoved the crying child into her arms. She raised the rifle to her shoulder and pointed it at her husband. 'Drop it.'

Rees looked at her. He took the roll-up he had made earlier from his top pocket and put it unlit between his lips. 'You could hurt someone with that.'

There was a small click as Lucy released the safety catch. A cloud shifted. Tiny shards of broken glass scattered across the terminal's tarmac glinted silver in the sudden sunlight. Across the bay gulls rode on air pockets, swooping and climbing through the sky, flashes of white against the blue.

Rees said, 'Lucy, for fuck's sake—'

'Don't swear in front of the baby. I want her first word to be "Mummy", not "fuck", "shit", "cunt", "thief", or "selfish-bloody-child-peddling-daddy".'

Rees's voice was soft and coaxing. 'Lucy . . .'

His wife shook her head to show him there was no point in appealing to her.

'You tried to make a deal over missing children . . . a missing baby. How could you, Rees?'

'I told you, I—'

'Don't say anything.' Lucy looked at her husband along the gunsight. 'We're all going inside and we're going to leave our weapons by the door. If you want Mercy and me to stick around you will tell these people anything you know that might help them find their children. Is that clear?'

For a moment Stevie thought Rees was going to argue, but he lowered his gun. 'Everything I do is for you and Mercy.'

'Not much point in chasing us away then, is there?'

Lucy emptied the rifle of cartridges. She walked past her husband to the shipping container and went inside, propping the gun inside the door. Rees's slumped shoulders reminded Stevie of the way Pistol hung his head after she had caught him in some act of disobedience. The trader followed his wife, disarming his pistol as he went.

Magnus looked at Stevie. 'You okay?'

'Fine.' She held the crying child out to him.

Magnus stroked a tear from Mercy's cheek with the tip of his finger, but did not take her.

'What would you have done if the gun had gone off?'

Stevie shrugged. 'I don't know. Killed myself, I suppose.'

'Suicide isn't your style. You're a survivor. A nuclear bomb could explode and you'd still be standing, bruised but unbroken.'

'Like a cockroach.' She tried to pass Magnus the baby again. He turned away and she realised that he was angry.

Magnus took the clip from his gun. 'You hold on to her. Maybe it'll do you good to be aware of someone else's heartbeat for a while.'

Stevie followed him into the container, still carrying Mercy. She thought about taking the knife from her boot and placing it inside the door with the rest of their arsenal, but the weight of it was a comfort and she kept it there.

Twenty-Three

Lucy lit a storm lantern and they followed her past the imprisoned ridgebacks, which greeted them with slavering enthusiasm, and through the complex of shipping containers, into a series of rooms loaded with sealed boxes. Rees unlocked and locked each connecting door. Every tumbler that clicked home tightened a screw in Magnus's chest. He breathed through his mouth and kept his eyes on Rees's keys. Mercy was asleep, her head resting on Stevie's shoulder. The presence of the couple's child should have reassured him, but the containers' metal walls were a weight on his lungs.

The storm lantern cast wedges of light, illuminating boxes stacked in the shadows: *Copper wire, AAA Batteries, AA Batteries, Smoke Detectors, Aluminium, Dried Milk, Freeze Dried Rations, Pasta, Baked Beans, Tonic Water, Bottled Water . . .*

The merchandise had been arranged with similar logic to now abandoned supermarket aisles. Magnus wondered if they would reach a room labelled *Fresh Meat* and find themselves suddenly thrust onto butcher's hooks. There had been stories of cannibalism after the Sweats. He had not thought he believed them, but they came back to him now. Men and women held captive for their flesh. He looked at Mercy, a white scrap in the dimness. Who was to say that she belonged to the couple? Perhaps her real parents had fallen fate to butchery; cut and jointed.

He tried to laugh at himself, but the containers' roofs were only a hand's stretch from his head. The air was stale. He recalled stories of stowaways vainly trying to cross borders, suffocating to death inside the backs of container lorries. He stared at Stevie's back, the tanned nape of her neck, but could not tell if she shared his unease.

Phone Chargers, Sim Cards, 3AMP Fuses, Routers, Candle Bulbs, CDs, Headphones . . .

Lucy's lantern wavered as she waited for Rees to open yet another door.

Stevie said, 'Quite a collection.'

Rees unfastened the padlock. 'Who's to know what might be useful in the future? We can throw everything away, leave it to rot or we can preserve it. At the very least it might tell future civilisations something about how we used to live.'

Lucy looked over her shoulder at Stevie and Magnus. 'One of the things I like about Rees is his optimism. He can imagine future generations.'

Rees was holding the door open, ready to lock it after them. 'How can you doubt it when we have a member of the next generation right here?' He touched his sleeping daughter's hand as Stevie carried her through.

The new cabin was different from the rest. Boxes were still stacked along its sides but its metal floors had been covered in rugs. A couch and a couple of easy chairs clustered around a wooden coffee table in the centre of the space.

Lucy set the lantern on the table. 'Take a seat.'

Stevie deposited the child onto the couch and herself into an easy chair. 'What is this? A panic room?'

'Got it in one.' Rees sat beside Mercy and lifted her onto his lap. The child stirred, but did not wake. 'I got the idea from a movie I watched once. High rollers used to have them. A place to hide out with your valuables if something bad goes down.' He pulled a throw from the back of the couch and laid it gently over Mercy. 'The ferry port is a good place to trade. People pass through. But that makes us vulnerable. I don't want anyone knowing how much gear I've got and I don't want them knowing that Lucy and Mercy exist. As far as any visitors are concerned, I'm just a sad old git who lives alone with his dogs, useful if you need provisions to see you on your way, but not worth ripping off.'

'You'd think he was Josef Fritzl the way he keeps us hidden.' Lucy sat on the couch beside her husband. She squeezed his hand. It was hard to believe that only a few minutes ago she had threatened him with a gun.

Magnus knuckled his forehead; shifting skin against the bone. A headache wavered beneath his skull. This must be how it felt to be locked in a submarine, plunged beneath an ocean's depths. He pictured their guns, abandoned by the door, inside the first container.

'You'd be trapped if anything happened.'

'Cool it, Rees.' Lucy delved into a box, took out four cans of Coca-Cola and gave them each one. 'You're making him nervous.'

'These are emergency rations.' Rees shoved his can back at her.

Lucy sidestepped him. 'I dare say this feels like an emergency to them. Their kids are missing, remember?' She popped the lid of her can, took a sip and grimaced. 'Old-style capitalism. If you thought that was bad wait till you get a taste of post-Sweats economics.' She saw Magnus hesitating, took the can from his hand and swapped it for hers. 'I'm not trying to poison you.'

Magnus lowered himself into the spare armchair. The Coke tasted horrible; warm and aluminium-tainted, but it was a flavour of the old life: hot, dusty summer pavements; the smell of diesel; bass-thumping-eardrum-busting car stereos.

Stevie clicked open her can. She put it to her ear, listened to the fizz of out-of-sell-by-date bubbles and then drank. 'Thanks.' She looked at Lucy. 'Sorry for frightening you.'

Lucy's face set. 'You were taking a big chance. I would have shot you if I could.'

'I know.' Stevie's voice was soft. 'I had no intention of shooting you.'

Magnus set his drink on the table. 'We don't have much time.' He looked at Rees. 'You mentioned a woman with an injured eye. Had you seen her before?'

The trader shook his head. 'Not that I recall and I would recall her. She was damaged goods, but she was a looker.' He stole a quick apologetic glance at his wife. 'The men with her were less memorable, but I make a point of remembering everyone who passes through. I hadn't seen them before.'

Magnus said, 'What makes you so sure they planned to traffic the kids?'

Rees leaned back on the couch. He brushed his sleeping daughter's fuzz of hair gently with his fingertips.

'They were being too nice to them. It was excessive. I've got cartons of clothes in one of the outhouses. I let the teenagers rummage in there while we sorted out provisions for their trip. They came back dressed like loons – silk scarfs, crazy colours, hats, feathers. They looked like they were on their way to Woodstock in sixty-nine.'

Lucy whispered, 'Kids playing dress-up.'

Rees ignored her. 'The woman was all over them, primping and pimping. She wanted to know if I had any make-up. I pointed her to a tea chest of the stuff. She took what she needed and showed the girls how to put it on. She even suggested the boys try some lipstick.'

Shuggie was vain, but Magnus could not imagine him in lipstick.

'Did they?'

'No, they pretended to be full of swagger, but they were shy.' Rees met Magnus's eyes. 'They seemed like nice kids.'

Mercy shifted on her father's lap. She started to gurn and he passed her to Lucy who pulled up her top and put the child to her breast. He said, 'That woman was basting them like a Christmas turkey.'

Magnus tamped down the urge to ask more about Shug. 'What can you tell us about Bjarne?'

Rees was playing with his daughter's feet, letting the child curl her toes around his finger and then pulling it away. The child giggled, but the Cornishman's face was serious.

'Bjarne's a blowhard. He boasts about how he's got Orkney tied up, but there isn't much island trade to speak of. You guys seem to have pretty much what you need – except for the occasional nostalgic luxury. The last thing I traded him was a few crates of out-of-date Stella Artois. I thought it tasted like piss at the best of times, but he seemed confident it would go down well.'

Magnus remembered the Easter celebrations, the pain in his head the following morning.

'It did. What did he give you in return?'

'A young ram. He said he'd had a hell of a job getting it over on the boat.'

Magnus said, 'Sounds like a deal in your favour.'

Rees shrugged. 'Stella's a finite resource. The Sweats passed sheep by, so they're hardly an endangered species.' He looked from Stevie to Magnus. 'Do you think he's involved with your missing kids?'

Magnus tipped the warm Coke to his lips. 'What makes you ask that?'

'You're looking for them and asking about him. Is Bjarne mixed up in this somehow?'

'You could say that.' Magnus set his can back on the table. 'He's dead. Someone took the top of his head off with a twelve bore.'

Lucy whispered, 'Shit.'

Rees took his rolling papers and tobacco from his pocket and started to put a cigarette together. If he was surprised by the news he did not show it. 'I only met Bjarne a few times. I thought he was a prick, but most people I meet are pricks. It doesn't mean they deserve to get murdered. The last time I saw him, he told me he had a big deal going down. He boasted it would make him king of the Orkneys. I said I probably had a crown somewhere in the stores that he could use.' Rees sealed the cigarette with his tongue. He gave Stevie a sideways look.

'I assumed he was full of shit – was he?'

Stevie said, 'We're having elections soon. He'd put himself forward.'

'I'd heard you were organised over there. Must be slim pickings, if Bjarne was in with a shout.'

Stevie gave a wry smile. 'He'd promised to sort out our fuel and electricity problems.'

Rees tried to put the cigarette behind his ear and discovered the one he had rolled earlier lodged there. He set both roll-ups on the table. 'That would do it. Given the choice most people will vote for the prick with the petrol over the prick without the petrol.' He took the cigarette out of his mouth and put it in his top pocket. 'Fuel is what people want most of all. It's hard to get and easy to sell. I made a decision early on not to touch it.'

Lucy took her husband's hand. 'Rees thinks it would make us too vulnerable.'

Rees kissed Lucy's fingers. 'The only way to deal in that stuff is to build a gang, arm them to the teeth and prepare for war.' The cigarette was back in his hand. 'Okay, I sell the odd gun, the odd bullet, even an occasional grenade, but fuel? I leave that game to the big boys.' He stuck the roll-up in his mouth. It had a slight bend in the middle, its unlit tip pointed upwards. 'My bet is it was a big fuel deal that killed him.'

'Maybe.' Magnus kept his voice non-committal. 'Who would we go to if we wanted to set up something like that?'

'There's only one outfit round here, the Petrol Brothers, ten miles inland at Eden Glen. You only exist round here if you're in their grace and favour.' The trader took the cigarette from his mouth and straightened the kink in its centre. He turned it around in his hand, as if he was trying to make up his mind about something. His eyes met Magnus's. 'I sent them there.'

It took a second to sink in. 'Our kids?'

Rees nodded. 'I sent the adults, but the kids went with them.'

Magnus leaned forward in his seat. The air in the cabin seemed thinner, the pressure in his ears denser. 'You sent our kids to an outfit called the Petrol Brothers?'

'The woman said they needed a van and fuel to drive it.' The belligerence was back in the Cornishman's voice. 'My responsibility is to my own family, not a bunch of teenage runaways. The two guys with her were beginning to nose about. I wanted them gone. Telling them where they could get a van and some petrol seemed like the surest way to get rid of them.'

Stevie said, 'How did they intend to pay for the van?'

Mercy had finished feeding. Rees lifted her from her mother's lap and kissed the top of her head. The child chortled and he kissed her again.

'That was none of my business.'

Twenty-Four

The horses Rees lent them would never win a race, but they were steady mounts, surefooted on the fractured road surface. Stevie had forgotten how trees obscured the landscape. From the right vantage points in the Orkneys, when the weather was with you, you could survey whole swathes of the islands. Even on a slow horse, the mainland's horizon rushed towards you. She found it hard to remember how the countryside had looked before, but was sure there were more trees now; hillsides that had been brown with bracken had given over to forest.

The map Rees had drawn before they left took them along what had once been the main artery between Scrabster and the south. On one side of them, cliffs sheered down to tumbled rocks and crashing waves. On the other, armies of trees trembled on hillsides so jammed with new growth it was easy to imagine the banks of woodland sliding towards them.

Stevie and Magnus followed Rees's map away from the road, where lorries had once negotiated sharp bends and gear-crunching inclines, onto a forest path. The wind was up, the trees caught in its sway; branches exalting in the strong gusts blowing in from the sea. Stevie's horse bent its ears back and whinnied, unnerved by the rush of air and roaring branches. She stroked its neck. The wind rose again. It carried fierce spatters of rain that fired through the canopies of leaves, ice cold and sharp against her skin. Stevie wrapped a scarf around her head, covering her mouth and nose, leaving a slit for her eyes. Pistol ran on ahead. She was worried about the dog. He was intrepid, but the distances they planned to travel were long and it would be a struggle for him to keep up.

Neither of them talked much on the journey. The weather was against them, the forest path narrow and there was little point speculating on what lay ahead. Stevie let her mind drift. She remembered her friend Joanie's manicured hands moving across her computer keyboard, fingers surprisingly sure against the keys, as they swiped through Tinder profiles. Joanie fluctuating between imaginative tortures intended for her ex-husband Derek and critiques of the self-catalogued men on display. Stevie had laughed until she had feared she would stain Joanie's lemon sofa. Joanie had died in the first wave of the Sweats, before anyone had realised how far things would go. Stevie did not know if Derek had survived, but doubted it. No one else from her past had lived.

Magnus stopped his horse. 'That could be it.' They had left the shelter of the forest and emerged onto a ridge at the top of a steep gorge. There was a gap in the clouds and sunlight glinted against a river below; a gush of deep water surging over a rocky bed. High beyond the far bank a turret rose above the treetops. Magnus pointed at it. 'A grand place for a fortress.'

Stevie shielded her eyes from the sudden sunlight.

'Rees and Lucy hide out in shipping containers, these guys live in a castle. They don't care who knows they're doing well.'

'They've got front.' Magnus turned his horse away from the ridge, back onto the path that would take them down the valley towards the river. 'Bjarne had front too. Look where it got him.'

Stevie disliked the bitter edge to his voice. She pressed her knees against her horse's sides and followed. The path led them back into the shade of the forest. They moved at walking pace, mindful of tangled roots and fallen branches.

'We don't know why Bjarne was killed.' She bent forward to avoid a low hanging branch. Her cheek touched her horse's neck and she smelt its clean, animal scent: warm and peppery. 'I didn't like him any more than you did, but we shouldn't jump to conclusions.'

Magnus looked back at her. 'I've been meaning to ask, was it you?'

The light in the forest was dim and faintly green, the smell of new growth and old rot heavy on the senses. Sunshine after rain had brought out the midges. Stevie flapped them away from her eyes.

'If you really thought I'd murdered Bjarne you would have accused me before now.'

'I didn't accuse you, I asked. It's not the same thing.' Magnus kept his back to her and Stevie had to strain to hear his words. 'You had a strong motive. There was a good chance Bjarne might take your place as president.'

'A slim chance.' Stevie was surprised to discover she was more irritated by the suggestion that Bjarne could have won the election, than the suspicion that she had murdered him. 'I would have won and even if I hadn't, the presidency isn't worth killing for.' She batted at some persistent midges. 'Why ask now?'

Magnus glanced over his shoulder at her. 'There was something about the way you held the gun to that child's head that made me think you had it in you.'

Stevie brushed her hair away from her face, looking at Magnus full on. 'I wouldn't have hurt her.'

'Wouldn't you?' The forest's dim light cast shadows over the Orcadian's features. For a moment his face looked like a tribal mask. 'Once you point a gun at someone's head you're only a trigger away from killing them.'

The conviction in her voice as she threatened Lucy still frightened Stevie. During the chaos of the Sweats she had killed to stay alive, but she had thought she had left her talent for violence behind.

'Save your sermons for your son, when you find him. He's the one who's on the run. I didn't kill Bjarne but if I had I wouldn't flee the consequences.'

'Shug had nothing to do with Bjarne's death. The boy doesn't have murder in him.' Magnus's voice was fierce. 'Even if he'd wanted to, he was too hurt from the beating Bjarne gave him. The bloody bastard battered the boy black and blue.'

He turned his back to her and they went on in silence. Neither of them mentioned Shug's quick recovery or that he had been well enough to leave the island with Willow and his friends, taking Evie with them.

There was a flash of movement in the bushes ahead. Stevie caught a quick glimpse of a nut-brown face fringed by greenery. She pulled her horse up, but the figure was gone, absorbed once again by the forest. She called to Magnus, but he was further up the trail and her words were drowned by the sound of the wind in the trees.

Twenty-Five

The Petrol Brothers' house was an ancient castle keep, high-walled and sharp-cornered, backed so closely by cliffs that it looked as if it had been hewn from the rock. The place was fronted by an ill-tended lawn, overgrown and pitted with bald patches. The only approach was across open ground or up the sheer cliff-side. There were no cars parked in the driveway, no chink of light in the arrow-slit windows. The heavy wooden door had FUCK U scored in tall, wobbly letters across its surface. It was shut and presumably bolted. The only sign of life came from a few hens, pecking their way across the grass.

Magnus and Stevie stood, hidden behind gorse bushes at the edge of the forest, and stared across the clearing at the fortification. They had tethered their horses some way back and come the rest of the way on foot. Their disagreement was a presence between them, unfinished business.

'We won't catch up with the kids if we stick to horseback and that hound of yours isn't going to last the pace,' Magnus said.

They had lost Pistol somewhere in the woods. Stevie knew the dog would track her, but Magnus was right, the speed of the journey was too fast, the distance too long, for him to keep up. She blamed Magnus for Pistol's presence. She would have turned back on the quayside at Stromness and put the dog ashore, had it not been for the Orcadian.

Magnus looked again at the map Rees had drawn. 'This is definitely it.' He sounded unsure.

Stevie crouched low and stared through a gap in the bushes.

'Looks like they're not universally loved. How do we get in?'

Magnus crouched beside her. 'Through the front door. These guys are traders. They need customers and we need what they're selling.'

'You're forgetting we have nothing to trade.'

'We've got a pair of borrowed horses, a couple of second-rate rifles and a heart-warming mission.' Magnus wished he felt as confident as he sounded. 'Maybe they'll have some kids you can threaten.'

'Drop it—' Stevie was interrupted by a creaking sound. A slim young woman slipped through a modest wooden door, set into the unwieldy, brass-studded castle entrance. Her hair was pinned in coils on either side of her head. She was dressed in a long evening gown made of a silvery, sparkling fabric that caught the light as she walked. A sequinned evening bag dangled from one hand and a red plastic bucket from the other. The effect was outer space and medieval, as if the Knights of the Round Table had imposed their tastes on a future race. The hens bustled towards the girl and she started to fan scatterings of corn across the lawn. Now and then she dipped to pick something out of the long grass which she wrapped in a cloth and placed gently in her evening bag.

Stevie whispered, 'All dressed up and nowhere to go. She's collecting eggs.'

Magnus gestured at the castle with his gun. 'She left the door open. Think we can get inside without her raising the alarm?'

Stevie shook her head. 'Not unless we silence her.' Magnus's face flushed and she said, 'For fuck's sake, Magnus, I meant put a hand over her mouth, not kill her.'

The girl's attention had been on the busy flurry of hens at her feet. Perhaps the wind carried a breath of Stevie's impatience to her because she looked up and stared in their direction, revealing a pale, round face, dark eyes and a rosebud mouth, too small for the rest of her features.

'Moon?' Stevie got to her feet and stepped from the bushes. Magnus grabbed the hem of her jacket but she pulled free, knocking him into the gorse. 'Moon?' Stevie ran across the grass towards the girl who reached into her red bucket, took out a gun and aimed it at her.

Magnus was on his feet too. He saw the gun, saw Stevie running towards it and hurtled after her. The girl was not distracted by the sight of a second pursuer. She had chosen her target and calmly settled her aim, sure as a seasoned hunter.

Stevie shouted, 'Moon, it's me.' And the girl pulled the trigger.

Pistol seemed to come from nowhere. The hens scattered and the dog leapt at the girl, knocking her to the ground, sending her shot wild. He sank his teeth into her arm and she screamed. Stevie had thrown herself onto the lawn when she saw Moon aim the gun, but she was on her feet in an instant, ordering the dog from her and pocketing the gun.

Pistol sank to his haunches, wagging his tail, desperate to be reassured he had done the right thing. '*Good dog.*' Stevie rubbed his ears. He licked her hand, the girl's blood still on his teeth. '*Good dog.*'

Magnus dragged the girl to her feet by her undamaged arm. 'Moon, what the fuck were you thinking?' The gorse had scratched his face and a bloody tear ran down his cheek. 'You could have killed her.'

'Pistol bit me.' The girl was crying. 'I was aiming into the bushes, not at Stevie.'

Magnus held Moon by the shoulders. The urge to shake her was almost overwhelming. 'I was in the fucking bushes.'

'I just wanted the old bitch to go away and leave me alone.' Moon tried to break free of his grip. 'I'm not going back.'

'*Good dog.*' Stevie had her face in Pistol's fur. She rubbed his sides with her hands.

A man was striding across the lawn towards them. His shotgun hung harmless and broken over his arm. 'In the old days we used to put down dogs that bit people,' he said. He was in his late twenties, dressed in a Barbour jacket, mustard corduroys and green wellington boots. 'Are you okay, Moonbeam?' His accent suggested the scent of leather armchairs and lingering cigar smoke. A couple of spaniels completed the country squire look. They ran barking towards Pistol and then dropped low, wiggling their rears, ready to play. The stranger shook his head at them. 'Typical bitches, suckers for a bad boy, bloody tarts.'

Magnus let go of Moon. 'The dog was only doing what he was trained to do.'

The girl dried her face on the extravagant gown and went to the stranger's side. She held her bloody arm out for his inspection. 'It bit me.'

Stevie said, 'You're lucky he didn't rip your throat out.'

The newcomer raised his eyebrows at Stevie. 'I'd be careful if I were you.' He gave Moon's wound a bleary inspection, and plucked at the soiled stuff of her gown. 'Good job Mother's in the family vault. She loved that Schiaparelli more than she loved me.' He took a hip flask from his pocket, knocked back a nip and passed it to Moon. 'Have some medicine. It'll take the sting out of things.'

The girl drank, spluttered and drank again. Raw egg dripped, yellow-viscous, from the sequinned bag still hanging from her good arm.

Magnus made a grab for the flask. 'For fuck's sake, she's only fourteen.'

Moon sidestepped him and took another swig. 'You don't know how old I am. No one does. Harry and Laura found me in Berwick and took me to that crappy island. Moon isn't even my real name.'

'It's a lovely name,' the young man murmured gallantly. He relieved the girl of the hip flask and offered it to Magnus who shook his head.

The girl's voice was aggrieved. 'My real name's Jennifer. There was a harvest moon the night they found me. They nicknamed me Moon and it stuck.'

Stevie muttered, 'I always thought it was because of your fat face.'

The hens were back, pecking at the scatterings of corn at their feet.

Magnus said, 'Surely to God you didn't run away because no one calls you Jennifer?'

'I didn't *run away*. I'm not a baby. I left.'

It started to rain, a soft shower that brought out the scent of grass and chicken shit.

Stevie pushed a damp strand of hair away from her face. 'And took Evie with you? She is a baby.'

For the first time Moon looked shamefaced. 'That was Willow's idea.'

The stranger had been watching them with interest. He took another nip from his flask. 'This is better than a play, but I for one am feeling the chill. Shall we continue indoors?'

Magnus glanced at the castle. A moment ago they had been keen to get inside, but its strong walls and heavy door would be good for keeping people in, as well as out.

'We can talk here.'

'Up to you.' The man took the ruined evening bag from Moon and flung it tumbling across the clearing. He put an arm around the girl. 'We're going inside to disinfect that bite.' He glanced to where Pistol was playing with the spaniels. 'I was serious. You should shoot that dog.'

Stevie took a step towards him. Her voice was dangerously calm. 'He was protecting me from your little Moonbeam. She took a shot at me.'

'Bad Moonbeam.' The man rubbed the girl's shoulder affectionately, his eyes still on Stevie. 'Doesn't matter whose fault it was. You should still kill it. Once a dog's bitten a human it loses track of its place in the pack. They begin to get a taste for it.' He kissed the back of Moon's neck. 'You know how it is with bad habits, they're hard to shake.'

He led Moon into the keep and after a moment Stevie and Magnus followed.

Twenty-Six

The man's name was Ramsey Fergusson. His father had been a lord, which he supposed made him one, '. . . not that any of that matters any more'. He laughed when Magnus asked if he was one of the Petrol Brothers and said he supposed he was, 'which proves that the blood of my robber baron ancestors runs through my veins'. He thought 'little Moonbeam' 'delightful' and was 'quite frankly, incandescent' that she had been hurt. He told them all of this in smooth, unhurried tones as he tended to Moon's bite. Pistol had caught the fleshy part of her arm. His teeth had drawn blood, but the girl's bones and tendons appeared undamaged. Lord Ramsey finished bandaging the wound, made the girl swallow an antibiotic and said again, 'You really must have that dog shot.'

Moon was sitting on Lord Ramsey's knee at the large, oak table in the castle's kitchen. Stevie and Magnus had both refused a seat and leant instead against granite worktops. A large picture window, double-glazed and incongruous, showed a view of sea and sky. The sun reappeared from behind the clouds and the waves shimmered; flashes of white foam against grey-green-aqua-water. The sun caught the sequins on Moon's dress, sending tiny glimmers of mirror-ball light around the room. The kitchen would have seemed a convivial place, were it not for the age of the girl, the shotguns propped in easy reach.

'You should find someone closer to your own age.' Stevie pulled herself up onto a worktop. Her muddy boots dangled a few inches from the tiled floor. 'For Christ's sake, Moon, get off his knee.'

Lord Ramsey's smile was amused. 'Beautiful Moonbeam is the new Lady Fergusson of Eden Glen. She's kindly promised to help me continue the ancient family line, if she doesn't die first of septicaemia.'

Moon's face clouded. The silver dress clung to her boyish, heroin-chic contours.

'What's septicaemia?'

Magnus said, 'I'll tell you when we're back on the road.'

Lord Ramsey laughed and Moon snapped, 'I told you. I'm staying here. Joe married us yesterday, with a Bible.'

Stevie swung her feet to and fro; specks of mud flicked onto the clean floor. 'Your parents will be delighted to know it's official.'

The girl nestled against Lord Ramsey's chest, her eyes trained on Stevie, defying her to interfere. 'My parents are dead.'

Stevie said, 'Harry and Laura are worried sick.'

Moon fiddled with the sequins on her dress. 'They both got over their own kids dying. They'll get over me too.'

Somewhere a door slammed and footsteps sounded in the interior of the keep.

Lord Ramsey looked towards the passageway. 'Here's the Reverend Joe.'

The newcomer ducked to avoid the kitchen doorway's low lintel. His eyes slid over Magnus and Stevie. He ignored them and touched Moon on the shoulder. 'Hello, Planet. Are you being a good little wifey?'

Joe was tall and skinny, dressed in black jeans and a leather motorcycle jacket. He had a knitted watch cap pulled low over his brow and the type of Scottish accent that had once attracted subtitles in documentaries about drug abuse and gang culture.

Moon's defiance was gone. 'I think so.'

She glanced at Lord Ramsey who pushed her gently from his knee. He looked self-conscious, as if caught in the act of doing something silly.

'She's behaving with perfect decorum, despite being savaged by a wild dog.'

Lord Ramsey held a hand out to the newcomer who pressed it briefly to his cheek before kissing its palm.

'Wild dogs are a menace, right enough. Did you shoot it?'

Lord Ramsey grinned. 'Not yet.'

Stevie braced the soles of her boots against the cupboards below her perch, leaving two muddy footprints on the doors. 'Pistol was protecting me. No one is going to shoot him.'

'Who are these?' Joe gestured towards Stevie and Magnus. He pulled his cap off and his hair fell to his shoulders.

Lord Ramsey's smile had a new edge to it, as if the alcohol that had previously mellowed him was beginning to sour his stomach. 'They've come to break up the happy home.'

An Alsatian trotted into the room, fur damp, tongue lolling. It surveyed the company, sniffing each of them in turn. Moon put an arm around its neck and buried her face in its thick ruff of fur. 'I'm not going with them.' The dog nosed her face and pulled free. It flopped onto the kitchen floor and closed its eyes.

Joe looked at Magnus. 'What's the kid to you?'

Stevie said, 'She was brought up in our community. She and some other teenagers disappeared suddenly with a baby that didn't belong to them. We've come to take them home.'

Joe glanced at Stevie, but directed his question to Magnus. 'Is the baby hers?'

Magnus shook his head and Joe said, 'Yours?'

'No, but one of the boys is my son.'

Stevie said, 'The baby's name is Evie. We promised her mother we would bring her home.'

Joe turned to Moon. 'You never told us the baby was stolen.'

Moon was standing awkwardly by Ramsey's side. 'It wasn't me, it was Willow.'

Lord Ramsey took a bottle of whisky from one of the kitchen cabinets. He unscrewed the cap, tossed it across the room in the ancient gesture that signalled the bottle was for emptying and poured himself a dram. 'Willow was the dark one, wasn't she? I liked Willow. She was fun.'

The lord pushed the bottle along the table. Joe ignored it. He drew out a chair and pulled off his boots. 'Willow was trouble.' Joe looked at Moon. 'Why did she take the baby?'

Moon shrugged. 'Sometimes Willow just does things. Maybe because she thinks it'll be funny or make her look cool. Lots of kids are like that. It's boring where we come from, nothing but grass and mud and sea. People do stupid things to stop from killing themselves.'

Stevie said, 'You're trying to tell us that you stole little Evie to stop yourself from committing suicide?'

Moon's voice sharpened. 'I told you. I didn't steal her. I didn't even know Willow had her until we were on the boat. She was upset about her stepdad beating up Shug. They were leaving with Belle and the rest of us decided to go along.' She glanced up at Ramsey. 'I'm glad I did. I wouldn't have met you if I hadn't, but I had nothing to do with them taking Evie.'

'There you have it, straight from the horse's mouth.' Ramsey slapped Moon's rump. He had lost his previous assurance and there was something forced about the gesture. 'Why don't you trot off and find another pretty dress to wear?'

Joe put a hand on his friend's arm. 'Let her speak.'

Magnus had known Moon since she was a bewildered

seven-year-old orphan. She had been Willow's on–off best friend, close as shadows one day, bitter enemies the next.

He gentled his voice. 'Moon, we need to find Evie and take her home to her mum. She's only a baby, even littler than you were when you lost your real mum and dad.'

Moon looked away. 'I don't know where they took her.'

'I believe you, but maybe you can help us work out why they took her. Had Willow talked about stealing Evie before? Even as a joke?'

The Alsatian trembled in his sleep. Moon sank onto the floor beside him and ran a hand lightly across the raised fur on his back.

'We used to joke about how annoying Evie was.'

Magnus noted the past tense. 'How was she annoying?'

'It wasn't her really. It was everyone else, all the grown-ups.' The girl seemed to have forgotten that she counted herself amongst the adults. Her voice was softer, her features less guarded. 'They acted like she was so special.'

'And you didn't think she was?'

Moon laid her face against the dog's neck. 'She was only a baby and babies are cute. I get that.'

Joe said, 'I had a cute wee brother, he was the baby of the family. He got all my ma's attention. I was jealous as hell of him.'

Moon cast him a grateful look. 'No one would ever look at Evie and wonder why she lived but their kids died. No one would ever ask what she did to survive.' She raised her head and looked at Magnus. 'Willow felt it worse than the rest of us. We're not meant to know, but people say she was starving when they found her. They say she was locked in a room with her mum and dad's dead bodies and that she—'

'Whoever says that is a liar,' Stevie said. 'I was there when they found her.'

Moon ignored her. 'Willow told me once that she doesn't remember what happened. She knows that she dreams about it, but the memories are always gone when she wakes up.'

Lord Ramsey looked at Stevie. 'You should have had her put down, same as you should put down that dog of yours. There's no coming back from some things.'

Moon's voice was all breath. 'She didn't do it. People just said she did behind her back.'

Magnus asked, 'Could that be why she took little Evie? To get revenge on the island? All those people who thought Evie was better than the rest of you because she'd been born after the Sweats?'

Moon stroked the Alsatian's nose. 'I told you. I don't know why Willow took her, but I know she wished she hadn't. She told Belle she wanted to turn the boat around and go back.'

'But Belle wouldn't?'

'She said it was too late. Stevie would have us shot.'

Stevie looked at Moon. 'And you believed her?'

'I don't know.'

Magnus slid from the worktop where he had been sitting. He crouched beside the girl and touched her good arm, his eyes level with hers. 'Did you really think Stevie would have you shot?'

A pale strip of fur ran the length of the Alsatian's spine. Moon stroked a finger along it. 'Not now that I see you both, but Belle made it seem like it could be true. We stole a baby. That's a big deal.'

'Did you hurt her?' Joe's voice was casual, as if it might be natural for the child to somehow be hurt.

Moon kept her head low. 'No.'

Joe leant forward in his seat. He put a finger beneath Moon's chin and raised her head.

'Look me in the eyes.'

Moon whispered, 'I didn't touch her.'

'Did anyone hurt it?'

The girl fought back tears. 'No. She cried a lot, but I think it was just because she missed her mum.'

Joe stared at the girl's face a moment longer and then let her go. He turned to Magnus. 'If you know Moon, you'll know she's not much of a liar. She didn't steal the baby and no one hurt it while she was around.' He nodded to the girl. 'Okay, go and raid the wardrobes.'

Magnus stood up. 'Just two more questions.'

Lord Ramsey gave an elaborate sigh. 'Aren't we meant to be desperados? I bet Pablo Escobar didn't have to put up with this kind of shit.'

Joe said, 'Ramsey's right. What are you? The new law?'

Magnus took a seat opposite the Petrol Brothers.

'I'm a crofter. Before the Sweats I was a stand-up comic. I was never much of a friend of the law, but my son Shug is one of the missing children.'

Joe asked, 'How old is he?'

'Fifteen.'

'Not a child by the standards of these times.'

'Maybe not, but he's my boy. I need to make sure he's okay. You'd do the same if he was yours.'

Joe looked away. Perhaps he was thinking of a young brother. He said, 'Keep it quick. There are things needing done around here.'

Magnus reached out to Moon and guided her to the seat opposite his. Her plaits had come undone and her hair hung in corrugated strands. He brushed them away from her face. The girl's eyes met his and he remembered how she had been greedy for sweet things as a child.

'How was Shug?'

Moon bit her bottom lip. 'He was quiet. Bjarne beat him up.'

'I know. He was in a bad way when I last saw him.'

Moon caught a strand of hair in her fingers and wound it into a knot. 'He had fallen out with Willow, so he was in a bad mood. You know how he gets.'

Magnus did. Shug would sink into long silences that might blow away suddenly like clouds in a northern sky or explode into violence. There was a fury in the boy that Magnus blamed on the Sweats. When he was little it had been easy to hold Shug down and talk to him until the urge to violence passed, but Magnus had long worried how his son would handle his temper as he got older.

'Had they fallen out over Evie?'

The girl put the strand of hair into her mouth and sucked it. 'Maybe. It was like they fell out before they got on the boat. I don't think it was because of Willow's dad. Everyone knows Willow hates Bjarne.'

Magnus saw Joe and Lord Ramsey's eyes meet at the mention of Bjarne's name. He filed the glance away, beside the observation that the girl spoke as if the trader was still alive.

'Did Shug say why he left?'

'Same as the rest of us, I suppose. He was sick of living on a shit-heap of an island. I guess Bjarne giving him a beating didn't help.'

Lord Ramsey pushed his chair back. 'It doesn't sound like she's got anything more to tell you.' He sank the last of his glass. 'Do you want to purchase any of our wares or just fuck off?'

'Don't worry, we're customers.' Magnus turned to Moon. 'Where were they going?'

Joe said, 'I can answer that. We traded them enough petrol to get to Glasgow.'

Stevie said, 'What did they give you in return?'

'None of your fucking business.' Lord Ramsey looked at Moon. 'For Christ's sake, stop sucking your hair like a sodding kitchen maid.'

Tears sprang into the girl's eyes. She got to her feet, ready to bolt from the room. Magnus caught her by her good arm. Moon had been a pudgy child, prone to runny noses and tantrums. She had been the tag-along kid. The one no one warmed to. Now she had surrendered to the first man to call her beautiful.

He said, 'I'm sorry if we let you down. The Sweats made a mess of everyone.'

Moon brushed away a tear. 'What do you think it would be like, if it had never happened?'

Magnus shook his head. 'I've trained myself not to ask that question.' In his dreams he lived a different life, dazzled by stage lights, the audience's laughter gusting him upwards, riding on a roar. 'We have to play the hand we're dealt. Shug and the rest of your friends are headed towards big trouble. You've got a choice. You can answer my questions and maybe help me find them, or you can turn your back on everyone.'

Moon looked at Lord Ramsey. He shrugged, 'Make it quick.'

Magnus said, 'What did Willow think of Candice?'

'Willow thinks Candice's a fool. She lets Bjarne treat her like shit.'

'And Bjarne?'

'She wishes he was dead.'

Magnus did not try to soften his words. 'She got her wish. They're both dead.' The girl's breath caught in her throat and he pressed his advantage home. 'Someone shot them.'

Moon's eyes were wide. 'Willow hated Bjarne, but she loved Candice. Maybe she would have killed her dad in self-defence, if he was attacking her or something, but she would never hurt her mum. Willow thought Candice was stupid, but she felt sorry for her. We all did.' The girl put her arms around Lord Ramsey's neck and laid her head against his chest. 'Poor Candi.'

The lord flinched and then folded his arms around Moon. His elbows and wrists stiff, like unoiled mechanisms. 'You should have told us you were investigating a murder.' He patted Moon awkwardly on the back and then pushed her from him.

Stevie said, 'Moon, I know you think you're in love, but so did Candice. She tied herself to Bjarne. Look where it got her.'

The girl rounded on her. 'What would you know about it? You never loved anyone except that bloody dog. Maybe Candi shot Bjarne and then shot herself. Did you think of that? Bjarne was a pig, but she loved him and they died together. I wouldn't want to live without Ramsey. He could beat me, tie me up and put me in a dungeon, but I'd still love him.'

Lord Ramsey touched her hair and twisted his mouth into a smile. 'A dungeon's a little old-school.'

Moon got up from the table and tucked her hair behind her ears. Her spine was straight and for the first time since they had come across her in the garden it was possible to imagine her as lady of the castle. 'I'm sorry Candice and Bjarne were killed, but I don't know anything about who might have killed them. I hope you find the others, but don't expect them to want to go back with you.' She looked at Stevie. 'Please say thank you to Harry and Laura for all that they've done for me. Perhaps I'll visit one day, when I have children of my own.' She gave Magnus a quick, unexpected kiss on the cheek and darted from the room, her high heels ringing against the tiled floor. The door slammed behind her, waking the Alsatian who got to his feet and whined to be let outside.

Ramsey wiped his mouth with the back of his hand and downed another dram. 'She's young, but I think she's up to the job.' His eyes were glazed, his lips whisky-glossed. 'My mother was young when father married her. He probably had even less of a choice than I did. He always said it was lean pickings in Debrett's the

170

year mother came out.' His hand searched for the bottle and found it.

Joe said, 'We came by the girl fair and square.'

Stevie pushed herself from the kitchen unit and let the dog out. 'You got her in return for petrol, didn't you? Moon was Belle's side of the deal. Before the Sweats you would have been jailed for trafficking.'

Lord Ramsey's voice was slurred. 'She seems closer to sixteen than fourteen to me. Survivors always underestimate the age of the kids they find. Why do they do that?' He filled his glass to the brim and took a sip, spilling some on his shirt. 'And as you may have noticed, times have changed. Girls, or should I say women, of her age, have the best chance of giving birth to healthy children and remaining unscathed.'

Joe leaned back in his chair and looked up at the ceiling as if the subject bored him.

'Ramsey's keen to carry on the family line.'

'Joe disapproves.' Lord Ramsey reached out and gave Joe's hand a squeeze. 'I daresay I would have disapproved too, before the Sweats. I never used to give a damn about that kind of thing. I had three brothers and a sister, all happy breeders, so I was free to gad my giddy life. Ironic I should be the only one left standing.'

Joe said, 'He thinks it's his duty.'

Lord Ramsey's eyes were closing, his eyeballs waxy slits. 'We've returned to the days of yore. I'm king of the castle. Little Moonbeam is my Guinevere and you're the unlucky Lancelot, destined to love unwisely.'

Joe put his foot on Ramsey's lap. 'We'll see about that.'

Stevie said, 'Moon thinks she's in love with you, but you're just using her to get a child.'

Ramsey squeezed Joe's toes. 'I'm fond of the little squirt. I daresay I'll be even fonder after she gives me an heir.'

'She could be carrying Ramsey's child already.' Joe slid his foot away. 'We're not going to let you take her. We can shoot it out, but you'd be fighting an army. She wants to stay with us. Even if you won, you'd have to carry her kicking and screaming.'

Magnus's eyes met Stevie's. 'We have to discuss this in private.'

Joe shrugged, 'Do what you need to, but I'm telling you straight, she stays here.'

Lord Ramsey set his hands on the table. 'I'm guessing you want the same as they did, a van and fuel.'

Stevie said, 'We'll get what we need elsewhere.'

Joe snorted. 'I doubt it. Why do you think they nicknamed us the Petrol Brothers? Go to any town, any village, any farmhouse or caravan park in a fifty-mile radius. Wherever there's fuel, you'll find one of our guys.'

Ramsey gave a boozy grin. 'Remember, I'm the God-anointed laird of this district. My ancestors have been in charge for aeons, so even though I may strike you as a silly ass, I know a thing or two about ruling. You'll find no one willing to trade you petrol in these parts without my say-so.'

Stevie whispered, 'There aren't enough people left alive for you to have tied up a fifty-mile radius.'

'How many people does it take? We've had seven years to get our stockpiles in order. Seven years to get the message across that we're in charge.' Lord Ramsey tilted the bottle, surveying the kitchen through a whisky filter – amber and gold. 'Joe, why don't you take them outside so they can have their private chat about how to steal my young bride from me and zoom off to the big city?' Lord Ramsey put his feet on the kitchen table and looked at Stevie. 'I'll make you a generous deal. I'll give you a van and enough petrol to get you to Glasgow if you shoot that dog.'

Stevie said, 'Get to fuck.'

Magnus stood by her side. 'That's not going to happen.'

Through the window in the distance the sea crashed and foamed. The tide was going out, a strip of white sand beginning to appear on the other side of the headland.

Joe got to his feet. 'Moon is happy here and unlike on your island there are no murders in our jurisdiction.'

'None that we haven't scheduled.' Lord Ramsey laughed. 'If you want to arrive in Glasgow in time to track down your runaways, you'd better give me that hound's head on a plate.'

Stevie leaned across the table, putting her face close to his. 'I'd shoot you first.'

Lord Ramsey took his feet off the table and leaned towards Stevie. Their breath touched.

'I'd be careful who you say that in front of. A lot of people want to catch the eye of power. They might decide to impress me with a present. Could be the dog's head, could be yours. It depends how ambitious they are.'

Twenty-Seven

The walls of the keep were thick and made of stone. Magnus and Stevie followed Joe through the darkness of the winding staircase that led up from the kitchen, into the shadows of the entrance hall. The space was cool as a cistern and silent, except for the sound of their footsteps against the flagstones.

Magnus said, 'Can you carry out your own negotiations, or are you just his boy?'

Joe's laugh was amused. 'I'm his boy, or did you not work that out?'

Stevie said, 'Aren't you jealous?'

'Of wee Planet? She's far out in the solar system. The poor wee thing's jealous of me, but she's young yet. It'll change when she has a wean. She'll not have time to be jealous then.'

Joe opened the small door cut into the castle's heavy wooden entrance. He led them out into the pink close-of-day and a hubbub of noise and laughter. Twenty or so men were camped on the scrub of lawn. A deer was being barbecued on a spit over an open fire, scenting the air with roast meat and wood smoke. Some men tended to horses, others erected brightly coloured nylon tents. Small clusters gossiped amongst themselves. But more than one soldier sat alone, staring into the darkening landscape. Eyes followed them as they stepped from the castle. Stevie found herself scanning the groups, looking for faces she might recognise from before. There was no one she knew, only hunger.

Joe said, 'This is just one of our divisions. Our army isn't big but it's loyal. We promise our people security and they give us their fealty in return. Most of them have turned to crofting. We come together every couple of weeks for training. It keeps us connected. They enjoy it.'

Magnus said, 'I'm guessing "fealty" is one of Lord Ramsey's words.'

'Wrong again, it's one of mine. I was studying political science at Durham University when the Sweats broke out. Machiavelli's *The Prince* was a set text. It's been a good friend to me. As the man says, "He who wishes to be obeyed must know how to command."'

The division was dressed in looted sports clothes and army surplus. They were a raggle-taggle bunch that recalled the civil wars that had spread across Europe before the outbreak of the Sweats.

Stevie said, 'No women in your army?'

Joe shook his head. 'Women are in short supply around here, hence Planet's good luck.' He grinned. 'I'd keep my hand on my ha'penny if I were you. There are men here who haven't seen a female in a while.'

The face Stevie had glimpsed in the woods could have belonged to a boy or a girl. She said, 'Who graffitied the castle door?'

'Every Prince has his irritants.' Joe nodded towards the army. 'Tonight's exercise will fix some of that. I've promised the men that if it goes right they'll be sleeping in warm beds tomorrow.'

Stevie was about to ask what he meant, but Pistol ran from the direction of the woods, a dead rabbit in his mouth. He dashed to her side and dropped it at her feet. She gave him permission to eat and he started to rip the flesh apart.

Joe grinned, 'The condemned prisoner made a hearty meal.'

Stevie rubbed the dog's head. 'I won't shoot him.'

Joe shrugged. 'I'll do it for you, if you like.'

Magnus said, 'That's not what she meant.'

'Then you're stuffed. Ramsey won't change his mind.'

Stevie straightened up and looked Joe in the face. 'I'll tell Moon about the two of you. I'll tell her you bought her for a tankful of petrol. That you only wanted a womb for hire.'

Joe shrugged. 'Go ahead. She knows most of it already. The rest she'd forgive or disbelieve.'

Stevie wondered if she could put a gun to Joe's head and force Lord Ramsey to give way. The tactic had worked on Rees, but there were too many armed men in the park for her to bring it off and Lord Ramsey's warning was still fresh. *Could be the dog's head, could be yours.*

Magnus looked across the green to where a blacksmith was examining the hooves of a chestnut mare. He narrowed his eyes, taking in the familiar cut of its ears, the slope of its back and jut of its tail. Stevie's mount stood close by. 'They're our horses.'

Joe shook his head. 'I think you'll find they're ours. You got them from Rees, didn't you? We've a good relay system across the district. Otherwise the horses get knackered. Rees only keeps his independence by paying fealty. It wasn't chance that I brought the boys back to make camp when I did. He caught us on the road and told me yous were on your way.' Joe grinned. 'Never take another man's map at face value. He sent you a long way round and set off full pelt on the direct route. He's a wise man. He didn't want to come home and find his secret wife and wean slaughtered.' Joe put a consoling hand on Stevie's arm. 'Ramsey meant it when he said kill the dog or walk. We can't have big beasts biting our wee princesses and getting off scot-free. It would make us look weak. As Machiavelli says, "It's safer to be feared than loved." ' He looked from Stevie to Magnus. 'Better you do it yourself, but if you can't I'll do you a favour and do it for you.'

Stevie said, 'I'll do it . . .'

'Good woman.' Joe slapped her back.

'. . . in return for one more thing.'

Joe grinned. 'I don't think you're in a position to make extra demands.' But he did not walk away.

Stevie said, 'You knew Bjarne, didn't you?'

'I was glad to hear he got what he deserved.'

Magnus said, 'Someone blew off the top of his head.'

Joe's grin grew wider. 'Enough to make you believe in karma.'

Magnus said, 'I'm guessing you weren't bosom buddies.'

Joe spat on the ground. 'Bjarne was good at spotting people's weaknesses. It helped make him into a successful trader. It also made him an utter cunt.' Joe hesitated, but perhaps possibilities for discussion were limited, because he continued. 'He knew we were short of women and promised us a dozen, if we could sort him out with enough fuel to help him win the election.'

Stevie's cheeks flushed. 'He promised you young girls from our islands?'

'He didn't promise they'd all be young, but he gave his word there'd be some virgins amongst them.' Joe snorted. 'Like I said, not a nice guy.'

Magnus nodded towards the brightly coloured tents on the green. 'Married men are easier to handle than single blokes. Were you tempted?'

Joe shook his head. 'Ramsey would have gone for it. You know what the upper classes are like. Their own upbringings are so fucked up they think you can breed people, the same way you breed cattle or horses. Ramsey likes the idea of filling his territory with a new generation of serfs.' A shadow crossed his face. 'I don't disagree. We need a new generation, but Bjarne was all about power. I wasn't about to give him any kind of foothold into our operations. I reminded Ramsey the islands have their own president and that it might put ideas into the men's heads if we went around helping to depose leaders. We'll fix the woman problem in our district our own way.'

The flush that lit Stevie's cheeks had spread across her neck and down her chest.

'You seem pretty sure you could depose the president of Orkney.'

Joe shrugged, 'It was Bjarne who was sure. He said people were desperate for technology to be restored and that there were girls of the right age on the islands who no one would really miss. He reckoned that if we could do a swap, he'd be president.'

Stevie said, 'Bjarne was a shit who judged people by his own standards.'

Joe said, 'How many of you are there on Orkney?'

Stevie looked him in the eyes. 'Enough.'

'Fifty settlers?' Joe raised his eyebrows. 'Maybe a hundred?' He shrugged his shoulders. 'A bunch of your kids go missing, but no one launches an armada. I only see two of you here and I'm guessing you're going to leave little Moon in our tender care. It looks to me like Bjarne wasn't as far off the mark as you'd like to think.' He nodded to where Pistol lay on the grass, sleeping off his meal. 'You're not even sure your kids are worth the life of one dog.'

Stevie snapped, 'That's not fair.'

'Isn't it?' Joe shrugged. 'It makes no odds to me but remember Ramsey will want proof. I think he specifically mentioned something about the head.' His mouth gave a quick twitch of disgust. But whether it was prompted by the vision of Pistol's severed head, Stevie's devotion or Lord Ramsey's lack of a princeship was unclear. 'You've got until morning.'

He turned his back on them and walked towards the encampment.

'The power behind the throne.' Magnus sank to his haunches and watched Joe pick his way through the camp, talking to people as he went. 'It makes sense now why Bjarne hated Willow hanging out with Shug. He wanted her isolated and intact.'

'Do you think she knew?' Stevie sat on the ground and called Pistol to her. The threat to the dog knotted her stomach.

'If she did, I wouldn't blame Willow for killing him.' The miles still to be travelled and the impossibility of crossing them in time weighed on Magnus. He looked to where the dog lay, sleek and untroubled, on the grass. 'Will you do it?'

'Do you think I should?'

Pistol felt Magnus looking at him and beat his tail lazily.

'If it's between finding Shug or saving your dog . . .' Magnus slipped into ashamed silence.

'And Moon? Do we abandon her as well, to save your boy?'

'I don't see we have much choice. She wants to stay.'

Stevie put a hand on Pistol's head. She felt the aliveness of him. 'He probably saved my life back there, Moon would have shot me.'

'Shooting him might help save more lives.'

'I'm too tired to think straight.' Stevie put her head in her hands. 'Christ knows what fucked up deal Bjarne was trying to put together, but he had a vision of life beyond Orkney that I don't possess.'

'For what it's worth, you had my vote. I know Brendan was going to vote for you too and plenty of others.'

'More fool them.'

A wood store stood flush against the castle wall, a simple structure, formed of three plank walls and a corrugated iron roof. Stevie went to it. She pulled off her jacket as she walked and folded it into a cushion.

Magnus followed her. 'We need to make a decision.'

Stevie put her jacket on the ground and curled up in the shadow of the shed. She took her gun from its holster and slipped it under the makeshift pillow, within easy reach.

'When I wake up, I'll know what to do.'

Pistol shifted and lay against her, lending her some of his warmth. She draped an arm across the dog's back and closed her eyes.

Magnus sat beside her. Stevie's breathing grew even. He wondered if she had gone to sleep so that he could absolve her of responsibility and shoot the dog. He glanced at Pistol. The dog opened one eye and returned his gaze. The croft had taught Magnus respect for animals, but he knew he would kill the beast in a heartbeat, if it would make a difference to Shug's survival.

Joe was talking to the men at the barbecue. Magnus's stomach groaned at the thought of roast meat, but he sat where he was, travelling the map south in his head. If there had been no mishaps the kids would be in Glasgow by now. His imagination stalled. He barely knew the city, could not envisage how it would look after the Sweats. Instead he saw Shug standing on a platform, his mouth forced open, teeth being examined by rough hands, the bidding beginning.

He got to his feet and whistled to the dog. Pistol raised his head, unsure about leaving Stevie, but Magnus knew how to command dogs and the second time he whistled, Pistol got to his feet. Magnus expected Stevie to wake, but she had perfected the soldier's trick of sleeping where she fell. She merely stirred and dropped into a deeper slumber.

'*Here, boy.*' He patted his leg. The dog came to heel and he led it through the camp towards the woods.

Twenty-Eight

Magnus felt eyes following him as he made his way across the camp with Pistol at his heels. The woods waited up ahead. Cool and dark. He had shot poor Mira, but the dog had been in pain and ready for death. Killing her had been a kindness of the sort he would seek for himself. Shooting Pistol would be a pointless waste.

Joe had quoted Machiavelli, 'better to be feared than loved'. Magnus wondered if Shug might still be safe if he had been a stricter father. But Bjarne had been a hard man, a disciplinarian, and look where it had got him – killed with a shotgun, a murdered wife and a foster-daughter on the run.

Pistol trotted off to greet another dog. Magnus called him to heel. *Better to be feared than loved.* Pistol butted his leg and he stroked the dog's ears. Pistol obeyed out of affection, not fear. Would Lord Ramsey really furnish them with a vehicle and a full tank in exchange for the dog's head? Magnus distrusted the promise, but it was his only hope.

Joe was still standing by the barbecue. He saw Magnus and held out a hunk of venison, speared on his dirk. Magnus was hungry, but his stomach gave a queasy flip at the sight of the meat. He shook his head and kept moving.

Joe's teeth tore at the chunk of meat. His lips were glossed with grease, his mouth full.

'I hope your knife's sharp. That dog's got a thick neck.'

A fat man in a red tracksuit top and jeans called, 'How much for half an hour with your woman?'

The fat man's companion punched him in the arm. 'Ten minutes would do me.'

Another man laughed. 'Three minutes.'

The reverse auction continued. Magnus glanced towards the woodshed. Stevie was hidden in its shadows. The men's tone was jokey, but there was an edge to it that made him want to walk back to where she slept. What he had to do would not take long. He bunched his fists and walked on.

The woods were full of shadows, a good place for a killing. Pistol snuffled through the undergrowth, stopping occasionally to mark his territory. Magnus's knife was sheathed on his belt. He had sharpened it on the whetstone in his cottage a week before. It was a hunter's knife, designed to cut through flesh and gristle. *Better to be feared than loved.* His own fear was born of love. He feared what might happen to Shug, dreaded the consequences of not reaching the boy in time. Magnus called to the dog and it came to him. '*Good boy.*' He patted its head, then crouched down and put his face against the dog's muzzle.

Magnus's childhood dog had been a cairn called Robbie. He had often buried his face in Robbie's fur when he was young and thought the world was against him. The cairn had been put down not long after he left for London. Magnus had elected to stay in the city and let his mother take it to the vet. Guilt at his neglect could still touch him, despite all the other guilty deaths wrought by the Sweats and its consequences.

He held Pistol's collar, wondering the best way to go about things. Pistol wriggled and growled. His strong front legs almost flung Magnus to the ground, but he held on tight. *Shhhhhhh*, he could not lose it now. Pistol barked and tried to bolt. Magnus reached for his gun and felt the cutting edge of a cold blade against the back of his neck.

He almost laughed out loud. Was this how it was going to end? With his throat cut in some dingy outcrop of wood; the boy he had nurtured and raised abandoned to the cities? He whispered, 'Stevie?'

A voice he did not recognise said, 'Keep that dog under control or I'll stick you.'

Something clinked in the trees above. Magnus looked up and saw rows of small mirrors, dangling from branches by invisible threads. Naked, pink plastic dolls hung by their necks, amongst the tinkling glass, and amongst them half-a-dozen severed male heads, their features twisted and grotesque. Magnus let out a small cry, but even as it escaped him he realised that the heads were false, fashioned from clay or papier-mâché. The mirrors reflected the last, pink rays of the sinking sun, forcing his eyes shut.

He lowered his gaze and relaxed his grip on Pistol's collar. '*Good boy.*' He patted the dog, reassuring it, wondering if the better plan might not be to allow the hound to let rip and damn the consequences.

'Get to your feet and turn around.'

Magnus did as he was told. The girl was about Shug's age. Her cheeks had been darkened with mud. Green leaves and twigs were tucked into her hair and clothing in an attempt at camouflage. She held a Bowie knife in her hand, big enough to cut a man's head from his shoulders. Pistol strained at his collar. Magnus swallowed. His throat was dry, his voice cracked. 'I'm going to have to let the dog go soon. He's too strong to hold for much longer.'

The leaves in the girl's hair shivered. 'If he bites me you're dead.'

'That's understood. If you put the knife down he'll feel less threatened.'

'He might but I won't.' The Bowie knife trembled in the girl's grip.

Magnus said, 'I'll keep my hands where you can see them.'

Pistol strained and whined. The wind played through the tree-tops sending the glass mirrors jingling. A distant sound of laughter echoed from the encampment.

The girl slowly lowered the knife. Her voice shook. 'Good dog.'

Magnus patted Pistol's head and let him go. The dog gave three short barks. Delight mingled with admonition. He bounded through the undergrowth, back towards the encampment and Stevie.

Magnus raised his hands. 'Joe knows I'm here.'

The knife was back in the air, the blade pointing at him.

The girl gave a nervous grin. 'I hope he doesn't fucking know I'm here. We're going to slaughter your lot.'

Magnus was about to ask who 'we' were but the trees and undergrowth around him were moving. Faces appeared from the forest. Someone said, 'You're meant to knife him, not have a fucking banter.'

The girl's eyes met Magnus's. Panic beaconed from them. 'He seems all right.'

'Most of them probably are, on their own. But put them together with a bunch of their mates and they're death to us.' The speaker was a short girl with cropped hair and a sweet face. 'Go on, stick him. The first one's the worst. You'll be fine once you've done him.'

Magnus felt his waters shift. 'I'm not with that army out there. I'm trying to get to Glasgow. I was told I could get petrol and a car at the castle. That's the only reason I'm here.'

'See, he's all right.' There was a plea in the first girl's voice. 'He's just passing through.'

The short girl said, 'They say anything to get away. He'll start crying if you don't do it soon.'

The group were gathering around Magnus. They were all young, all camouflaged with mud and greenery. Their hair was cropped, their expressions fierce, and it was a moment before Magnus realised that they were all female. The realisation turned his fear up a notch.

'He's with them all right and even if he's not we can't let him go now. He'll warn them.' The short girl took her own knife from her belt. 'Let's cut his head off and stick it in the tree with the rest, that'll be a proper warning.'

Magnus tried to load his voice with conviction, but all it sounded was frightened.

'I promise you, I won't tell anyone you're here.'

'He promises,' the girl with the Bowie knife echoed.

'I'm just a traveller heading to Glasgow.' Magnus's hands were in the air. He tried to step backwards, but the small group of teenagers had surrounded him and there were knives at his back too. 'This is none of my business.'

'Leave him alone.' Someone was pushing their way forward, through the cluster of young guerrillas. 'I know him. He's from my island.' The newcomer shoved the hand wielding the knife away. 'It's okay. Magnus is one of the good guys.'

The new girl was camouflaged like the rest of the children, her face muddied. It took Magnus a second to detect her features. 'Sky?'

Sky grinned, her teeth gleamed white in her dirty face. 'Hello, Magnus, what are you doing here?'

Magnus's fear shifted to anger. 'Searching for you and your bloody brethren.'

Sky's face clouded. 'My what?'

'Your fucking pals.' Magnus scanned the grimy faces surrounding him, looking for his son. 'Shug, Willow, Adil and little Evie? Are they with you?'

The twigs and leaves in the teenagers' hair trembled and more knives were drawn from belts.

'No need to get agitated.' It was not clear if Sky was addressing her new comrades or Magnus.

'Everyone on the islands is worried about you.' Magnus moderated his voice. The young guerrillas followed the conversation with their eyes. 'Are the others here too? Are Shug and little Evie okay?'

Sky shook her head. 'I'm the only one of the Orkney crew here. I went along with them for the adventure, but it started to get a bit weird, so I legged it. I told Shug he should come too, but he won't do anything without Willow and she buys all the shit they're dishing out.'

The short girl said, 'Cut the crap and get his gun off him.'

Sky turned on her. 'Shut up, Olivia. I told you, Magnus is one of the good guys.'

Olivia's sweet face turned vicious. 'You've only just showed up. Why should we listen to your say-so?'

''Cos I'm part of the rebellion, same as you are. Kill every stranger you meet and you might as well be that bloody laird we're meant to be fighting.'

Confusion flickered across Olivia's sweet-cruel face.

Magnus said, 'You're going to attack Lord Ramsey's men?'

Olivia said, 'We're going to wait until dark. Then we'll sneak up on them and cut a few throats.'

The girl's teeth were small and strong. Magnus could imagine them filed into points. He shook his head. 'You'll be committing suicide. There are more of them than there are of you. They're better trained and better equipped. People don't die silently. Even if you get past their lookouts someone will hear you and raise the alarm.'

Olivia took a step towards him. 'You're just saying that 'cos you're one of them . . .'

A tall, skinny girl interrupted, 'Shut up, Livy, I want to hear what he has to say.' There were murmurs of agreement.

He squatted on the ground. Sky and a couple of the group crouched beside him, but the rest remained standing. His eyes flickered over their hunting knives. Magnus tried not to show that he was afraid. He wondered if the teenagers had resolved to stick to the cutting blade, or simply been unable to lay their hands on guns. His own weapon was still on his hip, but the thought of shooting any of them sickened him. Anyway, the kids were wary. They would fillet him before he had time to kill more than a couple.

Magnus said, 'You're passionate. Maybe you've got right on your side, but that won't be enough to save you.' He nodded to the treetops above them where the papier-mâché heads swung with the breeze. 'I'm guessing you made these things and stuck them up there to frighten people away?'

Olivia said, 'Just until we got the chance to cut off some real heads.'

'You're not the only ones who like to frighten folk. Lord Ramsey will skewer your heads on spikes from here to Aberdeen, as a warning to anyone else who doesn't like his way of doing things.'

The image seemed to catch the girls' imagination. They looked at each other.

Olivia said, 'Henny could have killed you if she wasn't such a baby. I've killed before.' She dragged a finger across her neck. 'Slit their throats from ear to ear.'

Magnus looked at the small hands holding the knife and wondered if it could be true. He said, 'It takes a big person to show mercy. Henny caught me fair and square because she sneaked up on me. If she'd rushed me full force, I would have taken her.' He cast an apologetic look at Henny. 'You'll be a fine fighter one day, but I'm older and more experienced.' Magnus focused on Olivia. 'Your advantage lies in speed and surprise. If you want to hurt Lord Ramsey, be sneaky. Steal his vehicles, make off with his horses, pinch his whisky supply, raid his petrol depot. Do the deed and make a quick getaway. But remember, most of the guys over there are crofters, just trying to get by. If you start killing them you'll lose any goodwill you have in the district and the army will come after you like the hounds of hell.'

Olivia sank the point of her knife into the earth, overwhelmed by an urge to stab.

'You think we don't do all that already? We're like flies buzzing round a horse's arse. Every so often the horse flicks its tail and sends us flying.'

'Or shits on us,' a high voice peeped.

Some of the girls giggled.

'It's not funny.' Olivia's voice was fierce. 'I don't care if you all run scared. I'll sneak into the castle and kill him myself.'

Magnus said, 'I'm not a big fan of Lord Ramsey, but he seems to be doing an okay job of organising the district. Plenty of people are on his side. Why are you so against him?'

The girls looked at each other. There was something shame-faced in their expressions. The tall girl was the first to speak. 'I was only little when the Sweats came, but the older folk say that when everyone started to die, Lord Ramsey came home to the castle from the big city. He organised teams to clear the homes of the dead and halls to house the sick. They say that without Lord Ramsey there would have been chaos. He found people to look after children like us, whose parents had died. He led groups of survivors to guard the supermarkets and petrol stations and made sure no one took more than their fair share of supplies. The older folk still talk about the good he did. But then the Sweats ended and he was still in charge.'

'And that's what you object to?'

Olivia said, 'He keeps everything to himself. There's plenty of petrol, but only his guys are allowed to use it. There are houses and cars and clothes and shoes and anything you can think of, but they call it looting if you help yourself. My friend Danny took a car. They followed him until its tank ran dry and then they brought him back to Eden Glen and shot him up against the wall as a warning to everyone else.'

It was the kind of stupid prank Shug or one of his mates might have got up to.

Magnus said, 'Did no one try to stop them?'

'Danny's foster mother screamed and shouted, but they locked her up and did it anyway.' The girl looked at the ground. 'Some people were too scared to speak, but others thought they were right to shoot him. Danny had done things before. They said he needed to be made an example of.'

The tall girl said, 'That's not the only reason.' She looked embarrassed. 'He wants us all to get married and have babies.'

Someone giggled and one of the girls said, 'You didn't have to tell him that.'

Olivia's face was red in a way it had not been when she had talked of killing.

'It's the truth. He thinks girls exist to make little soldiers for his army.'

Henny whispered, 'And little wives for the little soldiers.'

The group chanted softly, 'To make little soldiers and little wives for little soldiers who need little wives . . .'

The chorus had a well-rehearsed rhythm.

'. . . to make little soldiers . . .'

The chant gave Magnus a shrinking feeling, his own image caught in the multiple reflections of his ancestors.

'. . . who need little wives, to make little soldiers . . .'

Magnus interrupted. 'Did none of your foster parents object?'

Olivia shrugged, 'Some did. Others thought it was a good idea. They liked us when we were little, but we're not so cute any more. My foster mother said that if I had a baby she would look after it. She went on and on about it – said I could have the extra rations all to myself.'

The tall girl was sitting cross-legged on the far side of the group. She picked up a leaf and tore along its central vein. 'He made a chart of all the boys and girls in the district and posted it on church doors. A few kids that were keen on each other signed up, but most of us ignored it. Lord Ramsey said we were too bashful and that he'd do the matchmaking himself. He started to set dates for the weddings. That's when we took to the woods.'

Magnus looked at Sky. She had been a scrappy girl, a good-natured tomboy, with a surfeit of energy that propelled her into fisticuffs and tumbles.

Magnus said, 'This isn't a playground rumble. This is the real deal. Lose and you're properly dead, lights out.'

Sky grinned, 'I always wanted to be a soldier. Now I've got a cause to fight for.'

The rest of the girls had joined them on the ground. Magnus looked around the circle of dirty faces and saw determination. They were lean and hard-bodied. As eager for adventure and as inexperienced in battle as any cannon fodder.

'Why don't you leave?'

A blonde, pixie-faced girl who hadn't spoken before piped up, 'This is where we live. And some of us have little sisters. If we go he'll just wait till they're older and do the same to them. We need to break Lord Ramsey, kill him or take away his power and show everyone else that they can't fuck with us either.'

Magnus lifted a fallen twig from the ground and drew a cross in the mud.

'If this is the castle, show me where Lord Ramsey's petrol store is.'

Olivia took the twig from him and started to draw a network of roads and buildings.

'My foster dad said it used to be an abattoir. He's got other places where he keeps fuel, but that's the main one.'

'Why would he choose there?'

'Lord Ramsey's dad wanted to make a place where lots of beasts could be killed and all of their parts used up, even bits people wouldn't normally eat. My foster dad said there were big protests, people coming from all over to try and stop him. Lord Ramsey's old man wouldn't give in. He fortified the building and stuck high fences around it.'

'Is there any easy way in?'

Olivia shrugged. 'We want to stick it to him where it hurts, but none of us has a death wish. We keep away from that place.'

Foliage crashed and Pistol bounded towards the group. The young guerrillas reacted like one organism, each reaching for their knives.

Magnus raised a hand in the air. 'Don't worry, he's friendly.'

Stevie followed in Pistol's wake. She looked tired, despite her nap, and was wearing different clothes from when he had left her: a man's shirt and trousers a trifle too large for her. She ruffled Pistol's head. 'Good dog, you found him.' Stevie looked at the camouflaged teenagers and then at Magnus. 'And looks like you found Birnam Wood.'

Magnus nodded, 'The kids are showing me where Lord Ramsey keeps his fuel.'

Olivia stared at Stevie, her eyes wide. 'Have you come to destroy him?'

Stevie took something from her pocket. 'Maybe I have.'

Twenty-Nine

Stevie had woken with a stab of panic, the scent of pine sharp in her nostrils. Pistol was gone. Three men stood inside the woodshed, staring down at her. She propped herself up on one arm, relieved to feel her gun still beneath the makeshift pillow.

'Hello.' She gripped the gun beneath her folds of her jacket and forced a smile onto her face.

The soldiers looked surprised, as if they had not expected her to talk. They mumbled a greeting. One of them crouched on the grass beside her.

'Your man left you alone, has he?'

Stevie's smile hurt her face. 'Looks like it.'

'I wouldn't leave you alone. Not if you were mine.' The soldier was in his forties, lean-faced with the tobacco complexion and deep lines of a heavy smoker. He touched her hair with his fingertips. 'Don't be frightened. We're not going to hurt you.'

Stevie caught sight of the knife in his free hand and tried not to wince. One of the other men, a sad-looking fellow with caved-in cheeks, shuffled his feet and Stevie saw that he was nervous. She sat up, hugging her jacket in her lap like a comforter, the gun bundled inside. The third soldier had a powerful torso and short legs. He reminded Stevie of a bull, ready to charge. She said, 'I'm a guest of Lord Ramsey's.'

The smoker raised his eyebrows. 'Lord Ramsey's guests don't sleep in the wood store.'

Pistol bounded from the forest towards them, tail wagging. He saw the soldiers and growled. The nervous man took out a gun and pointed it at the dog.

Stevie adopted her command voice. '*Pistol, stop!*'

The dog halted, but it was against his will and the growl was still in his throat.

Stevie got to her feet. 'I should get back to the castle before they miss me.'

The smoker put a hand on her elbow, as if he wanted to take her right there on the piles of logs. She shrugged him free, her eyes on the encampment, scanning the field of men and tents for Magnus or even Joe.

The bull said, 'They won't miss you for a while yet.'

The dog growled again. The bull raised his gun.

Stevie pointed away from the castle, towards the old main road. '*Pistol, go!*' The dog took three, slow steps and stopped. He looked over his shoulder at her, eyes doleful. She repeated the command, putting all her authority into her voice. '*Go!*' The dog trotted reluctantly off. She knew that he would not go far.

The smoker said, 'A well-trained dog.' He touched one of her breasts tentatively, plucking at her nipple, and smiled when it hardened. 'Don't worry. We won't tell your old man.'

She said, 'My husband's a killer.'

The smoker nodded. 'Aren't we all?' He put his knife against her neck and tugged the jacket from her arm. 'Bob, do us a favour and grab her gun, will you please?'

The bull took the gun from her. Stevie saw other soldiers watching them from the encampment. It would not be long before they built up the courage to join them.

The smoker said, 'Bob will give it back to you when we're through.'

Stevie knew then that they would kill her to ensure no reprisals. 'Let's go somewhere more private,' she said and grinned.

The smoker lowered his knife and put an arm around her, as if they were lovers taking a stroll. She encouraged him to go in the direction that Pistol had taken. His two companions followed a respectful distance behind.

'You should be more careful.' His voice was concerned, as if he was not about to rape and murder her. 'You're lucky it's us doing this to you and not some of those other guys. Some of them are right cruel bastards.'

A set of low wooden stables stood a small distance away from the main building. The man steered her towards them.

Stevie said, 'I'll go with you, but only one at a time. I don't want an audience.'

'Suits me.' The man looked back at his companions. 'I'll call you when I've finished.' His grin was nervous.

Stevie said, 'Are you sure you want to do this?'

He leaned in and kissed her neck. He smelt of sweat and desperation.

'We only get one life and it's too short to never have a little loving.'

She softened her voice. 'Did you have a family, before the Sweats? A wife? Kids?'

The smoker's knife pierced her shirt. It touched the soft skin above the waistband of her jeans, its point sharp and warning.

'I know what you're trying to do. Don't bother, unless you want to upset me.' He kept his knife pressed against her side. 'We're here for a good time.' It was dark inside the stables. The stalls had been ripped out, in their place stood a row of vintage cars, shrouded in plastic. The man said, 'Lord Ramsey would blow his stack if he knew we were in here. These belonged to his dad. They were his pride and joy.'

He kissed her again, his tongue alive and searching. His hands were on her now, tugging at the buttons of her shirt. Stevie whispered, 'Why don't we get into one of these cars and drive away?'

'He'd tear out our innards and make us eat them.' The man's lips were on her neck, his hands on her breasts. 'Anyway, he's had them all disabled.'

The smoker pressed her onto the bonnet of a Rolls-Royce. The plastic shroud crackled beneath Stevie. Her shirt was undone, her bra ripped. The man sucked at her breasts, his teeth sharp and biting, his breath stale. The weight of him was crushing. Stevie's heart hammered in her chest, panic rising. He was too heavy for her to push away. The smoker's fingers fiddled awkwardly with the fastenings of her jeans. Stevie wriggled a hand down towards his crotch. She unzipped his fly and released him.

The smoker's breath was a ragged wheeze. 'It's been a long time.' The knife was still in his right hand. The fingers of his left still struggling with her jeans.

'I'll do it.' There were tears in Stevie's eyes. She reached down, unfastened her Levi's and forced a laugh. 'Let me get them off.'

She wriggled her trousers halfway down her hips and bent forward, as if to unfasten her boots. The smoker pulled her to him. Stevie smelt the piss-sweat scent of him and tried not to gag. She reached for the knife in her right boot, but he was pushing her further up the bonnet of the car, trying to force her legs apart. The urge to shove him away almost overwhelmed her, but she mimicked his short, fast breaths and whispered, 'We won't get anywhere with these jeans on.'

Stevie could hear a low murmur of conversation from the two men waiting outside and guessed that it would not be long before they grew impatient for their turns. The smoker swore and tugged at her left boot, but it was fastened with a combination of buckles and laces and would not come free. He lifted his knife ready to cut the laces and slice her clothes from her. Stevie took her chance and scrambled away from him, further up the Roller's long bonnet. The man lunged at her.

'Come here you black bitch.'

The plastic shrouding the car was slippery, the man's skin bathed in sweat. He lost purchase and slithered backwards, down the bonnet. She pulled up her jeans and tugged her knife from her boot. She kicked the tobacco-stained face with the heel of her boot and threw herself onto the man, falling with him to the floor. The plastic car cover came with them, tangling them in its folds. The man's knife clattered against the concrete. Stevie's weapon was clutched tight in her hand. She sat on his chest, pinning his arms to his sides with her thighs and jammed the blade against his Adam's apple. The plastic crackled beneath them. Their breaths mixed, shallow and rapid.

'Everything okay in there, Mike?' one of the waiting men called.

Stevie hissed, 'Tell them you're fine or I'll slit your throat.'

The smoker shouted, 'She's got me by the fucking balls.'

The men outside laughed and a voice she recognised as the bull's said, 'Leave some for us.'

'I mean it, she's killing me.'

The men's laughter grew louder. It had a raucous edge.

The smoker hissed, 'Get off me, you bitch.' He bucked beneath her and reached for something in his jacket. Stevie's thigh muscles sang. She felt her grip on his arms loosening. In a second he would pitch her free and call on the other men.

'Fucking bitch.'

Stevie raised the knife and stabbed it into his carotid artery. Blood geysered from the wound and he made a drowning sound, wet and surprised. Stevie grabbed the edge of the plastic sheeting and held it over his face, covering his mouth and nose. Blood bubbled beneath, red and frothing. The door opened and light filtered into the converted stables. Stevie slipped a hand into the rapist's jacket. She snatched the gun he had been reaching for from his pocket, scooted beneath an old Aston Martin and hid behind the skirt of its plastic cover.

'Mike?' It took the bull and his companion a moment to see the smoker's body. Stevie watched from under the car as the men knelt beside him. The bull pulled the plastic from his friend's face. The smoker made a liquid sound, his feet drummed against the floor.

The nervous man said, 'I'm out of here.'

The bull caught him by the arm. 'She's just a lass,' he whispered. 'Joe will fuck us up if he finds out we took a woman out of turn. This way we can blame poor Mike, may he rest in peace.' Stevie saw him take a gun from his pocket. He raised his voice and addressed the silent stables, 'Sorry Mike frightened you.' The bull's tone was ludicrously gentle. 'Come out and we'll make sure you get back to the castle safely, no more monkey business. I promise you.'

Stevie checked the clip in the smoker's gun and pulled the safety catch off. She could hear the bull walking between the cars, lifting their shrouds to look inside and beneath them. He would find her soon.

There was a shift of landscape beyond the Aston Martin's plastic cover, a distortion of colours. Stevie recognised the anxious face staring at her. The nervous man said, 'She's here . . .'

Stevie shot him in the centre of his worried expression. Blood spattered the car cover, obscuring the view of what she had done. She rolled free of the Aston Martin, and lay flat on her stomach next to an electric-blue Lamborghini. The bull was running for the door. She took aim, fired and he fell against it, his hand scrabbling for the handle as he sank to the ground.

Stevie leant against the boot of the Lamborghini, trying to catch her breath. She vomited and then took off her bloody shirt and wiped her face. Blood was still pumping from the smoker's neck. She wondered if he was alive, appalled at her urge to kick him in the guts. She took the men's guns, bundled them in her shirt and zipped up her jacket. The path outside was empty, except for Pistol, sitting by the bushes. She called him to heel and walked away from the stables, down the driveway.

A gatehouse stood at the end of the rutted drive, a Victorian Gothic addition to the old castle, decorated with miniature turrets. An ornately carved archway branched from it, embracing the drive. Beyond that lay the road. Stevie wanted to be on it.

She stood under the arch, the knapsack she had fashioned from her shirt a weight in her left hand. To turn right was to turn towards home. To turn left was to head southwards, towards danger, with no guarantee of finding the kids. Stevie closed her eyes. Killing had made her numb. Pistol trotted through the arch onto the road beyond, sniffing at some unmarked trail. Birds piped in the slow dusk, a prelude to summer. Stevie's shadow stretched long and thin towards the tarmac. She called the dog to her, turned her back on the road and walked to the rear of the gatehouse.

The house's windows were boarded up, but there was a shed at the bottom of its small kitchen garden, unlocked and stacked with gardening tools. Stevie selected a spade, prised the board from the kitchen window and climbed in. She checked her Timex. If Magnus was still at liberty he would come looking for her. She would give him three hours and then head south.

The house was cast in dust and shadows. It smelt damply of earth, as if the woods were pulling it down into their roots. Stevie unlocked the back door with a key someone had left neatly in the lock and let Pistol inside. The dog wagged its tail, greeting her as if they had been parted for weeks.

Stevie knelt and drew the dog to her, feeling the warmth of his body – alive. He tolerated her for a moment and then pulled away, keen to explore the new scents of the house. Stevie followed him into a musty hallway where a barometer pointed to rain. The living room was dark behind its boarded-up windows. Her eyes adjusted to the dimness and she saw a pair of two-seater velvet couches facing each other from either side of an art-deco fireplace. Stevie's stomach did a quick flip-flop and she thought she might vomit again. She plonked herself on the nearest couch and put her head between her legs.

When she looked up her gaze met a photograph propped on the coffee table in front of her. It looked out of place. Stevie wondered if it had been the last thing the inhabitant of the gatehouse had focused on as they succumbed to the Sweats on the same couch. She lifted the frame from the table. The image trembled in her hands. A group of five children stood outside the castle: four boys and a girl. Something about the girls' hairstyles suggested the photo had been taken a decade before the Sweats. The children shared the same sandy-coloured hair and pale skin as Lord Ramsey. Their ages varied, but they were all in school uniform, the girls solid in Barathea blazers, the boys with side partings and puppety heads too large for their bodies. Each one sported a tie, knotted at the throat, and a smile that suggested mild strangulation. Stevie guessed the group was Lord Ramsey and his siblings, the 'happy breeders'. She tried to find him amongst the children, but they were too similar. All of them were dead except one, and she did not know who he was. She placed the photograph face down on the table.

A delicate writing desk with drawers too small to be useful sat to the left of the window. A bookcase at its side contained a shelf loaded with telephone directories. The gatehouse had been occupied by someone who had never learned to love the Internet. Stevie took a local telephone directory from the shelf and leafed through it, with no idea of what she was looking for. Pistol whined, keen to be on the move again. She shushed him.

Rees had tricked her and Magnus easily because they had no idea of the geography of the district. Stevie slid the directory back onto the shelf, as if neatness mattered, and walked her fingers along the book spines, looking for a road map. She found an AA Guide and set it beside her improvised bag. There were other maps and travel guides on the same shelf. A lost geography: *Paris, Berlin, Toronto, Auckland, Crete, New York, Amsterdam, Beijing, Chicago.* The names sang. Stevie slid a guide to Rome from the shelf. It opened at a photograph of the Trevi Fountain surrounded by tourists (all dead now, presumably). Something fell from the book. She bent and picked it up. A handwritten receipt for two cappuccinos. She remembered a sun-splitting morning, hot city air threaded with dust and petrol, coffee frothing against the rims of two white cups set on a metal table, the high-pitched buzz of Vespas zipping through narrow streets, people, people, people: walking, loitering, holding hands, carrying bags, children, umbrellas, little dogs, falling in love, arguing, making love . . .

Stevie slammed the guidebook shut. The sitting room was dark and quiet. Not even the sound of birdsong reached inside its walls. She let the book drop to the floor.

A little later she was in the bedroom, changing her bloodstained clothes for a man's shirt and walking trousers, when an advert she had glimpsed in the local directory tugged at her thoughts. Stevie fastened the shirt's buttons up to her throat and stepped quickly back into the sitting room, Pistol at her heels. There had been so many fires since the Sweats, so many explosions and razed cities, it was likely that the premises and its stock were long gone, but the advert kindled a gleam of an idea. She flipped through the book until she found the right page, ripped it out and went in search of Magnus.

Thirty

The plan was simple and destructive. Stevie pulled the torn page from her pocket and passed it to Magnus.

Relief at seeing her made his voice gruff. 'What am I looking at?'

'Bottom right-hand corner.'

It had grown dark in the woods, but they had not made any torches for fear of giving away their presence. The only light came from the full moon shining through the canopy of leaves above them. Magnus held the advert close to his eyes.

'Festival Fireworks?' He battened down a jolt of irritation. 'Is there something I'm supposed to be getting here?'

Olivia plucked the advert from his hand. She read it slowly, her lips silently spelling out the words. 'You want to set them off.'

Stevie nodded. 'Joe and his army keep their fuel stocks well guarded. We can't outgun them, so we need a distraction. What could be more distracting than an exploding fireworks factory? We set them off, Joe's guys go running and in the meantime . . .'

Olivia grinned. 'In the meantime, we get busy.'

The girl's smile shone in the darkness.

Stevie squeezed her shoulder. 'Think it'll work?'

'Maybe.' Olivia passed the advert to the girl next to her. 'I think the factory's still there, leastways I never heard of a load of fireworks going off. But we should keep away from the estate. It's too close to the old abattoir.'

'The abattoir?' Stevie looked at Magnus.

Magnus saw a splash of something on her cheek. He checked an urge to wipe it away. 'Where Lord Snooty stores his fuel supply.'

The young guerrillas were passing the paper between themselves. A few of them gave it a cursory glance. Magnus wondered if they could read.

Henny peered at the scrap of paper. 'I never saw a firework before.'

Magnus said, 'Ever see the Northern Lights?'

Henny nodded. 'When I was little I used to think they were ghosts coming across the mountains to get me.'

One of the girls said, 'Henny's a baby.' And the others laughed.

Henny snapped, 'I said, when I was little.'

Magnus said, 'Fireworks are too loud and too bright for anyone to mistake them for ghosts. If this goes up, it'll be Northern Lights on acid.' He turned to Stevie. 'I don't like it. Even if the factory's still there and you manage to set it off, Joe's guys might decide to stay at their posts.'

The knife was back in Olivia's hand. She looked like a bloodthirsty young pirate.

'If they do, we'll cut their throats.'

Stevie said, 'If they do, we'll think of something else.'

They had been walking as they talked, slipping through the woods, feet sliding on rotting leaves, crunching against fallen twigs, away from the castle, towards the outskirts of town.

Magnus felt out of place, the only man in the troop. A few of the girls were nearly his height, but others were short and slight. He saw their camouflage headdresses bob and dip as they walked and felt like a white adventurer commanding a bunch of pygmies to their deaths. Sky fell into line beside him. She was tall and athletic enough to make a credible soldier, but she was too young to go into battle. They all were.

He looked at her. 'What did you mean when you said you left Belle and the rest of your gang because you thought things were getting weird?'

Sky shrugged. 'Why would a bunch of grown-ups want to hang around with kids like us? They acted like they were our mates, but they weren't really. They wanted something.'

'Any idea what?'

'I don't know. At first I thought Belle wanted little Evie. I was raging when we found out Willow had brought her.'

A fallen tree blocked the path. Sky vaulted the trunk in one easy move. Magnus felt the bark rough against the palm of his hands as he swung himself over and thought again how easily a small scrape, a splinter or a graze, could lead to death. Shug was out there somewhere, alone and rendered stupid by love.

He caught up with Sky. 'But it wasn't that?'

'Belle looked after Evie. She was good with her, but I could tell she didn't want to get too attached. It was like she could have loved Evie, but made a decision not to. I thought maybe she got Willow to steal her for someone else. Then I began to think that maybe they wanted the rest of us – me, Shug, Willow, our wee Orkney gang – for someone else too. That's when I decided to leg it.' Sky touched Magnus's arm. 'It's nice that you came after Shug. He lucked out when he got you for a foster dad.'

'We came after all of you.'

'Maybe she did. Stevie likes everything to be in order, but you wouldn't be here if Shuggie wasn't missing.'

The truth of her words made Magnus feel ashamed. He said, 'Iris and Bill want you home, it just wasn't possible for everyone to come, not with harvest due and the threat of invasion.'

'You think someone's going to invade our islands?' Sky's voice was warm with indignation.

'It's a possibility.'

Magnus had thought Stevie up ahead, but her voice sounded beside him in the darkness.

'You're needed on the islands, Sky. We won't try to force you home, if it isn't where you want to be, but I think you should go back and take as many of your new friends as will go with you.'

The line of girls had been making steady progress through the woods, now it faltered.

Stevie addressed them all, keeping her voice low. 'We'd welcome more young people and I guarantee no one would make you get married or have babies, if you didn't want to.'

Olivia said, 'We can't make raids on Lord Ramsey's men if we're off on some island.'

Someone said, 'Shut up, Livi.' There was a hiss of whispers and then a small voice asked, 'What about our little sisters? If we leave, he'll just wait until they get older.'

The trees murmured around them as Stevie reached for a plan and the young guerrillas waited to hear what she would say. Small creatures rustled through the undergrowth. The girls stood frozen, the stillest things in the forest.

Stevie squatted and the group gathered around her.

'We have to make this a hammer blow and we have to make sure that Ramsey and Joe don't suspect you're involved. We need to hit them so hard it's impossible for their army to follow us straight away. Joe thinks power lies in a show of strength. My guess is he'll rally his men and head south after us, meanwhile you'll be safely on your way north.' She looked at Olivia. 'How far south does Lord Ramsey's territory go?'

Olivia was playing with a twig that formed part of her camouflage. She looked anxious, as if now that the time for action was close she was less keen on cutting throats.

'My foster dad says they can't go further than Dingwall, not unless they take the whole army and are prepared to lose some of them. He says it's anarchy over there. That's why Dad likes Lord Ramsey. Him and Joe keep anarchy away, whatever that is.'

'Anarchy's what we're going to bring. Magnus and I will head for Dingwall as fast as we can. If we're lucky we'll outstrip them. Meanwhile those of you who want to will head to Orkney. It wouldn't be right to steal your little sisters away from their mothers, but you can come back in a year or two and if nothing has changed they can come to the islands too.'

Henny said, 'How would we get there?'

Magnus turned to Sky. 'Think you could sail a boat that far?'

'I took the helm some of the way here. I'd need charts, but I think I could make it.'

He looked at the rest of the group. 'Anyone else a decent sailor?'

The girls shook their heads.

'My boat's waiting at Scrabster.' Magnus tossed Sky the keys to the cabin. 'You'll have to board in the dark. There's a man named Rees living on the quayside. Avoid him if you can. He'd like to hand you in, but I reckon his wife won't let him.' Like all of their plans it was full of ifs, but Sky had been sailing since she was tall enough to reach the boom and Magnus would trust her with his own boat. He looked at the girls. 'Say "Aye" if you want to go.'

A chorus of voices whispered: 'Aye.'

He felt rather than heard Sky's silence. 'Sky? Will you take them?'

The girl sat mute beside him.

He asked again. 'Sky?'

'I'll take them, but only if we set off the fireworks and do the petrol raid.'

The gang of guerrilla girls gave a muted cheer.

Magnus said, 'It's not a game.' But the small squad were already moving towards a break in the foliage – the wood's end.

Thirty-One

Festival Fireworks was half a mile from the abattoir. Magnus and Stevie were to make for the petrol stockpile. Sky, Olivia and the rest of the girls to the factory. Stevie's stolen map helped them estimate how long it would take to reach each location. The fireworks factory was nearest. The guerrillas were to lie in wait there, long enough for Stevie and Magnus to get into place at the abattoir, then set the sky on fire.

The girls stripped themselves of their greenery, rubbed fresh mud onto their hands and faces and emerged from the woods into the moonlit night, like slender seal-women slipping from the water. Stevie and Magnus ran with them, down a grassy hill, wet with night-dew, into the black and silent town. At the bottom of the hill they came together in quick goodbye hugs, then the girls trotted away, light and sure on their feet. Pistol wanted stay with Stevie, but she commanded him '*Go*' and he scampered in the girls' wake, his tail curving wide arcs against the night. A small part of her went with the dog. She would miss him, but it was better he return to the islands with Sky and the other girls.

Stevie watched them fade into the darkness and then started in the direction of the abattoir. She was used to early morning jogs. The air quick in her lungs, feet slapping a steady rhythm against the ground. Sometimes in the dawn, she could almost pretend she was still in her old life. Running past dazed club kids, contract cleaners, road sweepers, shop assistants, still jet-lagged tourists and blank-faced city workers; London going to bed and waking up around her. She heard Magnus stumble and slowed her pace.

Magnus felt his breath bunching in his chest. They were miles from the town centre, but he could smell death. Despite their efficiency with fuel and fighting men, it was clear Lord Ramsey and Joe had not managed the removal of all of the dead from the town's houses. Magnus wondered what diseases hung in the air.

They were approaching an overgrown roundabout. A sign declared *Fergusson Meat & Poultry*. Stevie and Magnus slowed their pace. High wire fences waited beyond the roundabout and beyond that, a large car park, flat as the veldt. The sound of howling came from somewhere in the distance, stretching through the dark, sad as an old blues song. Stevie remembered Rees's talk of wolves and felt a quick stab of fear for Pistol and the girls.

The abattoir looked vast. A huge white shed with loading bays sealed behind metal shutters. They squatted on the ground outside the perimeter fence. The gun in Magnus's shoulder holster was heavy. It seemed to pull at some muscle in his heart.

Stevie said, 'Remember all those action movies?'

'Mel Gibson, Bruce Willis and the like?' He had relived the *Die Hard* films with Shug, retelling them as bedtime stories to the boy when he was little.

Stevie's eyes were trained on the abattoir.

'There was always a scene where the heroes walk away from a massive explosion.'

Magnus said, 'No one looked back and no one got their balls blown off. This isn't a movie.'

'No, but if we take what we need and torch the rest, it'll cut the chance of us getting caught . . .'

'. . . And up the chances of us getting shot.' Magnus narrowed his eyes, searching for any glimmer of movement outside the building. 'Even supposing we walk away from the explosion, we'll have the hounds of hell on our back. Lord Ramsey's a spent force. He might have been a marvel when the Sweats first hit, but he's become too fond of the bottle to stick to anything for long, including chasing us. But Joe's a different banana. He's the kind of guy to bear a grudge. I wouldn't bank on him stopping at some unofficial border.'

'Joe and his buddies are rapist fucks.'

Magnus turned to look at Stevie. 'Did something happen while I was in the woods?'

'Nothing I couldn't handle.'

The howling took on a new note, soft and keening. It raised the hairs on the back of Magnus's neck. He touched Stevie's arm. 'I shouldn't have left you alone.'

Stevie's mouth tasted sour. She saw the smoker's bloody face, his features flattening as she pulled the plastic tight around his head.

'I can look after myself.'

Magnus took out his knife and pressed it experimentally against the fence in front of him, although he already knew its blade would be no match for the metal wire.

'Burning up all that fuel would be a waste. Joe and Lord Ramsey won't always be in charge.'

'They might be, if we don't precipitate a crisis.'

Magnus dug the blade of his knife into the soil, trying to test how deep the fence went. It touched concrete and he swore quietly.

'I'm not a politician like you or Joe. I don't give a damn about running elections or toppling regimes. I just want to get Shuggie home safe.'

'Don't compare me with Joe.' Stevie turned to look at Magnus, her face sheened in moonlight. 'I know you're here to find

Shuggie. But whatever Bjarne was up to was bigger than the kids' disappearance. It may mean we don't have a safe home to get back to.' She nodded towards the old abattoir. 'As soon as we invited the girls to take refuge on Orkney we made an enemy of Joe. We've got to put him out of action; land a body blow that sends him after us, or he'll follow them to the islands.'

Magnus saw the dirty streak on her face that he had noticed earlier, in the woods. It was a splatter-mark, dark and horribly familiar. He whispered, 'He won't know the girls have gone there.'

'He could make a shrewd guess, or one of them may be caught and confess.' Stevie gave a deep sigh. 'There's something else . . .'

Magnus waited for her to tell him. When she didn't he asked, 'What?'

'I killed three of his men.'

Stevie's fatigue and fresh clothes when she joined him in the woods made sense now. Magnus stretched out a hand towards her smeared face, but could not bring himself to touch it.

'What happened?'

'They were normal-looking guys. The kind I used to pass on the street or sit next to on the Tube and think nothing of.' Stevie could still feel the texture of the smoker's flesh as she stabbed her knife into his neck. His blood had been warm and slick beneath the plastic. 'It was them or me.'

Magnus sheathed his knife. He took Stevie's hand in his and got to his feet, drawing her with him.

'I'm glad it was them.' He spat on his scarf and forced himself to wipe it against her cheek, rubbing away the blood. 'Let's find a way inside and blow this place to fuck.'

Thirty-Two

The fence was old and not as well maintained as it had been when protesters had lined the abattoir's perimeter. Magnus found a breach in the links and slipped inside. Stevie followed, close behind. They had copied the girl guerrillas and rubbed mud into their faces in the hope of fading into the night, but the moon was full. It turned the car park's concrete surface gunmetal silver. Magnus and Stevie might have been actors, running across a stage.

Fear had been Stevie's friend in the stables. Now she knew that if she let it in it would become her enemy. She clung to Magnus's moon-cast shadow and thought only of the next step and the one after that. The girls had been sure that the building was well guarded, but there was no sign of any sentries. It occurred to Stevie that the place might be a decoy, a rumour created by Joe or Lord Ramsey to protect a real stockpile located elsewhere.

They skirted the loading bays where truckloads of animals had once been delivered to their deaths and made for a modest side entrance. It was padlocked shut. Magnus took a Swiss army knife from his pocket, selected a screwdriver and tried to unfasten the screws securing the hasp. The screwdriver was too small, the screws too firmly embedded.

'Shit . . .'

He heard a crack and a distant popping sound that recalled childhood bonfires. The sky glowed: pink, lilac, orange. The air whooshed and banged. Stars scattered in chrysanthemum bursts and a faint cheer reached across the night towards them. It was raining silver, scarlet and gold. Cocktail-coloured heavens rushed towards the ground and rockets whistled up into space. Magnus looked at Stevie and saw her features flit through a tropical spectrum. The night sounded like a final machine-gun battle; eye-to-eye contact and scattered limbs. His heart quickened. The world blazed: alarm-bell blue, hospital red, amber warnings.

Stevie pointed across the car park. Magnus looked at the expanse of concrete and saw half-a-dozen men with their backs towards them, staring up at the miraculous sky. Stevie jogged in the opposite direction and he shadowed her, around the abattoir's brick walls until they came to a half-open roller shutter. She ducked beneath it and Magnus followed, into a dark, damp chill, colder than the air outside.

Stevie whispered, 'Do you think they got away?'

There was no way of knowing. Magnus said, 'They're clever girls.'

He bumped against something in the dark and swore under his breath.

A pinpoint of light illuminated the abattoir. Magnus saw mechanised meat hooks hanging from the ceiling and shadows of machinery he supposed had been responsible for rendering meat. There was no sign of petrol cans or barrels of fuel.

Stevie shoved his arm. 'Turn your torch off.'

Magnus said, 'It isn't me.'

The source of the light turned its full beam onto their faces, blinding them. It dipped and Magnus saw a cadaver-thin man, with a battery torch in one hand and an axe in the other.

The man said, 'Welcome to the funhouse.'

Thirty-Three

They jumped beyond the light, but the torch caught them again in its beam. Black dots danced in front of Magnus's eyes.

Stevie whispered, 'Split up,' and dodged to the left.

Magnus went right, still blind, aware of his boots, harsh against the concrete floor.

The torch beam followed Stevie. He saw her outline spotlit against the abattoir wall, her shadow stretched behind her, thin and black. Magnus reached for his gun, but he remembered the petrol stores and grabbed his knife instead.

'Hey, you fucking prick. Pick on someone your own size.'

He waved his hands in the air, but the light stayed glued to Stevie. Magnus tried to run towards its source. He brandished his knife and let out a warrior yell that drew the beam to him. His eyes sank into his head and he heard Stevie gasping for breath somewhere on the other side of the hall. Magnus ran, expecting to hear the whizz of the axe followed by the thud of its blade between his shoulders. Fireworks were still cracking and banging outside, but not a flicker of light penetrated the building. Magnus stubbed his toe against something, and then his whole body slammed hard against metal. He was like a bug in a box, trapped in some schoolboy experiment.

Stevie shouted, 'Over here, arsehole!'

But the light was on Magnus now. The collision had winded him. He bent over, gasping for breath. The beam grew bigger, the axeman closer. He thought of Shug and drew himself up. Some unseen machinery was hard at his back. He moved to his right and then his left, but he was hemmed in. The light was closer, the man still hidden behind it. The axe had a longer reach than Magnus's hunting knife. The man would be able to swing and chop without ever letting Magnus get close enough to strike.

He braced himself. The axeman would have to drop the torch before he hit and then they would both be in the dark. An axe was unwieldy, his knife quick and sharp. He listened for the assailant's breaths, trying to pinpoint where he was.

The torch fell with a clatter. The beam of light bounced, illuminating belts of machines and went out. There was a slicing noise, the wet wheezing sound of an open windpipe and a thump as the man's body fell to the ground. Magnus was keyed to strike. He leapt forward. Strong hands grabbed him and his knife rattled against the floor.

A deep voice said, 'It's all right, lad.'

Magnus was shaking. The hands held him by his elbows, firm in the dark. The voice said again, 'It's all right, lad, I've got you.'

He fought against the stranger's hold, but the other man was stronger.

Stevie shouted from the darkness, 'Magnus? Are you okay?' Her voice was high-pitched and frightened.

Magnus cleared his throat. 'Stay where you are.' He felt an urge to sink, sobbing, into the stranger's embrace.

The stranger called, 'He's fine.' The hands loosened their grip. 'You're fine. Just a bit of a fright.' He let go and gave Magnus a friendly pat between the shoulder blades. 'Deep breaths.'

Magnus heard the stranger bend and pick the torch up from the ground. He fiddled with it for a moment and then the light was back. The man shone it on his own features, illuminating a round, blood-spattered face with a high forehead and bushy beard.

'I'm Col.' He held out a hand.

Magnus shook it, aware of the dead man's blood, warm and sticky between their grips.

'Thanks.' Magnus retrieved his knife from the ground and slipped it into its sheath. 'That was a close call.'

'Aye.' Col's accent had a north-country burr. He nodded to where the thin man lay ruined on the floor. 'Help me get him out of the way before the others come back. They took a foot each and slid the corpse beneath one of the redundant machines. 'His name was Matti. He was one of those guys who loved the Sweats. It made him feel special, everyone dead and him still here and what passes for healthy. Before, he was one of those guys who hung around bars getting drunk and starting fights. Afterwards, he was a valued member of society.'

'I thought I was a goner.'

'Aye well, Matti was still a drinker, but it didn't seem to affect his aim. I daresay he could have knocked your head from your body, given half a chance.' Col tucked Matti's legs beneath the machinery and shone the torch on the ground, making sure the body was out of sight. 'How many are you?'

'Just two,' Stevie said, beside them in the darkness.

'Ha.' Col shone the torch briefly on each of them and clicked it off. He gave an unhappy laugh. 'I thought you were the vanguard of the glorious revolution. I might not have killed him if I'd known there were only two of you.'

Magnus bit back an impulse to apologise. 'We're trying to get to Glasgow. My son and some of his pals are headed that way. We want to catch up with them, before they get into trouble.'

Col clicked the torch back on and shone it on his own face, showing them his sad expression. 'Too late.'

Magnus's heart seemed to twist in his chest. 'Do you know something?'

'I know it's impossible to get anywhere without landing in trouble. Look at you now.'

A cheer came from outside the abattoir. The guards applauding an especially spectacular explosion.

Stevie said, 'We're running out of time. We need petrol and a van. Can you help us?'

Col shone the torch on his face again. His hair was as bushy as his beard. The torchlight gave him a lionish aspect.

'Why don't you let the kids do what they want, spread their wings? This is a new world. They've got to learn how to make their own way in it.'

Magnus said, 'They went with people with doubtful motives. They took a baby with them. Her mother's frantic.'

Col pressed the torch off and on again. 'Steal from Joe and he'll come after you.'

Magnus looked at Stevie, wondering if he should come clean about their plan. She read his expression and gave a small nod. He said, 'We'd intended to blow this place up, so they couldn't chase us so easily.'

'Ha.' Col laughed again. 'You do realise I'm meant to be one of the guards here?'

Magnus remembered the ease with which the big man had sliced open Matti's throat.

'It was just an idea. We wanted to make sure there was no one inside, before we set the fire. That's what the fireworks are about.'

'Aye, that was a neat touch. But it didn't work on the likes of Matti, nor me for that matter.' Col aimed the torch at the floor, keeping the beam small, like a cinema usherette leading patrons to their seats after the film had started. 'Follow me.'

He led them through the vast abattoir, his torch picking out meat hooks, conveyor belts, rendering machines and animal pens.

Col's voice was deep and warm in the chill damp of the windowless halls. 'You must think us a pretty feeble lot around here, letting Lord Ramsey and his boyfriend rule the district?'

Stevie said, 'We know not everyone's for him.'

Col's voice was rueful. 'More than you would think. He's alienated a lot of the youngsters, but most survivors still seem to think he's their best chance of stability.'

Stevie said, 'The Sweats were a shock. I guess people want to get back to some sort of normality.'

'Funny kind of normality. Armies traipsing across the country, girls getting married off, whether they like it or not, people paying *fealty*.'

Col spat the last word out like grit. He led them into a second, grand hall and danced the torch beam around the space. Three petrol tankers were parked side by side. Lines of jerrycans stood along the walls, like troops on parade. It was more fuel than they had on the islands, much more than they needed to make their escape, but Stevie said, 'I thought there would be more.'

'Maybe there is.' Col unscrewed a lid from one of the jerrycans and sloshed its contents around the hall. 'Matti seemed to think so.'

Stevie sprang back, the scent of petrol strong in her nostrils.

Magnus put a hand on her arm, drawing her further from the fuel. Something in Col's voice made Magnus ask, 'Were you and Matti already fighting when we arrived?'

'Matti was an argumentative kind of bloke.'

More petrol splashed across the floor. Outside the fireworks continued to whizz and shriek. Magnus wondered if Joe would think the firework display the result of a spontaneous fire, or if he and his men were already on their way to check their fuel supplies.

Col said, 'Before the Sweats I worked for the Postal Workers' Union. I'd given up hope of the crisis of capitalism ever precipitating a revolution. Big corporations could screw up as many times as they wanted. They'd always get bailed out.' More petrol splashed against the concrete floor of the abattoir, rivers of the stuff, irreplaceable and more precious than gold. 'I spent my time trying to make the best of a bad job. When the Sweats came I'll admit there was a part of me thought we had a chance to forge a new way. Millions of deaths were a high price to pay. But I wasn't responsible for that.' He paused for a moment and looked up at them. 'Instead we got Lord Ramsey and Joe. Feudalism combined with a good dose of tyranny.'

Stevie said, 'Why didn't you leave?'

Col threw an empty petrol can to one side. It clattered against the wall. He unscrewed another.

'The usual story. I fell in love with a woman born and raised here. Her husband and kids are buried in the graveyard, her parents too. Once again I made the best of it. We kept a small orchard, farmed a couple of acres and paid *fealty*.'

He was working his way backwards, into the darkness of the first hall, petrol slopping in his wake.

Magnus followed him. 'We just want to get on the road. All we need is a van and a few of those petrol cans.'

Col reached into his pocket and drew out a set of keys. He flung them through the dark towards Magnus. They rattled against the concrete floor and he had to get down on his hands and knees to find them.

'I can do better than that. I can give you whole bloody tankers of the stuff.'

Magnus got to his feet, the keys in his hand. 'A tanker's too much. We'll be conspicuous enough in a van. A tanker would make us a target for everyone, not just Joe.'

Stevie was by his side. 'It'd be a precious white elephant. We wouldn't know how to get the fuel out of it.'

Col looked at Magnus. 'Matti would have chopped you into chunks if it wasn't for me.'

Stevie said, 'Maybe he would have chopped you up, if we hadn't interrupted him.'

Col grinned. 'Aye, could be. Could be someone else will finish the job, if you don't help me out.'

Magnus had been plagued by a recurring nightmare after his father's death. He was standing beside the combine harvester, watching as his father stepped down from the cab, ready to clear a blockage in the machinery. In the dream, Magnus saw what his father had forgotten. The combine's keys were still in the ignition. He knew that as soon as the blockage was freed, the blades would roar into life, slicing through his father's flesh, pulling him into the machine. The atmosphere of the nightmare reached out and touched him now. He needed to save Shug, but there were obstacles at every stage.

Col was still talking. '. . . I planned a two-pronged attack – politicisation married with a bit of thieving. Whoever owns the means of production has the power. I thought if I could get command of the petrol supply, I might have some sway. So I took it, bit by bit, and hid it away. There's only six guards including me and Matti and they're mostly grunts. We're meant to take inventories, but as long as the doors are locked, nobody bothers. I thought I was high and dry. I didn't reckon to the level of passivity amongst the workers. I wanted to make a revolutionary cell, but no one gave a toss. I didn't reckon with Matti either.'

Stevie was tempted to tell Col that if he had looked to the district's young women he would have had his cell. But if all had gone as planned at Festival Fireworks the girls would be on their way to the islands by now and she did not want them caught up in Col's mismanaged revolution. She said, 'Matti took an inventory?'

'Matti took objection to me talking politics with the lads. I was trying to unionise them.' Col snorted. 'I might as well have been talking to the birds, but Matti didn't see it that way. I guess he took it into his head to watch me. I had a neat system going. Each time Joe told us to shift fuel, I shifted some for myself too – vehicles are quickly spotted on these roads. It was still risky, but if someone had stopped me I would have pretended to have got the order confused. You know how it is – people are prone to confusion since the Sweats. As it was, I stole in plain sight and no one noticed.'

Stevie said, 'Until tonight.'

Col nodded. 'Until tonight. But it was only a matter of time until the shit hit the fan. I'd got too successful, stolen too much and not managed to get anyone to join me. You guys are my saviours and I'm yours.'

He fished in his pocket, found a second set of keys and held them out to Stevie.

'Either of you ever driven one of these big beasts before?'

Stevie kept her hands by her sides. 'We'd like to help, but our kids have to come first.'

'Do this and all being well you'll be in Glasgow soon after dawn.' Col was piling up empty cardboard boxes and bits of old packaging. 'I knew my luck was running out, so I organised myself an escape vehicle. Drive two of the tankers out of here, I'll set the rest on fire. Let me blame the explosion on you and you can have my van. I'll be high and dry and you'll be on your way. It's the same plan as you had before, with a small detour attached.' Col grinned. 'I'll still have my stockpile and who knows? If things get a little harder people might come around to the idea of a revolution.'

Magnus said, 'You don't think the Sweats were hard enough?'

'More than hard enough for me.' Col's smile was gone. His mouth had a bitter set to it. 'Maybe it was the speed of things that set us on the wrong path. Decent folk were left reeling and in the meantime the psychopaths took over.'

There was a noise from the other hall. The guards had grown tired of the fireworks and were returning to their posts. Or perhaps they feared that Joe might be on his way.

Col said, 'It might take you weeks to get to Glasgow without a car. Who knows what will have happened to your kids by then.'

Magnus looked at Stevie. 'I could take one of the tankers and come back for you.'

A faint light glowed in the previously dark adjacent hall; time was running out. Col glanced towards it, but kept his nerve. 'It's all or nothing.'

Stevie took the tankers' keys from his hand. 'I'm guessing we have to drive through the perimeter fence?'

Col grinned. 'Already taken care of. The padlocks on the front gates are unlocked. Just drive right at them, they'll give way.' He tapped his head. 'It's all about psychology, people see what they expect to see.' He took a nub of pencil and a notebook from his pocket and drew them each a quick map. 'I'd put my foot down if I were you. The roads are winding, but it's not like you have to worry about someone coming in the opposite direction.'

Stevie said, 'Unless it's Joe.'

Col grinned. 'Then all your worries will be over.'

Magnus climbed up into the cab of the nearest tanker and settled himself in the driver's seat. He adjusted his wing mirrors and glanced through the side window at Stevie, already in position in the next cab. She had found a baseball cap bearing the BP logo and set it on her head. Her hair was in a ponytail, the cap at a business-like tilt. She might have been one of the female models who used to liven up Formula One events, pouring glasses of champagne for laurelled racing drivers.

Stevie gave a quick salute, indicating she was strapped in and ready to go. Col had already opened the doors to the loading bays. They sailed through them and into a night that was still alive with flashes of rainbow-defying light.

Thirty-Four

Their headlamps were off but Stevie was aware of Magnus's tanker rumbling close behind hers in the dark. They were barely free of the perimeter fence when the abattoir exploded. Stevie looked in her wing mirror and saw the flash of light, so close that she caught her breath, scared their own vehicles would spark into flame. The flare of the explosion drowned out the kaleidoscope of fireworks. She saw the white tanker behind her, the abattoir ablaze, trees and roadside verges wavering in the shimmering light cast by the flames. Men ran from the burning building. Stevie hoped that Col was with them. There was another boom. A second flash of light fed the fire. Then she rounded a corner and all that remained of the explosion was a halo of brightness above the treetops and the distant bang of exploding petrol cans.

Col had retained a postal worker's fluency with roads and junctions. His map guided her off the main artery onto a network of minor roads pitted with potholes. The fireworks were a memory in her rear-view mirror, the view in front and beside her dark. The map took her onto a long, flat stretch of road. Stevie guessed they were crossing moorland and hoped she would not tip the tanker into bog and be sucked from one darkness into another.

She felt rather than saw the road rising and realised that there was a sheer cliff-side drop to her left and high, mountain rock to her right. The road was too narrow for the tanker to comfortably take the curves and she was forced to slow down on bends. She looked in her mirrors and saw the pale gleam of Magnus's tanker, a ghost-shadow, following her. There was nowhere for another vehicle to pass and she wondered what she would do if she were to meet Joe or his men coming from the opposite direction. She reached the top of the rise and the fireworks reappeared, distant flashes of colour, in her rear-view mirror.

The interior of Magnus's cab was black, but she knew he was there. Stevie remembered how Magnus had called to the man with the axe, drawing him from her, putting himself in mortal danger and realised that she had not thanked him.

A village appeared, abandoned and crumbling. Stevie saw the dark shapes of neglected buildings and wondered if a stubborn survivor, roused by the sound of their engines, was watching the tankers' progress from one of the darkened cottages. She thought of Pistol, Sky and the rest of the girls and hoped that they were well on their way to Scrabster.

A pink tinge crept across the sky. Stevie had an instant of panic, thinking that she had somehow turned back on herself and was catching the final glow of the fireworks. Then she saw that the sun was slowly rising. Col had lied when he had said they would make Glasgow before dawn. Soon it would be light. She wondered what else he had lied about. Her stomach knotted with hunger and misgivings. She was tired enough to envy the dead.

The road descended into a grassy valley dotted with sheep. The grass was frosted with dew, the morning fresh-washed and golden. She rolled down the driver's window. Birds chorused-in the new day. The blazing abattoir was far behind and the air smelt sweetly of wakened greenery.

Stevie could see Magnus reflected in her mirrors now. His face set, hands cemented to the wheel. A mascot hung from his rear-view mirror, swinging jauntily with every lurch of the cab. She thought she saw his head nod and hoped he would not fall asleep at the wheel.

The map sent her left, onto a muddy track, rutted by the passage of other vehicles. She knew they were reaching journey's end. The turn onto the track was tight and she took it slowly, rattling over one cattle grid and then another. The vibrations shook her to her bones and she was sure that the noise must have travelled across the valley.

Magnus misjudged the turn and had to back up and re-negotiate it. Stevie slowed to allow him time to catch up. The dawn was giving way to grey sky. She could see the farmhouse now. A flesh-toned building flanked by cattle sheds. A crack cut diagonally across the front of the house. It leant the facade an off-centre look, a scowling face.

Stevie adjusted her baseball cap. 'Welcome to Cold Comfort Farm,' she thought, and steered the tanker towards the cattle sheds marked with a heavy X on Col's map. Their shutters were down. She turned her engine off and waited while Magnus drew his tanker in, close behind hers. Their eyes met in the rear-view mirror. Stevie picked up her gun from the passenger seat, put it in its holster and stepped down from the cab.

Six petrol tankers were already parked in the cattle shed and it was difficult to manoeuvre theirs inside. Magnus guided Stevie in first, both of them wincing at the beep, beep, beep of the tanker's reverse warning, which neither of them could work out how to deactivate. They swapped places and Stevie helped Magnus slide the final tanker into place. He was pale with fatigue, but managed it on the second go.

'It looks like a box of panatellas.' He climbed down from the cab, stumbling on the final step.

Stevie caught Magnus by the arm. She saw what he meant. The cylindrical tankers stood side by side, inside the oblong box of a shed.

She said, 'I wonder what Joe's friend Machiavelli would say about this?'

Magnus gave a tired grin. 'Christ knows, but I don't think he'd be impressed.'

Stevie pulled out Col's map. 'The van's parked in the shed opposite.'

They crossed the yard swiftly. The farm was eerily quiet, even the birds seemed to have deserted the place. Stevie and Magnus's boots sounded loud against the gravel.

Magnus wondered why Col had chosen this place to store his plunder. If ghosts existed, the whole world would be haunted, but it seemed some places held on to the atmosphere of death more distinctly. He felt a prickling in his spine that made him remember Candice and Bjarne's house. The dogs slaughtered in the yard, Bjarne dead in his chair and poor Candice, lying butchered in her bed.

He wanted to ask Stevie if she could feel it too, but she was striding ahead. He put a sprint on and caught up with her. 'Let's stick together.'

She looked at him. 'I thought we were.'

It was the wrong moment, but he said, 'What happened back at the castle, when I was in the woods?'

Stevie was about to tell Magnus to mind his own business, but she remembered again how he had drawn the axeman away to save her.

'Some men tried to rape me. I killed them.'

'Did they hurt you?'

Stevie's body was covered in bruises. Her muscles ached from the violence of the fight, but she shook her head.

'No, they would have murdered me, but I shot them before they got the chance.'

Magnus nodded. 'I keep thinking, maybe that's what happened to Bjarne. He tried to rape Willow and she killed him in self-defence, but it doesn't explain why Candice would be shot too – not in her bed like that.'

The garage in front of them was padlocked. Stevie looked under a stone by the door as Col had instructed and found the key. Her back was to Magnus, her expression hidden. 'Perhaps the kids will be able to tell us something, when we find them.'

'I won't tell anyone you shot those guys. They got what was coming to them.'

'If we want to live in peace, we need a rule of law.' Stevie looked across the valley in the direction of Eden Glen. 'That's one of the things wrong with Lord Ramsey and Joe's set-up. If they suspected I'd killed their soldiers, there'd be no investigation, no inquiry, no trial. Joe would give me to the troops and when they were finished with me I'd be strung up.' Her eyes met Magnus's. 'I want to make sure Willow's safe. I want our community, everything we've worked together for, to be safe too. If we find Willow, I'll bring her home and ask her to give an account of what she knows about Bjarne and Candice's murders. If that involves putting her on trial, I'll make sure it's a fair one.'

She turned her back on him and slid the key into the padlock. Neither of them had mentioned Shug, but Magnus knew every word that applied to the girl applied equally to his son.

The van was a white Ford, the kind that used to be favoured by fast-driving, self-employed tradesmen. The keys were where Col had told them they would be, tucked beneath a wheel arch. She unlocked the back doors and took a quick inventory.

'Extra petrol, mattress, blankets, toolkit . . . fuck.'

Magnus had pulled the shed door not-quite-closed and was keeping lookout, his ears pricked for the sound of any approach. 'What?'

'No food or water.'

Magnus's stomach was tight with hunger, his throat parched. 'You're kidding.'

Stevie glanced at Col's map, but there were no overlooked instructions about secreted supplies. She shut her eyes, trying to focus.

Magnus said, 'I'll check the farmhouse.'

Stevie closed the van doors. 'I'll come with you. We can drive round, if there's anything we need to load.'

'Sure, let's stick together.'

It was the second time Magnus had used the phrase, since they arrived at the farm. Stevie glanced at him, but the stillness of the place was working on her too. She locked the shed and followed him into the yard.

Thirty-Five

The farmhouse's kitchen door was unlocked. Magnus pushed it open and peered inside. The room was cobwebbed and dusty, but it felt alive, as if the owners had just stepped out on an errand and would be back soon. Magnus had never got used to trespassing in the houses of the dead. He took a deep breath and stepped over the threshold. Stevie followed close behind.

It was like entering one of the farm kitchens of his childhood. A large pine table occupied the centre of the room. Five chairs were neatly tucked around it, a sixth was pulled out, as if someone had just risen. Magnus slid it into place. He took in the old range, the Ulster sink, the jars labelled *Flour, Sugar, Coffee, Tea*, the flowery curtains, surely hung in the 1970s. The floor was the same red tile as the floor in his croft kitchen, the rag rug set by the hearth.

A calendar, gifted by a feed supplier and decorated with rural views, hung on the wall. It was years out of date; halted in the month of May. The neat entries reminded him of his mother's handwriting and he could not stop himself from reaching out and turning the pages; *Dentist, Open Day, Jim's Birthday, Angie's Wedding* (this entry was surrounded by little hand-drawn stars in another, more exuberant, hand), *start of term* . . . The reminders continued into June and on, towards the end of the year, by which time whoever had recorded them was probably dead.

Stevie was already rooting through the cupboards. 'Looks like Col looted himself a decent stockpile.'

Magnus let the pages of the calendar fall back into place and turned around, just in time to catch the packet of crisps Stevie tossed towards him. The sell-by-date was years past. He ripped the packet open and started to eat – salt and grease. There was a time when he had lived off junk food bought from garage shops. Butterflies in his stomach as he sped along the motorway to the next gig. And afterwards, pizza and beer with other comics, adrenalin from the show keeping them high, bitching about venue managers and absent friends; each of them trying to top the last story.

Magnus went to the sink and turned on the tap. Water flowed from it, clear and magical. He drank some and splashed his face, trying to wash away unbidden memories. He turned the tap off.

'Looks like the house is connected to a well.'

Stevie was filling a bag with supplies. 'See if you can find some bottles to collect it in. A tin opener would come in handy too.'

Magnus pulled open cupboards and drawers, closing each one neatly. The crockery was the same oatmeal shade as the stuff he had inherited with the croft. It had been mid-range and popular when his mother had bought it, but it made him feel strange to see the same plates and saucers, same cups, same sugar bowl here. He found a plastic water bottle and a couple of flasks, sniffed them to check they had held nothing toxic and then filled them at the tap. The tin opener was in the cutlery drawer. Magnus grabbed a cotton bag from a hook in the pantry and stuffed his finds into it.

Somewhere in the depths of the house a door slammed. Stevie was crouched by one of the low kitchen cabinets. She looked up. Their eyes met. Magnus put a finger to his lips. He shouldered the cotton bag, and moved backwards towards the door, his gun in his hand. Stevie was ahead of him, carrying the carrier bag she had filled with food. She stepped into the yard and fresh air gusted into the kitchen, rattling the hall door.

'Is someone there?' The voice belonged to a woman.

Magnus froze.

Stevie whispered his name.

'Is that you, son?' The woman was in the hallway, just beyond the door. Her voice had a tremble born of fear, but it held determination too.

Stevie stepped back into the kitchen and pulled at his arm. 'Magnus.'

He did not move. The voice could not belong to his mother, but he was rooted to the spot by all the fantasies he had dreamt, that she and his sister Rhona had escaped the Sweats and were living elsewhere, never knowing that he had survived.

'Son?' The hall door was opening.

'Magnus.' Stevie tried to drag him into the yard.

He batted her away. 'I have to see.' He heard Stevie cock her gun and said, 'Don't, it'll be fine.'

The woman looked nothing like Magnus's mother. She was small, with long grey hair and a wrinkled face. Her white outfit looked like a combination of wedding dress and hospital gown. It gave her a witchy air. She said, in a voice more anglicised than his mother's, 'Oh, I thought you might be him.'

Magnus backed away. 'I'm not.'

The woman held a hand out towards him, as if ready to touch Magnus, to make sure he was not who she was seeking.

'No, he was taller than you and better-looking.' She seemed to see Stevie for the first time. 'Have you come to rob and kill me or just rob?'

Stevie said, 'We just need a few things. We're friends of Col.'

The woman sat at the kitchen table. She took a cigarette from the pocket of her dress and lit it.

'None of this is mine. I'm just looking for my son.' Her eyes met Magnus's. 'I thought you might be him, but you're shorter than he was and not as handsome.'

Magnus said, 'I'm looking for my son too.'

The old lady took a long drag of her cigarette. She stared at Magnus and nodded, as if she already knew of his mission. Her tone was matter-of-fact.

'He might be dead. Lots of them are. The Sweats keeps on carrying them off.' She balanced her cigarette on the edge of the table, lit end facing outwards, so as not to burn the wood. 'Give me your hand, palm up.'

Stevie said, 'We don't have time for this.'

But Magnus stepped forward and placed his hand in the old lady's, his palm open. Now that he was closer he could see the charms strung around her neck: rosary beads tangled with St Christophers, evil eyes and love beads. She traced his lifeline with her finger.

'It's all written here, if you know how to look.' Her washed-out blue eyes met his. A piece of ash crumbled from her still-burning cigarette onto the floor. 'He's not your boy, but you'll find him.'

Magnus slid his hand free. He had never believed in the super-natural, was contemptuous of séance-goers and spiritualists who claimed to be able to contact the dead, but the women's words calmed him.

'Thanks.' Magnus thought he should give her something, but could think of nothing. He nodded. 'Thank you.'

The lit end of the cigarette made contact with the edge of the table, blackening the pine. Stevie pulled at his arm and this time he went with her.

The old lady called, 'I'm going to find my son too. He's alive somewhere, waiting for me. I see him waiting, in the lines of my hand.'

Thirty-Six

Stevie drove south while Magnus slept on the mattress in the back of the van, his gun by his side. She stuck to B roads, her eyes flitting often to the rear-view mirror, alert for pursuers. Magnus had made Stevie promise to wake him after an hour, but his reaction to the old woman in the farmhouse had disturbed her and she let him sleep on, hoping rest would cure any creeping psychosis.

The countryside had returned to nature. It was still possible to discern that there had once been farmed land, but the neatly defined fields had lost their edges. Hedges were wild and tangled; dykes were crumbling, fences tumbled. There were no herds of grazing cattle, but sheep and fowl flourished and Stevie was often forced to slow the van to avoid them. The route took her past farmhouses and cottages, through market towns and villages. She sealed her windows and picked up speed in the deserted streets, trying not to focus on the decaying buildings, the stench of rot. They passed through districts razed by fire and lone buildings reduced to burnt-out skeletons. It was strange to think of whole streets alive with flames and no one there to see or care.

Occasionally Stevie saw signs of habitation; a row of washing on a line, a well-tended kitchen garden, a few cultivated fields; but she did not glimpse any people. She supposed the sound of her engine sent them into hiding. Orkney islanders were wary of newcomers too.

Stevie was two hours into the journey and making good progress when she came across the first warning. A metal sign that had once been used to halt traffic at roadworks was propped in the middle of the road. A wooden board, painted with red lettering, was nailed to it. The brushstrokes were thick and clumsy. The paint had run in places and it was difficult to make out the words. She idled the engine for a moment, wondering if it was best to exit the van and approach the sign on foot, or drive right up to it.

The change in the engine's rhythm woke Magnus. She turned the ignition off, took her gun from the passenger seat and stepped into the road. The sign was clearer now.

KEEP OUT
TURN BACK
PENALTY FOR TRESPASS
DEATH

Magnus crawled, bleary-eyed, from the back of the van. He had not shaved since they left Orkney and bristles had colonised his chin. He knuckled his face.

'Where are we?'

'Just outside Dounthrapple.' Stevie pointed at the sign. 'We may have a problem.'

Magnus had brought his gun with him. He kept it in his hand and walked to the side of the van.

'Ah, Christ.' His words were soft enough to be a prayer. He looked at her. 'Do you think it might be left over from the Sweats? Maybe someone realised they were infectious and tried to save other folk from entering town and catching it.'

'Could be.' Stevie sounded unconvinced. 'But it would be a long time for the sign to sit undamaged in the middle of the road, without getting knocked over by an animal or damaged by the weather.'

Magnus was used to his hopes being shattered. He gave a small, resigned nod.

'What happens if we go back?'

'A long diversion and no guarantee that we won't hit the same warning at another junction.'

'Shit.' Magnus slapped the side of the van. He rubbed his face again. Stevie thought he might be close to tears, but when he looked up his expression was resolute. 'We've come too far to go back now.'

They shifted the sign together. Magnus held out his hand for the keys and Stevie tossed them to him. He drove the van forward a couple of yards and then they each took a side of the warning barrier and dragged it back into place.

Magnus grinned at her from the driver's seat. His beard leant the Orcadian a reckless, piratical edge. Stevie thought that in another life she might have liked to kiss him.

He said, 'Who do you want to be? Thelma or Louise?'

Stevie returned his smile. 'Neither, they both die at the end of the movie. We're going to come out of this alive.'

Thirty-Seven

There were more warning signs on the approach to town. They were painted on walls, on the sides of buildings and the surface of the road itself. The words varied, but the message was the same: Death awaited trespassers.

Magnus said, 'I'll skirt town and rejoin the main route. We might still be considered trespassers, but at least I'll be able to put my foot on the gas.'

The deserted landscape, littered with threats of death, was beginning to spook Stevie.

She said, 'The anonymity makes it worse. I'd rather see who we're dealing with.'

Magnus glanced at her. 'Remember Internet trolls? They usually turned out to be sad fucks who lived with their mums. My guess is, whoever wrote these signs is the same type, cowards, trying to scare us.'

'They're doing a good job.'

The first roadblock took them by surprise. Abandoned container lorries were slewed across the carriageway. Cars had been deliberately crashed into them. They sat at whiplash angles, their bonnets crumpled, windows crazed.

Magnus backed the van up and executed a quick, three-point turn. He took a left that would steer them away from the town, but they were met by another roadblock of lorries and smashed cars. 'Shit.' An open road to his right led into an industrial estate. Magnus looked at Stevie. 'Do you have a map?'

'I lost it, somewhere at the abattoir.'

'Someone's playing silly buggers. There are no road signs, have you noticed?'

He turned the van into the estate, grateful for its grid system. It was closer towards town than he would have liked, but warehouses and workshops had always been located on the outskirts and if he followed the main drag through the estate he would eventually hit a fast road to Glasgow. Magnus rounded a corner and was confronted with another mash of bus, metal and cars. He hit the steering wheel with the heel of his hand.

'Jesus Christ.'

Stevie said, 'Can you imagine how long these roadblocks took to set up? Whoever did this, they're motivated.'

Magnus crunched the gears into reverse. 'I'd like to string them up.'

Stevie stared out of the window at the low-rise buildings. DEATH TO TRESPASSERS was painted across the front of a tile warehouse in incongruously cheerful bubble letters.

'I think it was a mistake to cross the first roadblock. We should have retraced our route while we still had the chance.'

'We've taken too many diversions already. Every minute we waste, the kids travel further away from us.'

Stevie took the clip from her gun. She checked it and slotted it home.

'Whoever erected these barriers will know we're here by now.'

They emerged onto a roundabout. All of its exits were blocked by a wall of wrecked vehicles, except for one that led uphill, into a street of older houses. Magnus had never been in Dounthrapple before, but he was familiar with the layout of enough Scottish towns to know that it would take them into the old part of the city. Once they were up there, amongst the twists and turns of medieval streets, they would be easy pickings. He circled the roundabout, heading back the way they had come.

'I feel like we're in a computer game.'

Stevie said, 'Do you hear that?'

He did. A heavy rumble of engines that seemed to make the road beneath them quake.

Magnus took the exit back into the industrial estate, but the street they had so recently left was no longer clear. Two trucks were manoeuvring into place halfway along it. They stopped, bumper to bumper across the tarmac.

Magnus's mouth dried. 'What the fuck's going on?'

Stevie said, 'I don't know, but if they catch us, they'll kill us.'

There was a gap between the truck on the left and the buildings that edged the street, a small unfenced lawn where workers might once have enjoyed tea breaks on sunny days.

'Hold on tight.' Magnus pressed his foot on the accelerator and raced towards the opening. He focused on the patch of grass, the edge of the building, the tail end of the truck, but he was aware of Stevie too, folding herself into a brace position in the passenger seat beside him.

He had mounted the pavement and was about to rocket through the gap, when an ice-cream truck slotted into the space. Magnus saw the jaunty plastic ice-cream cone on its roof, the cheerful ices decorated with hundreds and thousands painted across its bonnet, the instruction above the windscreen to *Mind That Child!* He turned his steering wheel hard right and did a doughnut turn into the middle of the road, wheels screeching and rubber burning. There was a second when he thought that he had lost control and the van was about to roll, but then he managed to straighten the wheel. Stevie was curled forward, her knees drawn up, her hands clenched over her skull, still holding her gun.

Magnus expected to see another roadblock being assembled, jamming the path ahead, but the way to the roundabout was clear. They were penned, their only possible route through the roundabout and up into the old town. Magnus was reminded of his father's sheep, herded into runs by insistent collie dogs, before being taken to slaughter.

'I've a horrible feeling someone wants us to go this way.'

Stevie's voice was raw, a marathon runner who had hit their limit. 'Let's ditch the van and make a break for it.'

They had gone through so much to get mobile, abandoning the van would feel like giving in.

Magnus said, 'They can't have blocked off all the roads. Maybe there's somewhere up ahead where we can loop back and get out another way.'

'I've got a bad feeling about this.'

'Really? I feel great about it.' It was the kind of stupid sarcasm he pulled Shug up for. Magnus was about to apologise when he saw a Humvee in his rear-view mirror. 'Where the fuck did that come from?'

The armoured vehicle was racing towards them. Magnus pressed his foot to the floor but the Humvee was already a breath away from his bumper. Stevie rolled down her side window. She drew her gun and he realised that she was about to aim at the Humvee's windscreen.

Magnus said, 'There's no point shooting at them. You'll only be wasting bullets. That thing's armoured like a tank.'

The Humvee held back on the roundabout, as if it was eager for him not to spin out of control before they reached their destination. Then it was back on them like a magnet, shadowing them through the winding streets of the old town. The van juddered over cobbles, past Edinburgh Woollen Mill, Marks & Spencer's, Greggs and once chichi boutiques that had catered to tourists.

The shopfronts were peeling, their displays emptied of merchandise, but there were none of the shattered windows and smashed-in doorways that had plagued cities in the wake of the Sweats.

Magnus's wheels lost purchase on the cobbles and the van's rear slammed against a metal bollard. Cans of petrol rattled in the back. His hands slipped against the gearstick as he dropped down into first and pulled away. He remembered the way the abattoir had erupted into flames – billows of fire, flowering against the night sky. An unblocked road forked off to their left. Magnus sped down it, the Humvee at his back.

'You were right. We've got to make a break for it.' He unclipped his seat belt and was aware of Stevie releasing hers. 'Get ready to run.'

Magnus drove as fast as he dared, one hand on the steering wheel, the other on the car door. The road was narrowing into an alleyway hemmed either side by brick walls. 'Fuck, fuck, fuck.'

Stevie curled into a ball. She shouted, 'Magnus!' but he had seen the wall at the end of the alley and was already slamming on the brakes. Stevie straightened up and looked at the reflection of the Humvee in the wing mirror. The vehicle rolled back a few inches and peeped its horn. She said, 'I think they want us to reverse.'

Magnus locked the doors. He put his forehead against the steering wheel, took a deep breath and then sat up and regarded the Humvee.

'If they wanted us dead they could shoot us right here. No fuss, no muss. We're like fish in a barrel, but they're just sitting there waiting.'

The thought gave him some hope.

Stevie said, 'This town must have been boring before the Sweats, imagine how dull it is now. Maybe they don't want the hunt to end too soon.'

Magnus shook his head. 'Christ, I hope you're wrong.'

There was nowhere to make a run to and so he reversed out, the Humvee still at his back, its black-tinted windscreen masking their pursuers' faces. Magnus was reminded again of his father's collies, programmed to keep herding until the job was done.

The Humvee backed out of the alleyway. It blocked the road they had driven in on, leaving Magnus no option but to continue the ascent to the historic centre. Stevie was checking her gun again. She tied her hair back from her face, readying herself for combat. 'What do you think they want?'

A tourist information sign pointed towards the cathedral. Magnus slowed the van to a crawl. There was no point in rushing now. 'I don't know, but we're about to find out.'

Thirty-Eight

Adil was hanging from one of a line of gibbets in Merkat Square. He had been a thin lad and his body looked insubstantial, turning on its rope. One of Belle's companions, the tall man called Rob, who had once worked for Kwik Fit, was hanging on a neighbouring gibbet.

A dozen or so people, dressed in black, were assembled in front of the cathedral. A woman stood at their centre. Her fair hair was coiled into a plait that hung down her chest. She held a long twist of rope, draped across her outstretched arms. There was a horrible sense of theatre to the arrangement: the black-clad group, the cathedral backdrop, the hanging bodies.

Stevie started to shake. She said, 'We have to get him down from there.'

Magnus could not take his eyes from Adil – his blackened face, his soiled clothes. He remembered the boy eating soup with Shug and the rest of the kids, in the kitchen of the croft, after a Saturday morning football match. They had been muddy. Their cheeks flushed by the sudden heat of the kitchen after the chill of outdoors.

Alive. All of them, alive.

The boy's feet were bare. Magnus could see his soles, the downward tilt of his toes. Adil had scored a goal that Saturday. He had lapped the green, arms outstretched like a champion.

Magnus took Stevie's hand in his and felt her judder. 'I'm sorry.'

It was his fault that they were going to die. Tears obscured his vision, but Magnus still could not take his eyes from Adil. The only good thing about dying would be not having to break the news of what had happened to Francesca, the boy's foster mother. Magnus wished he had been able to see Shug one last time and tell him, whatever he might have done, that he was loved.

Stevie pulled her hand away. She released her seat belt and primed her gun. 'Fuck.' The heels of her boots scrabbled against the floor of the cab, the way Adil's must have on the rope.

Magnus wiped his eyes and saw what she had seen. The crowd was moving towards them. He crashed the gears into reverse, but the Humvee was blocking his only exit.

Stevie punched his arm. 'Drive at them.'

His hands were slick with sweat. Magnus revved the engine and accelerated at the crowd, but the square was too small to allow him to build speed. The black-clad assembly scattered, without a single scream. He was a bull, they the matadors. Unless he killed them all, he and Stevie would be raised on the empty gibbets beside poor Adil and Rob.

Magnus turned the van, gears crunching, tyres spinning against the cobbles. The crowd had fled to the shelter of the cathedral doorway. He twisted the steering wheel, aiming towards them. There was a crack of gunfire and the van went into a sickening spin. Magnus tried to steer into the skid, but the van kept whirling, the world a slur of smearing colour. He remembered the cans of petrol in the back and unlocked his door, ready to bale.

Stevie's gun flew from her hand into the footwell of the cab. She swore and tried to grab it, but the spin pitched her back in her seat and the gun slid out of reach beneath her chair. Another shot cracked the air and the van slumped. The skid slowed. They hit a metal refuse bin that had been cemented there by a long-ago council for the benefit of tourists, and came to a halt.

Stevie groped for her gun. 'Fucking drive.'

The van's front tyres were blown. Black-clad men were smashing the windscreen and side windows with hammers. Magnus reached for his gun, but strong arms dragged him from the cab. He looked for Stevie and saw her bucking and kicking as she was pulled into the square. Magnus feared the hammers in the men's hands more than he had ever feared a bullet; more than he feared a noose around his neck.

He shouted, 'We're outnumbered. Don't fight them.'

Stevie was in the air now, two men holding her arms, another two her legs and ankles. Her body went limp. She shouted, 'I'm unarmed!'

Her captors looked towards the blonde-haired woman, who still held the rope draped across her arms. She nodded and they lowered Stevie to her feet. Two of them kept a bruising grip on her arms.

Magnus was pressed in amongst a group of men. They held him by his neck, arms and back. They were warm, trembling from excitement, like men about to have sex. These were the people who had killed Adil. Magnus knew that he and Stevie were dead.

Their captors steered them together across the small square to the cathedral steps, where the group had reassembled. Magnus turned to look at Stevie. Her hair had come undone in the fight. It hung in matted strands across her face, but he could see her strained expression, her skin dulled with fear and exhaustion.

'I should have ditched the van when you told me to.'

Stevie shook her head. 'We were damned from the moment we ignored that first warning sign.'

Two men stepped from the Humvee. They were in their late teens, lean and muscular.

Magnus called, 'Good driving, lads. I think we can say you won. We'd like to head on our way now.'

It was all bravado. The young men ignored him and took places at the back of the crowd. The woman had dropped her arms and was holding the skeins of rope, stretched taut between her hands. She looked at Stevie.

'Why didn't you turn back?'

Stevie returned the woman's stare. 'We wanted to get somewhere. Why did you murder that child?'

The woman's brow creased. 'He was warned and chose to ignore the warnings. The penalty is clearly stated.'

Magnus did not want to look at Adil's corpse. But he could still see the boy in the corner of his eye, swinging slightly in the breeze. It was too easy to imagine his progress across the square to the gallows; the firm hands propelling him over the cobbles; the boy begging for his life.

Magnus said, 'Adil was a good lad. He was only fifteen. He'd have gone away if you'd told him to. You didn't need to kill him.'

The woman twisted the rope. 'We take no pleasure in killing.' Magnus looked from the hands coiling and uncoiling the rope to the faces of the men and women in the square and did not believe her. The woman said, 'The Sweats were a penance from God. He destroyed our families; our mothers and fathers, our siblings, our children and grandchildren as punishment for ignoring His laws. We learned our lesson. Other towns have perished, but we survive, by God's grace. Were we to welcome anyone who does not follow His law, God would smite us.' The small group of people at her back were nodding. She repeated, 'We take no pleasure in it. We pray that God accepts each death as a sacrifice and welcomes the fallen into His kingdom.'

Stevie made a noise of disgust.

Magnus asked, 'Were Adil and Rob alone?'

The woman nodded to the corpses. 'If they had had companions, they would be with their friends in death.'

Stevie said, 'What was your job, before the Sweats?'

The woman raised her chin. 'I was a mother. I raised my children until they were taken from me.'

Stevie straightened her spine. 'What about your children? Were they sinners? Is that why they died?'

The woman lowered her eyes. 'It was God's will.'

Magnus had hoped that there would be some ritual before they were dragged to the gallows, a purification ceremony or prayer service that would give them a chance to escape, but the woman simply looked at the men restraining them and said, 'It's time.'

Stevie and Magnus bucked and struggled as they were forced across the square. Someone started to sing 'Amazing Grace' and the rest took up the refrain. Magnus had forsaken religion while he was still a teenager, but his mother had been strong in her faith. The song had been a favourite of hers and Magnus felt the insult of it in his killers' mouths.

He shouted, 'Better Christians than you died of the Sweats. If there's a God, you're all going straight to Hell.'

They were close to the line of gallows now. Magnus could smell poor Adil's body. He tried to dig his heels into the ground, but the men gripped him tight by his elbows and half-dragged, half-carried him across the cobbles. Someone had taken the rope from the woman and was expertly threading it into place. Quick hands formed it into a noose. Magnus strained to look at Stevie and saw the same procedure taking place at the adjacent gallows. Stevie was facing away from him, still kicking out at her captors, her head twisting, looking for a chance to butt or bite.

'Damn you.' Magnus sought for language they would under-stand. 'Damn you all to Hell. You're Satan's arrow. The Devil is working through you.'

The sound of singing grew louder in the square below. Magnus's guards remained silent, save for the odd grunt of exertion, as they forced him towards the steps that led up to the small platform. A hammer jutted from one of the men's pockets. Magnus struggled to free a hand and grab it, but the men tightened their grips on him. He heard a clatter and saw that Stevie had fallen against the steps to her gallows. Her captors righted her and shoved her onwards.

At first Magnus thought the throbbing noise was the sound of his own blood pounding through his head. When it grew louder, he thought it was the Humvee, revving up to capture other wayward souls. The singing stopped. Magnus's guards faltered. He turned to look at the square and saw the Humvee still outside the cathedral, where the teenagers had parked it.

A brace of motorcycles screamed into the old marketplace. The men at Magnus's back froze. The motorcyclists came to a halt. They were dressed in leathers, their faces hidden behind their visors. The lead biker reached up and removed his helmet.

Joe's face was red, his hair dishevelled. He pointed a gun in the direction of the gallows and shouted, 'These belong to me. Let them go and there'll be no trouble.'

The woman with the flaxen plait stepped forward. Her voice was clear as fresh water, calm as a still pool. 'They have broken our laws. The penalty is death.'

Joe turned towards her. The gun in his hand turned with him. It pointed at the woman's chest.

'Don't worry, cunt, they're going to die, just more slowly and painfully than this.'

The woman furrowed her brow. 'Didn't you see our warnings? The penalty for trespass is death.'

Joe looked at the woman, as if he was only now seeing her.

'You're fucking insane.' He took in the assemblage, their black clothes and still expressions. 'All of you. Mad as fucking hatters.'

The woman took a gun from the pocket of her dress and shot him in the stomach. Magnus heard her say, 'Slow and painful.' And all hell broke loose.

His guards relaxed their grip, unsure of whether to hold him or go to the aid of their comrades. Magnus snatched the hammer from a guard's pocket and smashed one of his cheekbones. The soft crunch of flesh and bone was horrible; the sound of a rotten apple, falling in an orchard. The man dropped backwards, clutching his face. The guards on the platform reached for their guns. Magnus hit out, aiming for knuckles, elbows, kneecaps, anything to keep them from getting a grip on their weapons.

The woman who had killed Joe shouted, 'Death to blasphemers!', and one of Joe's posse shot her in the head. The death of the woman hit Magnus's guards harder than any hammer blow. They let out a collective cry of pain and abandoned him for the fray.

Stevie had run up the steps to the gallows and taken the hanging rope. She was poised on the platform's edge, waiting for a chance to jump. Magnus began swinging the hammer like a claymore. Stevie saw him and leapt to the ground. She bent her knees as she landed, but lost her balance and tumbled into a roll. Magnus reached out and pulled her to her feet. He was out of breath, but managed to gasp, 'The Humvee.'

He had thought Joe's leather boys the likely winners, but the religious brethren were fighting hard. Stevie and Magnus kept their bodies low, skirting the small square until they reached the Humvee. Stevie tried the driver's door. It was unlocked. Magnus slipped into the passenger seat. There were no keys in the ignition.

'Fuck, fuck, fuck.' Stevie flipped down the sun visor and slid free the ignition card tucked inside. The Humvee growled awake.

Stevie turned it towards the battle. A bearded man fell across their bonnet. His face left a smear of blood on the windscreen. Stevie braked and he fell free. She pressed her foot to the accelerator and steered down into the town. Magnus searched the Humvee for weapons, but there were no guns in the glove compartment, no hidden rifles in the back. His only weapon was the hammer he had stolen, still clutched in his hand.

He said, 'The roadblocks.'

A bruise was turning damson on the side of Stevie's face. She shook her head, as if trying to throw off the pain inside it.

'I'm hoping they've moved those lorries. The roadblock that trapped us was designed to be opened and closed like a drawbridge. That woman and her followers wanted people to disobey their warnings, so they could maze them in. How else would they have the thrill of stringing blasphemers up?'

Stevie steered the Humvee into the industrial estate. She was right. The lorries were gone, the jaunty ice-cream float no longer there. She drove on, towards the main route to Glasgow.

Magnus watched the empty road retreat in the wing mirror and thought of Adil, swinging on his rope, food for the birds. It was hours before either of them spoke. By then the landscape was softening, the mountains replaced by rolling hills.

Magnus said, 'If we make it home, I'm not going to tell Francesca the truth. I'll make something up.'

An abandoned car rested in the long grass by the roadside. A vestige of a figure was slumped in the driver's seat. Stevie focused on the way ahead.

'Adil was a sweet boy. He was a team player. I can't imagine him wandering far from Shug and Willow.'

'Do you think that mad bitch was lying?' Magnus turned the hammer in his hands. 'Do you think they murdered the rest of them as well?'

Stevie stared straight ahead. 'I think Belle used Adil and Rob, the same way miners used to use canaries. She sent them on ahead and when they didn't come back, she took another route.'

A road sign appeared on their left: *Glasgow 60 Miles*.

Magnus said, 'Shug wouldn't . . .'

The sentence tailed away. Once he had been able to predict his son's actions, intuit his thoughts. Now he felt he no longer knew the boy.

Stevie said, 'You should sleep. We'll be there soon.'

'I can't. You rest. I can drive.'

Stevie's face was drawn. Greenery had grown from the roadside verges and she was obliged to drive along the centre of the highway.

'I feel like I did when the Sweats first hit London. I'm scared to close my eyes, because of what I might see.'

They drove on, the white lines on the road speeding towards them like arrows, the encroaching countryside flashing by.

Thirty-Nine

They descended into Glasgow in the late afternoon. The sun had been with them on their journey, but now it was hidden behind clouds. Stevie saw the city laid out in the basin below, a mosaic of tenements, greenery and tower blocks. There were gaps in the view; whole districts laid black and wasted. Fires had stripped some high rises to their metal frames. They crumbled upwards, skeletons dissolving into the glooming sky. She kept her foot pressed to the accelerator and sped the Humvee on, down towards the ruined city.

Abandoned vehicles had clogged the approach to all the cities and towns on the journey. Several times Stevie was forced to divert onto minor roads to avoid jams that stretched to the horizon. She remembered her own panicked flight from London and knew they were remnants of an exodus that had failed to outrun infection.

As they neared Glasgow the numbers of vehicles multiplied. For the last thirty miles, broadening lines of stalled traffic bore witness to the panic at the pandemic's height. The exit routes to every city in the world would look the same Stevie realised: Athens, Paris, Rome, Tokyo, Manhattan, Chicago, San Francisco . . . She had seen disasters played out so often in Hollywood movies that it was easy to picture American cities. Other countries had receded into landmarks: the Acropolis, Eiffel Tower, Colosseum, Godzilla . . .

Stevie had feared that the final stretch of road would become impassable. But though the traffic deepened, the way remained open. Eventually the motorway shrank to one narrow lane. She saw that cars had been shunted to one side to keep the way clear. Her skin tingled. The job had taken manpower and organisation. The people who had carried it out would be waiting, somewhere up ahead.

Magnus had fallen asleep after all, the hammer cradled in his lap. It was their sole weapon, primitive and only good for close combat. Stevie reached out and touched him gently on the shoulder. Magnus jerked awake. His grip tightened on the hammer and he looked at her without recognition. Stevie felt a flash of fear, then Magnus's eyes focused. He rubbed a hand across his face. His bristles rasped. 'Where are we?'

'Almost in Glasgow.'

The city rose around them. Slip roads fed into new carriageways, each clogged with abandoned cars. Trees wavered on the banking, but the Humvee was the only thing moving on the road. They crossed a bridge over a broad river. White gulls swooped and dived above the water.

Magnus said, 'There are people down there, mending nets.'

Stevie slowed the Humvee to a halt. She peered at the riverbank below and saw brightly painted boats moored by the river's edge. Men and women were hunched around fishing nets, spread across the boats' decks. The wretchedness of Adil's death and dread at what might come next had coloured everything. The sight of the fishing folk prompted a guilty flutter of excitement in her.

One of the fishermen lifted his head and looked towards the sound of the Humvee's engine. He pointed towards it. Others paused to look in their direction. Stevie raised a hand in greeting, but they lowered their heads and returned to their nets.

Stevie let her hand fall. 'I've been driving this stupid tank so long, I forgot it has tinted windows. I guess they couldn't see us.'

A faint note of disquiet sounded inside her. She pressed her foot on the accelerator and drove on, trying to shake off the sense that there had been something defeated about the hang of the heads of the people mending nets.

A road sign listed the distances to places Stevie had never been; faint memories from vanished traffic bulletins. The motorway branched into swooping curves that stretched above and below them. This was where traffic would have jammed in the mornings and early evening, with commuters travelling to and from work. Now there were only lines of derelict vehicles.

Stevie said, 'Have you noticed, there are hardly any bodies in the cars?'

Magnus had not spoken since the people repairing their nets had failed to return her greeting. She sensed him surveying the windows of the rusting, metal carcases.

He said, 'Do you remember how hard it was, clearing the dead from Orkney?'

'I'll never forget it.' Stevie felt another faint sliver of hope. 'People are cooperating with each other.'

Magnus's voice was wary. 'Perhaps, but so were people in Eden Glen and Dounthrapple.'

'We're trying to make a better future on the islands, why shouldn't people be trying to make one here too?'

'No reason.' Magnus tapped the head of the hammer gently against his palm, as if testing its weight. 'But this is a big city. It's too soon to let our guard down.'

'My guard's been up so long its hinges are rusted stiff.'

Warehouses and tenements rose like giant megaliths either side of the motorway, some so close that it felt as if the road had been blasted through a fully formed city. The Humvee was still the only car moving, but the fishermen and women had heard the engine and somewhere other survivors would be observing their progress from darkened windows.

Magnus said, 'Do you think I was too soft on Shug?'

'You're a good dad. You wouldn't be here now if you weren't.'

His face was turned away from Stevie, looking out at the piles of cars.

'My father used to beat me. Not badly and never for no reason. He was brought up to believe that boys needed discipline. I loved him, but there were times when I hated him too. I swore that if I had children I'd never raise a hand to them. Maybe if I had . . .' He faltered. '. . . maybe if I'd set firmer limits . . .'

Stevie remembered Shuggie as she had last seen him: sulky and half-drunk, sitting at the Stromness Hotel bar at the Easter cele-brations, waiting for Willow to arrive. Magnus had been sulky and drunk that night too, because of something to do with the boy. She said, 'Did you rebel when you were Shug's age?'

Magnus leaned his head against the passenger window and looked at Stevie.

'I got a motorbike when I was sixteen and drove it full pelt, the length of the main island. My poor mother thought I was going to come home in a body bag – several body bags. How about you? Were you a problem teen?'

'No one ever hit me, but I got tired of being the only mixed-race girl in a small town. People kept telling me I could be a model, so I packed my bags and headed for London when I was seventeen. I guess that was my act of rebellion.'

Magnus had never asked Stevie about her life before the Sweats. He said, 'How did that work out?'

She smiled. 'There were lots of pretty girls in London, more exotic than I was. I didn't become a model, but I made a life.'

'I guess that's what we've all been trying to do since the Sweats, make a life.' Magnus looked away again. 'I keep thinking of poor Adil. He was a good lad and they killed him just for being in the wrong place.' He let out a long, juddering sigh. 'I don't care who killed Bjarne and Candice any more. I just want to find Shug, Willow and little Evie and bring them home.'

Stevie measured her words. 'I want to find them too, but we won't have a home worth the name, if we don't try to get justice for Candice and Bjarne.'

Magnus's voice had a bitter twist. 'Candice was a poor, put-upon soul who didn't deserve to die. But Bjarne was a shit. It's a miracle no one gave him what he deserved sooner. If somebody had, perhaps poor Candice would still be alive.'

Stevie steered the Humvee slowly along the narrow stretch of cleared motorway, careful not to graze against the scrapyard of abandoned cars, piled high in the lane beside her.

'Is that the kind of place you'd want to live? Somewhere anyone can murder people they dislike and get away with it?'

The motorway bent into a long curve designed to slow speeding traffic. The piles of abandoned cars stretched on, blocking their view of the road beyond.

Magnus said, 'You killed three men in Eden Glen, but I don't see you volunteering for a trial. Christ, you put a gun to a baby's head at Scrabster. I'm guessing that used to be considered against the law.'

The Humvee edged to the left and scraped against an articulated lorry. There was a screech of metal on metal, but the armoured vehicle held steady. Stevie swore beneath her breath and touched the brakes.

'Eden Glen is lawless. That's why those men felt free to try and rape me.' She sensed contradictions in her argument, but pressed on. 'If the district had a rule of law, I'd step before its court and accept its judgement.'

Stevie didn't mention baby Mercy. She felt ashamed of the way she had put the gun to the child's head and held it hostage.

Magnus let out another sigh. 'You say that, Stevie. You probably even believe it, but I know you. You're always convinced you're on the side of right.'

She was about to remind Magnus that he had vouched for Belle and the men with her, but the curve they had been travelling on straightened out and the view was clearer. The roadblock she had been half-hoping for, half-dreading, waited up ahead. Stevie slowed the car. She saw Magnus slip the hammer into his pocket and knew his hand would stay wrapped around its handle, ready to strike.

Forty

The blockade was different from the ones they had encoun-
tered in Dounthrapple. Three men and a woman, wearing
black sports gear beneath high-vis jackets, waited by a barrier that
spanned the motorway's free lane. They each cradled semi-auto-
matic rifles of the kind issued to the armed police who had
haunted airports and large railway stations in the years before the
Sweats. A sign was fixed to the barrier. Magnus read the words
painted across it out loud: 'Glasgow Smiles Better.' Mr Happy, a
grinning, yellow ball of a figure, equipped with stumpy arms and
legs, was painted next to the slogan.

The female border guard held up a hand and stepped into the
middle of the road, confident of her power to halt their progress.
Her rifle rested against her large chest. Her face was soft and
pleasant; worn by familiar marks of suffering. Stevie stopped the
Humvee and rolled her window down a couple of inches.

The guard's lips were frosted with pink lipstick. Her smile was
warm, her hands steady against the metal of her gun. She looked
somewhere in her late forties, but it had grown hard to age people
since the Sweats.

'Welcome to Glasgow.' In the streets beyond, tenements were
blackened and derelict, but there was no irony in the woman's
voice. She glanced behind her at the three men, still clustered
around the barrier. 'Am I on my own here?'

The guards looked at each other with affected nonchalance. The tallest of them gave the man on his left a not so gentle shove. The man muttered something that might have been *piss off*, but he picked up a clipboard from the bonnet of a car and sauntered towards the Humvee, hips pitching an unconvincing swagger, eyes lowered. Stevie sensed Magnus's grip tightening on the handle of the stolen hammer.

'Thank you, Billy.' The woman rolled her eyes at Stevie. 'You'd think these boys would be keen to meet new folk, but they're the laziest set of fearties I've met. They're scared you're going to gun them down, but they cannie be bothered to run away.' She put a hand on Billy's arm and pulled him closer to the Hummer. 'See Billy, it's only a nice, young couple come to help with the clean-up.'

Billy looked in his early thirties, broad-shouldered and ruddy from outdoor work.

'Piss off, Maureen.' His voice was free of rancour. He nodded to Stevie. 'Are yous healthy?'

Stevie gave him one of her best salesgirl smiles. 'Yes, we're both well.'

Billy's cheeks flushed a deeper shade of red. He reached into the pocket of his jacket and produced two glass thermometers.

'Stick these under your oxters please, next to the skin.'

Stevie slid her hand down the neck of her shirt and pressed the thermometer in her armpit. The glass was cold against her flesh. A musky, unwashed scent rose from inside her clothes.

'Is the city free of the Sweats?'

Billy shrugged. 'Seems so. For now, anyway. There was an outbreak last year, but they caught it quick and isolated the folks that had it, poor buggers.'

'It was a false alarm if you ask me.' Maureen crossed herself. 'Not like the first waves, folk falling down dead in the street with no warning, kids coming home from school and finding their parents had passed away.'

Billy pulled on a pair of latex gloves.

'People still died, Maureen. You wouldn't be calling it a false alarm if it was you who was deid.' Billy held out his hand for the thermometers. Stevie and Magnus passed them over. He glanced at the mercury scale. 'Aye, yous're fine.' Billy lowered his eyes to the clipboard and made a note. 'Where have yous come from?'

'Orkney.'

'Orkney.' Maureen repeated the name. Her smile was wistful. Stevie thought she was going to tell them that she had holidayed on the islands before the Sweats, but she simply said, 'A long way.'

Magnus leant across Stevie. He pressed a button on the driver's side door, scrolled the window down further and flashed the woman a grin. A breeze carried the smell of a distant fire from somewhere down below the motorway. Wood smoke filtered through a chemical tang that reminded him of London burning.

'Anyone else from our neck of the woods passed through?'

Billy gave Magnus an apologetic look. 'We're not meant to share details of comings and goings. People post photos and contact details in George Square if they want to be found. You can check there, once you're registered.'

Maureen nodded. 'Once we've got your details, the boys will take you to the corpo offices. Someone will sign you up and find out what your skills are. They'll assign you a job and a billet. You can check the notices after.'

Stevie looked at Billy. 'What do you mean, *if* they want to be found?'

The guard shrugged. 'There's been trouble. Folk beaten up . . .' He stared across the interconnecting roads towards a bridge curving through the air; testament to a lost civilisation. '. . . killed.'

Maureen's smile was tight. 'Some people come to the city to get away from bad decisions they made after the Sweats . . . men they hooked up with . . .' She gave Magnus an apologetic look. '. . . or women. You remember how it was.' Stevie sensed a personal story behind Maureen's upside-down smile. She said, 'People were confused, looking for comfort.'

Magnus interrupted. 'We need to find some people. My son is . . .'

Maureen rested a hand against the Humvee and leant into the cab. Her weapon swung gently on its strap.

'We're not being difficult. When we started trying to get the city back on its feet everyone thought reuniting people was top priority. Then it dawned. Families hadn't survived, friends were kaput, workmates weren't there any more. The only people getting together were folk who'd met since the Sweats. Like Billy said, reuniting people wasn't always a good idea.' She looked from Stevie to Magnus and back. 'Have you met anyone you knew from before?'

Magnus said, 'It's not like that . . .'

Stevie threw him a look. 'No, but . . .'

Maureen talked over them. 'I've never met a married couple who both survived or a child who still had a parent.'

Stevie took Magnus's hand in hers.

'There are new families since the Sweats. Sometimes they need help.'

Magnus pulled his hand free. He fixed his eyes on Maureen's.

'I'm looking for my foster son. Someone beat him up. He and his girlfriend went on the run with some strangers they'd just met. A woman called Belle and a bloke who looks like a tough nut. Shuggie's a naive lad. He's not been beyond the Orkneys since he was seven years old. He thinks he's grown-up, but he's not. I need to make sure he's okay.'

A shadow crossed Maureen's face. 'How old is he?'

'About fifteen.'

Billy said, 'Old enough to know his own mind. Old enough for privacy.'

Maureen nodded. 'It's hard for kids that survived, but Glasgow's a small city, smaller than it was. If he's here and wants to be found, you'll run into him.'

Magnus held her gaze. 'They took our daughter with them. Her name's Evie. She's eighteen months old.'

Stevie widened her eyes, the way she'd been taught to on a sales training course, back when she was starting out.

'Shug's a good lad, but he's jealous of Evie. The beating unhinged him. We're worried he might harm her.'

Maureen's brow puckered. She looked from Magnus to Stevie, as if trying to make her mind up about something. She said, 'It hits them when they reach puberty, everything we've lost. They don't know how to handle it . . .'

Billy spoke quietly, too low for the men at the barrier to over-hear: 'Don't ask me to bend the rules, Mo. It's not fair.'

The woman straightened up, the rifle back against her chest.

'Remember Stevo? Maybe if we'd bent the rules he'd still be here, taking his turn holding the clipboard.'

Billy hissed, 'Don't fucking start . . .'

His voice must have carried. One of the men loitering by the barrier called, 'Everything all right, Mo?'

Maureen threw him a smile. 'Just getting their details, Davy. They're from the islands.'

Davy nodded as if that explained everything. Maureen turned her attention back to Billy.

'If they came this way they'll be on the register . . .' She turned to Magnus and Stevie. 'The New Corporation are trying to keep track of who's here, so they can assign them work tasks and the like. It'll take a while, but we want to get the city back to what it was. The population's rising.' Maureen's smile was proud. 'It'll take more than a plague to destroy Glasgow.' She looked at Magnus. 'What did you say your boy's name was?'

'Shuggie McFall. He was probably travelling with a woman called Belle, a man, a teenage girl called Willow and a toddler called Evie.'

'Go on, Billy, you can see they're beside themselves. The wee one's only eighteen months old.' The woman gave her colleague a nudge. 'It'll do no harm and it might do some good. Maybe they came in when the other team were on.'

Billy's feet shuffled against the tarmac. He glanced back at the other guards, before meeting Magnus's eyes.

'No offence, but for all I know you could be a bounty hunter, a ganger or a whoremaster on the lookout for escapees. I'd like to help but . . .'

Stevie whispered, 'Please . . .'

Maureen's voice hardened. 'We don't have time for foreplay, Billy.' She rolled her eyes, indicating the other guards, still loitering by the barrier. 'Davy and Malcy will be over in a minute to find out what's taking us so long.'

Billy made a face. 'You'll get me shot one of these days, Maureen,' he said but he was already turning the pages pinned to his clipboard, moving quickly now that he had made the decision to help. 'Four people and a baby, that'd be a red-letter day.' His face clouded. 'Sorry, mate. After all that, they're not on the list.'

Maureen plucked the clipboard from his hands. 'Give it here.'

Billy said, 'For fuck's sake.' The men by the barrier went for their guns. Billy held up his hands. 'It's all right, lads, just Maureen having a carry-on. You know what she's like.' He gave her a pointed look. 'A bloody, silly twat who'll get us wur heids blown aff one of these days.'

Maureen was flipping back through the surprisingly thick sheaf of pages pinned to the clipboard. She paused and ran a finger down a column. The friendliness fell from her face.

'What did you say the woman's name was?'

Magnus tried to catch her eye, but Maureen looked away. He said, 'Belle.'

Maureen shook her head. 'There's no mention of her or the others here.'

Stevie said, 'Yes, there is. You saw something.'

Maureen passed the clipboard to Billy. 'Put that away. You'll not be needing it.'

Billy hissed, 'I'm meant to write their details down, Mo. Their names and all that.'

'You don't need their names. They'll be heading back the way they came.'

Maureen's eyes met Stevie's. 'My gran was from somewhere on Orkney. She died before I was born. I never went there, but my mum said it was a lovely place. Glasgow's a good city, but it's not for everyone, especially since the Sweats. You'd be better going back to your island.'

Magnus's voice was resolute. 'I'm not going home without my boy.'

'Your boy is on his way and there's nothing you can do about it.' If Maureen wondered why Magnus did not mention Evie, she gave no sign of it. She cast a sympathetic look at Stevie. 'Take my advice. Go home and have more babies while you're still young.' She glanced down at her own body, the rifle cradled in her arms. 'That's what I'd do if I were you.'

Billy touched the older woman's arm. 'Mo . . .'

Stevie said, 'Who's head of the city corporation?'

Maureen shook her head. 'You don't want to see him. Anyway, Mr Bream's a busy man.'

Stevie looked towards the barrier where the other border guards had each lit up a cigarette. She raised her voice. 'I'm the elected president of the Orkney Islands. I'm here on a diplomatic visit and I demand to meet the head of your council.'

The guards looked at each other. They took a last drag of their cigarettes, then tossed them to the tarmac and ground them out. There was something comic about the synchronisation of their actions, their perfect timing, but nobody smiled. The guards ambled towards the Humvee.

Maureen shook her head. In a voice too low for the approaching men to hear she whispered, 'Why the fuck did you have to go and do that?'

Forty-One

They were down in the centre of the city, travelling past neglected tenements and derelict shops, each window a dead soul. Stevie had relinquished control of the Humvee. She was sitting in the back, a hand's breadth from the border guard Maureen had addressed as Davy. Magnus was in the front passenger seat next to the other guard, Malcy.

Malcy was driving, his rifle hanging by its shoulder strap from a peg beside the window. Maureen had argued that she and Billy should ferry them to the City Chambers, but the two men had held firm. These guards were of a different stamp from the woman and her clipboard-wielding colleague. They had patted Stevie and Magnus down and confiscated the stolen hammer. The guards found it hard to believe it was the only weapon in their possession and had searched them and the Humvee twice.

'Can't be too careful.' Malcy's eyes watched Stevie in the rear-view mirror. 'I could tell you tales that would curl your hair.'

They were driving along an empty road, lined either side by four-storey tenements. Sycamores and other greenery had colonised the buildings' gutters and their facades were water-stained and crumbling. Abandoned shops regarded the street from the ground floors. A few were secured by aluminium shutters, but most sat grimy and abandoned. Windows had been smashed in the panic that had hit at the peak of the Sweats and its aftermath. Premises had been stripped of stock and left to fester. Some walls were blacked by fire. Others graffitied with cryptic messages: *TONGS YA BAS, GOVAN YOUNG TEAM 5 ALIVE, BREAM IS THE FISH AND THE TREE AND THE RING.*

Stevie met the driver's gaze. 'Maybe I could tell you a few hair-curling tales of my own.'

Malcy's skull was freckled beneath a short buzz cut, a brown egg ready for smashing.

'I bet you could.' His grin was hungry. 'I've a nice bottle of malt hidden somewhere safe. We could swap war stories over a dram.' Malcy glanced at Magnus. 'If your man doesn't mind.'

Magnus kept his expression closed. 'We're looking for our kids.'

Malcy snorted. 'And you think seeing Mr Bream will help you find them?'

Stevie said, 'You don't?'

The shoulders inside the high-vis jacket shrugged. 'There are folk who go to the top when they want to find something out and folk who start at the bottom. Starting at the top might seem like a good idea. These guys know a thing or two, right?'

Stevie kept her voice the not-quite-sunny-side of bright. 'I'm guessing you think wrong?'

'The boys at the top of the ladder may have some information, the names, facts or figures, but are they willing to share them? A working man on the other hand . . .' The driver let his sentence tail teasingly away. 'Let's just say, sometimes you get a better view of the street when you're closer to the ground.'

They were passing the entrance to a park. Wrought-iron gates slumped on rusting hinges. Trees reached beyond the railings, their branches casting leaves and shadows against the pavement, their roots crazing the concrete.

Magnus turned to look at Malcy. 'You do realise we're talking about children? A wee girl, less than two years old? A couple of fifteen-year-olds?'

'You must be beside yourself,' Malcy said with false solicitude.

Stevie gentled her voice. 'They went off with a woman called Belle. She's distinctive, long, blonde hair – good-looking, but her face is badly scarred.'

'I might have seen her.' Malcy's eyes met hers in the mirror again. They were pouchy and soft-looking, like molluscs deprived of their shells. 'Have a dram with me and I'll tell you.'

Magnus said, 'You're fucking kidding me. We don't have time for this.'

'I'm talking to her, not you.' Malcy looked at Stevie again. 'What about it, love? I promise I won't bite, not unless you want me to.'

Davy spoke for the first time. His accent was Glaswegian, diluted by travel or aspiration. 'The Teuchter's right. We don't have time to muck about. If you know something, tell them. If you don't hold your *wheescht*.'

Malcy's laugh was forced. 'Don't you get it, Davy? The world's over. All the rest is just marking time.'

Davy was the oldest of the pair by a good decade. He looked like he had been weathered in a windswept landscape. His hair was tangled, cheeks a mess of broken veins, large ears sticking out, as if caught from behind by a force-ten gale.

'Cut it out, Malcy. I know what you're at. It's not on.'

Stevie said, 'I'll have a drink with him, if he can tell me something that'll help us find the children.'

Davy had unstrapped his gun from his chest. It lay across his lap, the muzzle pointing towards the street.

'I know you would, love. You'd let him fuck you up the arse if you thought it might get you your kids. I'd let him fuck me any which way too, if there was a ghost of a chance it'd bring my son back. But Malcy's just winding me up and leading you on.'

They were climbing a steep street sandwiched between high office blocks, the sky a thin strip of grey above them. Buildings slumped beneath their neglect. Lintels were crumbling, window frames untrue, sills rotting, glass cracked. Rain had seeped into the structures' fabric and water stains bloomed across their facades like Rorschach blots.

A couple of skinny horses, harnessed to a cart, waited patiently by the kerb, their eyes shielded by blinkers, their long faces obscured by nose sacks. They made Magnus think of his own horses, steady Straven and his pride and joy, Jock the Clydesdale. A rook landed by the cart and hopped towards fallen sprinklings of grain. One of the horses stamped a hoof. The rook cawed and bounced away, its button eyes still on the prize. Two men dressed in fluorescent vests stepped from one of the buildings carrying boxes loaded with wires and computer equipment. The rook took to the air.

Magnus followed the men with his eyes. Their loads recalled Rees's stocks of obsolete technology. 'Looters?'

Davy's speech had left Malcy unruffled. He slowed the Humvee and looked at the laden men.

'Salvage crew. Bream and the corporation keep us busy.'

Stevie leaned forward. She whispered into Malcy's ear. 'Do you know something about our kids?'

The driver turned to look at her. 'Have a drink with me and I'll tell you.' His voice was half tease, half threat. 'You look like a girl who knows how to cut loose.'

'Ach, Malcy lad, I fucking warned you.'

Davy grasped Stevie's shoulder and pushed her gently but firmly back into her seat. There was a click clack of metal, the unmistakable sound of a mechanism setting and he stuck the barrel of his gun against Malcy's skull, just below his left ear. The interior of the Humvee shrank.

Malcy batted at the muzzle with his hand. 'For Christ's sake, Davy. That's not a toy you're playing with.'

Davy jabbed the gun against the driver's skull. 'This is me cutting loose. How do you like it? One squeeze of the trigger, you'll stop marking time and start marking the car seats.'

Malcy batted at the gun again. 'You're not funny.'

'I'm not trying to be fucking funny.'

Malcy slowed the Humvee to a halt outside an abandoned Italian restaurant. 'What's this about, Davy? It can't just be because I chatted up some lass.'

'You don't get it, do you?' Davy's face held the calm expression of a maniac dispensing logic. 'Do you remember the History Channel? All those programmes about the Nazis? I'd watch them of a night with a beer in my hand and think about how we were on the right side of history. Looking back, I think I might have been a tad smug.' A bead of sweat trickled down the side of Davy's face. He blinked, but did not loosen his grip on his gun to wipe it away. 'Recently, I've not been feeling so sure about things. I've not felt like I'm necessarily on the right side of history. Do you get my drift? Working for Bream and the New Corporation doesn't give me a warm fuzzy feeling.' He set the gun on his knees. 'If you know something about where their kids are, tell them.'

Stevie felt the interior of the Humvee shrink a little further. She could detect the scent of the men's individual sweat. She touched her face. Her hand came away wet and she realised that she was sweating too. She said, 'You'd remember Belle. She's tall and slim with lots of blonde hair. One of her eyes is injured and she has a long scar down her face but like I said she's still beautiful.'

Stevie recalled Belle as she had last seen her, the wind lifting strands of her hair as she perched on the ruined walls of Cubbie Roo's Castle.

Malcy let out a long sigh. 'I saw her yesterday. I recognised her, from way back.'

Surprise lightened Magnus's voice. 'From before the Sweats?'

'Afterwards.' Malcy gave him a quick sideways glance then turned his attention to the broken shopfront, the weed-choked pavement. 'Everyone I knew from before is lost and gone.'

Davy's gun was still resting on his lap. He stroked its handle as if fascinated by the texture of its patina.

'Stop feeling sorry for yourself.'

'I'm just trying to explain how things were. The Sweats hit me hard.'

'The Sweats hit everyone hard, you narcissistic twat.'

'I didn't even notice it was the end of the world at first. I worked in a warehouse, a fucking hundred aircraft hangars long. They were automating our asses. Demanding one-hour delivery times. Fucking drones buzzing through the warehouse carrying impulse buys. We knew there were going to be layoffs, so when less people started turning up at work, I put it down to that. It wasn't until the orders packed in that I realised something was wrong.'

Davy booted the back of the chair. 'They're not interested in your life story. Tell them where you saw the woman.'

'I need to get it straight in my head, Davy,' Malcy said. 'Stuff from back then gets jumbled. I hated my job, but the weird thing was, I kept going in, even when I was the only one left. I didn't know what else to do. After a while I stopped going home. The streets were too quiet. I'm not a soft touch, you know that Davy, but being outside scared me. I made myself a nest in a corner of the warehouse. Everything I needed was there. Food . . . drink . . .' He paused, as if trying to remember other things necessary for survival. 'There was a TV in the staffroom. When it stopped working I hooked up a DVD player. There were centuries of films in stock. All the box sets you could want.' His voice grew wistful, the way another man's might remembering lost family. 'I even built myself a nice big bed. No one to share it with, but that didn't matter. First time I got in it I slept for three days straight. Didn't even get up to piss.'

Davy said, 'I clocked you for a lazy bastard the first time I saw you. What does all this have to do with the female they're looking for?'

'That's what I'm trying to tell you. She was with a gang that broke into the warehouse. I say gang, but they were more like a party.'

Stevie sounded bemused. 'A political party?'

'No, a party, party. Balloons, jelly and ice cream, pass the parcel . . . except instead of all that they had drink, drugs, sex and music. They called themselves the Kinfolk.'

Davy was still examining his gun. He looked up. 'Sounds like the Sweats did you a good turn, Malcolm.'

Malcy closed his eyes. An expression that might have been grief or perhaps fear fluttered briefly across his face, like rain smeared across a windowpane.

'I was glad to see them, if that's what you mean. It was beginning to hit me, everything that had happened. I was having dark thoughts. I'd started to wonder if I was the only one left. I stayed with them for a few weeks. We travelled and partied and picked up a few more survivors along the way. There must have been a dozen of us by the end. I tried to get with Belle a few times, but she didn't want to know.'

Magnus said, 'Sounds like a good set-up. Why did you leave?'

Malcy shook his head. 'We ran into the wrong people, somewhere not far from Birmingham. At first they were friendly. We thought they were up for a party, like us. They broke out a decent stash and we got stuck in.'

Stevie said, 'A stash?'

'Weed, cannabis, hash, shit – whatever you want to call it. Later I realised we did most of the smoking. I guess that was their plan. When everything kicked off, we were too out of it to fight back.'

Stevie knew what was coming next, but she let Malcy go on.

'Other men arrived when it got dark. They were strangers to us, but they knew our new pals all right. They were after our women. One guy, a fellow called Richie, a good guitarist, stood up to them. He'd been playing most of the night, so maybe he hadn't smoked as much as the rest of us. He laid into the raiders with his guitar, trying to give the girls a chance to get away. They caught him, slit his throat and kicked him into the fire. I didn't wait to find out what happened next. I legged it into the woods. I never saw any of the Kinfolk again, until yesterday when I saw Belle.'

Stevie said, 'Where was she?'

Malcy's voice wavered. 'At the corpo offices. I don't think she recognised me and I didn't say hello. I didn't spot any teenagers, but she had a toddler bundled up in a papoose in the front of her jacket. I thought maybe it was the kid she was due to have when I knew her, but then I realised, it would be older by now.'

Stevie took a quick intake of breath. 'Was the toddler okay?'

Malcy's voice was vague. 'I guess so. I'm not interested in babies. I didn't really pay attention.'

Magnus blinked. 'Belle was pregnant when you knew her?'

Stevie wondered if there was a chance the child might be his. She asked, 'How old would it be now?'

Malcy gave a small shrug. 'How long is it since the Sweats? Five years?'

'Seven.' Davy shook his head. 'How can you not know that?'

'Time passes. I don't count the days.'

Stevie repeated. 'So the child would be how old?'

'I don't know. Time changes when you're on your own. Maybe I met the Kinfolk six months after the first Sweats, maybe it was a year. It felt like a long time. After I met the gang, time speeded up. It felt like I was only with them for a few weeks, but maybe it was longer. Then the raid happened. I was back on my own and time slowed down again.'

Magnus said, 'How did Belle look?'

Malcy shook his head. 'I don't know. Scared . . . excited. The way everyone looks when they first arrive. I was holed up in a cottage somewhere outside Newcastle when I heard the broadcast. It took me a week to get here. I was so keyed up, I sang all the way.'

Stevie and Magnus said, 'What broadcast?' in not-quite unison.

Davy gave a small laugh. 'I guess the signal doesn't reach as far as Teuchterland. Turn on the radio, Malcolm.'

Malcy did as he was told and a female voice sounded faintly through crackling airwaves, like a ghost reaching out from the past.

Come to Glasgow . . . help us make a new society . . . Come to Glasgow . . . together we can make a new and better world . . . Come to Glasgow . . . if you are old, lend us your experience . . . if you are young give us your strength . . . Come to Glasgow . . . the Sweats are over and we are rebuilding the city . . . Come to Glasgow . . . there is work to be done . . . Come to Glasgow . . . help us rebuild the city . . . Come to Glasgow . . . help us make a new society . . . Come to Glasgow . . . together we can make a new and better world . . . Come to Glasgow . . . if you are old, lend us your experience . . . if you are young give us your strength . . . Come to Glasgow . . . the Sweats are over and . . .

'Turn it off, please,' Stevie said.

Malcy leaned forward and pressed the off button. The voice died in mid-sentence.

'Gives you the willies, does it?' Davy nodded. 'It gets some people like that, but it's beginning to work. For good or for bad, people are starting to drib drab back.' He sank into his seat. His posture suggested a man about to grab forty winks, but his eyes were bright. 'We're meant to take you to the City Chambers, but if we do, I guarantee you won't find your kids. Maureen might buy all this guff about making a new society, but things are going the same way they always did. One rule for the rich, another for the poor.' He looked from Stevie to Magnus and back. 'You two are late to the party. You might be president of some island, but you're in the big city now. The prime spots have all been bagged. You'll be assigned to a work party. They'll tell you you're doing your bit for the New Tomorrow, but when you try to leave there'll be someone like Malcy or me with a gun to your back. Your kids'll be long gone.'

Magnus said, 'We'll take our chances.'

Davy grinned. 'You're not listening, are you? You have no chances.'

Magnus turned round so he could look Davy straight in the face.

'The female guard seemed to think everything was okay.'

Davy sighed. The manic gleam in his eyes had dulled. His eyelids looked bruised and heavy.

'Maureen's a nice woman. She hasn't woken up to the fact that the world is still a shithole. She suspects it, but she won't give in.'

Stevie said, 'What changed Maureen's mind? She was all for helping us, then she checked the registration documents and it was as if someone had blown out a light.'

Davy sighed. 'There are two lists. The first list is professions that Bream is keen to recruit: doctors, nurses, engineers and the like. That's the good list – the useful list – the list you want to be on. The second list is a record of names of people who he wants brought to him for other reasons. That one's a bit hit or miss. Sometimes it's famous folk he's heard a rumour survived, but mostly its people who have blotted their copybook in some way. Generally speaking, you don't want to be on that list. I'm guessing your girl Belle's name was there.'

Malcy started the engine and swung the Humvee out into the empty road. 'We need to get going or there'll be hell to pay. City Chambers?'

Davy shook his head. 'I think not, Malcolm.'

Stevie saw Malcy's eyes glancing at his companion in the rear-view mirror.

Davy grinned. 'I'm out of here. I've been thinking about it for weeks. I reckon this could be the incentive I need.' He put his hand on the driver's shoulder. 'Remember I told you about my scrapyard? Fifteen happy years I ran it for. It was my own wee kingdom, a little goldmine. I didn't survive a plague to become a lackey. You might be happy running errands for Bream, but I'm losing my religion.'

Malcy glanced at him in the rear-view. 'What does God have to do with it?'

'I don't mean God. God's neither here nor there. I'm losing faith in the system.' They were driving along a wide street lined either side by Victorian office buildings decorated with carved figures and curlicues. A bearded St Andrew hefted his cross above a doorway to a bank, buxom Patience and Justice loitered in clinging robes on the facade of an insurance office, their expressions implacable. Davy said, 'How long do you think we have? Three years? Five? Ten? The Sweats are still out there and precious few scientists survived to find a cure. I'd like to sign off on the right side of history.'

Magnus saw a sign for George Square. The City Chambers were nearby. 'Drop us here. We'll take our chances.'

Malcy glanced towards the back seat, looking for Davy's approval.

The older man shook his head. 'Turn right and head towards the river.'

Magnus tried the car door, but it refused to open. 'I told you, we want out.'

Stevie remembered the men who had attacked her at Dounthrapple. Panic lit her voice. 'Where are you taking us?'

They turned into a dank road, below a section of motorway. Concrete pillars thrust upwards, supporting the freeway above. Stevie saw something move in the shadows. She thought at first it was a person, then a black dog ran into the open with something limp dangling from its jaws.

Davy heard her quick intake of breath. He squeezed her hand. 'Don't worry.' He touched Malcy's shoulder. 'Through the inter-section and left at the river.'

A traffic light switched from amber to red. Malcy ignored it. Other traffic lights lined the way. All of them dead.

Davy said, 'There's been a bit of unrest, a split in the New Corporation. Word is that an opposition is coming together. Bream pretends not to be bothered, but I reckon he's shitting it.'

Malcy said, 'Are you burning our boats, Davy?'

The older man shrugged. 'Maybe I'll head for the islands, see what's going down there. Fancy it?'

Malcy grinned, pleased to be invited. 'More than I fancy telling Bream we've been giving guided tours of the city.'

Magnus said, 'I'm delighted you two have worked out your holi-day plans. Why don't you find a vehicle of your own and get going?'

'Turn left.' Davy patted the driver's left shoulder, as if he was a horse that needed to be nudged in the right direction. A hint of mania had returned to his face. 'We're doing you a favour. You can do us one in return.' He grinned at Stevie. 'Fair's fair.'

Malcy turned the Humvee into a narrow street. It was the kind of place Stevie would have sought out on a city break. A much publicised 'hidden corner' designed to tantalise in-flight magazines and tourist guides.

Davy tapped Malcy's shoulder. 'Here'll do.'

Malcy drew into the kerbside, outside Curl Up & Dye, an abandoned hairdresser's shop.

Magnus turned towards the back seat. 'This is our car.'

Davy shrugged. 'Armoured vehicles like this are hard to come by. We've got guns. You haven't. Suck it up.' He pointed outside. 'Last sighting of the opposition was somewhere around here. I reckon you don't have to do much. Just let yourself be seen. They'll find you.'

Malcy said, 'They're unarmed, Davy. It's not safe.'

The older man shrugged. 'They were unarmed when we found them.'

Malcy pressed a button on the dashboard and the vehicle's doors unlocked with a click. Stevie saw Magnus's fists bunch. She touched his arm.

'It's not worth fighting for.'

Magnus got out of the front passenger seat. Stevie opened her door and stepped onto the pavement outside the salon. She leaned back into the Humvee and looked at Malcy. 'Check the petrol gauge. You've got about three miles left in the tank.'

Davy started to say something, but she shut the door on his words, his feverish smile. The Humvee's engine revved, loud in the quiet street. It sped towards the corner and was gone.

Forty-Two

The Humvee had barely disappeared from sight when they saw the dogs. The pack ran in their direction, a snarling body with many slavering jaws and wavering tails. The dogs were generations from the pets that had been left to fend for themselves when the Sweats took their owners. Magnus followed Stevie, leaping over the jagged glass of the hair salon window, into the gloom of the shop. Women with fabulous hair scowled at them from skewed pictures on the walls. Rows of tall mirrors had been smashed, their fragments muted beneath dust. Magnus's boots slipped against the scree of shattered glass. He bumped into a lamp and sent it toppling to the ground.

Stevie was ahead of him, barrelling through the salon. 'Scissors . . .' She rifled the surface of a cutting station, swearing under her breath.

Magnus swept his hand across a counter littered with debris: combs, brushes, kirby grips, tubes of dye, a hairdryer; but not a cutting blade in sight. The dogs were in the shop now. A brown and white beast with pit-bull ancestry was at the head of the pack, its mouth foaming with rabies froth.

Stevie picked up a bottle of shampoo and hurled it at the dogs. She barged through a door at the back of the salon and Magnus followed, into a small, windowless room, barely bigger than a cupboard. There was no lock on the door. They flattened themselves against it and felt the weight of the pack batter and bark against the other side.

Magnus whispered, 'How long will they keep this up?'

It was too dark to see Stevie's face, but the door was untrue and a little light leaked into the small room. He could make out her body. The flare of her hips beneath the too-large pair of men's trousers she had looted in Eden Glen.

'Until an easier target comes along.' The door jumped at their backs as the dogs kept up their assault. 'Or until they break through this matchstick wood and have us for dinner. They'll stop when our bones are clean.'

'Thanks for that.'

Magnus pressed his full weight against the door. The walls of the small room were made from hardboard, the ill-fitting door from the same flimsy material. It had been bashed together by somebody with no pride in his work. Magnus's eyes were beginning to adjust to the dark. He made out an aluminium sink set into a single kitchen cabinet. A microwave sat to its right. The sink was littered with mugs and plates. Where there was crockery there might be a knife. He stretched towards the worktop, but it was a hand's breadth too far for him to reach with his back against the door.

Stevie saw what he was reaching for. 'Think you can hold them off by yourself for a moment?'

'I'll do my best.'

She darted away and started to look through the abandoned plates and mugs.

'Shit, shit, shit . . . fucking hairdressers . . . forks and butter knives.'

She remembered that rabid dogs were afraid of water and tried the tap, but it was dry. The pack was howling now.

Magnus said, 'Any chemicals? Ammonia or bleach or whatever it was women used to dye their hair with?'

Stevie was rooting through the cabinet beneath the sink.

'Washing-up liquid and cloths.' She kicked the cabinet shut.

The dogs heard the noise and slammed against the door with renewed force. The door juddered at Magnus's back. It seemed looser than before and he worried about its hinges. It was too dark to see what Stevie was doing, but he could hear her knocking against something. The dogs heard her too.

'This is just a partition.' She was back inside the kitchen cabinet, pulling at the pipes beneath the sink. 'If we rip it out, we might be able to smash our way into the next room.'

'Let me try.'

Stevie braced herself against the door. Magnus put his arms around the cabinet and hauled. A long ago leak had rotted the hardboard behind it and it came away more easily than he expected. Plates and cutlery clattered to the floor. The dogs bayed. The hairs stood up on Magnus's body. This pack would be one of many roaming the streets. He wished for a gun and thought of Shug. It was only a few years since he had bathed the boy each night in the kitchen sink, cautious of the temperature of the water, careful not to scald his tender skin.

He shoved the kitchen cabinet across the small space. There was a tricky moment while Stevie slid aside still holding the door and Magnus scooted the cabinet into place, but they managed it, both of them drenched in sweat.

Stevie lent her weight to the barricade. 'This won't hold them off for long.'

Magnus pulled at the wood, widening the gap.

Stevie said, 'I'd rather die running than crouched in a hole.'

Magnus kicked at the rotten partition, braced for an assault from the other side of the wall. He wanted to remind Stevie about

Thelma and Louise, her resolve to live beyond their adventure, but it felt too much like tempting fate. The damp wood crumbled and split. He glimpsed a pale sheen of light, distant grey in the darkness.

'I think there's another exit.'

'How far?'

'Too far to tell.'

They worked quickly together, slotting bits of broken partition between the base of the kitchen cabinet and the uneven floor, trying to jam the barricade in place. The dogs heard them moving and hurled their bodies against the door, snarling. The cabinet rattled. Soon it would give way. Flesh was nothing against sharp teeth and strong jaws.

Magnus missed the weight of a gun in his pocket. He said, 'Dogs are stupid animals,' although he had known plenty of smart dogs in his time.

'Let's hope so.' The hole had grown big enough for them to squeeze through. Stevie crouched, ready to go first. Something rustled in the darkness beyond and she hesitated.

Magnus squeezed her shoulder. 'Let me.'

He crawled forward on his hands and knees, exposed to whatever lurked there. It was a small hole and he was forced to turn sideways to get his shoulders through. The floor beneath his hands was cool tile, his face gritty. Magnus got to his feet, coughing. He was in some kind of hall. Light leaked dimly from the ceiling. He stared upwards and saw large windows set in a vaulted roof, high above; their glass rendered almost opaque by grime and fallen leaves. He thought of the red sandstone of Kirkwall Cathedral, the building's atmosphere of permanence, which had been a comfort, even though he was not a religious man. There was a whoosh of air, so solid he raised his hands against it and let out a small cry. A flock of pigeons swooped through the space, a swirl of dust and feathers. They circled, regrouped and glided back to their roosts.

Stevie was quick behind him. 'We need to find something to cover the gap.'

Magnus said, 'What do you think this place was?'

'A shopping centre.'

Stevie spoke as if it was obvious and Magnus realised she was right. Retail units circled the central hallway. His eyes sharpened and he saw that the hairdressing salon they escaped had a locked and shuttered entrance onto the shopping area. The soaring roof space above them was interrupted by a mezzanine housing more stores and cafes.

Stevie was dragging at a counter that had belonged to a concession stand. He took the counter's other side, pleased by the solid weight of it. Together they shoved it against their escape hole.

The sound of the dogs had receded, but there were other noises, too faint to grasp. Magnus scanned the atrium and realised that any resemblance to Kirkwall Cathedral was superficial. The shopping centre was falling apart. Its ceiling had been decorated with bronze, artichoke-shaped lamps which now hung precariously amongst exposed cabling. Some had fallen to the floor where they lay shattered, like doomed spacecraft. The roof was breached in places, the walls blackened with damp, the floors buckled. The usual looting had left traces of plundered goods in its wake; clothes flattened against the floor like atom bomb shadows.

The most arresting thing about the shopping centre was not its damaged shopfronts, peeling display boards or toppled benches. It was not the bird shit and feathers that clumped and spattered beneath roosts of cooing pigeons. A thick layer of grey dust coated the space. It lay smooth against the floor, ruffled in places by the scurryings of small creatures. The dust had crept across abandoned furniture, settled in cracks and grooves, had slid, thick and silent, across every fold and scratch. It gave the centre a grainy atmosphere: black and white TV footage, fuzzed with static. It caught in the back of Magnus's throat, powdered his skin.

He had imagined Shug and Willow somewhere like this. Had secretly thought they might be glad to be found and returned to the relative comfort of Orkney. But it would be exciting to be young and at the centre of a city's rebirth. For the first time it occurred to him that Shug might have been right to leave the islands. Wrong in the way he had gone about it. Certainly wrong to be involved in little Evie's kidnapping, but right to make a grab at life.

Stevie touched his arm. 'Let's get out of here.'

She walked towards a phalanx of stalled escalators and the faint glow of light beyond them. Magnus followed her, reminded again of the shoot-em-up computer games he had played as a boy. They had been located in cityscapes like this. Desolate buildings, full of corners and hidden cells, where enemies could hide unobserved. He missed his lost Glock, regretted the confiscated hammer.

The shopping centre had been designed to allow crowds to sweep through its halls. Magnus looked up at the mezzanine and saw they were exposed from every angle. A snatch of video footage returned to him. People running across the open concourse of a mall, while gunmen with concealed faces mowed them down; bodies dropping to the ground; white tiles smeared red.

Stevie's voice was soft. 'Do you remember all this? These shops?'

He saw what she meant. *The Body Shop*, *Next*, *Boots*, *Clintons*, *Lush*, *H. Samuel* . . . The once familiar shopfronts made him think of Christmases past, the squash of crowds in Oxford Street as he struggled to find presents for his mum and sister Rhona, the rush to get his parcels to the post in time.

Their escape from the dog pack seemed to have exhilarated Stevie. Her voice was brighter than it had been since they left the islands.

'I used to love shopping.'

'I couldn't stand it.' Magnus had owned two smart stage suits. One midnight-blue, the other black, both lined with scarlet satin. The rest of his wardrobe had been the same as he wore now: jeans and T-shirts, a jumper when the weather required.

Stevie said, 'Would you wish it all back, if you could?'

Magnus was trying to tread carefully, but the floor was gritty beneath its layers of dust. Every footstep announced their presence.

'There are people I miss. I'd wish them back. I'd wish back medicine too: dentistry and hot water, comedy clubs and pubs, TV, cinema, trains . . .' He let his words tail away. It was a foolish question and he was foolish for answering it.

The exit was in sight, an outsize, revolving door that would once have magically spun when customers approached.

Magnus said, 'Here's hoping that's not locked.'

Stevie was no longer paying attention. She touched his arm. 'Did you hear that?'

They froze in mid-footstep. Magnus forced himself to stay still. To run blindly might be to run towards danger. The noise sounded again.

Stevie nodded towards the dim of a shop unit. 'There.'

Magnus heard it. A single note plucked on a guitar string. He glanced back the way they had come.

'Keep moving.' He put a hand on Stevie's elbow, as much to steady himself as to urge her on. A chord twanged. It was a G followed by an F and an E.

Magnus was no longer master of his limbs. He halted. 'I know that song.'

Stevie was a step beyond him. 'What?'

'"Wade in the Water".'

Stevie screwed up her face. She looked as if she wanted to hit him. 'So?'

Magnus felt stubborn and stupid; unsure of why he needed to stop, but certain that he must. 'I've got to check it out.'

Stevie pulled Magnus to the shelter of one of the escalators. The staircase offered poor cover. They were exposed from three sides and the mezzanine above. They hunched down, instinctively making themselves smaller.

'You were the one who told me to keep my guard up. Someone could be trying to lure us.'

The fear of cannibalism he had been prone to since the Sweats flitted across Magnus's mind again. He shook his head. 'It sounds stupid, but that song means something.'

'For fuck's sake, Magnus. We're only a few miles from the City Chambers. Belle might still be there, she could lead us to the kids. We can't afford to lose any more time.'

He knew Stevie was right. They had come so far, it would be tragic to spoil it by dying now, like an ancient explorer drowning on the stretch of sea between his galleon and a newly discovered land.

Wade in the water, wade in the water . . . The guitar picked out the notes and the chorus sounded in Magnus's head.

'It's a protest song, an old protest song.'

He thought Stevie was going to tell him to pull himself together, but a stillness came over her. The song stopped too, as if the guitarist were allowing them time to think. Outside the sun must have emerged from behind a cloud. The interior of the shopping centre brightened and the exit glowed like a promise. Something rustled close by, breaking the spell.

Stevie got to her feet. 'Okay, we'll trust your instincts. No one wants to find the kids more than you do. And if there is some kind of opposition, we should find out what it's about, before we walk into the middle of it.'

The music started up again, low and tentative, the bones of the song played in a nervous staccato, like a distress call from the rubble of an earthquake.

Forty-Three

The shop unit was in a twilight gloom that recalled illicit afternoon pints in London snugs. It took Magnus a moment to realise where they were, then he saw the decals peeling from the walls. Sweet-faced princesses, amiable beasts and animals with grins that were all personality. Magnus had forgotten the franchise existed, had never been in one until now. He whispered, 'It's the Disney Store,' though Stevie had probably already realised the place's identity.

The shop's stock had been ransacked. The unit was empty, except for bare display cases and a few overlooked toys. Magnus's foot crunched against something. He looked down and saw a plastic tiara snapped in two beneath his boot. The tiara was small, designed to crown a child. He picked both halves up and examined the false jewels moulded to its silvered peaks. Once there had been whole factories dedicated to such fripperies; teams of workers packing plastic gewgaws snug in boxes, for distribution across the globe. He thought he should be disgusted by the waste of industry, but a wash of nostalgia pricked his eyes. He set the broken pieces gently on a display case, treating the toy like the artefact it was.

Stevie nudged him. He followed her gaze and saw a slight figure sitting cross-legged in a corner, cradling an acoustic guitar.

The guitarist was dressed in black. They wore a wide-brimmed felt hat and despite the gloom, a pair of dark sunglasses. There was something of the self-conscious troubadour about the guitarist's style. Magnus wondered if they had chosen the Disney Store because they were attracted by fairy tales and romances.

He crouched on the floor, keeping his distance, and spoke softly.

'My name's Magnus and this is my friend, Stevie.'

The guitarist looked up; they were young. The hair beneath the hat was long and parted in the centre, the guitarist's eyes hidden behind the sunglasses. The face might have been sweet, were it not for the wry cast of the rosebud mouth.

'Aren't you scared?' It was a pink voice, small and sugar-coated.

The question threw Magnus. 'Should I be?' His answer sounded stiff, more aggressive than he meant.

Stevie crouched beside the child. 'All the time. Are you?'

The guitarist looked at the fretboard balanced on their knees and drew their fingertips across the strings.

'I try not to be. It helps to accept that you're going to die. If you're not afraid of death, you're not afraid of anything.'

It was the kind of adolescent philosophising Magnus had grown used to from Shug. He said, 'Pain can be worse than death. Everyone is afraid of pain.'

The guitarist nodded. 'Maybe.'

The hat and glasses were like a disguise, the long hair a curtain in the shadows. Magnus realised he did not know whether the small figure was a boy or a girl.

'What's your name?'

'Briar. Sometimes people call me Bri. I don't mind.'

The name gave no clues to the child's gender.

'My name's Magnus and this is Stevie. We're looking for some lost kids. We heard your guitar and I recognised the tune, "Wade in the Water". Why did you play that song?'

Briar ignored Magnus's question. 'What do you mean lost?'

Stevie said, 'They went off with some people – dangerous people. They took a baby with them. Her name is Evie. Her mother wants her back.'

Briar plucked at the strings. The words of the song sounded in Magnus's head again.

Wade in the water, wade in the water children, wade in the water . . .

Briar said, 'I've not seen any new kids. Just you.'

Stevie said, 'But there are others around? Other young people?'

'Why aren't you in a work team?'

The carpet of the shop was black and decorated with stars that had once been bright. It was powdered with fine sprinklings of dust. Dust clung to the guitarist's oversized dark clothes and floppy hat too, making them look as if they'd been there a long time.

Magnus got to his feet. 'We need to go. They could be anywhere by now.'

Briar raised his/her head to look at him. 'It's good that the song called you, but it's not enough. You don't look like gangers, but looks aren't enough either. I need something more.'

Stevie said, 'What do you mean?'

'I need something more, before I can trust you.'

On the wall behind Briar's head a fairy princess lifted the hem of her long white gown. The princess's butter-yellow hair was wound into a knot. A blue ribbon was pinned around her throat by a diamond clasp. She held a matching bluebird on the finger of one hand. The bird had a coy expression on its face, as if it suspected it would not be long before he and the princess got down to doing the dirty.

Magnus said, 'If you're thinking of sending us off on a quest, forget it. I've got my hands full in that department.'

Briar's smile was sudden. Dentistry was a dead art, but it was still a shock to see the jagged teeth behind the sugarplum lips.

Stevie got to her feet. She opened her jacket and pulled the lining out of her pockets.

'We're unarmed and we want nothing, except any news you might be able to give us about Willow, Shug and little Evie.'

Briar said, 'You want more than that. You want weapons. You want to know how things are organised here. You want to stay alive. You want a lot.'

Apart from Shug, a gun was what Magnus wanted most in the world. He shook his head. 'We didn't ask for any of that.'

'But you want it. Or would you prefer to step outside with nothing to protect you from the dogs? The New Corporation are trying to get rid of them, but the packs keep getting bigger.'

The sweet voice was grating on Magnus's nerves. He took a deep breath. 'This was a mistake.'

Briar held up her/his left hand. A small cross was tattooed in the centre of the palm.

'Want to know why I played that song?'

The thought of Shug was like a magnet, pulling Magnus from the store, but the song had been the thing that lured him there. 'Yes.'

The child got to his/her feet and took off the dark glasses. Briar's irises were so pale they were almost translucent.

'It's about escaping slavery. Slaves told each other to wade in the water, because it would throw the dogs that were hunting them off their scent. But it's also about the Israelites crossing the River Jordan and escaping their slave masters.' Briar added, 'Israel was a country. The Israelites came from there.'

Magnus made no reply. He already knew the history of the song.

Stevie said, 'You stand for freedom. So do we. If Shug and Willow decide they want to stay in Glasgow, we'll let them, on condition they give us little Evie.'

She made no mention of making them account for the murder of Candice and Bjarne.

Briar shook his/her head. 'It's not enough to be for something. To be truly effective, you have to be against things.'

Magnus laughed. 'What are you against?'

Briar flashed the wide grin, revealing the jagged, bomb-blast teeth. The laconic air was gone.

'Pretty much everything.'

A howl stretched across the mall followed by a chorus of barks. Briar shoved the guitar onto his/her back and drew an assault rifle from the folds of the dusty, black jacket. Magnus swore and Stevie took a step forward, ready to grab the weapon.

'Take it easy.' Briar aimed the gun at them and held up his/her tattooed hand. 'This isn't for you.' The howling sounded again. Fear tugged at the guitarist's mouth. 'Swear I can trust you?'

Magnus drew a cross over his heart with his finger. 'You can trust us.'

Briar looked at Stevie who held up her right hand. 'I swear.'

The barking was close enough for them to hear the dogs' individual timbres – high yelps and gruff, snarling growls.

Briar looked in the direction of the noise. 'I guess I either trust you, or let you become dog food.'

It felt wrong for Stevie and Magnus to shelter behind the small figure, but Briar led the way, out into the main shopping centre, the assault rifle clutched in both hands. They jogged through the hall, raising plumes of dust, the brim of Briar's black hat bobbing. Magnus felt the dust catch the back of his throat and tried not to cough. It was affecting the guitarist too, he noticed. The child set a brisk pace, but as they crossed the hall, he/she held a hand up to their face and coughed.

He had thought they were heading outside, but Briar led them across the atrium towards a door marked STAFF ONLY. A broken keypad was fixed to the wall by the door, wires lolling from it. Briar gave a quick glance towards the noise of the dogs, then took a key from a bag at his/her waist, unlocked the door and ushered Magnus and Stevie into a small stairwell.

'This way.'

Briar's running shoes were dusty black too, silent against the concrete stairs. Magnus felt his chest bunch. The guitarist must have heard his laboured breath because he/she turned to look at him. 'Not long now.'

They reached a landing and another locked entrance. Briar led them along a white corridor punctuated by doors. This section of the building had clearly been the centre of the mall's operations. Instructions for employees to *BE VIGILANT* still hung on the walls. *Are they wearing a big coat to hide something?* asked a poster, decorated with the image of a swarthy man bundled in an over-sized parka: *SEE IT, SAY IT, SORT IT!*

Magnus heard a movement from a room beyond and felt a sudden panic.

Briar raised a fist and gave a complicated series of knocks. There was the sound of a key turning in the lock and the door opened.

Forty-Four

Magnus braced himself for a room full of young revolutionaries, but the man on the other side of the door was in his sixties: lean, with a weathered face and grey beard. He ushered Briar into the room with obvious relief.

'You made it.' The old man gave the small figure a hug that knocked the wide brimmed hat sideways. He kissed Briar on the forehead, both cheeks and the rosebud mouth, and then shook Magnus and Stevie's hands. 'Welcome, I'm Ivan.'

Stevie and Magnus mumbled their names. Ivan clapped them both on their shoulders, as if making sure they were real.

'We saw you from up here and were worried the dogs might attack you. Briar volunteered to go to your aid.'

Magnus looked at the guitarist. 'So all that, about not trusting us, was a game?'

Briar shrugged. 'Not a game. Ivan's too trustworthy. That's why I volunteered to go.'

Ivan was dressed in lightweight boots, walking trousers and a heavy shirt, topped by a fleecy gilet. It was an outfit designed for survival.

He shook his head. 'A slight exaggeration.'

Briar's eyes met his. 'You took me into your home before you knew me. I could have slit your throat easy.'

The old man stroked the child's hair. 'Just as well I'm a good judge of character.'

The room was bigger than the modest door had led Magnus to anticipate, its far side dominated by a large, bow window that looked down onto the central shopping hall. A bank of switches and microphones sat beneath the window. Most of the furniture in the room had been pushed to one side, except for a couch standing in the middle of the room. A figure lay on it, bundled beneath blankets. An old lady sat by their side, her white hair cropped short, like a nun's. She too was dressed in walking gear. She spoke to Briar without acknowledging Stevie and Magnus.

'Grace is no better. I think she may be slipping away.'

Briar went to the couch. Stevie and Magnus's eyes met.

Ivan caught their look. 'It's not infectious. Grace has reached the end of her time. I suspect she won't be sorry to go.'

Stevie went to the window and looked down on the abandoned mall, as if a natural death was nothing to remark upon.

'The dogs have found their way in.'

Magnus joined her. A dozen or so dogs were lolloping across the concourse, raising clouds of dust. They nosed the ground, keeping close to each other, making their own looping trails through the space. Magnus searched for the pit bull that had been at the head of the pack but could not find it.

'I think it's a different lot.'

Ivan joined them at the window. 'The dogs are one of the city's biggest problems, but they help un-allied people like us. Bream's squads are reluctant to patrol, except in numbers and numbers are what he still doesn't have.'

The old lady tending to dying Grace started to hum a song. Magnus did not recognise the tune, but it made him think of home; the outgoing tide sucking the shale with it; a hiss of waves, a tumble of sand and stones. The pink sky streaked with gold as the sun went down. It would be good music to die to.

Briar had taken off the wide brimmed hat and placed a hand on the dying woman's forehead. The guitarist's long hair fell forward as he/she bent over the couch, whispering a prayer. The sound of Grace's rattling breath reached over the song.

Ivan said, 'Excuse me.'

He knelt beside the couch and took one of the dying woman's hands in his. Briar reached for Ivan's spare hand and the old man joined in the whispered prayer. It was a scene worthy of Rembrandt. The old couple and the dying woman an augur of what was to come; the young guitarist a reminder of what had been.

Down below, the dogs circled the shopping centre concourse, lean and battle-scarred, their ribs visible, bellies concave. They reminded Magnus of photographs that had once illustrated appeals for rescued pets.

Briar had unstrapped the assault rifle as they'd entered the room and set it on a filing cabinet next to the door. Magnus glanced at it. Stevie followed his gaze. She raised her eyebrows. Magnus gave a small shrug. The rattling breaths coming from the couch had grown louder. It would be a simple thing to make for the door, grab the rifle, demand the building's keys from Briar and be gone.

He whispered, 'I don't think I can do it.'

Stevie nodded. 'Me neither, but these aren't the people we were hoping to make contact with. There's no point in staying here.'

For a moment Magnus thought she was going to summon the ruthlessness she had shown baby Mercy at Scrabster, but Stevie crossed to where the trio were holding vigil. She crouched beside the guitarist and whispered something in his/her ear. Briar nodded and spoke softly to Ivan. The old man closed his eyes. He leaned over and placed a kiss on Grace's forehead, then gripped Briar's shoulder and used it to help him get to his feet. He touched the dying woman's cheek and walked slowly to the window where

Stevie and Magnus stood. Gravity had won control of his face. The bags beneath his eyes sagged, his mouth drooped.

'Briar says you're looking for a kidnapped baby.'

Magnus nodded. 'Two teenagers and a kidnapped toddler. We know they came to Glasgow, but we don't know where they are now.'

Ivan spoke gently, like a man used to breaking bad news.

'The baby will have been given as a reward to a childless couple unable to have children. There are a lot of them since the Sweats, so many I've wondered if there's a link between infertility and immunity.' He took off his glasses and wiped his eyes. 'You won't get it back. Are the teenagers male or female?'

Stevie said, 'We have to get Evie back . . .'

Ivan put a comforting hand on her arm and repeated his question. 'Are the teenagers male or female?'

Magnus said, 'One of each. They're both around fifteen years old.'

Ivan slipped his glasses back onto his nose. 'The boy will probably be in one of the recycling factories. The girl . . . if she's lucky, she'll be there too.'

Stevie rubbed her face. 'And if she's unlucky?'

Ivan looked to where Briar was crouched over the dying woman.

'Girls are especially vulnerable. There are comfort stations on Glasgow Green. The sex workers are meant to be volunteers but . . .'

Stevie said, 'I'll shoot anyone who touches Willow.'

Magnus squeezed her arm. 'We'll find her.'

The old man took off his spectacles again and rubbed the bridge of his nose before replacing them.

'The baby will be well looked after. I advise you to let it go. Your chances of getting the other children back are slim. Life has become labour intensive since the Sweats. There's a lot to do and not enough people to do it. Some newcomers are . . .' Ivan hesitated, searching for the right word. '. . . disadvantaged. There are rewards for people who can supply the city with workers.'

Magnus remembered the salvage workers he had seen loading a cart; their weary trudge and slumped shoulders. 'By workers, you mean slaves.'

The old lady had resumed her song. Ivan looked towards where she and Briar were hunched over the dying woman.

'Provost Bream is an exceptional man, charismatic, single-minded. He's determined to get things up and running again and he won't allow a little squeamishness to get in the way. We might not agree with his methods, but we have to accept that he has a point. The world was always unfair. Since the Sweats, divisions have simply become a little starker.'

Magnus took in the dreary office, the dying woman shuddering her last breaths on the couch.

'You talk like you know Bream personally.'

Ivan looked towards the window, down into the shopping centre where the dogs had settled in the dust, small groups curling against each other for warmth and comfort.

'I do . . . did. We were amongst the first to return to the city. I thought we were going to build a place worth living in. Instead . . .' His words tailed away.

Magnus recalled his own poor judgement. He had welcomed Belle and her companions to the islands. Now Adil was dead, Sky risking her life on the journey back to the Orkneys, Shug and Willow enslaved and little Evie lost, perhaps for ever. He rubbed a hand across his face.

Stevie said, 'We were told there was an opposition. We came here looking for them.'

Ivan frowned. 'Here, specifically?'

'We were told the opposition was located in this district.'

'Then I fear we're in trouble. We need to move as soon as . . .' Ivan glanced at the couch where the old lady lay and his meaning was clear. He turned to Stevie and Magnus again. 'During the Sweats some people claimed to have seen Jesus walking down streets where the dead were piled high. In times of trouble, rumours and superstition abound. There are pockets of opposition. I've seen signs. Anti-Bream graffiti on walls, valuable salvage scattered across roads. But most people are relieved to have a strong man at the helm. They see a group of kids being brought into the city and believe we're saving them from starvation.' Ivan raised a hand to his mouth and coughed. He took a handkerchief from his pocket and spat into it. 'Odds are, your kids have been processed and put to work by now. I'd check the main recycling plant. It's down by the river in the old Fish Market. Bream has an idea that cold helps preserve salvage, but it's hard on the recruits. They sleep where they work.'

Magnus shook his head. 'Shug and Willow have been brought up with freedom. They're rebellious, mouthy – they won't knuckle under and accept orders.'

Ivan made a face. 'You'd be surprised.'

The old woman's singing had been wavering on softly in the background. Now it faltered. Briar called Ivan's name. The old man muttered an apology and hurried to the couch.

Magnus felt the uselessness of it all. He sunk to his haunches.

Stevie crouched beside him. 'We'll find them.'

Magnus shook his head. 'I keep seeing Adil swinging from that rope. Christ, we don't even have a gun between us.'

The sound of gentle sobbing reached across the room. Magnus stood up and wiped his face with his sleeve. The rattling breaths had ended. The body lay flat on the couch, a sheet smoothed over its features. Briar was crying. Ivan put an arm around the small figure and said, 'Would that we could all have such a peaceful death.'

Magnus looked at Stevie. 'We've got to go.'

Stevie ran a hand through her hair, smoothing it behind her ears in a calm way that did not quite hide her fear.

'No point hanging around.'

'Wait.' The old woman who had been tending to dying Grace rose to her feet. Her face was pale and wrinkled, but age had not touched her fine bone structure, her sharp cheekbones. Magnus felt a shiver of déjà vu. A single tear ran down the woman's cheek. Her voice was clear. 'No one gets far without a gun these days.'

Magnus said, 'We'll have to do our best.'

The old woman bent stiffly to her knees. Magnus thought she was going to resume her prayer but she dragged a rifle and a pistol from beneath the couch and placed them by her dead companion's body.

'Grace would have wanted these to go to a good home.' She pulled herself upright with the aid of one of the couch's arms. 'There's not much ammo, so you'll have to get more or go easy. I find that if you shoot the lead dog it can keep the rest of the pack at bay, depending on whether they're rabid or not.' She made a face. 'There's a lot of rabies these days. I imagine it came through the Chunnel.'

Stevie took the weapons from the woman. She weighed the rifle in her hand and passed the pistol to Magnus. 'Thank you.'

'*De nada*, as we used to say.' The woman met his eyes and Magnus realised that he had spent hours in the dark watching her face appear in close-ups on a screen twenty-feet high. Her hair had been darker then, cropped just as short, but in a more sophisticated style.

He said, 'I remember you, from before.'

The woman's smile dazzled years from her face. She covered her mouth with her hand and closed her eyes in mock self-deprecation.

'Vanity is the last thing to die.' She put a hand on the still sobbing Briar's head. 'It's all dust now, but there's some consolation in knowing my films still exist, even if only in a few people's memories. I'm not going to spoil things by asking which ones you saw.'

It was an invitation, but the substance of films escaped Magnus and there was something dreadful about the sight of the woman grinning at him from across the fresh corpse.

Briar pulled free of the actress's touch and joined them by the window, wiping away tears. 'Ask them, Ivan.'

The old man draped an arm around the small figure, pulling the child close and putting his lips to his/her cheek in a way that made Magnus uneasy.

'If we could increase our numbers we might be able to begin forming a credible opposition. Natalie and I are too old to become commandos, but we have a lot of valuable experience between us.' Ivan looked fondly at the guitarist. 'Briar's young and untried, but willing to learn.' His eyes met Magnus's. 'We would make good comrades.'

Stevie slung the rifle the old woman had given her over her shoulder. 'We can't turn back now.'

Ivan nodded, as if her answer was inevitable.

Briar had put an arm around Ivan's waist and was leaning against him, hip to thigh. He/she seemed younger in the old man's embrace.

'You could come back, once you've found your kids. They could join us too.' Briar's words came out in a rush. 'We saved you.'

Ivan returned Briar's hug. 'They don't owe us anything.' He looked from Stevie to Magnus. 'Don't mistake Bream for a movie villain or a deranged psychopath. He's not Hitler or Stalin, conniving for the greater glory of himself or some messianic ideology. Bream sincerely believes he's acting for the good of the community. His solution to the city's labour problems may trouble him, but he's willing to shoulder an uneasy conscience in order to do what he believes is right . . .'

Magnus's voice was tight. 'So your advice is to give up?'

The old man stroked a hand through Briar's long hair.

'Let me finish. Bream has two weaknesses and two corresponding fears. Much as he believes in what he's doing, Bream would rather the nature of his workforce wasn't too widely known.'

Stevie said, 'Word gets around. If the city's as small as you say it is, people will already know he's using slave labour.'

Ivan gave his small, sad smile. 'People know what they want to know. Most of them will convince themselves the system benefits the slaves. Bream is leader of the city by popular consent. It's in his interest to keep people in the dark. And when it comes to uncomfortable truths, in the dark's exactly where most people want to stay.'

Stevie said, 'Are you suggesting we threaten to expose him?'

Ivan snorted. 'Threaten Bream with exposure and you'll wake up dead.'

Magnus said, 'You said he wasn't a psychopath.'

'Everything's relative.' Ivan dragged a hand across his face. His features drooped further, then moulded back into shape. 'The city's approaching a crucial stage. Bream's determined to convert salvage into new resources. He's making progress. His workers—'

'Slaves,' Stevie corrected him.

Ivan stumbled over the word. 'His *slaves* have succeeded in reclaiming valuable assets but, despite his radio broadcasts, he hasn't attracted new settlers in the numbers he'd hoped.'

Magnus thought of the desolate countryside they had driven through. He recalled Lord Ramsey's men and the brethren tearing each other apart in Dounthrapple's Merkat Square.

'Maybe there aren't as many survivors as he thought.'

Ivan sucked in his cheeks. His thin face and white beard gave him a goatish aspect.

'Could be. But Bream fears he's open to attack. He's got assets and not enough personnel to protect them. It's made him prone to paranoia.'

Briar's grin was bold. 'That's why he threw us out. He didn't like Ivan and me being friends. It made him paranoid.'

Magnus looked at the small body, hugged so close to the old man's they were almost entwined and felt unexpected kinship with Bream.

Stevie said, 'What do you mean he threw you out?'

Ivan winced. 'We disagreed on how to run things.'

Briar talked over the old man. 'Ivan was Bream's deputy. I was working in the recycling plant when he found me and recognised my potential. Ivan made me his assistant, but Bream didn't like it. They quarrelled and we had to run away. Natalie and Grace came with us.'

Natalie had been brushing her dead friend's hair. She paused in her task.

'Old prejudices reassert themselves in times of trouble. People in the New Corporation wouldn't accept that Ivan and Briar are in love.'

Magnus resisted the urge to take the small figure by the shoulders and prise them free of the old man's grasp.

'How old are you?'

The child threw him a defiant look.

'What difference does it make?'

Magnus nodded towards Ivan. 'He's taking advantage of you. You're too young to realise it, but he knows.'

Ivan put his hand on the curve of Briar's skull, almost cradling the child's head.

'Our age difference would have been considered a problem before the Sweats but—'

Magnus's voice was ice. 'You would have been put in jail.'

Natalie said, 'Oh for God's sake.'

Ivan released his hold on Briar's head and raised his hand in the air, silencing her. His voice was gently reasonable.

'Relationships like ours were forbidden, but the Sweats put everything into perspective. What does the difference in our ages matter? We're both alive in a world full of the dead. I help keep Briar safe and Briar makes my life worth living.' He squeezed the guitarist's shoulder. 'Tell them your story.'

Briar twisted his/her head away.

Ivan said, 'Don't be shy. It might help them understand.'

The old man's gentle coaxing invoked old tabloid reports of minicabs cruising darkened streets and charmed teenagers climbing from the windows of children's homes; vodka bottles, pills and friends-to-be-kind-to.

Magnus said, 'You don't have to do anything you don't want to.'

Briar disentangled his/her body from the old man's and sank cross-legged to the floor. Ivan followed suit, using the child's shoulder to steady himself. He drew his knees up with the aid of his hands. Ivan's old head looked ghastly on top of his thin body. As if he had transplanted himself into the corpse of a teenager, but been unable to alter his face.

Natalie began brushing Grace's hair again. She hummed to the dead woman in a light, wavering voice. There was a brittle edge to the melody that suggested her teeth were clenched. Magnus wanted to tell her to shut up. He stayed on his feet, too angry to join the storytelling circle on the floor.

Briar's voice was low. 'I used to live with some kids in the railway arches down by the river. I lived somewhere before that, but I don't remember where. The arches were cold and damp. The rats wouldn't leave us alone. Sometimes they brought the dogs with them. Rats and dogs hate each other, but they travel together. We'd collect stones and fight them off with catapults and slings.' A boast entered Briar's voice. 'I killed more dogs than anyone. Wham!' The guitarist shot a clenched fist into the air, miming a punch. 'Once I killed a lion or a tiger; a big cat with teeth like a trap. I sent a rock between its eyes and it dropped like a stone. I ate its heart to get its power. We ate the dogs too, so we could grow strong and fierce like them.'

Now the tale had begun Briar's mood was reckless, his/her grin wild. 'After I ate the lion's heart, I could feel it alive inside me. I ran faster. My teeth were sharper.'

Ivan sucked in a long, whistling breath. 'They were feral children, abandoned and half-savage.'

Briar looked at him. 'I was whole savage, couldn't hardly speak except in tunnel-talk.'

The sound of howling came from the mall below. Natalie's song died, the hairbrush lay still in her hand.

Ivan touched Briar's hand. 'Tell them how you ended up in the recycling plant.'

Briar's smile faded. He/she looked towards the sound of the dogs.

'Some men came. We hid, but they knew we were there. They lit a fire and started to cook dog stew. The men sang songs while they waited, songs we didn't know. We were scared as puppies, but the smell of the stew and the heat of the flames called us. We sneaked close enough to hear their songs and steal warmth from the fire. We could hear the men chewing the meat, crunching the bones. We crept closer. The men spoke our tunnel language. They offered us food and talked, while we filled our bellies. They said they knew a place where we would always be warm and well fed. There were women waiting for us there; kind women whose children had died and who wanted new sons and daughters. Some of the kids said the men were child snatchers. They gobbled their stew and ran away, but when the sun came up, four of us followed the strangers into the city.

'It was exciting at first. We marched across town, singing our tunnel songs. We travelled further from our den than any of us had travelled before, but we weren't afraid. The men had guns. When dog packs came for us they shot the king dog and the rest went running. We cheered and the men gave us sweets to eat.' Briar paused. 'I knew what my new mother would look like. I could see her face. She had clean, blonde hair that smelt good and a smile that made you feel happy. No one showed me a picture, but I knew that was how she would be.'

Shug had gone through a phase, when he was around eight years old, of suggesting women Magnus might marry. Nothing had come of it. The women the boy liked had tended to be too motherly for Magnus's tastes and the women Magnus fancied were never the mothering kind.

He looked at Briar. 'I'm guessing she didn't exist?'

'I think maybe she does, somewhere. But the men didn't take me to her. They led us to a big building full of stuff. There were different men there, three of them. They didn't smile or give us nice things to eat. They took us to piles of salvage and showed us what to pick out. They said that if we did as we were told, we'd be fed. We tried to leave and they beat us until all we wanted was for them to stop.' Briar stalled again.

Ivan put a hand on the child's arm. 'There was more, wasn't there?' Briar looked away. The old man said, 'You need to tell them, if they're to understand.'

Briar stared out into the middle distance, somewhere beyond the control room of the mall. The rosebud lips were pursed, the shrapnel teeth hidden.

'It made the men angry that I was different. At first they only called me names, tripped me up and gave me tangles of razor wire to separate.' Briar opened his/her tattooed hands to reveal a cross-hatch of white scars, thin as threadworms. 'I wanted to make them like me so I smiled and did as I was told, but it only made them hate me more. There were other kids there too, not just our tunnel squad. One night the men set up a boxing ring and made us fight. I knew the other kids would hurt me, but I thought my friends would only pretend.' Briar looked at his/her hands again. 'My friends had learned to hate me too. They beat me until all I had was pain. After that they hurt me even when there was no one there to watch. There were other things too.'

Magnus had a premonition of what Briar was about to tell them. He closed his eyes, as if not seeing the child would lessen his dread.

'One of the men liked to get me on my own. He told me I was pretty and promised to protect me, but then he hurt me more than all the others.' Briar looked at the adults. 'Ivan saved me. He took me away from the salvage centre. He washed me, dressed my wounds and when they were healed he found me a guitar to play. Ivan gave me my freedom. I would have loved him anyway, but I love him more because he rescued me.'

Ivan took Briar's hand in his. He raised it to his lips and kissed the tattooed cross in the centre of the child's palm. 'I love you too.'

The sight of the old man's lips against the guitarist's scarred hand burned in Magnus's craw.

'Briar's a child. You haven't saved anyone. All you've done is swap one type of abuse for another. You're a criminal and if it was up to me . . .' Magnus was about to say he would like to see Ivan hanged, but an image of poor Adil, swinging on his rope, visited him and he choked on his words. '. . . If it was up to me you'd be locked up.' Magnus took Briar by the shoulder and pulled him/ her upright, beyond the old man's grasp. 'You're coming with us.' Ivan made a lunge for the child. Briar struggled to get free, but Magnus was stronger than both of them. 'You've been taken advantage of so many times you can't tell kindness from abuse.' The child kicked and bucked, swearing and calling for Ivan. Magnus gripped a hand under each of Briar's armpits. 'You'll thank us for this one day.'

No one had ever put a gun to Magnus's head before, but the sudden cold shaft of metal against his cheek was horribly familiar. He froze, still clutching Briar.

Natalie said, 'Let him go.'

Magnus released his grip and the child ran sobbing to the rifle resting on the filing cabinet by the door.

Stevie unslung her new rifle from her back and aimed it at the woman, but Natalie's finger was snug against the trigger of her revolver, the gun's muzzle pushed against Magnus's cheek.

Magnus raised his hands in the air. His bladder was full. He turned his eyes and looked at the woman without moving his head.

'This isn't a movie and they aren't star-crossed lovers. One of them is a child. The other's an old man, a paedophile.'

The actress's voice was dangerously calm. She pressed the gun into Magnus's face, forcing his nose to one side, distorting his features.

'I've had my fill of moralisers. I lost friends – good friends – to people like you. You've no idea what it was like. Ugly old whores coming out of the woodwork, complaining they were interfered with decades ago, when everyone knew they were star-fuckers and that the "abuse" they were whining about was the most significant moment of their pathetic lives.'

Stevie lowered her weapon. 'We've got the message. He'll think before he speaks in future. Let him go and we'll be on our way.'

Briar's face was flushed. He/she put the sight of the rifle to his/her eye and aimed it at Magnus. The weapon made the child look younger. Natalie's hands trembled, but Briar's were steady with intent.

Magnus closed his eyes, shutting the guns out. 'Why don't you come back to Orkney with us? There are other children there. We've got a school. You could learn to read and write.'

Briar's voice was flat and cold as the tundra. 'Your children have run away. They hate you.'

A tear slid from Magnus's eye. It skated the gun barrel pressed against his face and made its way down his cheek.

'They don't hate us. They've just lost their way.'

Ivan struggled to his feet. He placed a hand on Natalie's shoulder.

'We've had enough of death for one day.' The actress did not move, but when the old man reached out and took the gun from her, she offered no resistance. Magnus opened his eyes. Briar was still aiming the rifle at him. Ivan held up a hand, self-consciously saintly. 'Let them go in peace.'

For all her gentleness Magnus's mother had been clear on the guises the Devil could adopt. Her insistence that the De'il could masquerade as a religious minister or even Christ himself had bemused Magnus when he was a boy. Now he understood.

Stevie gripped his arm. 'We're leaving.'

She pulled Magnus towards the door. Briar's rifle followed them; a weathervane steered by the breeze.

Magnus let himself be led like a lairy boyfriend being dragged from a nightclub. He trained his eyes on Ivan.

'That child will despise you when it grows up.'

Ivan's voice was calm. 'The way your son despises you?'

The keys were in the lock. Stevie turned them and pushed Magnus into the corridor beyond. He caught a last glimpse of the child, already back in the old man's embrace; the elderly actress with her arms around them both. Their three bodies fitted together, snug as a puzzle carved from one stone. The door slammed and they were gone.

Forty-Five

The landscape beyond the rear of the shopping mall was an expanse of fractured concrete, wrought with vegetation. Stevie had expected the same high buildings that had hampered the view of the horizon on their drive through the city. The unbroken stretch of grey sky startled her. She paused on the shopping centre steps, her attention captured by the swoop and turn of a flock of starlings. The birds pitched and rose, the flock folding and unfolding; scattering and then regrouping into shapes she no longer knew the names of.

Magnus sprinted down the steps. He paused when he reached the pavement and pulled the knitted cap he had worn on the boat from his pocket. Stevie saw that he did not know where to go. She followed him and put a hand on his shoulder. The Orcadian was trembling beneath his jacket. He tugged his cap low over his brow. It made him look like a burglar on the prowl.

Stevie said, 'We're close.'

He did not look at her. 'We may as well still be on the islands, or on the moon, for all the good we've done.'

The misery in Magnus's voice touched her own despair. Stevie put an arm around his waist. He gave a small judder and hugged her to him.

She said, 'At least Evie is probably being well cared for.'

Magnus nodded, but did not speak.

The concrete expanse was a car park. Vehicles ranged across it in scattered ranks. The vegetation that colonised the cracks in the ground had crept around their wheels and hubcaps. Shoots stretched inside the cars' engines and reached into their cabs, rooting them there. Mould muted the vehicles' metal exteriors beneath a skin of brown-green.

Beyond the car park a clock-tower, its spire crowned with a golden ship, reached towards the glooming sky. Low-rise pubs squatted beside it, looking like they had been there since the first citizens stumbled, thirsty, into the city. The tower's clock was figured with gold numbers. Its hands had stopped at five to midnight.

Magnus touched Stevie's arm. 'Look.'

She followed his stare and saw a shambling figure dressed in black, walking across the bleak expanse. Stevie thought it was a man, though the loose-fitting coat gave no clue of the person's shape and a hood concealed the features. She pulled free of Magnus and took her rifle from her back. The oncomer raised their face to the sky and screamed something that was all pain and anger. Magnus reached into his pocket and Stevie knew he was going for his gun.

She kept a tight hold on her rifle, 'They might be harmless.'

The figure crossed the car park towards them, their limping walk fast, despite their bent back and hanging head. They were making for the steps where Magnus and Stevie stood, sure as mercury rising beneath a flame.

Magnus aimed his gun. 'Keep your distance.' His voice melted into the open space.

The wind rose, trembling the weeds and fanning the skirt of the approaching figure's coat. Somewhere a dog howled. The stranger raised their head and sent another scream into the gloaming. Stevie caught a glimpse of deep sockets set in a grey face; hollow cheeks and a black, depthless mouth.

The fluid in her spine shifted. Magnus caught her elbow and they retreated backwards, up the steps. The stranger was close enough to be sure that it was a man. He raised his head and looked at them. His mouth opened in a grin that revealed teeth more broken and blasted than Briar's. 'Are yous alive?'

Magnus kept his voice and his gun level. 'For now.'

'For now, that's a good answer, now's all we've got, this moment, now.' The man's voice was gravel. 'No use looking forward, no use looking back, live for the present, the moment, this moment, now, for tomorrow, we may die.' He turned his grin on Stevie and touched a hand to his forehead. 'We who are about to die salute you. What is it, but a step in the dark?'

The wind carried a spatter of rain. The man coughed and spat a gob of phlegm onto the ground. He turned towards the wind, black coat flapping; raised a hand in farewell and screamed.

Magnus shouted after him, 'We're looking for the old Fish Market!'

The man was limping away from them, his shoulders and head pitching to the rhythm of his stagger. He made for the alleyway by the side of the shopping centre where his death might wait in the form of a rabid dog, a stranger with a knife or countless other guises. His hand was still in the air, raised in a long goodbye.

Magnus shouted again, 'Do you know where the old Fish Market is?'

At first it seemed that the man had not heard him. Then he turned and pointed towards the spire.

'That's it there, the Briggait. It's a flesh market now, tender flesh, easy on the gums.' He raised his head to the sky and howled.

Forty-Six

For a man who had not eaten or slept in a long time, Magnus was running fast. Stevie followed him across the car park. The open space left them dangerously exposed, but he hurtled on, racing across the broken concrete, towards the spire. Stevie shouted, 'Magnus, for God's sake!' but she matched his pace, the rifle strapped to her back jarring against her spine. The vegetation that had colonised the car park was slick beneath her feet, more like seaweed than grass. A blast of rain hit her face. She shoved a strand of wet hair from her eyes. Up ahead she could see the name of a pub, The Westering Winds, and beside it the Fish Market, where Ivan had said the teenagers might be held.

'Magnus . . .' Her voice was lost in another gust of wind, another spatter of rain.

The Fish Market was large, built from blond sandstone and decorated with crests and other carvings. Two bearded faces stared through the smir from high on the building's frontage. Water stains and verdigris darkened their features, recalling the mould that had crept across the corpses of Sweats victims who, only seven years ago, had lain unburied in the streets.

Magnus faltered to a halt at the edge of the car park. Stevie caught up with him and saw the wrought-iron gates padlocked ten feet high across the building's triple entrance doors.

She shoved his shoulder. 'Come on.'

There was a modest doorway to the left of the grand entrance. They sprinted across the road and huddled side by side in its scant shelter, bodies touching, jackets streaming with rain.

Magnus's face was pale beneath his woollen hat. 'I know they're in there. I can feel them.'

Stevie blotted her face with her scarf. 'Wanting them to be there isn't the same as knowing they are. If this place has lookouts, they'll have seen us coming. I'm not risking my life on a hunch. You shouldn't either.'

A mechanical thrum rattled the air. They looked up and saw a helicopter wasp-like, high above them.

Stevie shrank deeper into the doorway. The sound of the helicopter's rotors coiled a knot in her belly, but she could not take her eyes off it. She tried to tamp down her fear.

'The propaganda effect of that thing could be worth the petrol it eats.'

Magnus gave a grim smile. He had lost weight. His cheeks were hollow, the hinge of his jaw more prominent.

'Thinking of getting one, pres?'

She had almost forgotten she was president of the Orkney Islands, had barely thought about Alan Bold deputising for her. 'Islanders aren't so easily impressed.'

Magnus's eyes were trained on the miracle above them. Planes and helicopters had once been commonplace, but it was years since either of them had seen one in the air.

'Islanders can be impressed – they just don't like to show it.' He settled his cap lower on his head and looked at her. 'I'm one of the few born and bred Orcadians left, so this isn't something I'd say lightly. You impress me, Stevie, you always have.' He looked away. 'I'm not coming on to you. I just wanted to say, I appreciate everything you've done for me and Shug.'

The compliment sounded too much like a leave-taking for Stevie to find any pleasure in it. A burst of wind loaded with rain and gravel assaulted the doorway where they were hunched. She tried to wipe the wetness from her face with her scarf, but it was sodden.

'Save the speeches for the homecoming ceilidh. Remember what we promised each other. We're both coming out of this alive.'

Magnus gave her another of his skull-like grins. 'You always were ambitious.'

The sound of the helicopter's engines was growing louder. Stevie looked upwards and realised that it was lower than before.

Magnus showed his teeth. 'They're landing.'

He was right. The helicopter was descending onto a cleared portion of the car park. Stevie could make out the air ambulance markings painted across its body. It was bigger than she had realised, designed to accommodate equipment and medics. They watched as it wobbled above the weed-choked concrete. The wind caught the helicopter and it seemed it might tumble like a leaf, but the pilot held firm. Its feet touched the ground and stayed there.

Stevie's hand sought Magnus's. 'They might not notice us.'

The engine died; the rotors slowed. The door to the cab opened and a man jumped down onto the concrete. It was a rock-star entrance, but he was soberly dressed in a long, waxed coat, ideal for concealing a rifle beneath. The man faced away from them, scanning the distance between the helicopter and the shopping centre. Stevie thought they were going to go unnoticed, but then he glanced towards their doorway. The distance between them was too far for Stevie to make out his features but she saw him freeze and knew that they had been spotted.

The man turned and spoke to someone inside the cab, cupping his hands around his mouth to funnel his words away from the wind and rain. Stevie reached for her weapon and felt Magnus do the same beside her. The helicopter rotors were still turning; their slipstream trembling the brim of the man's hat. He steadied it with one hand and ran towards the Fish Market in a half crouch. Three people followed from the helicopter.

Stevie looked at Magnus. His eyes were red with tiredness, his features drawn. There was something reckless in his expression that made her whisper, 'Remember, we're not Thelma and Louise or Butch Cassidy and the Sundance Kid. We're survivors.'

The bodyguards, if that was what they were, reached for their guns as they drew close. The man turned his head and said something that made them lower their weapons. They were close enough for Stevie to see that they were all men, bulkier and better-fed than the soldiers who had attacked her in Eden Glen.

Their leader took his hat from his head and, mindless of the rain, walked to the doorway where Stevie and Magnus were waiting, his hands raised in the air to show he was unarmed. Stevie could see his face more clearly now. He was clean-shaven with pale skin and dark hair, cut short in a way that emphasised the roundness of his head. The newcomer's expression was mild, his features open and honest. He nodded at their weapons.

'Keep your guns to hand if it makes you feel better, but you'll not be needing them.' He had a Borders accent; a lilt of lowland Scots; round English vowels.

Magnus said, 'Are you Bream?'

'I am.' The provost's smile was measured. 'From your accent I'm guessing you're our Orcadian visitors . . .' He paused and wrinkled his forehead, as if searching his memory. '. . . Stevie and Magnus. I heard you were headed for the City Chambers. We were waiting for you. What happened?'

Magnus's hat was still pulled low over his forehead; the growth of his beard had thickened. Only his eyes were exposed and they gave nothing away.

'Our lift dropped us off earlier than expected.'

Bream raised an eyebrow, but did not ask him to elucidate.

'Which one of you is president of the Orkneys?'

'I am.' Stevie did not return his smile. 'If you know our names, you already know why we're here.'

Bream met her gaze. His eyes were a sharp, Icelandic blue.

'I'm hoping you've come to build an alliance between the City of Glasgow and your islands.'

Stevie had expected him to mention the children. She stumbled over her words.

'I'm not sure how practical that would be. We're not exactly neighbours.'

Rainwater ran down Bream's face, slicking his hair to his head.

'It's true. Badlands lie between our two territories, but the people who live in them are largely the same people who lived there before the Sweats. I've heard about Orkney and the work you've done. You've managed to maintain a democratic process. So have we.'

Stevie said, 'I can't take credit for democracy on Orkney. The community works together.'

Bream nodded. 'No doubt, but a successful community requires a strong leader. From what I heard, yours would have fallen apart without you.'

Stevie looked at the ground. 'No—'

'Who did you hear it from?' Magnus interrupted.

The provost levelled his gaze. 'Someone who fancied himself in your friend's job.'

'A man called Bjarne?'

Bream replaced the broad-brimmed hat on his head. 'Sounds like he's not flavour of the month.'

Magnus said, 'He's not anything. He's dead.'

Bream lowered his head for a moment. It was impossible to see his expression, but when he raised his face to look at them again, it was calm.

'How did he die?'

'Shot with a shotgun from behind.'

'He was executed?'

Stevie said, 'Not officially. Our community doesn't approve of capital punishment, but someone obviously had it in for him. It was our first unsolved murder.' She corrected herself. 'One of our first two unsolved murders. Whoever shot Bjarne also killed his wife.'

Bream made a face. 'I only met him once, a month ago. He talked big about trade agreements and alliances, but he struck me as a man who would be better at making enemies than deals.'

Something in the provost's denial made Stevie ask, 'You've no idea who might have killed him?'

Rainwater dripped from the brim of Bream's hat. 'I didn't even know he was dead. Like you said, we're not exactly neighbours.'

The bodyguards had stood a respectful distance from the conversation, but now one of them stepped forward.

'They'll be gone, if we don't get there soon.'

'Thanks, Simmy.' Bream turned to look at him. 'It's a big building. Start on the ground floor and work your way upwards. I'll meet you back at the Chambers.' The provost saw that Stevie and Magnus were following his conversation. 'Every family has its troubles. One of our council members decamped with a kid young enough to be his grandchild. We had bother with that kind of thing in the early days – people exploiting children they were pretending to help. We imposed a policy of zero tolerance.'

The mention of zero tolerance, so soon after Bream's enquiry about whether Bjarne had been executed, made Stevie draw breath.

Magnus said, 'We met them.'

'Where?' Simmy was all heat and eagerness, as keen on the hunt as the dogs they had outrun.

Stevie hissed, '*Magnus*,' but he pointed towards the shopping centre.

'In the mall, bunked up in a control room on the upper floor. There was an old woman with them, an ex-actress called Natalie.'

Simmy nodded. 'Thanks, mate.' He clapped his companions on the shoulder and the three of them jogged off, moving quick and sure across the riven concrete.

'Don't hurt them.' Stevie's words were snatched away by the wind.

Magnus waited until the men were at the far side of the car park.

'We're not here to make an alliance. We're looking for three children who were stolen from our islands by a woman called Belle. Your friend Ivan said two of them are prisoners in this building.'

Stevie saw the gun in Magnus's hand and knew he had sacrificed Ivan and the others for the chance of getting Bream on his own.

'Stolen children being held prisoner is a serious accusation. You believed a man who took a child as his lover?' Magnus's weapon did not seem to bother the provost. He stepped closer, shortening the gap between them. 'I don't know anyone called Belle and my corporation does not imprison children.' He raised his hands, palms outwards and looked at Stevie. 'There's a set of keys in my left-hand pocket, get them for me. This is a good coat. I don't want Magnus here getting the wrong idea and ruining it with bullet holes.'

Stevie reached into Bream's coat pocket, fished out a heavy assortment of keys looped together on a chain and handed them to him.

Magnus kept his gun trained on the Provost.

'It's nothing personal. I can't take any chances, not now we're so close to finding them.'

Bream picked through his bunch of keys, until he found the right one. 'Guns have a way of making things personal.'

He unlocked the door and led them into a long corridor lined on one side by numbered doocots. He saw Stevie looking at them and said, 'This place was being used as artists' studios when the Sweats hit. Do you remember how councils used to bribe artists into gentrifying poor neighbourhoods by offering them cut-price workspaces?'

It was an attempt at camaraderie but Stevie did not return his smile. 'I suppose having artists around made things more interesting.'

Bream made a wry face. 'Making things interesting is something we don't have to worry about any more.'

He led them through another door into a hall that had once racketed to the sound of fishmongers selling their wares. A glass roof arched overhead, curving from a central spine, like a massive whale skeleton. Grime and leaves had accumulated on the glass, dulling the daylight seeping in from the already dull sky. The fishmongers of Glasgow must once have got rich, paddling in fish blood, their white coats flaked silver, counters sparkling with ice. The Fish Market had been magnificent. Now it was a leaky warehouse, stacked with jagged mounds of harvested technology. People bundled in waterproofs and woollens were sorting the junk into piles. Hats and balaclavas obscured their faces, but Stevie got the impression that they were all young.

Magnus grasped one of the salvage workers by the shoulder and pulled back his hoodie. He was slight, with slim hips and a sullen droop to his shoulders. Stevie caught his resemblance to Shug. But when the worker turned towards Magnus, he was a stranger, with pale skin and pinched features. The worker pulled word-lessly away. Magnus mumbled an apology and let him go.

He called his son's name, 'Shug . . . Shuggie . . .', his voice breaching the soft echoes of the building, harsh as a seabird's cry.

The salvage crew turned to look at Magnus, each one of them a stranger.

Bream said, 'He's not here.'

Magnus's face was raw with hardening rage, his eyes damp with frustration.

'You told us you'd take us to them.'

Bream held up his hands in apology. 'I'll take you to the City Chambers, but first I want to convince you we're not running a prison.'

The workers had returned to sorting the salvage. They moved slowly, conserving their energy. Occasionally one of them would carry a piece of equipment to the far side of the hall, where half-a-dozen people were busy at a bank of tables. Stacks of manuals sat amongst solar battery packs, coils of wire, fuses, half-disman-tled radios, junction boxes and other bits of electronica Stevie could not identify. There was an air of bemused industry about the people tinkering with the equipment. Their workstation might have belonged to a bomb factory, toymaker's workshop or an art installation.

Stevie nodded towards them. 'What are they doing?'

Bream shrugged. 'They're learning. We all are. The Sweats didn't discriminate, but sometimes it feels like they wiped out every engineer, doctor, plumber, electrician and anyone else who knew how things worked and left us with accountants, middle management and salespeople. We're all that remains. We can live as if the industrial revolution never happened, as if microchips were never invented and satellites never launched, or we can try and educate ourselves.'

A rash was flaring on the line of flesh above Magnus's beard. Magnus scratched it, his bristles rasped.

'Nothing you've said proves these people are here voluntarily.'

Bream reached out an arm and, without looking, caught the sleeve of a passing worker, a slim girl whose ancestors had hailed from somewhere in the Indian subcontinent. It was a random choice, like reaching into a tombola. The girl flinched and almost dropped the box of circuit boards she was carrying. Bream released his grip. 'Don't be frightened. I just want you to tell these people, you're not here against your will.'

The girl cast her eyes to the ground. Her head was swaddled in a blue- and red-striped scarf edged with gold fringes. They tipped forward, shrouding her features. 'I like being here.'

The provost said, 'No one forces you to stay?'

'No.'

'Nobody hurts you?'

The girl shook her head. The gold fringes on her scarf shivered. Her voice was a whisper. 'No.'

Stevie put a hand on the girl's arm. She could feel her trembling beneath her bulky clothing.

'Why are you so scared?'

The girl raised her head. She looked at Bream, who gave her a nod of encouragement.

'When I was a baby, everyone died.' Her voice held the faint trace of a Birmingham accent. 'The fear got into me and never left.'

There were people on the islands who had not fully recovered from the shock of the Sweats. Candice had been one of them; never quite able to escape the anxiety the pandemic had induced.

Stevie said, 'What's your name?'

'My foster mother called me Blessing.'

'Where is your foster mother now?'

'She died in the third wave of the Sweats. After that, I was on my own. I thought the dogs would get me. Then I met some people who told me things were good in Glasgow. They played me the radio broadcast and I followed them here.'

Stevie glanced at Bream. 'The third wave?'

'Last year. It didn't hit you?'

Stevie shook her head. 'No.' There had only been one major outbreak of the virus on the Orkneys. She turned her attention back to Blessing. 'You're happy here?'

'They feed us and keep us warm.' The girl spoke as if that was all there was to life. 'The dogs can't get us.'

Magnus took the box of circuit boards gently from her and set it on the ground. He had lost the easy-going smile that had helped make him a hit with Shug's pals, but the vulnerability that was the key to his empathy remained.

He crouched level with Blessing. 'I'm looking for my son. He's about your age. Slim, with dark hair. His name's Shuggie, Shug for short. He was travelling with a girl named Willow and a toddler called Evie. Have you seen them?'

Blessing bit her lip and looked at Bream. The provost's smile plumped his cheeks. It was late in the afternoon, but his face was smooth and hairless as a Roman general's.

'You don't need my permission to speak.'

The girl lowered her head again, avoiding Magnus's gaze. 'I didn't see a toddler, but the other two were here. They didn't like it. They went away.'

Magnus exhaled. 'How did they look?' The girl's expression was bemused. He scrabbled for the right words. 'Were they healthy?'

This time Blessing met his eyes. 'They looked okay, but they didn't like it here. The girl was angry, the boy was . . .' She shrugged, out of her depth. 'The boy was quiet.'

Magnus looked like he wanted to ask her more questions, but the provost interrupted.

'Like I told you, no children are being held prisoner in this city.'

Stevie gave the girl an encouraging smile. 'Did you ever meet someone called Briar? A small kid with sandy hair; a good guitarist.'

Blessing glanced at the Provost again. Stevie looked at him too but if anything had passed between him and the girl, she was too slow to catch it.

Blessing said, 'I don't know them.'

'How about a woman called Belle. She's pretty, but she lost one of her eyes in an accident.'

The girl knotted her hands. Her voice wavered. 'I never met any of these people.'

Stevie said, 'Don't let Mr Bream dictate what you say. If you're unhappy here, tell us and we'll help you.'

Magnus forced a smile. 'We live on an island. It's nice there – blue sea, green grass. We have a school. You could learn to read and write.'

The girl's face puckered. She picked up her box of circuit boards and held it in front of her, shielding her body.

'There was plenty of grass where I used to live. You can't eat grass. It makes you sick. I'm happy here.'

Bream touched his fingertips to the girl's cheek, gently dismissing her. 'Thank you.'

The sky outside was growing darker as day slipped towards night. Blessing flitted away from them and joined the other salvage workers, slowly moving through the bone-chilling hall.

Magnus's eyes followed her. 'She's too thin . . .'

'We have enough to feed everyone, but not enough to get fat.' Bream risked an arm around Magnus's shoulders. 'Let's go to the City Chambers and see if we can get you reunited with your kids.'

Stevie cast a last look across the dimming hall at the workers, moving like figures in a Lowry landscape. She remembered the well-fed bulk of the bodyguards who had gone in search of Ivan and Briar and thought that Magnus was right. The salvage workers were too thin. She followed the two men towards the exit. Magnus had shrugged free of Bream's hold. Stevie saw how his jacket hung loose on him and thought that if their journey did not end soon, he would edge from thinness into frailty.

Magnus and Bream passed through the connecting door, into the narrow passage that would lead them outside. Somewhere behind her one of the workers started to cough. Others took up the sound, their throats hacking; the chambers of their bodies resonating in the hollow gallery. The sound recalled the Sweats, the machine-gun rattle that preceded death. Something rose in Stevie's chest. There was a shout and the sound of coughing collapsed.

She looked back into the hall. The salvage workers were ghosting between the mounds of dead technology, going slowly about their business as if nothing had happened. She could not tell if the chorus had been a protest or a ghoulish joke, but felt that somehow it had been directed at her. The door ahead swung closed. Stevie broke into a trot and ran towards it.

Forty-Seven

The helicopter pilot was a middle-aged man with a face like a brick. He had a skip hat on his head and a cigarette between his lips. Stevie buckled herself into one of the passenger seats. Magnus sat next to her, Bream beside the pilot.

She saw that Magnus was having trouble with his seat belt and leaned over to help.

'I'm surprised you fly such short journeys.'

She was addressing Bream, but it was the pilot who answered.

'You're privileged. What you saw earlier was our maiden flight.' The engine rattled into life and he raised his voice to make himself heard above its din. 'We reckoned it was better to do a few short hops before attempting anything more ambitious.'

The pilot pulled on the joystick and the helicopter lurched upwards. It gusted with the wind. Stevie felt her stomach reel queasily with it and remembered how the helicopter had looked in danger of tumbling out of control when it had come in to land. She was squeezing Magnus's hand, but could not say if he had reached for her, or if she had grabbed him.

The pilot shouted, 'Hold on to your hats.'

They rose, tremulously at first, then gloriously into the rain-lashed sky. The wind caught them again and she called, 'Should we be going up in this weather?'

Bream turned his head to look at her, his face the colour of oatmeal.

'Finn's been flying these things for over thirty years.'

Finn pushed his hat back on his head. He took the cigarette from between his lips and exhaled through his nose, filling the cab with a second-hand fug of tobacco.

'I used to hop regular across the North Sea in weather worse than this, taking men backwards and forwards to the rigs. Before that I did a spell in Dubai. Over there it was sandstorms you had to look out for. Too much grit in the mechanism and these things drop like a stone.'

Magnus leaned back in his seat and closed his eyes. 'I think I'm going to be sick.'

Stevie looked down at the city. It was a sight she had never thought she would see again; the landscape laid out like a child's play-set, buildings reduced to the size of Lego; cars smaller than the nail of her thumb. They circled the old Fish Market, the weed-choked car park and derelict shopping mall. She saw the River Clyde snaking beyond the city. There was a gap in the clouds and she caught a glimpse of fields and the sea beyond them. The helicopter settled on its course. The view of countryside was left behind and they were flying over tenement rooftops, tiled with grey slate. They flew above a graveyard, toppled tombstones crowded together on a hillside busy with deer. An ancient cathedral stood in the shade of the hill and close by a turreted, Victorian hospital half-collapsed in on itself, like a neglected wedding cake left to rot.

Stevie turned to Magnus, but he was asleep, his mouth slightly agape. There were flecks of grey amongst the red in his beard that she could not recall noticing before. She heard his chest wheeze and felt an unexpected stab of tenderness.

The helicopter was already descending. There was a square beneath them, its focus an elaborate building Stevie guessed was the City Chambers. Three large objects she could not make sense of stood in a line outside the Chambers. The other roads that formed the square's perimeter were empty, except for a single car. She wondered if Briar had been captured. Ivan was the type to go quietly, but Stevie could imagine the old woman and the child fighting to the death. The wind buffeted the helicopter and Magnus woke with a start. He rubbed his face with his hands.

'Did I miss anything?'

'Nothing worth writing home about.'

The helicopter wobbled a few feet above the ground. Finn hummed a triumphant, military-sounding tune Stevie could not identify. They touched the tarmac, rose into the air again and landed with a jolt.

Finn killed the engine and slapped Bream on the back. He turned to look at Stevie and Magnus, a grin splitting his face.

'Ladies and gentlemen, we've got ourselves a flying machine.' He turned back to Bream, his expression serious. 'Won't be long before we can take your old lady and your sproglets up for a birl, but there's a rattle in the guts that I don't like. I'd rather not take her up again until I've had a chance to give the engine another once-over.'

Bream nodded. 'You're the expert.'

Stevie had thought the pilot's accent cockney, but now that the engines were silent she realised it was Australian.

'You're a qualified engineer as well as a pilot?'

Finn was lighting another cigarette. He waited until he had inhaled his first pull of nicotine.

'Qualified pilot. Self-taught engineer.'

Bream said, 'Finn spent the last year studying books on helicopter design salvaged from the university library.'

Magnus rubbed his face with his hands again, massaging his temples as if he had a headache.

'Congratulations. But I wish you'd left us out of your trial run.'

Cigarette smoke and misplaced adrenalin narrowed the pilot's eyes.

'This is a fucking triumph, mate. You should be over the moon.'

Stevie gave Finn one of her best smiles.

'He is. We're looking for our lost kids. We've travelled a long way; seen a lot of things we wish we hadn't seen. It's made us both jumpy.'

It occurred to her that she had not looked in a mirror for days and that her smile may no longer have the effect it used to.

Finn drew on his cigarette. 'A lot of kids end up here. Mr Bream's radio message pulls them in. I hope you find them.'

The provost opened the helicopter door and jumped down onto the tarmac. A blast of cold air rushed into the cab. Magnus patted the pocket of his jacket, checking for his gun. Stevie wondered if they would be asked to surrender their weapons inside the City Chambers and what they would do if they were.

Finn said, 'I've been in the square working on the copter for weeks. Maybe I saw your kids. What do they look like?'

Magnus drew a photograph Stevie did not know he had from his pocket. It was a Polaroid printed from an Instamatic camera. She glimpsed it as he handed it to the pilot – a group shot taken on one of the island's hillsides. Shug and Willow with Connor and a bunch of other island children. She saw Adil in the middle of the group and felt tears prick her eyes.

Magnus said, 'That's a couple of years old. Shug's the dark-haired boy on the left. Willow's the brown girl with the curls. She shaved her head recently.'

'Nice-looking kids.' The pilot passed the photograph back. 'I don't remember them, but that doesn't mean they didn't come by. I spend half my life with my head in this old bird's engine. It helps keep me what passes for sane.'

Finn opened his door, tossed his cigarette out and undid his seat belt, ready to follow it onto the tarmac. Stevie touched his shoulder, keeping him there.

'They vanished from our island at the same time as a woman called Belle. She's good-looking, late twenties – tall, with long, blonde hair. She had an accident, it damaged her . . .'

Finn touched a hand to his left temple. '. . . her eye?'

Magnus pitched forward. 'You know her?'

'I don't know her, but I saw her crossing the square a few days ago. She's the kind of woman you notice.' He smiled at Stevie, making it clear that she too was noticeable. 'She went into the City Chambers. There was something about her that made me think there goes trouble.'

'Did you see her leave?'

'No, but like I said, that means shit all. I've been focusing my attention on Rachel.' Stevie and Magnus must have looked bemused because Finn added, 'That's what I call the helicopter.' He looked away. 'I named her after my wife.'

Finn snatched a walking stick she had not noticed, hooked to a grab handle above the door and swung himself out of the cab. There was an awkward tilt to his movements that suggested smashed hips or broken vertebrae.

Stevie said to Magnus, 'Keep Bream busy.'

She followed Finn out onto the tarmac. The large objects she had seen from the helicopter were three tanks, queued outside the City Chambers like taxis at a rank. Their guns were muffled beneath khaki covers, but their shape was impossible to camouflage. They angled outwards; proud Nazi salutes.

Tattered Christmas lights were still strung precariously around the perimeter of the square; dead outlines of bells, stars and sprigs of holly tilting with the breeze. Statues of ancient worthies had fallen or been deliberately toppled. They lay on the ground, black and metallic, three times life size. The dead statues looked beyond human, yet it was easy to imagine them creaking awake, their footsteps shaking Glasgow's foundations.

The hotels, office blocks and restaurants ranked along adjoining streets suggested this had been the centre of the city. The commuters and tourists who must once have busied the square were gone, but the place was still full. Buildings were papered with tattered photographs and pleas for information. The gleaming eyes and smiling mouths that shone across the square were a reminder that death had come for the young as well as the old; the rich, poor and comfortably off. It had not cared what colour people were or whether they had good looks and style. Death did not adhere to a political party. It had taken clever clogs and dunces; the religious, drug-addled and only-at-the-weekend crowd.

One similarity united the lost. Almost all of them were caught in a moment of celebration, a party, wedding, bar mitzvah, communion or graduation, as if the people seeking them had wanted to put their loved ones' best faces forward. Time and weather had torn at the posters. Some were so stippled that to look at them was to know how it might be to have eye cancer. Others had been mutilated into Dadaist collages: a nose, a staring eye; gaping lips.

Stevie caught up with Finn. What she had taken for the ravages of teenage acne was a web of old scars, pitting his face. He had gone through a windscreen, she guessed, and wondered if his wife had died of the Sweats, as she had assumed, or on some country road, the victim of a corner taken too fast or a moment's lapse in concentration.

She brought out her smile again and kept her voice low. 'Is everything on the level here?'

'Why ask me?'

'You seem like a good guy.'

Finn shrugged. 'I've only been here twelve months or so. I had a few lost years after the Sweats. I took a plane up when I shouldn't have and hit the ground with a bang. It bent me out of shape.' He gestured to his body. 'I didn't think I'd fly again, but then I heard the broadcast and came here. Bream has a way of enthusing people.'

Stevie glanced to where Magnus was in conversation with the provost. Bream looked towards the door of the City Chambers, eager to go inside. Guards were stationed at the building's entrance and at ill-defined intervals around the square. They were men of the same stamp that had gone in search of Briar and Ivan: bulky and broad-shouldered, dressed in a combination of outdoor gear and camo. They had been nurtured on better rations than the workers in the Fish Market, but there was something jaded about their complexions that suggested ill health. Both pale- and dark-skinned men looked vaguely bleached, as if a layer of pigment had been removed.

Stevie said, 'We've heard it's not all good.'

The pilot shrugged again. 'I travelled the world before the Sweats and never found nirvana.'

Magnus waved at her from across the square. 'Come on.'

Stevie raised a hand in acknowledgement but stayed where she was.

'We heard that first settlers are treated well, but that some new arrivals, especially the younger ones, are slaves.'

Finn shook his head. 'No way. I only got here a year ago and I've been welcomed like a long-lost son.'

'You have a rare and desirable skill. I'm talking about kids.' She remembered how Ivan had described Briar. 'Some of them are half-feral, barely literate, angry. All of them are desperate for love.'

She glanced at the door to the Chambers. Magnus was walking towards her, fish belly pale, his face set in a scowl. She knew him well enough to know that he was play-acting for the benefit of the provost.

Finn said, 'They're asked to work hard and not given a great deal in return, that's true, but then there's not a lot to go round.' He sounded less sure than before. 'They're not slaves. Slaves are forced to stay. People here can come and go.'

'Are you certain?'

He shook his head. 'Yes . . .'

Magnus was almost level with them.

She said, 'Our kids are in there. If you know anything, tell me now, for their sake.'

Finn shook his head again. 'It's nothing . . .'

'But?'

He sighed and looked at the sky, perhaps wishing he was up there again.

'. . . but I see lines of them . . . little kids . . . skinny-looking teenagers being led through the town . . . work parties. I asked Bream about it. He said they were being taken care of, but it made me feel . . .' He shook his head as if he was trying to dislodge the image. '. . . it made me feel . . . uncomfortable.'

Magnus touched her shoulder. 'He's getting antsy. Best go now, if we're going.'

Stevie fixed her eyes on the Australian's. 'That's all?'

'That's all.'

She touched Finn's hand. 'Don't worry. You're on the side of the angels.'

The pilot snorted. 'The same airspace maybe – if I get lucky.'

He walked to the rear of the helicopter and started to examine the rotor blades on its tail, as if it would hurt him to look at her any longer.

On a frieze above the door to the City Chambers, an elderly Queen Victoria was being presented with gifts from envoys of the Empire. The old queen stared across the square, complacent and regal.

Magnus raised an eyebrow as they walked together towards the building.

'The side of the angels?'

'Never underestimate sales technique. It's where he wants to be; where we want him to be too.'

Bream was talking to one of the guards stationed outside the City Chambers, a horse-faced man with a red nose and rheumy eyes. Stevie felt the guard's gaze on her and was glad of the too-large trousers and shapeless jacket she had adopted in Eden Glen.

The provost gave her a tight smile. 'Making a date?'

'Just thanking him for the flight.'

Bream opened the door for her. Stevie had grown used to places drifting into darkness with the dying of the day. The abundance of oil lamps illuminating the place startled her almost as much as the interior's riot of marble, gilt and stained glass. She had never been to the Vatican, but the entrance hall reminded her of it. Stevie wondered if the pope had survived or if the line of succession had continued down a toppling chain of cardinals, the last one worshipping on alone, in pomp and magnificence; small groups of survivors assembling in St Peter's Square, hoping for his blessing; his brief, involuntary hesitation before he touched the sick. She could put a crew together, sail to Italy and find out. Or perhaps Finn could fly her there. Nothing tied her to Orkney except affection and Stevie was not sure that would last.

Guards loitered inside the building too. The provost had been frank about the city's scarcity of manpower, but there was a surfeit of muscle idling around the City Chambers. A couple of beefy men sauntered towards Stevie. They shared the same red eyes and dull skin as the men in the square. Stevie wondered if Bream's cohort had discovered a cache of drugs somewhere. They moved as if their bodies were heavy, their muscles dead weight.

Bream held up a hand and the guards let her and Magnus be. There was a proprietorial edge to the provost, as if he had designed his headquarters himself. He caught Stevie's eye and gave a self-deprecating laugh.

'Impossible to heat and a bugger to light, but this building's an important symbol of survival and regeneration. It's the first place we bring newcomers.'

Stevie thought of the small souvenir shop in Stromness, where she and Alan Bold had established their parliament.

'Some people must be overwhelmed by it.'

Bream nodded. 'They are. But they're inspired too. Survivors see all this and trust we know what we're doing.'

A white, marble staircase dominated the centre of the building. Candlelight glimmered against its surface, illuminating dark networks of veins. Bream bounded up it, towards the first landing, the picture of a no-longer-quite-young politician keen to show himself in good condition.

'The offices are this way.'

Magnus was overtaken by a fit of coughing. There was a whoop in the back of his throat. It seemed he would never catch his breath, but then he sputtered to a halt.

Stevie said, 'Are you okay?'

Magnus rubbed his throat.

'It's the change in temperature, coming indoors from the cold. It hit me.'

The air inside was as cool as a mortsafe, but Stevie nodded.

'It can do that. Are you able for this?'

Bream's footsteps echoed in the upper landing. Magnus started to say something, but a voice called his name from above.

336

'. . . Magnus? . . . Magnus?'

Their eyes met, but only for an instant. Stevie turned and ran towards the landing. Magnus overtook her. He slid on the marble stairs and righted himself, whatever ailed him forgotten in the dash to get to his son.

Forty-Eight

Shug had lost weight. His bruises had faded to a sallow yellow, but he was pale and even in the candlelight they stood out against his skin. Magnus registered all of this as he grabbed his son and folded him in a hug. Willow was standing by the banister. He extended his other arm and pulled her close. The teenagers felt light as driftwood. He forced himself not to squeeze them too tightly.

'I thought you were dead.' Shug and Willow's bodies were stiff. He sensed their resistance and made himself let go. 'Jesus Christ, Shug. You've led us a dance.' Magnus had forgotten the boy was almost a man, had pictured them falling into each other's arms. Anger bubbled up inside him. Magnus knew the love that had made his own father raise his fists to him and his hands shook with the effort of not hitting the boy. 'Jesus Christ,' he repeated.

Shug's voice was barely audible: 'I'm okay. You look like shit.'

'I'll be fine, now we're heading home.'

Stevie said, 'Where's Evie?'

Relief at seeing Shug had pushed Evie from Magnus's thoughts. His stomach leapt at the remembrance. He caught his son by the shoulder. 'Where have you put the bairn?'

Shame at forgetting about the toddler made Magnus rougher than he had intended. The boy pulled away.

Willow spoke for the first time. 'She's okay.'

Stevie put a hand on each of Willow's shoulders and said, 'Can you go and get her?'

Willow tried to take a step backwards, but Stevie held her there. The girl's eyes teared. 'I can't.'

Bream was still on the landing, leaning against a wall as if the scene was no big deal.

Stevie turned to him. 'These children are wanted for questioning about two murders on mainland Orkney and the kidnapping of a baby.'

Magnus said, 'We don't need to . . .'

The provost's voice was rough, as if he was coming down with a cold.

'You're full of accusations. I'm a slave-runner. These kids are murderers and kidnappers . . .'

Stevie took a step towards Bream. 'Willow and Shug are under my jurisdiction. I'm taking them back to the Orkneys where they will receive a fair trial.'

Magnus started to speak, 'Let's not . . .' but he was overtaken by a fit of coughing.

Bream held a hand to his face, as if it was defence against infection.

Stevie resisted the urge to take the gun from her back. The building was full of bored, armed men with nothing to lose and it was too easy to imagine blood slicking the City Chambers' marble floors. She met Bream's eyes. 'We're leaving and taking these two with us, as soon as they tell us where we can find the toddler they kidnapped.'

Bream turned his attention to Shug and Willow. He had lost some of his vigour, his eyes were bloodshot, his voice parched. 'Do you want to go with these people?'

The teenagers looked both younger and older than they had on the islands. Their cheeks were hollow, eyes sunken, features sharpened by weight loss. Their former cockiness was gone. They shook their heads, neither of them meeting the eyes of the adults grouped on the landing. 'No.'

Magnus stretched out a hand. 'Shug . . .' The boy stepped beyond his reach. Magnus let his arm fall to his side. It struck him that with Bream's help the teenagers could walk away. He might never see his son again. 'We've been through a lot to find you. At least talk to us.'

Stevie looked at the provost. 'Any alliance you hope to make with our community is dead before it's begun, if you harbour people who are under suspicion of kidnap and murder.'

Willow's voice was high. 'We're not kidnappers or murderers.'

Bream ignored her. His eyes were fixed on Stevie. The other people on the landing might not have been there.

'You're President of the Orkney Islands, but I am Lord Provost of Glasgow. It's my say that goes in this city. You can talk to them. But remember, they're under the protection of the New Corporation.'

Bream took a battery torch from a pocket in his coat. He clicked it on and led them into an unlit portion of the City Chambers, along a corridor lined either side with closed doors. The beam of light slid across the nameplates of dead councillors. It glided over empty chairs, where people had once waited to be seen; picked out intricately patterned floor-tiles laid over a hundred years ago, by men who had lived out their allotted span. The torchlight glanced over noticeboards bearing timetables for meetings no one had gone to. Bream stopped at a door marked *BOARDROOM*. He shone the torch at Stevie, Magnus and the teenagers. Their shadows rose, monstrous against the walls. Bream opened the door and led them into a musty room.

Three candelabras sat on the long boardroom table. The provost struggled for a moment with his tinderbox. A paper spool sparked into flame and he lit the candles. The room took on a mellow glow, revealing walls hung with portraits of men and a few women; all decorated with the same gold chain.

The provost saw Stevie taking in the paintings. 'The chain's locked in a safe. I toyed with the idea of wearing it – it's a symbol of office after all, the kind of thing people might find reassuring. Turns out it's pure gold, weighs a ton.'

He coughed into his handkerchief, then took a seat at the table and nodded for them to do the same.

Magnus said, 'We'd like some privacy.'

Bream's smile might have held a sliver of regret, or he might have been enjoying himself.

'I owe these kids a duty of care. You can talk to them, but only with a chaperone.' He looked from Magnus to Stevie and back. 'I haven't forgotten that you're armed. I'm showing you the same respect I'd expect if I visited your islands. For all our sakes, let's keep our discussion peaceful.'

The sound of shouting echoed from somewhere deep in the building.

Stevie got to her feet. 'That's Briar.'

It was clear the name meant nothing to Willow and Shug. They looked at each other blank-faced.

Bream said, 'Sit down. No one's going to hurt the kid. As far as we're concerned, he's the wronged party. '

Magnus leaned across the table, 'And Ivan?'

Bream shrugged. 'Do you care?'

'I'm the one who told you where he was.'

'Ivan will be given a fair trial.' The provost glanced at Stevie, as if checking that she approved. 'He'll be found guilty and we'll deal with him.'

The shouting rose in pitch. Stevie opened the door and took a step into the corridor.

The provost said, 'Sit down. Screaming won't hurt him. Neither will anyone here.'

Magnus coughed into his hand and then wiped his face with his scarf.

'How can you know the outcome of a trial before you've held it?'

Bream gave the weary sigh of a man who had honed his patience over years of working with idiots.

'We know how Ivan was with the kid. We saw him. You did too, or you wouldn't have handed him in. Sometimes a trial is just for show. You know that, so does she.' Stevie had one foot in the corridor, torn between the need to keep Shug and Willow in sight and the urge to go to Briar. The provost turned to look at her. 'If you don't, you're not fit to be president.'

Stevie stepped back into the room, slamming the door behind her, shutting out the sound of Briar's protests. She went to the table and leant across it, facing Shug and Willow.

'I don't know if the provost is talking about show trials because he wants to plant doubts in your minds, or because he sincerely believes in them. You've known me since you were children. You know that when I say you'll be given a fair trial that's exactly what you'll get – a fair trial. No foregone conclusions. You'll be judged by people who have known and loved you all your life; people who will remember what Bjarne was like. We need to find out what happened. If we don't, we're condoning murder.' She softened her voice. 'It would help if you told us where Evie is.'

Shuggie whispered, 'They took her away.'

Willow hissed, 'Shut up, Shug.'

Magnus fixed the girl with a hard look. 'The bairn's mother is beside herself.' He turned to his son. 'Away, where?'

The boy looked close to tears. 'I don't know. Belle said Evie deserved a better home than she had. You know what Breda's like

– half-daft. Belle said she knew people who wanted children but couldn't have them. People who could give her the kind of childhood she deserved.'

Magnus's voice was close to breaking. 'And you agreed with her?'

Shuggie wiped his face on his sleeve. 'We said no, but then, when it happened . . . there was blood everywhere and . . .'

Willow ran a hand over her head. Her hair had grown and her curls were beginning to grow back, not loose like they had been before but tight, like lamb's fleece.

'Shut up.' Tears brimmed over her eyelashes. She wiped them away. 'Remember what we promised.'

Tears were running down Magnus's face too. He reached a hand across the table towards Shug. 'Why didn't you come to me?'

This time the boy met his grip. 'It was a mess. My head was still hurting. All I could think of was running. Belle said she could only take us if we brought Evie along to pay our fare. We said no, then she explained, about the good homes and everything . . . she said people would hang us if we stayed . . . that she'd seen it before . . . that it was always what happened.'

Magnus gripped the boy's hand tighter. 'You know I'd never let anyone hurt you.'

'She said you wouldn't be able to stop it, that you would end up getting blamed too. They'd kill you as well.'

The thought that the boy had wanted to protect him scalded Magnus's heart. He dreaded the answer, but asked, 'Did you shoot Candice and Bjarne?'

Shug's head drooped. 'No . . . but . . .'

'That's all I need to know, for now. You can tell me the rest later.'

'Dad . . .' Shug looked up, his face streaming with tears. 'Dad . . . I think Adil might be dead. He went into a town. There were warning signs, telling people to keep out. Belle said a couple of us should check it out. We drew straws. Adil and Rob got the long ones. They went . . . but they didn't come back.'

Magnus wiped his face. 'Aye, son, they killed them.'

The candlelight flickered against Stevie's face, illuminating the fine lines creasing the corners of her eyes, the worry scored across her brow. 'Adil and Rob were hanged in the market square. They tried to do the same to your dad and me.'

Willow's voice was dazed. 'The others just came along for the adventure. Once Belle knew we were bringing Evie, she wanted everyone to come. Adil would have stayed at home if it wasn't for us. He'd still be alive.'

Stevie said, 'Moon is tied to a man who only wants to use her for breeding and God only knows where Sky is.'

Willow covered her face with her hands. When she took them away her eyes were wet.

'We were scared. We thought we'd be safer in a gang. The others didn't know Bjarne and Candice were dead or that we'd taken little Evie. We didn't bring her up on deck until we were underway. They were angry. Sky blew her top, but by then it was too late.' Willow snuck a look at Bream, sitting scrubbed and relaxed in his chair like a man not long out of a warm bath. Only a thin sheen of sweat on the provost's forehead suggested any tension. Willow went on, 'Belle told us there would be a price to pay, but we didn't know what she meant. When we got here, they took little Evie and sent us to work in the salvage centre.'

Magnus leant forward. 'How did you escape?'

Willow turned on him. 'You don't know anything, do you? We didn't *escape*.' She emphasised the word. 'People don't *escape* from the salvage centre. Someone came and got us.'

Bream addressed Magnus. 'I asked for them to be brought here when the checkpoint sent word of who you were and who you were looking for.' He shifted one of the candlesticks closer, casting his face in the light. 'Perhaps it's time for me to say something. There is no slavery here, but the girl's right in one respect. We require everyone who comes to the city to work. In the early days, when there were just a few dozen first settlers, it was easier to pull together. As our numbers grew, so did the complexity of our needs. Reclaiming salvage is just the start. There are mines that need to be reopened and worked, roads that must be cleared. Bodies are still festering in some of our buildings. The city is falling apart around us. I reckon we've got five years before it's beyond saving. We need more people – especially young people – than our radio broadcast is pulling in. Bjarne reckoned he could get us plenty.'

Stevie said, 'From Orkney? Then he was conning you. There aren't that many people on the islands and those who are there wouldn't swap what they've got for life down the mines or heavy labour in your salvage plant.'

Bream shrugged, 'Life in the countryside isn't for everyone. Look at your kids – they were desperate to get away.'

Willow's voice was small. 'Orkney was just the start. Bjarne was planning on getting people from all over the place. Remember his manifesto, all his promises to make the island self-sufficient and restore technology? That was how he planned to do it. Bjarne reckoned there were tons of kids like us, kids no one really wanted, who could be fooled into coming to the city. And if he couldn't fool them he could force them. The way he saw it, he'd be doing the kids and the rest of the world a favour. "If we don't make them into a resource, they'll use up all reserves we have." That's what he said. He was going to bring as many Orkney folk as he could to Glasgow and indenture them to the city in return for fuel and technology.' Willow's words gained speed. 'He wanted to marry me off to Lord Ramsey of Eden Glen and form an alliance,

345

as if they were a couple of kings.' She gave a small, self-conscious laugh. 'He should have asked Moon. Turned out she was desperate to be wedded and bedded.'

Stevie said, 'You should have known we wouldn't let Bjarne buy and sell people just to make the island more comfortable.'

Candlelight touched Willow's face. A scattering of spots had broken out on her forehead, her lips were dry and cracked, but none of that, not even her angry expression, could cancel out her prettiness.

'You don't think he'd have broadcast it, do you? You wouldn't have known and everyone would be so happy to have things getting back to what they call normal, they wouldn't have asked.'

Bream took a handkerchief from his pocket and wiped the sweat from his forehead. He cleared his throat; it made a grating noise that recalled old drains.

'It wasn't like that. We were planning a mutually beneficial alliance. People would come to Glasgow of their own free will, as you did. We'd give them somewhere to stay, feed and clothe them and in return they'd agree to work for us, the community they were becoming a part of, for a set number of years. My hope is that now that Bjarne is gone you and I can come to a similar arrangement.'

Magnus turned on Bream. 'You've got kids of your own. I guess you won't be sending them down the mines, or into the salvage plant.' He stretched a hand across the table towards Willow. 'You are wanted. Come back with us.'

Willow snorted. She was close to tears and mucus bubbled from her nose.

'Candice wanted me when I was cute and little, but Bjarne only ever saw me as an asset. That was why he hated me being with Shug.'

Stevie was focused on Bream. 'Where does Evie fit into all this?'

The provost wiped his face. He looked suddenly old and tired. Less like he had stepped out of a bath than a sauna.

'We were presented with a minor too young to care for herself and did what any decent society would. We gave her a home.'

Shug had been quiet. Now he leant across the table. 'Bullshit. Belle was desperate to bring her here. She wanted us for extra heft, but Evie was always the main show.'

Bream wiped his face again. 'You're wrong.' But his voice wavered. He turned away from the table, seeking solace in the cool dark, as if the heat of the candles and the four people gathered around the table were too much to bear.

Willow caught Stevie by the arm. She whispered, 'I think Evie might be in the building. I heard a child crying earlier, before you arrived. It sounded like her.'

Stevie nodded to show that she had heard. 'Are you okay, Bream?

The provost turned to face the table. He looked worried. 'I'm okay . . .' His sentence dissolved into a cough.

Bream's coughing seemed to set Magnus off. He bent double in his chair, trying to catch his breath. When he eventually straightened up, a telltale sheen of sweat coated his face too.

Stevie's stomach pitched with horrible realisation. She got to her feet. 'Shug, find an empty room on this floor and take your dad to it. Listen for a commotion and get ready to help him leave in a hurry.'

Magnus held up a hand. 'Keep away.' He hugged his arms around his body. 'I didn't think it was . . . I wouldn't have come near any of you if I'd thought . . . not for a moment . . .'

His voice was wavering, his body trembling, but he was in better shape that the provost who was bent forward, caught in the grip of a spasm.

Stevie's voice was sharp. 'Shug—'

'No, Stevie.' Magnus was on his feet. 'I came here to save the boy, not kill him.' He took another step away from the table, reeling like a man not quite on top of his drink. 'I'll find somewhere to hide and let things take their course. Maybe it will pass.'

Stevie had been infected in the first outbreak of the Sweats. The virus had laid her so low, she had been certain that she would die. Three days later she had woken in her soiled bed, to discover that she was alive and most of the world was dead. The virus had hit the provost faster and harder than it had hit Magnus, but the Sweats were capricious and it was impossible to know whether either of them stood a chance of survival.

Shug held up his hands, reassuring his foster father that he would not come any closer. 'I'll go with you, Dad. I'll sit at one end of the room and you can sit at the other. I won't touch you, I promise. We'll just keep each other company.'

Magnus shook his head. He had lost his hat somewhere and his hair trembled with the motion.

'I'm not leaving Stevie. We promised to stick together. She needs me to make sure she doesn't get herself killed.'

'You'd be a liability right now, Dad.'

Despite his promise not to touch him, Shug had a hand on Magnus's back and was ushering him towards the door.

Magnus looked back at Stevie. His eyes had the glassy sheen of a fever victim.

'Remember, we're not Thelma and Louise.'

Stevie tried to force her best smile. Her mouth wobbled.

'We'll be home soon, all of us.'

Shug opened the door. He put an arm around Magnus's back. The boy looked too thin to support his father, but working the croft had lent him stamina and his slight frame was corded with muscle.

Stevie said, 'Shug, there's a gun in the pocket of your father's jacket.'

The boy nodded. He and Magnus slipped into the dark of the corridor together. The door shut softly behind them.

The provost was struggling to his feet. Stevie pressed him back into his chair. She patted Bream down, feeling in the pockets of his coat, and drew out a neat revolver.

She whispered, 'Here,' and passed the gun to Willow. 'Be careful.'

The girl stowed the gun in her pocket. Stevie turned her attention back to Bream.

'We're going to get you some help.'

The provost had been showing symptoms for a shorter time than Magnus, but the Sweats had a stronger hold on him and he was already in the grip of a fever. He looked at Stevie with panicked eyes.

'She doesn't belong to you any more. I told Belle that too.'

'Who are you talking about? Little Evie?'

'Evie . . . Melody . . . they don't belong to you.'

'Who do they belong to?'

The provost shook his head. 'There are men in this building who would kill for me. You won't get a hundred yards.'

Stevie said, 'Do you think they'll still kill for you when they know you have the Sweats? Loyalty only goes so deep. I'd hide from them if I were you and hope you recover. People can get over it. I did.'

'It might not be the Sweats. It might . . .' The provost was struck by a bout of the shivers. He clutched at his body and bent forward in his chair, juddering. 'It might be something else . . .'

'Is there someone I can get? Your wife? Tell me where Evie is and I'll find help.'

The provost stared at her. He moved his lips, trying to work up some saliva. He was about to speak when Willow tugged at Stevie's sleeve.

'Let's go. He's not going to tell us anything.'

'Shhhh.' Stevie batted the girl away and sank to her haunches, her face dangerously close to Bream's. She pictured the ill-looking men loitering in the square outside, the guards stationed in the lobby and knew that it was not drugs that had dulled their skin and weighted their limbs.

'Another wave of the Sweats is coming. If Evie stays here there's a good chance she'll die. Our islands are free of infection. We'll spend a month in quarantine and then, if we're all well, we can go back to our community. We'll reunite Evie with her mother.'

Stevie had been sure the provost was about to tell her where Evie was, but Bream gave a ghastly grin.

'My wife loves those kids more than her own life. Losing them would kill her.'

The provost forced himself to his feet. This time Stevie did not stop him. He staggered to the door. After a moment, she and Willow followed.

Forty-Nine

This time the provost did not bother with his torch. He lurched along the unlit corridor, like a mummy risen from the tomb in some old movie. Willow had picked up one of the candelabras as they left the boardroom and their shadows flickered weirdly against the corridor walls. The girl took the gun from her pocket and pointed it at the departing man's back.

Stevie hissed, 'Put that away. If we meet anyone, the story is he was taken ill and we're following at a distance, to make sure he doesn't fall and hurt himself.'

The girl slipped the weapon back into her pocket. There was something reluctant about the gesture that made Stevie wish she had not given it to her.

The central staircase glowed softly up ahead. Voices echoed from below, indistinct, like the sounds of swimmers calling from a distant pool. The provost reached the landing. He staggered to the stairwell, clutched the wrought-iron banister and looked down into the entrance hall. He groaned, though whether it was in pain or at something he had seen there, Stevie could not be sure. She blew out the candles and held Willow's arm, keeping them both shielded in the corridor's shadows.

Bream caught his breath and reeled towards the stairs that led to the upper floors. He climbed them slowly, clinging to the banister for support. Stevie kept her hand on Willow's arm. She felt impatience running through the girl's body like a current and whispered, 'We'll catch him up. We want to be in the open for the shortest time possible.'

A faint wheeze sounded in the girl's chest. Stevie turned to look at her. Willow was exhausted, but her eyes were focused, her skin free of telltale prickles of sweat.

Bream reached the next floor. Stevie touched the girl's shoulder and they ran quickly together up the stairs, moving quietly on the balls of their feet like assassins making for the kill. The provost picked up speed. He headed for a corridor, a reflection of the one that had led to the boardroom. His feet patterned a drunken waltz against the tiles. Willow reached for her gun again.

Stevie nudged her. 'Leave it.'

The girl kept a tight grip on the weapon. 'You still think you're in charge, but you're not. Why do you think Shug and me ran? To get away from you and your petty, fucking rules.'

Stevie cast a glance at Bream. The corridor was dark, but she could still make out his shape, weaving up ahead.

'I thought it was because you shot your foster father and mother dead.'

Willow's eyes brimmed, but the hand that held the gun barely trembled.

'I didn't shoot Candice.'

'But you murdered Bjarne?'

'It wasn't murder.'

'What was it then . . .?'

There was a noise of a door slamming and something that might have been a sob, cut suddenly short.

Stevie looked for the provost. He was gone. She pulled her gun from her back and ran into the dark. Door after identical door lined the corridor, each one anonymous and unmarked.

'Shit.' The girl had followed her and they hesitated together, in the centre of the unlit passage, uncertain of where to go next. Shouting from somewhere deep in the building broke the spell. Stevie whispered, 'Cover my back.'

The nearest door opened into darkness – the shapes of office furniture, gloomy corners. She took a deep breath and opened the next door and the one after that, onto the same black nothingness. Willow tapped her shoulder. The girl put a finger to her lips and touched her ear with her other hand, telling Stevie to listen. Shouts of panic were still rising from the entrance hall, but another, fainter sound reached through the dark – the sound of a child crying. Stevie tried to isolate the noise. She could hear the blood beating inside her head, the clatter of something falling. Her breaths were quick and shallow, high in her chest.

Willow tiptoed to one of the doors. She pressed an ear against an oak panel, met Stevie's eyes and nodded.

Stevie motioned with her gun for Willow to move out of the way. Adrenalin brightened the girl's smile. The hand that was not holding the pistol went to the door handle and turned it. Stevie breathed, '*Willow.*'

Everything happened at once. The door opened onto golden light, the girl's body was silhouetted for an instant in the doorway. There was a bewildering hiss of noise and air, a fracture in the atmosphere, a crack of cordite. Willow dropped to the ground at the speed of gravity. Stevie threw herself to the floor, falling with the girl.

'Willow?' She touched the girl's chest and felt heat and sticky wetness. 'Willow?' Stevie pressed a hand to Willow's neck. A faint pulse flickered. 'Willow?' The pulse glimmered and was gone. Stevie forgot about finding cover. She snatched her scarf from around her neck and pressed it to the girl's chest. The wound was bleeding badly. 'Willow?' They had come too far for the girl to be dead. She was going to take her home for trial. It had been manslaughter, not murder, and she would go free. 'Stay with me, Willow.' Stevie's scarf was filthy, but it was all she had. She pressed it against the girl's breast, whispering something that sounded like *shshshshshshshshshshsh*, trying to stem the bleeding.

'Is she okay?'

Stevie looked up. She had forgotten where she was and the glowing, candlelit room was a shock. She registered a woman sitting on a couch with a child cradled in one arm and a gun, capped with a silencer, in the other. Somewhere a child was crying, but it was not the one in the woman's arms. That child was so silent it might have been a doll. Stevie went back to her task. '*Shshshshshshshshshshsh* . . .' Willow's eyes had rolled back in her head. Her mouth was open and stupid, in a way it had never been in life.

'Is she okay?' the woman asked again. Her voice was light and surprised. 'I didn't mean to hurt her. My husband told me to make sure no one came in.' She gave a nervous laugh. 'People should knock.'

'She's dead.' Stevie's voice cracked. 'You killed her. She was only fifteen.'

The child cradled by the woman was older than Evie. It had a vague, swimmy look on its face, as if caught between waking and sleeping, life and death.

Stevie put her face to Willow's and rocked backwards and forwards, backwards and forwards. She clamped her teeth together, trying to lock the scream inside her, but it escaped in a long keening moan.

'You're getting yourself covered in blood.'

Stevie realised that the woman was speaking to her. She took her scarf and tried to wipe some of the blood from her face, but the fabric was drenched. Shouting echoed in the halls below them, a scatter of panicked footsteps. Soon someone would wonder where Bream was and come to fetch him.

'*Shshshshshshshshshshshsh* . . .' Stevie touched Willow's face again. She had lost count of the dead people she had seen since the first outbreak of the Sweats, but it was still impossible to grasp that a living-thinking-being, full of the power of love and fear, could be so easily transformed into an object of decay.

'*Shshshshshshshshshshshsh* . . .' Stevie straightened Willow's body. She placed the girl's lifeless hands one on top of the other, draped her scarf over the dead face and then forced herself to sit up.

The room was an upmarket bedsitter. Its ceilings were high and iced with white cornicing, its furniture oversized and regal. The couch the woman was sitting on had gilt legs and marigold, brocade cushions. Her eyes held the same glassy sheen as those of the child slumped across her lap. She looked like a junky Madonna who had gifted her child her addiction in the womb.

The woman said, 'What was she doing with a gun, if she was only fifteen?'

Stevie's body was trembling. Her voice shook. 'I gave it to her.'

'That was a bit silly.'

'I'd forgotten how young she was.'

A large bed sat in the far corner of the room. Bream lay huddled on top of it, his knees pulled up towards his chest. Two cots stood by the bedside. Stevie stroked Willow's hair: '*Shshshshshshshshshshshsh* . . .' The girl's curls moved beneath her palm, still alive, though Willow was dead.

She remembered her first sight of the girl, a ragged child, huddled beneath the bed, where her dead parents lay. Later, someone had let slip about how Willow had been found, covered in her parents' blood. The other children had gone through a phase of teasing her about being a cannibal, but it had not lasted long.

They were a small group and Willow had charisma. When she walked away from their taunts the others had discovered that they wanted to follow her. Willow had not reported the bullying to any of the grown-ups, Stevie remembered. The same pride had prevented her from telling anyone about Bjarne.

'I'm sorry,' she whispered. 'I should have known. If we'd taken you out of that house, none of this would have happened.' Stevie was too tired to cry. Too tired to do anything except put her head on the child's lifeless body and close her eyes. The race was over. Willow was dead. Magnus had the Sweats and would soon follow. Little Evie was lost. Shug was destined for hard, life-shortening labour. Willow's gun had fallen not far from her body. Stevie reached out a hand and pulled it close. She did not have the energy to use it yet. She didn't dare look at Willow again, the dead thing she had become. She lifted one of the girl's hands to her lips, kissed it and repeated, 'I'm sorry.'

Out of sight on the other side of the room, in a cot by the bed where Bream lay, soiled and shivering, the unseen child resumed its cries. Stevie opened her eyes. Sleep was her only desire, but the child's cries were rising, harsh and panicked. She hauled herself to her feet and took a step towards the cot. The woman on the couch raised her gun and pointed it at her.

'You're intruding on my family.'

Stevie took a deep breath, trying to lower her heart rate. 'I just want to help. Can I look in the cot please?'

'It's time for my daughter's nap. I don't want her disturbed.'

Stevie looked at the gun barrel, pointing towards her and was surprised to discover that she was afraid.

'What's her name?'

'Anne.' The woman looked down at the child, still and pale on her lap. 'And this is Elizabeth.'

'Are you married to Mr Bream?'

The woman smiled and Stevie saw that she was beautiful in a way that men liked and fashion designers had despised: soft and voluptuous with long, dark hair and red lips.

'No one really gets married any more, do they? There are no vicars or registrars left. John says we jumped the broom.' The woman glanced vaguely towards the bed. 'He's not very well – flu or something.'

'What's your name?'

'Ruby.'

Stevie had lifted the gun from the floor as she got to her feet, but Ruby's gun was pointing at her, the child still cradled on her lap.

She kept the weapon by her side. 'My name's Stevie, short for Stephanie. I've travelled a long way, looking for a little girl called Evie. Someone stole her from her mother.'

Ruby sounded indifferent. 'Poor woman, she should have taken better care. No one could take my children from me. I'd kill them first.' She gave a glassy smile. 'Well, you know that already.'

Stevie took another step towards the cot. Ruby cocked her weapon.

Stevie froze. 'A new wave of the Sweats has hit the city. Your husband is dying from it. Anne and Elizabeth will catch it and die too, if they stay here. I've come to take your daughters into quarantine on our islands. They'll be safe there. We'll return them to you when the crisis is over.'

'You must think I'm stupid.' A strand of hair clung damply to Ruby's face. 'I told you, my children aren't going anywhere.'

Bream groaned on the bed. He rolled onto his side, sat up slowly and placed his feet cautiously on the floor, as if afraid that the parquet might slide from beneath them. His words came out in staccato gasps.

'We need to get away. Take the kids and go to the islands, with her.'

'We're city people.' Ruby gave Stevie a complicit smile, as if she had not just murdered Willow in front of her eyes. 'Flu makes Johnny feverish.'

A voice from somewhere behind Stevie said, 'He's dying, Ruby. You and the girls will too, if you stay here.'

Stevie looked round. Belle was thinner than before, her scarred face too skull-like to be beautiful any more.

Belle saw Willow's ruined body on the floor, dropped to her knees and put her hand to the dead girl's wrist, seeking for a pulse. 'Christ, Ruby. You killed her?'

'It was self-defence.'

Belle stared, pale-faced and shivering, Willow's hand on her lap. 'She was only a kid.'

Stevie kept her eyes on Ruby, waiting for a flicker in her concentration. 'Willow was only here because you brought her, Belle. Her blood's on your hands too.'

Belle pulled the scarf from Willow's face, as if she could not believe that the child was dead. 'It's on all our hands. You gave her to a power-mad bastard to look after.'

Stevie shook her head. 'I gave Willow to Candice. She was desperate for a child. I thought she'd take good care of her.'

Belle linked her hand with Willow's, their fingers nested together, dead and alive. She stared at the child in Ruby's lap.

'She did. Then the girl hit puberty just as Candice began to feel she wasn't going to hold on to her man.'

Guilt sat bitter and heavy in Stevie's chest.

'Candice thought every woman on the island was after Bjarne.' She wanted to tell Belle to let go of Willow's hand, but her own part in the child's death was crashing in on her. 'I promised Candice I'd take Willow, but I was late. I took the boat to Wyre and fell asleep at Cubbie Roo's Castle.'

It seemed a lifetime ago.

Belle whispered, 'I remember. Your dog was there. He liked me.' Her eyes were still trained on the child, pale and sleeping in Ruby's arms. 'Candice told Bjarne that Willow was going to live with you. They had a big fight. She took her sleeping pills and went to bed. Bjarne started drinking. Normally Willow left the house when he hit the bottle, but she was waiting for you, so she hid in a cubbyhole she'd made in the attic. Bjarne was too fat to make it up the ladder into the roof safely, especially after he'd been drinking, so Willow felt secure there. She fell asleep and woke up to the sound of him calling to her from the landing. He said he knew she was there, and that if she didn't come down, he would shoot the dogs. Willow didn't believe him, not even when she heard two shots, one after the other. He said he would shoot her horse next. He'd killed the dogs cleanly, but he took longer over the horse. She heard it screaming and knew that he was telling the truth.'

Ruby rocked the child on her lap. One of its arms fell free of its blanket and flopped by its side. Belle let out a small moan.

Ruby lifted the child's arm and tucked it back in place. 'Why would I go to your islands? They sound hellish.'

Stevie said, 'They're beautiful.' She glanced at Belle. 'Willow stayed in the attic?'

Belle's skin sagged, as if the process of decay had already begun and her flesh was pulling away from her bones.

'Of course she did.' She touched the back of the girl's perfect skull, the curve where, when Willow was little, Candice had cupped her head with her palm as she rocked her to sleep. Belle's eyes were still staring at the child in Ruby's arms. She bit her lip. 'Willow was brave, but she wasn't stupid. She burrowed into the nest she'd made in the attic and when she heard a shot coming from Bjarne and Candice's bedroom, she tried to pretend it was only a trick to get her to come down. Later, when she heard Bjarne sobbing and wailing, she knew he'd murdered the nearest thing to a mother she'd known. Willow hoped he would kill himself next. She waited a long time, but there was no shot after that. Eventually she sneaked down from the attic. You know the rest.'

Ruby gestured with her gun.

'I hope she got him.' She was on Willow's side, even though she had shot the girl dead.

Belle took a deep breath. 'Bjarne was snoring. His head had fallen backwards and Willow could see the top of his skull over the backrest of his armchair. The gun he had used to shoot Candice was on the floor beside him. The sight of his skull seemed to set something off inside her – Willow said it was like a mechanism clicking into place. All that potential for violence, the killing, was waiting, stored inside Bjarne's brain. Willow said that if she had seen his face she might have been too frightened to do it, but she sneaked round the side of the chair, picked up the gun and shot him in the back of his head, before she could change her mind.'

The baby in the cot had stopped crying. Ruby was crooning tunelessly to the child in her arms, rocking it gently to and fro.

Stevie whispered, 'I would have helped her. Bjarne was a crude pig. I hated him, but I didn't know he was so dangerous . . . I should have known.'

Belle said, 'Willow thought no one on the island would believe her.'

Stevie wanted to shout, but she could hear voices rising in the building's hallways. She spoke softly, for fear of discovery. 'Willow was a frightened child whose mother had just been murdered. You could have advised her to come to us. Instead you tempted our children away. You knew they would be in danger. You knew that even if they survived the trip, they'd be treated like slaves. You took advantage of them.'

Belle looked away. 'I knew the trip would be dangerous, but I didn't think any of them would die.' She raised the dead girl's hand to her lips and kissed it, her eyes still trained on the listless child in Ruby's arms. 'I didn't hide anything from them. I told them they would have to work in return for bed and board.'

'They were island kids. They had no idea of what they were letting themselves in for. You made Moon into a baby-factory. Adil was hanged because of you.' Stevie's voice rose. 'What about little Evie? Were you helping her too?'

Belle let go of Willow. She folded the girl's hands back in place.

'You don't have children of your own. If you did, you'd understand. A mother will do anything to save her child.'

'You stole Evie from her mother.'

'Melody is the only child I'll ever have.'

Ruby said, 'Her name is Elizabeth. You gave her to us. She's mine now.'

Belle sounded weary to her bones. 'I didn't have a choice. We were both going to die if we stayed in the salvage centre. When I heard the provost's wife was desperate for a baby . . . it seemed the best way to save us both. I didn't know how much it would hurt, not having Melody with me.'

Stevie said, 'How could you steal poor Breda's child? You knew the agony you were subjecting her to.'

'It didn't seem so wrong to try for just a little happiness, even if it cost someone else some pain.' Belle's look was plaintive. 'Bream likes to give his wife presents. When I saw Evie, I knew what I had to do. She was such a pretty baby. I knew Ruby would fall in love with her. When we got to Glasgow I hid Evie away, somewhere safe where the dogs wouldn't get her. I came to the City Chambers and begged Bream to let me have my daughter back. He promised to give me Melody in exchange for Evie but in the end he took them both.' Her eyes met Stevie's. 'I couldn't afford to think about her mother.'

Ruby shook her head. 'Her name's Elizabeth now. You shouldn't have given her away, if you wanted her so badly. You could have worked in the salvage centre and kept her with you. Instead you moaned about how hard the work was and gave her to us, so you could go gallivanting. You abandoned Elizabeth. She's mine now and I wouldn't swap her for the world.'

Belle's grin was ghastly. 'I've come to take them away, Ruby. Both of them. They can't stay here, not now the Sweats are back. You know that.'

Bream had been sick on the floor. He lay on his side, on top of the bed, his glassy eyes trained on the women.

'Let her take the kids, Ruby. I need you.'

Ruby raised her gun so that it was pointing at Belle's face. She tightened her grip on the child on her lap. Its head flopped backwards revealing dull, half-closed eyes.

Belle took a step forward. Her voice was raw. 'Have you killed her?'

Ruby pulled the child close. 'She's got a cold. All children get colds.'

Bream retched again. He tried to sit up and failed. 'Ruby, please. I think I'm dying.'

Ruby glanced at the bed, but stayed where she was, motionless on the couch.

Belle took another step towards her. 'Your husband needs you, Ruby. Give me Elizabeth. Save yourself and Evie.'

Ruby said, 'A mother lives for her children, not her husband.'

Bream raised his head from the pillow and looked at his wife. His face was glossed with sweat, his voice ragged.

'You were headed for the Comfort Dens on Glasgow Green when I found you. I brought you to the City Chambers and gave you everything you wanted. I gave you these kids.'

Ruby kept the gun pointed at Belle and Stevie, but she turned her head and looked at him.

'You got what you wanted, John. Men like you always think it's nothing. But I gave you a lot.'

'Ruby . . . please . . .' The provost's mouth was flecked with foam, his tongue swollen and thick. 'My bones are grinding. Can you hear them?'

The woman got to her feet. She seemed unaware of the beads of sweat prickling her own brow.

'You don't have long to go, John. I'm sorry for you, but what can I do? They'll be making wooden huts on the green again. Like you got them to do last time. I'll ask them to take you there. Remember what you said? "It's not so bad. After a while they don't know where they are. It's just like falling asleep."' She smiled sweetly at the child in her arms. 'Just like Elizabeth, falling asleep.'

Bream's jaw was swollen, the glands in his neck hardening. Each word was a battle, hard-fought and only half-won.

'I'm still provost. I'll tell them it was your kids who brought the Sweats. Simmy will throw them in a couple of sacks and drown them in the Clyde like rats.'

Ruby lifted her gun and fired towards the bed, but the provost was lying flat against the mattress and the shot went wild.

The room was large, the distance between the door and the couch several yards. Stevie took it at a run. She knocked the gun from Ruby's hand, punched her in the mouth and snatched the child from her. Ruby grabbed for the child and scrabbled for the gun. Stevie kicked her in the head and she fell against the couch, blood spurting from her nose. Ruby's hands flew to her face. Snot and tears distorted her words.

'Elizabeth has a cold. She needs her mother.'

Belle staggered towards Stevie. Fever had swallowed her strength and she moved with the same staccato gait that had propelled the provost through the corridors of the City Chambers. She held out her arms.

'Her name is Melody. You're right, she needs her mother.'

The child was about six years old. Skinny, with long limbs that suggested she might have grown tall, like Belle. Her hair was white-blonde, her half-open eyes blue, her skin brown. Melody's pupils shifted, but the virus was in its final stage and she could not focus.

Belle said, 'Please, give her to me.'

Stevie placed the little girl in her arms.

Belle sank to the floor. She put her face to her daughter's. 'I'm sorry I left you.'

Ruby was on her feet. Her nose was still bleeding and the lower half of her face was a bloody mask.

'You're not having her.'

She lurched towards Belle and Melody. Stevie split her knuckles against Ruby's skull. The provost made a sound that might have been *no* or some word of encouragement. Ruby reeled forward. Stevie hit her again. The woman fell. Her head slammed against the tiled floor with a noise that was a combination of a thud and a sickening snap. Stevie pulled back her boot, ready to kick her again, but she caught sight of the blood on her toecap and stopped.

Bream was on the bed, Belle on the floor, keening to her daughter. Stevie went to the cot. She lifted Evie from beneath her blankets. The toddler's face was red from crying, her cheeks slathered with snot and tears, but she was alert, her temperature normal. Stevie kissed her on the forehead. The child tried to wriggle from her grasp. Stevie zipped the child inside the front of her jacket, so

364

that only the top of her downy head showed. She kissed her again and whispered something soft and soothing.

Bream was mumbling. He might have been calling to her, but Stevie did not spare the provost a look. She lifted the baby blanket from the bed, draped it over Willow's body and went in search of Magnus.

Fifty

The City Chambers was fractured, as sure as if a fissure had cracked its walls apart. The voices of the men who had loitered confidently in the halls had grown to a pitch and then splintered into silence. Stevie ran along the unlit corridor, clutching Evie to her chest. The child was crying, her small body heaving with distress.

'Shhh, Evie, shhh.' Stevie rubbed the child's back through her jacket, trying to soothe the toddler. She shouted: 'Shug . . . Shuggie?' Her voice echoed against the Chambers' marble surfaces. 'Shug? . . . Magnus? . . . Shug?'

Stevie swore beneath her breath. She ran to the corner of the landing, a junction in the corridors that wrapped around the building.

'Magnus? . . . Shug?'

Stevie swivelled on the balls of her feet, sweeping her eyes across the atrium, trying to take in the corridors and landings. The movement soothed Evie who stopped crying.

'Shug? . . . Magnus?'

She saw them on the opposite side of the atrium. Magnus had one arm slung around Shug's shoulders. The boy limped unevenly towards her, buckling beneath his father's weight. Stevie jogged towards them, Evie heavy against her body. Magnus was muttering something, perspiration dripped from his face, but he showed none of the swollen pustules that disfigured Bream and so many other victims of the Sweats.

Stevie held the child's face against her chest and lifted Magnus's other arm around her shoulder, taking half his weight. She gripped his free hand. Magnus's breaths were rasping and laboured, his skin clammy.

Shug said, 'Where's Willow?'

'She went on ahead.' The words caught in Stevie's throat.

They were half-carrying Magnus down the staircase, their arms still linked around his shoulders, like a ghastly chorus line. Magnus's foot missed a tread and all four of them nearly tumbled.

Shug said, 'You shouldn't have let her.'

A sob rose in Stevie's chest. The child had fallen asleep. She hugged her closer.

'I didn't want to, but she wouldn't . . .'

Magnus lurched, almost tumbling them over again.

A man sat on the bottom step. He looked up, his face pale and sweaty, his chest bubbled with sores.

'I need you to . . .' He clutched at Stevie's leg as she passed. 'Please . . .'

She tried to pull free, but desperation lent the man a surge of strength. He held tight to her ankle and she was forced to kick him away.

Stevie whispered. 'I'm sorry.'

The man started to cry. He said, 'Why will you save him and not me?'

She had no answer.

The guards had vanished from the entrance hall, except for a big man sitting on a chair by the door. He looked up as they passed, but did not say anything.

It was dark outside. The air cool, shot through with stabs of rain. Fires burned in large oil drums around the square, illuminating the smiling faces of the missing pasted to the walls of the abandoned shopfronts and bars. A breeze trembled the photographs' ragged edges, as if the people in the portraits were applauding the Sweats' latest victory.

Stevie and Shug guided Magnus between the armoured tanks parked outside. His feet were becoming less sure, his weight heavier.

Shug paused to heft his father more firmly around his shoulder. He scanned the square and shouted, 'Willow?' The girl's name rang across the open space. He called again at the top of his voice, 'Willow?' He turned to Stevie. 'Where is she?'

Stevie touched Evie's head. The child was warm, but her skin was dry, her breaths even.

'I told you, she's waiting for us.'

Magnus was a dead weight. They would not be able to carry him much further. Her mission now was to get the child to safety on the islands, but Stevie would not leave Magnus to die alone on the street.

Shug sounded scared and suspicious. 'Where is she waiting?'

People were moving on the edge of the square. Stevie could see them, dark shapes, in the blackness.

'I told you, up ahead.'

Beyond the light thrown by the oil drums, there was darkness. Stevie hesitated, unsure whether to push onwards, or lead them back to the City Chambers and wait for dawn.

'Where up ahead?'

She turned on the boy. 'If you'd trusted me in the first place none of this would have happened. Your father and I have killed for you and now he's . . .' She stopped and drew in a deep, juddering breath. Somewhere a dog was howling. 'Willow is waiting for us, up ahead. Right now we have to think of what to do for your father and Evie.'

The shapes of the people hidden by the dark were coming closer. Beyond the square, towards the east, there was a hint of dawn. The sound of howling reached them again and from somewhere in the darkness came a shout of 'Plague-bringers!'

Shug took a step backwards, pulling Magnus and Stevie with him. 'Fuck.'

Someone else shouted, 'Feed the Sweats and starve the fever.'

Stevie reached for the revolver she had taken from Willow's corpse.

Shug shouted, 'Willow?'

Stevie readied herself to fire into the darkness. 'Shut up, for Christ's sake. Do you want to draw more attention to us?'

Shug's panic must have reached Magnus through the fog of his fever. He muttered, 'It's all right, son. Mira's waiting for us. It's home soon and light the fire.'

'Fucking plague-bringers . . .' A stone flew across the square towards them. It missed, but it was followed by another that caught Stevie on the shoulder. She let go of Magnus and ducked, putting both hands around Evie who woke and started to cry.

'Make for the Chambers.' She grabbed Magnus's arm and turned, ready to beat a retreat, but a figure was silhouetted in the firelight. The provost was standing in front of the line of tanks, leaning on the weapon Stevie had left behind, as if it was a walking stick. His voice was broken, but he raised it as high as he could and took up the cry.

'Plague-bringers!'

Another stone whizzed close to Stevie's head. It was followed by a bullet.

She shouted, 'Get down!'

Someone was running towards her. She raised her gun, the firelight caught against its metal surface and she squeezed the trigger.

An Australian voice shouted, 'Don't shoot.'

Shug said, 'Fucking shoot him.'

Finn grabbed Magnus. Shug tried to fight him off and the Australian delivered a push to the side of boy's head. 'It's all right, I'm a friend.'

They half-carried, half-dragged Magnus to the middle of the square, where the helicopter was waiting. Evie screamed at the top of her lungs. The stones were coming fast and thick, the crowd building. Stevie looked back and saw that the provost was on the ground, though whether he had been felled by a missile or had reached the end of his strength she could not know. At the last moment Shug refused to get into the helicopter until they found Willow. She put the gun to his head and forced him on board.

Finn shouted, 'All aboard the Skylark,' and started the engine. 'Let's hope none of the bastards' aim improves. All it needs is for a stone to hit the rotors and we're toast.'

There was no time to strap Magnus to the helicopter's stretcher. They settled him on the floor and buckled themselves in, Shug still protesting that they could not go without Willow. The engines started.

Stevie shouted, 'How did you know we'd be there?'

'I didn't.' Finn shoved his cap on his head and started fiddling with the controls. 'But after I talked to you, some things that'd been bothering me fell into place. I was coming to tell Bream to shove his New Corporation.' He pulled on the joystick and they rose, awkwardly at first, then wonderfully sure, into the night.

Over in the east the sky was turning pink. Finn righted the helicopter and set course towards the dawn.

Fifty-One

Magnus was not sure where the sky ended and the sea began. He was above them both, looking down on the blue-white as if he was in heaven. His mother took his hand and squeezed. It was a long time since he had seen her and the touch of her made his eyes tear.

'I thought you were dead.'

His mother did not say anything, merely squeezed his hand again.

He said, 'Is Rhona with you?' And there she was, his sister, not angry with him as she so often was, but smiling. He smiled back and held out his other hand. 'Rhona.'

'Dad . . . Dad . . .' Shug was calling him. 'Dad . . .'

He opened his eyes again and saw the sea below; bright-blue, tipped with silver. White horses shining like fish scales. His islands were coming into view.

After the Sweats he had thrown off the ambitions of his London life and remade himself as a man his ancestors would recognise. A robust crofter, unfazed by harsh winds and bleak weather, a man fond of a dram, with a stock of good tunes to brighten a dark night, but who never forgot he had beasts to feed in the morning. It was all gone. All that remained was the core of him, and that was love.

His mother was at his shoulder again, his sister Rhona on his other side. Magnus said, 'Is Dad with you?' Neither of them answered. He turned his head and saw Stevie. She looked like she had been crying. Magnus tried to tell her it was not as bad as it looked, that nothing was, not even death, which they had done so much to avoid.

Stevie tried to smile. 'We made it. We're almost home.'

'Dad . . . Dad . . .' Shug was in his ear again. 'Dad, don't go. Willow's dead. You can't go too. You're needed here.'

Magnus saw the blue sea, the brown and green of his islands. His mother touched his shoulder, his sister Rhona was by her side. He could feel his father's presence some way off.

Stevie said, 'We'll be home soon. A few more minutes and we'll be there.'

'Dad . . .' Magnus heard his son whisper. 'Dad . . . please, Dad . . . stay with me.'

He squeezed Shug's hand. 'I'll never leave you.' But his son was crying and Magnus could not be sure that he had heard him.

Afterword

The world has changed more than I anticipated in the five years since I first sat down to write about a contemporary, worldwide pandemic. As an imaginative child, raised in the seventies and eighties, I grew up with a consciousness of nuclear bombs, military coups and natural disasters. My apocalyptic vision has been honed by horror movies, thrift store paperbacks and genuine political discord. But my vision of the world is underpinned by the belief that most people are essentially good. Call it naive, but it's a conviction that helps me get through the day and like Stevie and Magnus, I refuse to let it go.

There are many people to thank. Eleanor Birne and Mark Richards for their astute editorial advice and patience in the face of drifting deadlines. Thanks too to Becky Walsh for her editorial input – especially for noticing that my characters all initially had curly hair – how did I miss that?

I am very grateful to the University of Otago and the Wallace Arts Centre for a three month residency at the Pah Homestead in Auckland. I met with a great deal of kindness during my stay in New Zealand and would like to thank in particular Professor Liam McIlvanney, Sir James Wallace, Matthew Wood and Zoë Hoeberigs. Thanks too to the Women's Bookshop, Ponsonby Road, Auckland for making Zoë Strachan and I so welcome when we were far from home.

My family are steadfast supports who are rewarded with neglect. Thanks for letting me disappear into the page.

Thank you, too, to my partner and first reader Zoë Strachan.

My agent David Miller died suddenly, soon after Christmas 2016. *Plague Times* is a trilogy full of death, but I find myself inarticulate when faced with the real thing. David was one of the anchors of my literary life. He was a man who held the whole of the London Underground in his head, who read widely, with enthusiasm and insight, often out loud, and who generally contrived to bring the conversation back to his literary love, Joseph Conrad. David was passionate about music. He knew about the world, was clear-sighted, but never cynical. He could be tough, but was kind by nature and never cut an unfair deal.

David Miller was there at the start of my career and I had assumed, without thinking about it, that he would always be there. He steered me through all of my books, including this one, which I have dedicated to him.

From Byron, Austen and Darwin

to some of the most acclaimed and original contemporary writing, John Murray takes pride in bringing you powerful, prizewinning, absorbing and provocative books that will entertain you today and become the classics of tomorrow.

We put a lot of time and passion into what we publish and how we publish it, and we'd like to hear what you think.

Be part of John Murray – share your views with us at:

www.johnmurray.co.uk

 johnmurraybooks

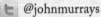 @johnmurrays

johnmurraybooks